W9-BSV-489

No Filter
and
Other Lies

No Filter and Other Lies

CRYSTAL MALDONADO

HOLIDAY HOUSE • NEW YORK

Library of Congress Cataloging-in-Publication Data

Names: Maldonado, Crystal, author.
Title: No filter and other lies / Crystal Maldonado.
Description: First edition. I New York : Holiday House, [2022] I Audience:
Ages 14 up. I Audience: Grades 10-12. I Summary: Seventeen-year-old Kat
Sanchez uses photos of a friend to create a fake Instagram account, but
when one of her posts goes viral and exposes Kat's duplicity, her entire
world—both real and pretend—comes crashing down around her.
Identifiers: LCCN 2021034367 I ISBN 9780823447183 (hardcover)
Subjects: CYAC: Social media—Fiction. I Online identities—Fiction. I
Popularity—Fiction. I Friendship—Fiction. I Family life—Fiction. I
Overweight persons—Fiction. I Puerto Ricans—Fiction. I LCGFT: Novels.
Classification: LCC PZ7.1.M346954 No 2022 I DDC [Fic]—dc23
LC record available at https://lccn.loc.gov/2021034367

ISBN: 978-0-8234-4718-3 (hardcover)

♥

To Grandma and Grandpa, who called me their own;

To Bub and the beautiful little family we have built;

And to anyone who has ever worried

they're not enough. You are.

* * *

Chapter One

You should know, right now, that I'm a liar.

They're usually little lies.

Tiny lies.

Barely lies.

Not so much lies as lie-*adjacent*.

Case in point: I lied to get my friends out here tonight. I told them there'd be food.

There's no food.

But isn't it more important for us to enjoy Lake Isabella together in the middle of the night than it is to sit at home?

Plus, I need photos of the stars.

"You done yet?" Luis emphasizes the *t* in *yet* so hard it almost sounds like a threat. "You didn't bring any snacks like you said. I'm *starving*."

I take a second to squint through my camera's viewfinder, adjusting my tripod slightly and focusing on the dark sky sprinkled with tiny specks of light. The universe. The abyss. The proof that existence is bigger than us. Awestruck, I stare at the twinkling black velvet unrolled in front of me and think: This matters so much more than that thing I said about there being food here.

"How can you be hungry?" I ask, not looking at him. "It's after midnight."

"Exactly. I haven't eaten in hours!" Luis snaps, and out of the corner of my eye, I see him put his hands on the back of his head, clearly frustrated. "Homegirl spends over an hour trying to get a good picture of the *sky*."

Hari looks up from reviewing the photos on his own camera (the newest Nikon—I *totally* covet it, even though my own Nikon does its thing just fine) and shrugs. "She's almost done, man. And, hey, why aren't you taking any photos? This can count for our art assignment, you know."

Luis scoffs. "Yeah, but I already took some dope photos at the beach. My assignment's done. *Been* done."

At that, Marcus pulls back from his camera, too. "Lemme guess. A selfie?"

Luis strikes a pose, showing off his arm muscles. "Mira, I *am* a work of art, after all." We groan. "Anyway, don't you guys think it's gonna be a little weird if you all submit the same photo for class?"

Marcus wrinkles his nose. "This isn't just for *class*. This is portfolio work. To show off my range."

Luis makes a face at Hari, and they both laugh. "Man wants to show off the range."

Marcus shrugs. "Hate on me all you want, but I'll remember this when I'm a rich globe-trekking photographer and you're begging me for a gig."

"Can we focus here?" I ask. "The sooner you let me get what I need, the sooner we're done."

"Fine, but all I gotta say is *of course* Hari defended you." That earns Luis a quick—and well-deserved, if you ask me—jab in the side from Hari. The insinuation causes heat to creep up my neck, and I stare into my viewfinder to avoid looking at anyone. If I don't make eye contact, maybe they'll all be quiet. "Ow! Cabrón!"

"Shut the hell up then," Hari mutters.

"Make me."

For some reason, that makes Marcus bust out laughing, even

2

though it wasn't even funny. A triumphant grin spreads across Luis's face.

"If you're gonna keep complaining, stupid, you can just walk your sorry ass home." Then I square my eyes at Marcus. "And don't encourage him, idiot."

Marcus widens his eyes at Luis like they're in on some secret Hari and I aren't and I suddenly regret so much that I invited them all out tonight. I'd been wondering if we might want to go camping out in Joshua Tree sometime to really enjoy the stars, sans light pollution, but forget that. I'll go alone.

"Jeez, relax, Kat," Marcus says, a smirk tugging at his lips.

And that annoys me even more. "Fuck off, Marcus." Can they just be cool for, like, one second of their pathetic little lives?

"That language." Marcus shakes his head.

"You kiss your mother with that mouth, Sanchez?" Luis asks, playing along.

Hari rolls his eyes. "Enough, guys."

Luis gasps and holds his hand to his heart. "Oh, no. Now we've gone and upset the happy couple!"

"We're not a couple!" I shout at the same time as Hari forcefully says, "Stop!"

Our voices echo through the dark and it feels like we've gone and disturbed the dead with our loud and obnoxious bickering. But then loud and obnoxious bickering makes up about ninety percent of what we do.

Marcus gives Hari a shrug. "We're just messing, man."

"Personally, I love to piss Sanchez off." Luis grins. "I'm killin' it right now."

He is and I hate it. Luis knows exactly how to get to me, and I always, always let him. So I take a deep breath and start scrolling through the pictures I've already taken—there are dozens—and just hope I've got one I like. They'll have to do. My concentration's shot.

There's a loud yowl in the distance.

Hari and I exchange looks. "Shit," he mutters.

Luis's eyes widen. "I'm *not* trying to die by coyote tonight!"

Marcus glances around us. "Seriously, I'm with Luis—can we go?!"

I snap my lens cap on my camera and grab my tripod, then sprint in the direction of the parking lot, not bothering to wait for the boys. "See ya!"

"Kat!" Hari yells, but I'm already off and laughing, leaving them in the dust. They've got to collect their things (Hari's tripod, Marcus's ginormous camera bag, Luis's big fat mouth) before they can take off, and they left their shit lying everywhere. Amateurs.

I make it back to Marcus's car first, out of breath but victorious. When my friends are within earshot, I yell, "You guys just lost to a *girl*!"

"You cheated!" Hari yells, but he's laughing, too.

"Not cool," Marcus says, rushing to unlock the car. "We could've been ripped to shreds by coyotes while you saved yourself!"

"You better hurry up and let me in," I say, watching him fumble with his keys.

Luis rasps, out of breath, "You know, for a fat girl, you can run."

I glare at him. "You know, for a boy who doesn't know shit, you sure do have a lot to say."

"Guys," Hari says. It feels like he's always saying that, trying to get me and Luis to stop. But we go back and forth like this a lot. Most of the time, I feel like I could kill Luis; if he isn't poking fun at my weight, he's teasing me for my poor Spanish-speaking skills or calling me a gringa even though I'm half Puerto Rican. He makes me so mad that sometimes I wonder why we're even friends.

I mean, there are good parts to Luis, too, I guess. I just can't think of them right now.

Marcus finally unlocks the car and we pile inside. It's a tight squeeze with all the gear, but we fit. (It helps that his car is impeccably clean.)

"I'm still hungry," Luis complains.

"Me too," Marcus agrees. "Didn't Kat say there would be food?"

"I have no memory of this," I say innocently, and from the front seat, Marcus scoffs.

Beside me, Hari's stomach grumbles. "Guess I'm hungry, too."

"Traitor," I tease. "So, we going to In-N-Out or what?"

The boys whoop in celebration, and it isn't long before we're chomping on burgers and fries (animal style) as we cruise down the nearly deserted freeway.

"*Don't* get my car dirty," Marcus warns.

"Too late," Hari says.

Marcus swivels his head almost 180 degrees to try and look in the backseat.

"*Pay attention!*" I yell as Luis shouts, "*Hey!*" because the car swerves into another lane.

Hari points toward the road. "I was just joking, man, chill!"

I don't dare say there actually *is* a piece of lettuce on the floor because I'd like to make it home alive tonight.

"You *better* be joking." Marcus refocuses his attention on the sprawling road ahead of us. "Fry."

Luis reaches into the bag and passes a fry to Marcus, who opens his mouth wide. Luis shakes his head. "Man, we talked about this. I am not feeding you!"

"I'm the one driving," Marcus reminds him.

"Doesn't matter!"

"Fry me!" And this goes on for a minute until finally Luis shoves a whole handful of fries into Marcus's mouth. Muffled with food, Marcus asks, "Was that so hard?"

Which just sets Luis off again, and then they're arguing over Marcus's rules of driving. To be fair to Luis, Marcus *does* have a lot of rules for the car, which he's named Honey (gag). Some make sense (keep the car clean; wear your seat belt) and others are a straight-up abuse of power (he *always* gets to pick the music; whoever is in the passenger seat has to feed him).

Hari and I exchange a smirk but don't intervene. He leans his head against the window, staring outside, and a few heavy blinks signal to me that he'll likely nod off soon, belly full. I could do the same, honestly, but I know I've got a long night of photo editing ahead of me—first for my assignment, which I've put off way too long, and then for the photos I took earlier in the day. My grandma and I had gone for a walk after dinner and, just as the sun set on Panorama Drive, I saw this cool-looking couple roller-skating together. Their confidence, the palm trees, and the sun hitting just right made me so, so grateful I brought my camera. I had no choice but to take a few photos.

That's the thing with this hobby of mine. Turns out, it's not much of a hobby at all—more like a compulsion, one I love. I'm always snapping life around me. Me and the boys are even in Photography Club together, which Marcus started. He loves the medium as much as I do.

I settle in with my camera and get to work reviewing what I've got.

TBH, there are a decent amount of duds, which I delete right away. Given that this was one of my first times trying to capture the grandeur of the Milky Way, though, I didn't do *so* bad. Especially for my first time trying in my city.

Bakersfield is not the fanciest place, okay? Let me just get that out of the way. It's a small, squat city of red-tile roofs and black-tar roads and midcentury offices, surrounded by oil fields and megafarms. Because it sits in a bowl between the Sierra Nevadas and the Tehachapis, the air pollution isn't the best. But the beach is pretty close. We have a dope food scene. Almost half of the city's population is made up of brown folks, so I never feel totally out of place when I go out. Everyone here loves dogs (I haven't seen that listed as an official quality of our city on any lists or anything, but I believe this in my heart). The people I care about most are here, too, and that counts for something. We have the best sunsets. On the clearest days, you can see the mountains rolling blue along the horizon. And at night, with just the right conditions, there are even a few breathtaking spots to see the night sky.

The key for those types of photos is to get as far away from artificial light as possible (like the reservoir we were just at). And then go with a medium-to-high ISO, low shutter speed, and tripod. If you don't have a tripod, don't even bother. You can't be trying to take pictures of the stars with your camera in your shaky-ass hands.

Once I've looked through all my star photos, I recheck the photos from earlier, admiring the way the brown skin on this gorgeous couple glimmers in the light, as if that's the real gift of the golden hour. Brown skin really is the most beautiful. Damn. And these photos will *kill it* on IG.

At least I hope.

Satisfied, I pull out my phone and start to scroll Insta: liking some photos, watching some Reels without sound, tapping through people's stories. Yet somewhere between the quiet of the road and the smooth thrum of the car, I doze off—next thing I know, I'm being gently shaken awake.

It's Hari. "Hey," he says, giving me a soft smile. "We're home."

I rub some of the sleep away before climbing out of Marcus's car. He's dropped the two of us off at the corner of the road where Hari and my parents live so we can walk home and get back into our houses undetected. It's late now—later than either of us should be out—so we'll each have to sneak back in.

Hari slings his bag over his shoulder and starts to walk down the street. I fall into an easy rhythm beside him.

We've got this routine down: Hari and I will walk right past my parents' house so I can go to my *actual* home one street over—my grandparents' house. Once he's dropped me off, Hari will double back and go home himself, and I'll text him to make sure he made it there okay, like a good friend always should.

"Think you managed to get something that'll work for Mr. Griffin's class?" Hari asks.

"Yeah, I think so. He's a pretty easy grader."

"That's true. And your stuff is great."

"Thank you." I smile at him, appreciating the compliment, even though I know my stuff is good. Better than Hari's (no offense!), despite him having a *way* nicer collection of camera lenses. Definitely better than Luis's; he phones every assignment in (often literally taking pics with his phone). It's on par with Marcus's work, and sometimes even better (though he has really nailed his style and I'm still figuring mine out).

"How about you?" I ask. "Did you manage to get anything before Luis started being the most annoying person on the planet?"

Hari laughs a little. "Yeah, I got a few, I think. Do you think Mr. Griffin's gonna be pissed we have the same subject for our assignment, though? Because I'll get something else."

I shake my head. "No, he's way too nice to care. He's an art teacher! Plus, you know we're his favorites."

"Makes sense. We're the best, after all," Hari says.

Right. The best. We definitely are, at least in art; no doubt the four of us are extremely talented.

But one thing has been gnawing at me, especially lately. If my work is so good, why does it flop *every time* I share it on Instagram? It pisses me off. I don't know what I'm doing wrong, but my account is practically dead: just over two hundred followers, (way) less than fifty likes per photo, and next to zero comments.

Yet my aesthetic on that account is AMAZING. Like, pull me up on your phone and look at my grid: every single picture is serving a *vibe* and a *color scheme* and a *mood,* and they look good *as a whole.* That is hard work! No one appreciates how much tweaking and editing goes into photos to make them all feel different enough to be interesting but similar enough to go together. And I've nailed that.

Plus, my photos are mostly street fashion with a focus on stylish Black and brown kids like my friends and me, which: COME. ON.

So...what is it, then? I see so many people effortlessly rack up followers. I don't want Twitter fame. I don't want to be a TikTok star. I want to be recognized for my art. I just want my perspective as an artist and a human being to mean something—to reach someone.

And the boys! The boys, who literally don't even care about social media, *all* have more followers on IG than I do.

HARI SHAH:
A RESPECTABLE 930 FOLLOWERS.
MARCUS BROWN:
AN ENVIABLE 2,301 FOLLOWERS.
LUIS DIAZ:
A DISGUSTING 5,843 FOLLOWERS.
KAT SANCHEZ:
A TRAGIC 209 FOLLOWERS.

I'm ashamed of the fact that I know these numbers off the top of my head because I check them so obsessively. But I can't stop.

The way they get infinitely more likes on their smoldering selfies or whatever the hell else they post gives me a complex. I tell myself it's because I'm the only one trying to use my account to promote my *photography* rather than my *life*. But I don't know. Marcus seems to weave both in pretty effortlessly. So maybe the problem is just me.

I've thought about trying to be more personal on my account. What life, exactly, would I share, though? Nights like this, out with these fools? Who would even care about that?

It's just like, IG is flooded with these perfect influencers and I could never compete. They style themselves perfectly and wear perfect clothes on their perfect little bodies; they have shiny hair and pristine makeup and, okay, kinda all look cut from the same mold but whatever. They're gorgeous, their photos are *premium,* and they clearly don't feel stupid when they pose with their arms up in the air looking at a sunset. They can write captions that start, like, *I've always had a thing for mermaids,* and somehow it's charming and you don't want to gouge your eyes out. People appreciate them. People hear them. People value them.

But all that...it's just not me. I have the striking photos, but I don't like selfies; I have the taste, but I don't live a fancy life. And I'm uncomfortable being the one in front of the lens rather than behind it.

Not that I'm not cute. Because I'm CUTE, okay? These brows? These curls? These eyes-so-brown they look like the rich soil of the earth? This melanated skin? This body? I do my best not to hide my belly and its rolls, which is probably why Luis is always calling me fat, but whatever. Rocking an oversized sweatshirt won't make me any smaller, so why try? I've photographed enough people to know there is beauty in everyone, me included.

But let's be real: no one's checking for the life of a fat seventeen-year-old Puerto Rican girl who lives in Bakersfield, California—two hours from anything that matters—and who kinda reeks of desperation.

So badly, I just want to be liked. I just want my art to be appreciated. I just want to be *seen*.

Ugh.

Hari interrupts my thoughts. "You good?"

"Oh, yeah."

"You sighed."

"Did I?"

He laughs a little. "Sure did."

"Well, I'm good. Just thinking, I guess."

"About what?"

"Stupid things." It's a cop-out answer, but I'm not sure I want to bare my soul here. Plus, saying aloud that I want validation on IG seems so . . . *pathetic*.

As we walk, my eyes wander to my parents' house out of habit, noting that the front porch light is on. My mom must be out. Or my younger brother, Leo. I wouldn't know; I rarely have any idea what goes on in that house.

I wrap my arms around my body and Hari reaches out to rub my shoulder. I almost pull away, the taunts from Luis and Marcus about us being a couple echoing in my mind, but don't. Hari's hand is warm and comforting.

He clears his throat. "They shouldn't have said shit, Kat. I never told them."

"I know you didn't," I say. "They're just idiots. They can't imagine a boy and a girl being close without it *being* something."

"Yeah." He pauses. "But, I mean. They're not really wrong." There's a coy smile on his lips when he says this. "Right?"

I stiffen. Technically, he is right. We make out. We do stuff sometimes.

But . . . being *something* with Hari? I don't know. I really don't. And I'm too much of a coward to be upfront and tell him that despite how hot he is, despite how much I like what we do, despite how kind he is to me, it's probably not gonna happen—not for real, anyway. Hari is my *best friend* and I don't want to lose him.

He presses. "Kat?"

"No, yeah. I just don't want them knowing anything," I lie. Always lying.

"Yeah," Hari says. Quietly, he adds, "But maybe it wouldn't be so bad?"

"Do you really trust them not to be weird about it? I love them, but...I don't know." I stop walking and jut my chin out in the direction of my grandparents' house, an aging California bungalow with pale yellow siding and a porch full of plants. It's a ways, and he normally walks me farther than this, but I cannot do a what-are-we conversation right now. "Anyway, I'm good here."

He looks surprised. "Oh, okay. Are you sure? I can—"

"Yeah, for real. I'm good," I say, forcing a smile. "Thanks. I'll text you?"

He swallows whatever words almost come out. "Sure. See you."

Chapter Two

Maybe I should've taken Hari up on walking me all the way home. It's late, I swear I heard a twig break behind me, and I'm suddenly spooked. Because of that, I'm not as careful sneaking back *into* my house as I was sneaking *out* of it.

Okay, so, should I have snuck out in the first place? Probably not. But my grandparents would have been upset if they knew what I was doing: late-night drives, a dark reservoir, coyotes...So, the way I see it, I was doing them a favor by keeping it a secret and just dipping out after curfew, which is an embarrassing 10 p.m.

I didn't want to worry them, you know? I'm basically *protecting* them. My grandma is a natural-born worrier and I'd rather she focus on other things, like her beloved iPad games.

That's why I get so annoyed at myself when I scrape my shin on my windowsill and make way more noise than I intend.

I'm normally an expert at stealthing (yes, even for a fat girl), but not tonight, obviously. Now my shin is throbbing and I can't even swear and hop around until it feels better because there's *no way* I'm risking waking Grandma or Grandpa! Instead, I squeeze my eyes shut and clench my jaw until the pain calms, straining to hear whether there's a noise across the hall indicating I've woken anyone up.

Thankfully, the house remains silent except for the whir of the air conditioner.

Phew.

In the comfort of my room, I slip out of my shoes, take off my signature hoop earrings, wiggle out of my jeans and bra, and plop in the middle of my bed with my laptop and camera. I inspect my shin (fine, but shit, that hurt). And then I start to transfer the photos to my computer.

I find myself excited to dig in and see what I'm capable of. Astrophotography is so new to me. I haven't had a chance to do it before—not that I ever have a chance to be one with nature in between school, hanging out with the guys, spending time with my family, keeping up with my street photography, homework, working...and wasting lots and lots of time on the 'Gram.

Whatever. This sort of photography is pretty sick. I love the serene feeling that washes over me when I see a photo of the night sky. It's not as thrilling as stumbling across a picture-perfect moment while I'm out living my life, but it's still pretty dope.

Before I forget, I shoot Hari a text to see if he made it home okay (he did) and I notice that Marcus has sent a few Snaps to the group about how he found a piece of lettuce in the backseat, complete with photographic evidence. I take a selfie giving him the middle finger and send it, then cycle quickly through a few stories before switching over to Instagram.

My feed is a mix of Instagram poets, aesthetic accounts, adorable animals, and photography. And lots of those influencers I was talking about.

Like I said, I keep up with the accounts of girls who are effortlessly beautiful; always surrounded by friends or family that could be plucked straight from Hollywood; constantly traveling; and notoriously adored, captioning their pictures with cutesy lyrics, or anecdotes from their lives, or cheesy quotes.

I'm actually embarrassed by how much time I spend on my phone scouring through these accounts, dissecting each picture and wishing I had their reach (and kinda that my life was like theirs, lbr). But it bears repeating that none of these girls look a thing like me. So few are brown. None are fat.

I don't get why I'm supposed to hate myself so bad just because I'm fat. The word used to make my ears burn with shame, every offhanded insult from Luis about how I'm whatever "for a fat girl" digging into me. I wasted so much time thinking about how I'm the only fat person in my family, even wondering if maybe I got switched at birth, because there's no way these thighs like dough and these soft back rolls came from my thin parents, right?

There used to be this part of me that wanted to get all defensive, too, like—no, I'm just thick. I'm *only* a size whatever, as if that was supposed to mean something. Hey, world, I don't have fluffy kaiser rolls, just, like, soft lil bakery buns, so be nice to me, K?

But that's stupid. People really do not give a shit what kind of fat you are, just that you are. If you're lucky enough to be one of the few "acceptable" fat girls, you gotta have perfect hourglass proportions, a flat stomach, flawless skin, pouty lips—and even then, you're def still getting comments on your account about how you're disgusting, you should eat less, and no one will ever love you.

So, yeah. Maybe that's part of why I don't want to get in front of the camera. I can project my confidence in that fake-it-till-you-make-it kinda way in my real life as much as I want, but it gets surprisingly challenging not to be critical when I look back on pictures of myself and worry what others might think. Comments sections straight-up terrify me.

Messed up or not, that's how it is.

From my bed, I can see my reflection in the mirror, my stomach protruding out from my body, my thighs that are faintly streaked with stretch marks, my skin that is pockmarked from a recent breakout. How is it that I somehow even manage to be the wrong kind of fat?

Whatever.

I look back at my computer to see that my photos have finally loaded, grateful to shift my focus toward something useful. I scroll through all today's pictures, marking the best. Of the many that I took, there are maybe twenty-five I've earmarked, of which I'll only edit ten or so. I'll submit just one photo of the night sky to class, and post just one of the roller-skating couple to my IG. But that one has to be *perfect*. Maybe this candid shot of city life might be what finally gets me some clout.

But probably not.

It's nearly 3 a.m. by the time I'm done editing, but I have my two favorites. I'll have to post tomorrow on IG; if I do it now, it'll be buried by the time I even wake up.

A soft rap on the door nearly startles my bones right out of my body.

I quietly walk over and open it to find the short, plump silhouette of my grandma, dressed in her housecoat and illuminated from behind by the hallway light.

"What are you still doing up?" I whisper.

She wordlessly hands me one of the two mugs she's cradling. I breathe in and smile. Sleepytime tea, my favorite. "It's nearly time for me to wake up for the day. What are *you* still doing up?" Her voice is playful, not accusatory in the slightest.

I give her a sheepish grin. "Editing some photos."

"Ah," she says with a nod. "I should know by now that creativity strikes at the most inconvenient times."

"Want to see?" I ask. (Even though the photos of the night sky kind of implicate me. Hopefully she won't ask questions.)

Grandma nods, coming into my room and peering over my shoulder at my laptop. She squints a little as her eyes adjust to my bright screen, and then she lets out a small gasp. "Oh, Kat. Just beautiful."

"You think?"

"I know." Her eyes linger over the photo to appreciate the detail.

I grin. "There's also this one…" And I pull up the pic for IG, then glance back at Grandma as she looks it over. The glow of my laptop casts a bluish light on her pale face, illuminating her soft graying hair; her brown eyes and button nose, both of which match mine; and the wrinkles developed from decades of expressions (which I appreciate, though she laments them, laughing and telling me, "Never get old!").

She's so confident in my greatness, I can't help but feel a wave of gratitude wash over me. My grandparents are always reminding me that I'm *enough* and, on nights like tonight, I could really use it.

Sometimes I wonder if I even deserve them, though I'm not about to say that out loud. They saved me. If it sounds dramatic, that's because it is. There's a reason I'm here, in the Mancini house, instead of one street over in the Sanchez house with a dad, a mom, a brother, and four dogs. (Yes, four.)

It's complicated. I don't know very much about my early life aside from what I've picked up by eavesdropping, but I do know this: more than seventeen years ago, my parents, Sarah Mancini and Anthony Sanchez, were just teenagers doing their thing.

My mom met my dad when they were fifteen. By the time they were sixteen, my mom was pregnant. Secretly. No one, not even my own mom, knew—or so goes the story.

At the time, my dad was going *through* it. He'd been brought here, to Bakersfield, from Puerto Rico by my abuela, along with my Tío Jorge and my Titi Grace. Abuela was here to help care for her sister, Victoria, who was sick with cancer. When the prognosis turned grim, Victoria decided she wanted to die in peace in the small town in Puerto Rico where she'd grown up, but Pop and Tío Jorge had gotten used to California and wanted to stay. So Abuela took Titi Grace and Victoria and let them.

Papi and Tío Jorge bounced around the homes of distant relatives and family friends, but nothing was permanent. Tío Jorge was eighteen then and able to work, but Pop relied on the kindness of near strangers, kindness that wasn't an endless well, kindness that dried up. Eventually, he started crashing at his buddies' homes until his "oops!"—me—made an appearance. He and Mom were seventeen by then.

I threw *everyone* for a loop. Legend has it I was born in an elevator because everything was so unexpected. Suddenly, here was this baby, and now everyone needed to figure out what that meant.

Ultimately, Grandpa invited my dad to move in with him and Grandma, because Pop had no place to live and he and my mom both needed support. The new arrangement came with rules, though. Mostly: Do not get pregnant again, okay?

Only…less than a year later, there was another baby.

I don't know what happened in between, but my eighteen-year-old parents—with my little brother, Leo, on the way—left. They took all their belongings.

Except for me.

I don't know why. And maybe I won't ever find out.

Have I found myself wondering? Imagining? Daydreaming? Picturing myself in that house just down the street, with what might have been a picture-perfect family? Thinking that maybe my brother could've been my best friend? That I'd have a lifetime of memories and experiences with the ones who gave me life? Of course.

But I'm lucky. I only see my parents and my brother at weekly dinners, but look who I ended up with.

I smile at my grandma wistfully.

"Thank you," I say, meaning it.

"You should be proud," she says, leaning down to give me a kiss on the top of my head. "Now, go to bed."

I smile and close my laptop. "You got it. Morning, Grandma."

"Night-night, chickadee."

Chapter Three

I squeeze the squeak toy in my hand in a desperate attempt to get the adorable caramel-colored Pomeranian in front of me to look my way. "Come on, Peanut. Over here!"

But Peanut is stubborn. He doesn't want to look my way. He doesn't want his photo taken. He doesn't want to be here.

I don't blame him. No one wants to end up rejected by their family. But if you're an abandoned dog in Bakersfield, One Fur All is genuinely the best place to be.

Here, at this small nonprofit, Peanut will be given the proper shots, brushed, cleaned, trained, and well loved—just like all the dogs that end up here. The work is tough and underappreciated, but crucial, and I'm lucky enough to get paid to hang out with the loving dogs, the badass owner, Imani, and the entire committed staff. One Fur All is the first Black-owned, no-kill animal shelter in town, and she is absolutely putting in the *work*.

From behind me, my coworker Becca laughs at my pathetic attempt to get Peanut to look at the camera—and that's what finally inspires him to do it.

"Gotcha!" I say, snapping a few photos.

"That was a pity glance," Becca teases.

I shrug. "I will absolutely take it." I show her the photos and she smiles.

"Peanut won't last long." Becca leans over to Peanut and ruffles his fur. "Huh, Peanut? You'll be out of here in no time!"

I nod. "I hope so."

But I know she's right. Peanut is disgustingly adorable, so even with crappy photos, he'd get snatched up quick. The nice photos I take with the beautiful lighting and soft bokeh background and silly props are really to help the big dogs get out: the pit bulls, the German shepherds, the Rottweilers, the ones who aren't so cuddly and cute but still deserve to find a loving family. I feel for them. Maybe a little rough-looking on the outside, but big softies on the inside. I count it among my greatest victories when I help get one of them adopted.

One Fur All needs lots of photos for its website and its social accounts, which I manage. We never post pictures of the dogs in cages or newly rescued. Instead we wait a bit, until they've gotten used to this new environment, feel a little more comfortable, and then I try to get photos of them when they're at their happiest—usually running in the field out back, chasing each other, bellies and hearts finally full. Sometimes we dress the dogs up in themes (costumes for Halloween, Santa hats for Christmas); sometimes there's a flower crown involved; sometimes I just snap as many joyful pics as I can while they play. I've even helped build up a whole prop studio that lets us show off these dogs as their best selves when we're ready to do their adoption photos.

Not to brag, but the adoption rate has *def* gone up since I started here over the summer. A few of our posts have even gone semiviral (not, like, millions of likes viral, but a couple thousand views and hundreds of comments), which has helped. Best of all, I get to work a job where I know the work I do actually matters. How many people get to say that?

Plus: dog snuggles.

"I think that's it for today. Peanut, Cash, and Cinnamon were the only ones who still needed photos, right?" I answer my own question by looking back at the text Imani sent earlier for confirmation. "Yep. Just those three. Round 'em up!"

Becca and I entice the dogs back into their kennels, and I give

Cash an extra chin rub for being such a good boy today. Unlike Peanut, Cash may have a little trouble finding a family. Not only is he a pit, but he's missing a front leg. Most families that come in don't want a pit bull, nor do they want to have to "deal" with an animal missing a limb, even though Cash is the biggest sweetheart in the whole entire world.

"I'm gonna water them," Becca says.

"Okay. I'll get to work on these photos."

With my bag slung over my shoulder, I head to the small, shared office so I can work on editing these pictures and popping a couple onto One Fur All's Facebook and Instagram. Once I have a few processed, I send them over to Imani to get her approval.

Yes! she writes back. **These are awesome, Kat.**

Thank you! They were all little angels. Cash especially, I text.

Can you add these to the site and social ASAP? Heading back now with two pits, so we need to try to get Cash adopted sooner rather than later.

I write, **On it!**

Becca slips into the seat next to me at our communal desk, peering at the photos I'm uploading. "Oh, these came out so good," she says, looking at the Facebook post I'm working on. "Look at Cinnamon!" She points to a picture of the brindle boxer with her tongue stuck out.

"Ugh, I know. I just love them all."

"You say that about all the dogs."

"Because I mean it about all the dogs!"

Becca laughs and I start to work on a caption: *Last week, you cleared out the kennels! But we've got three more beautiful dogs looking for homes. Meet Peanut, Cash, and Cinnamon: your new best friends!*

For Facebook, I add text to each of the separate photos (including info about each animal), plus a link to their profiles on our site, in hopes that we can get some families interested in adopting or, at the very least, fostering. For IG, our link in bio will do. Lastly, I add alt text to each pic, because I'm not trying to be exclusive about this shit. If you're not making your social content accessible for all audiences, what are you even doing?

"This sound okay?" I ask, pushing my laptop toward Becca.

While she reads, I steal a second to check my phone. I've been wondering how well my recent Insta post is performing. It went up this morning in hopes that that would give it maximum views over the day. My heart sinks when I see there are only eleven likes. I groan.

Becca looks away from my laptop and motions to my phone. "Everything all right?"

I make a face and turn the screen to her. "I took this amazing photo of this couple yesterday."

"Wow!" she says, leaning in closer to inspect it. "That's beautiful. Shit."

"Thanks, but it only has eleven likes so far! Can you please go and pity-like it for me?"

She shakes her head. "No way. You *know* I don't do Insta."

Right.

BECCA DUPONT:
0 FOLLOWERS.

Because Becca isn't on Instagram.
Or Snap. Or Twitter. Or Snow. Or even FACEBOOK.

How? HOW? I want to shout this at her, but I refrain. It's just truly something I don't understand.

I pull my phone away from her and start going through my feed. A girl on a swing in a mossy tree, wind rustling her flowy dress and hair, midlaugh. Double tap. Hari's new sneakers. Double tap. A new photo of Tessa Thompson. Double tap. A video I don't turn on the sound for that shows some puppies frolicking in a meadow of flowers. Double tap, DM arrow, sent to our group chat.

"Oh, right," I say. "I forgot you're an alien."

Becca uses the scrunchie on her wrist to pull her silky honey-colored hair back in a ponytail and rolls her eyes. "I'm an alien because I want to experience life rather than worry about how many likes I get on a photo?"

"No, it's because this is literally how the world communicates now and you're actively choosing to miss out."

"Well, I think too much technology is bad for you. It's rotting our brains," Becca says, shaking her head. "So greetings Earthlings, I guess."

"People have been saying that technology is rotting our brains for decades and it's never been true." I put my phone down and point at my laptop. "Is this okay or what?"

"Quit harassing me about my lack of social media presence and I will finish reading and tell you." She returns to the laptop; then she turns it back to me. "Okay, yes, all good!"

"Thanks. And I don't know why you're so anti-Insta, anyway. You have a TikTok!"

She wrinkles her nose. "I don't *post* on it."

"But you could," I say. "You could even start with a mash-up of the photos from our LA shoot! Imagine?"

I open a new tab on my laptop and navigate to where I keep all my photos, clicking on a folder I have labeled *Becca*.

I scroll through quickly. I've been trying to work on some more stylized, editorial shoots to help me gain experience, and Becca has very generously been the model, which is great, because she's the most model-looking person I know. In this shoot, I have her posed on a basketball court, with palm trees and a bright blue sky in the background. The juxtaposition of the faded court, with its tattered net, against the bright green palms—and Becca in a sunshine-yellow dress—makes for what I think is a pretty visually fascinating photo.

"God, these would probably *kill* on Instagram," I murmur.

"No." Becca's voice cuts in harshly.

"Right. Sorry," I say quickly, closing the tab. "I know I'm being pushy. I just have a hard time getting people to like what I post and I think you would be really successful."

Her expression softens. "It's okay. I just—social media has always been unhealthy for me."

I nod as if I understand, though I kinda don't. "Yeah, totally. I'm sorry, Becca."

"It's cool." And then she smiles. "That shoot *was* fun."

"Right?" I grin. "But we don't have to do the photo shoot at Hart Park."

"No, no; it's okay," Becca says. "We're good. It'll be fun."

"Thanks, Becca. I owe ya."

The truth is that Becca is gorgeous, and I *enjoy* taking photos of her. Not in a creepy way—although I would be lying if I said I hadn't admired her looks before—but photographing her is effortless, you know? By now, we've done more than a few shoots, and I should probably find new models to challenge me, but maybe I like having the excuse to hang out with her.

She taught me how to French-braid. She introduced me to boba. She let me borrow her favorite book (*On Earth We're Briefly Gorgeous*—get on it). We're not quite friend-friends, but I'd like to think we could be.

As someone who has struggled to make girl friends, I fully appreciate that Becca lets me hang with her. She's a college freshman. She's way, way cooler than I am. Yet she still makes time for me, and she lets me use her for composition practice.

So...why shouldn't I take a few pics of her here and there? I'm getting photos for my portfolio, right?

Chapter Four

My latest post has officially flopped and now I'm annoyed. First, I'm irritated on behalf of this gorgeous couple, because they deserve better. Second, I'm mad at Instagram for being so shitty. I swear to God, I must be shadowbanned. The reach on this post is embarrassing. Is it my hashtags? My timing? What?

A simple *selfie of Luis squinting in the sun* has done better—no caption, no hashtags, just Luis and that smug face and I *swear* I could punch him. Lovingly, but still.

It puts me in a real bad mood. And it's a little obvious, I guess, because while I'm having some breakfast with my grandparents, my grandpa suddenly asks, "Why the long face?"

I glance across the table at him. "What?"

Grandpa motions at my phone. "You've been staring at that thing like it just peed in your cereal."

"Oh." I give him a sheepish smile and turn my phone over. "Sorry."

Grandpa puts his fork down. "No need to be sorry. Just trying to figure out how that tiny little screen has hurt you so. Do you need me to take it outside and have a talk with it? Because I will."

I laugh a little. "It's just...I shared a photo and no one seemed to care about it as much as I do."

At that, Grandma shakes her head. "See, Ray? This is what I hate about that stupid Facebook. It makes people feel bad about themselves for no good reason!" To Grandma, Facebook is the internet. It's adorable. She turns to me. "If it was one of the photos you showed me the other day, then those are magnificent! Show your grandpa."

"Magnificent? I'll be the judge of that," Grandpa teases. He reaches into the breast pocket of his shirt and pulls out a pair of reading glasses. "May I?"

I unlock the screen, pull up the photo, and place the phone in his outstretched hand, noting how weathered it looks from years of working as a construction contractor. I make a mental note to try to catch a photo of his hands soon. In black-and-white. I think it'd be beautiful.

Grandma gets up from her side of the table and leans over Grandpa's shoulder to look, too. "Gorgeous, isn't it?" He lets out a low whistle in response as she continues, "Those colors! The sky! The fashion! I mean, I don't quite understand the ripped jeans, but we have such a talented granddaughter." She is practically beaming, the corners of her eyes crinkling.

"This sure is something," Grandpa says, nodding. "How do I make this bigger?"

"I think you click on it." Grandma reaches for the phone and taps the screen a few times with her fingers, and I see the Instagram heart light up over and over as she likes and unlikes the photo (as me). "Oh, for God's sake. Kat, it's not working."

"Okay, okay," I say, rising from my chair and rescuing them. "It's pinch to zoom, remember?"

Grandma waves a hand at me. "I'm never going to remember that."

"That's what we have you for," Grandpa adds with a smirk.

I exit Instagram altogether and instead hand him the phone fully zoomed on the photo from my camera roll. "Here you go."

He takes in the photo, chin jutting out, studying it like it's some kind of painting. My heart swells a little at their visible pride. "I mean, even if no one else cares, at least you guys like what I do," I say.

"We love what you do, Kat, and so should everyone else!" Grandma insists. "Don't let this little box tell you what's good and what's not. You're good. You should know that. Isn't that right, Ray?"

"Of course, Bethie. Kat is our superstar." Then he winks at me. "Plus, we know by now that your grandmother is always right."

Grandma smiles and starts to clear the table. She reaches for my grandpa's plate, which is nearly empty except for a few bites of toast.

"Hey, I was still working on that!" Grandpa says, looking at me with a grin. He loves to banter with my grandma and give her a hard time, in hopes that it will make her or me (preferably both) laugh.

"This toast has been on your plate for at least twenty minutes now!"

"I was *thinking* about eating it," he insists.

"Oh, for Heaven's sake! Have a bite now and I won't touch it."

"Well, maybe I don't want it now that you think it's worth throwing away." They both start laughing, and I use this as a chance to slip away and get ready for school.

Buuut, before I do that, I'm just going to check IG one more time. Maybe in the last few minutes several people have recognized my creative genius?

Nope. Stuck at a measly twenty-four likes, and one comment from a graying older dude that just says, *Nice!*

My heart sinks. I can't fully articulate why this was so important to me, but it was. I was really proud of that photo I took. Is it so wrong to want a little appreciation sometimes?

Doesn't my art matter? Doesn't my perspective matter?

With a sigh, I navigate over to my feed and absentmindedly scroll through. A photo from one of my favorite influencers shows up. Posted three seconds ago. Already dozens of likes. The picture shows her standing on the beach, the sun coming up behind her, sky on fire with pink and purple clouds. Everyone cares about her. Everyone cares about this shot.

A text from Hari comes in. **Ready?**

Shit. I forgot Marcus offered to give us all a ride this morning.

Gimme five? I text back, then rush into the bathroom and take the quickest shower of my life. I pull my wet hair back into two braids, fill in my brows, slather on a quick cat eye, then slip into a T-shirt, a plaid flannel, and my favorite pair of jeans. Good to go.

"Love you!" I call to my grandparents as I rush outside with my bag.

I hear my grandma yell, "Have a great day, chickadee!" as I open the car door. I lift my leg to climb into the backseat beside Hari but notice Luis's backpack in the way.

Annoyed, I ask, "Can you move your shit?"

"Can you ask nicely, *chickadee*? Coño. Not even a hello from this girl." Luis reluctantly grabs his bag and moves it down by his feet up front.

"Now that you're all in my car again," says Marcus, driving, "please let me reiterate the rules of riding in Honey."

I groan. "Here we go."

"We know the rules, Marcus!" Luis protests.

"Clearly not. Because I suffered *blatant disrespect* from some clowns in my backseat the other night," Marcus says. "Riding in Honey is a *privilege*, not a right."

From beside me, Hari scoffs. "I have a car, too, you know."

"Excellent. Then you can drive in your own car if you are going to be so flippant about my incredibly reasonable rules," Marcus says.

I roll my eyes. "It was just a piece of lettuce."

"No, it was the principle of the piece of lettuce." Marcus shakes his head. "And how about a little gratitude? Even after that serious lapse in judgment, I'm still bringing all your asses to school. In fact, you can't say anything, Kat! You made us late."

"Me?!"

"We *were* waiting for you for at least ten minutes," Hari says.

Luis turns around in his seat to look at me. "You know, Sanchez, a little consideration goes a long way."

"Oh my God, I had to shower!"

He squints at me. "Yeah, sure. That's why you took forever. Nah, lemme guess. You were obsessively checking IG again?"

"Shut *up*," I say.

Marcus grins. "You're addicted."

"I am not!" I insist.

"Not sure we can trust your judgment on that one," Hari teases.

I cross my arms. "Okay, well, screw you guys."

Hari pretends to be wounded. "Is that how you talk to the person who's about to invite you to a party on Saturday?"

"For real? During Halloween weekend?" Marcus asks, getting excited.

"For real," Hari confirms. "During Halloween weekend."

"You're having a party?" I ask, surprised—surprised that he didn't tell me first, honestly, and also because it's not exactly a thing we do. I mean, the boys and I aren't losers, but we aren't really the kind of kids that throw parties like you see in all those teen movies or whatever. Luis always argues that's for white people. We mostly shoot the shit together. Sometimes we drink, sometimes we smoke, but it's usually a just-the-four-of-us kinda thing.

I notice Hari swallow hard, his Adam's apple giving him away. "Don't sound so surprised, damn."

"Sorry, Hari. I didn't mean it like that."

"She def did," Luis says.

I ignore him. "I'm just a little surprised. You didn't tell me."

Hari usually tells me everything before he shares it with Marcus and Luis. Maybe he *is* a little mad after my abrupt end to our conversation the other night. "Are your parents away this weekend or something?"

He nods. "They'll be at my auntie's. It'll just be me and Dev, so yeah."

At the mention of Hari's twin brother, Dev, the party starts to make more sense...though I'd never say that out loud.

Dev is super popular, an incredible soccer player, and the blatant golden child in the Shah household, a fact he and Hari are forever fighting over. From what I've heard, Dev's parties are usually pretty wild, but I wouldn't know because I've never been invited. Neither has Hari.

For all intents and purposes, Hari should be considered the "good kid," as he excels in school, does what he's told, and rarely causes trouble. He's also a genuinely great person, kind, caring, and funny. But he's also shy, anxious, careful, and thoughtful.

Unlike Dev, who fully takes after their father and is confident, self-assured, charming, and driven. For twins, they couldn't be more different. I sometimes wonder if Hari's dad is so hard on him in the hopes that it will push him to gain more confidence, but the way I see it, his efforts inspire the opposite.

Whatever the real reason, the disparity in how Hari and Dev are treated has definitely driven a wedge between them. I mean, can you imagine your own twin brother not including you in plans? Devastating.

"Tight!" Marcus says.

"Are we gonna have to dress up?" Luis asks suddenly. "Because I don't really do costumes."

Hari laughs. "I'm sure some people will, but you don't *have* to dress up."

Luis nods. "Good. I want to come as myself."

"Sounds terrifying," I tease.

"More terrifying than that mug of yours?"

"Ooh, what if I show up as Chris from *Get Out*? I already have the camera, and I look even better than that actor," Marcus muses, not wrong, but not humble. "That'd be sick."

Luis shakes his head. "No one's going to get that costume. It's just, like, clothes."

"I don't need this kind of negativity in my life!" Marcus shoots back.

As they bicker over what an adequate costume might be, I sink back into my seat. A huge party sounds both incredibly exciting and absolutely exhausting. And what would my costume even be?

Maybe I'll just lie my way out of this one.

Chapter Five

Hari texts to ask if I'd be up for taking some photos at the street-fashion fair downtown. It's an obvious yes from me, and not just for the shots. I've been wanting some time with just Hari, away from Luis and Marcus, so I can get a better sense of how he's feeling and figure out whether we're okay.

After the awkward conversation the other night, Hari not only didn't tell me about the party, he also skipped meeting up with me after my last shift at One Fur All—an insult to me *and* to the dogs.

So it was a relief when he reached out.

Hanging out with Hari is one of my great comforts. We can both shed our skins a little and chill. When it's all four of us, we always have a good time, but there's this unspoken pressure to be "on" all the time, you know? We're constantly messing with each other and vying for the funniest joke or wittiest retort. It can be a little tiring.

But with Hari I can just...breathe.

It helps that we've been friends since middle school. We got paired up for tutoring after I was struggling in algebra. He was a kid from the "smart class" that I was fully expecting to hate, but we sorta clicked. Underneath his anxiousness was this genuine, kind, funny person. I admired how he always wore his heart on his sleeve—unlike me, who is always calculating who gets to know what about my life, forever afraid of what others will think.

Hari is patient with my extra ass. While I'm stressing over my follower count on IG, he's good enough to reel me back in and remind me that none of that shit matters, while also kind of understanding why I feel like it does. He also knows more about me than anyone else in the world—including the fact that I really wish I had a better relationship with my parents, something I perpetually downplay with everyone else.

He's helped me understand the definition of *best friend* like no one else has.

And, let's be real, he is cute, too. I get why so many girls are always eyeing him—lush black hair; deep brown eyes; a jawline that does not stop. We're about the same height and I've found myself checking out his body on more than one occasion, especially this past summer when we spent a lot of time hanging out at Marcus's pool. I have eyes. I'm gonna look!

That's absolutely how this mess happened. Me, with wandering eyes, looking at him a little differently because we're getting older now and can I help that he's cute?! It got the best of me when the two of us hit up the beach and I felt so self-conscious about rocking this new bathing suit I'd gotten. My boobs had really taken on a life of their own, and I felt so thick and awkward. But Hari told me I had nothing to worry about, that I was "kinda hot."

We made out. Because hormones are dumb yet surprisingly controlling.

Did we have a few additional hookups after that? I'd love to say no, that of course we sorted it all out, it was a one-time thing, we were just feeling some kind of way that night.

But that would be another lie.

It didn't happen often, just sometimes. Hari was a good kisser, having had lots of practice. It was *me* who was probably bad; I'd only kissed, like, one other boy before, whose hair smelled like coconut oil and the ocean. But you figure it out quick and...something kept Hari coming back, right?

It was good and it was easy. It was exhilarating feeling wanted.

But lately, I can tell Hari wants more from me.

So...a normal, just-friends hangout will help me feel like we can go back to the way it was. That we're fine. That we can pull back from whatever we are—were?—doing.

That we don't have to be a *thing*.

And, away from the prying eyes and ears of Luis and Marcus, I'm hoping I can work up the courage to vocalize that, just to be sure that there are no secrets, at least not between us.

"You're awfully quiet today," Hari says as we park.

"Yeah," I admit. "I was just thinking about how annoying it was that Mr. Griffin spent so much time talking about Marcus's photo in class."

Hari laughs, relaxing his shoulders a little. "That's what's got you all serious? I was worried it was something way worse."

"Destroying Marcus with my talent *is* serious." We get out of the car, our camera bags over our shoulders, and Hari locks the car behind us.

"Right, of course," he says as we start toward downtown.

As we walk, the ambient sound of laughter, music, and voices grows, even though we had to park far away. But the walk is part of the fun. Already, we see people showing off incredible outfits— vibrant colors; glittering jewelry; fabrics mixed and matched in ways I'd never have imagined. A boy full of piercings passes us, his hair in his eyes; then a pretty girl our age with braids down to her waist.

I pull out my camera and start to shoot. Hari does, too.

"I mean, Marcus's photo was good," I continue, snapping away. "But mine was the night sky, Hari. The galaxy! Is there anything better?"

He pulls his camera away from his face, thinking. "Ice cream?"

"You think ice cream is better than the *galaxy*?" I shake my head. "Pitiful."

It's then I spot three drag queens in full face and the tallest heels, all dressed in camo like Destiny's Child from their old "Survivor" video. Hari and I exchange a look and rush to them.

"You're gorgeous!" I gush. "May I?"

"You better," one says, and the three pose as if it's second nature. I take a few and then thank them before they're swept away by people who want selfies.

I grin at Hari. "Coming was such a good idea."

He pulls his camera to his face quickly, pointing it at me, and the shutter goes off.

My hand flies up. "Don't!"

"I had to! You just looked so happy!"

"Delete it," I warn.

Hari rolls his eyes but obliges. "It was out of focus, anyway. Who knew the key to your heart was drag queens?"

I grin. "Aren't they the key to everyone's heart?"

The bronze-skinned girl with the long braids walks past us and I take her in—the jean jacket she has draped over her crop top, the curve of her hips, her pout. For just a second, we lock eyes. She gives me a small smile, and my breath catches in my throat.

"Are you checking her out?" Hari's voice has just a hint of bite to it.

"What?" I ask, blushing. "No! I mean, she's beautiful, but yeah. No."

He laughs, though it sounds hollow. "*Okay.*"

"I'm not," I insist, but my pulse is racing.

We move into the heart of the street fair, surrounded by booths and food trucks and street performers. I spot an older man, probably in his sixties, wearing head-to-toe denim and absolutely killing the game. "Hey, look."

Hari follows my gaze and can't help but smile. "Awesome."

After we get a few photos of Denim Man, who tells us his name is Manuel and who is more than happy to mug for the camera, Hari spots something that makes his eyes light up. He pulls me to a sunglasses booth and hands me a teeny-tiny tiger-striped pair to try, and—the nanosecond I put it on—we both erupt into laughter. Abandoning the glasses, we weave our way through stands selling clothes, jewelry (I stop to buy new hoop earrings to add to my collection), and hats, pointing out things we love or things we're mortified by.

It's easy. Normal. The way best friends should be.

"There go your besties," Hari teases, pointing at the Destiny's Child drag queens, who are posing for another photo as I put the new hoops on.

"Me and them, we're like this." I cross my fingers. "How do I look?"

"Perfect," Hari says, sincerely.

I smile. "So, speaking of our friends, that reminds me to post the pic of them on Insta. One sec." We find a shady brick wall to hang out near so I can transfer that pic to my phone without being in anyone's way. I toy with the contrast and coloring until it's perfect.

"Did I tell you my parents have been waffling about going to my auntie's this weekend?"

"They are?" I ask, only half listening. I think I bumped the saturation a little too much.

"Yeah," Hari continues. "They're wanting to do some additional planning for college with us—well, mostly Dev—rather than leaving. Dev is pissed. He already told a ton of people to come over on Saturday and someone posted it on Snap, too. So... people are coming whether my parents are gone or not."

"Hmm."

"Are you listening?"

I glance up. "What?"

He peeks at my screen. "It looks fine! Just post it already."

"The coloring is a little off," I protest.

He shakes his head. "You're obsessed."

"I'm not!"

"You're not even listening to me," he says, far too knowingly.

"I was listening!"

He arches an eyebrow at me. "What was I saying, then?"

I bite my lip. "Umm..."

"Exactly."

"I'm sorry, Hari." I post the photo and then tuck my phone away. "All good. Sorry. Can you say it again?"

He rolls his eyes. "I was trying to tell you that my parents suddenly aren't going away this weekend, convinced they need to be home to help Dev with more college prep. I think they're envisioning some kind of family road trip to nearby schools, I don't know. But Dev isn't happy. He already told people he's throwing this party. So, we're fucked."

I make a face. "Shit. What're you gonna do?"

"I'm doing my best to convince my parents to still go. But, you know, they're torn. Do they give up their weekend at my auntie's so they can dote on *Dev,* or do they listen to their perfect angel, *Dev,* and go away like he's suggested? Basically: *Dev,* or *Dev?*" Hari shakes his head. "Nothing I say really matters one way or the other."

I look at Hari. "I'm sorry. That's so annoying. They *do* care what you say; they just show it weird."

"You know as well as I do that I'm not the favorite child. It is what it is." He shrugs, but I can tell he's bothered. Who wouldn't be?

"Well, *I* think you're pretty great," I say, offering a smile. "Weird as hell, but still great."

Hari smiles back. "I take pride in that."

"As you should. Oh!" I point to a food booth decorated with Puerto Rican flags. "Empanadas!"

"On it," Hari says, handing me his camera bag and striding off.

I manage to stake out a shady spot beneath a palm tree where we can eat in peace. I scroll through IG while I wait for Hari to return. No likes on my pic yet, which sucks.

"There you are!" he says, and I look up to see he's carrying a generous plate of food—rice and beans, empanadas, and tostones. All my faves.

"Oh my God, gimme!" I make dramatic grabby hands toward the plate as he settles beside me.

Hari reaches into his back pocket and holds up two plastic forks. "Shall we?"

I eagerly grasp an empanada and take a bite that's so crisp and flavorful it practically melts in my mouth. "I would do illegal things for empanadas."

"Hard same," he agrees, taking a bite of his. "Oh, this one's pork! Want a bite?" He holds it out for me to try.

I lean over and help myself, and as I do, he steals a bite from the one I'm holding. "Hey!"

He laughs. "So I'm just supposed to share mine but you won't share yours?"

"No, but how about a little warning before you take *half* of my empanada, damn!" I tease. "I get an extra tostone to make up for it." I swipe one from the plate and pop it in my mouth. Once I swallow, I say, "I know the party is feeling a little stressful, what with your parents going back and forth about staying in town. But... are you excited to possibly see Dev get yelled at?"

Hari shakes his head. "You know we'd both be on the hook if people started showing up."

I groan. "Ugh. That's so stupid. I'm sorry."

"Let's just hope my parents visit my auntie." He turns to me. "If they do, it'll be a fun time. You excited for *that*?"

I push some of the rice around with my fork. "Well...," I begin.

He eyes me. "*What?*"

"So you know I already have plans with Becca..."

"Oh, come on! Don't tell me you're not coming because of that?"

"I need more photos for my portfolio!"

Hari huffs. "Can't you come after?"

"I mean, I really don't know when I'll be back. And this is mostly going to be your brother's friends, which is usually a hard pass for us." As I say this, I realize that all the reasons that make me nervous about going to this party are probably the same for Hari—tenfold. I can't ditch him. "I'll be there, though. Late, but there. Promise."

"You better be. And, hey, you can bring Becca if you want?"

"Yeah? That would be great."

He reaches across me to snag the last empanada. "And—as payback for even *considering* not coming—this is officially mine now."

Chapter Six

The front door to my parents' house is always unlocked, but I still knock and wait until someone lets me in.

Maybe I should feel slightly more comfortable at the home where I tell people I live, but I don't. It's uncomfortably alien, this pristine Spanish ranch house with a two-car garage, one-and-a-half stories, walk-in closets, fireplaces, elaborate patio cover—and my family.

The lie about where I live takes up so much room in my life. It sometimes feels like it could eat me up if I let it.

But this lie isn't mine. It was given to me by my mother.

She, Pop, Leo, and I were at Pirate Playscape, a local kids' entertainment arcade (complete with singing animatronic pirates). I was only five or so, Leo maybe four, and he and I had just come off a fun afternoon of playing games, having foam sword fights, laughing at sea shanties, and running around the ship-themed playscape.

When my dad and brother took a bathroom break, my mom looked over at me and smiled. "Are you having a good time?" she asked.

I glanced at my giant pile of tickets, which I would soon use to claim a prize. I remember *really* wanting an eye patch. "Yes!" I shouted.

"Good. That makes me happy," she said. "And you know another thing that would make me really happy?"

"What?"

"If you could try your absolute hardest and stay the night at our house."

I felt my stomach drop as she said this. I was already embarrassed by how I could never make it through a sleepover at my parents' house. The daytime would go by easy enough—it was fun to play with Leo, racing his Hot Wheels or watching Disney movies—but, without fail, whenever night crept in, my stomach would start to hurt. By the time I'd be in my pajamas, I would have a full-blown stomachache, often crying and calling home to ask if Grandpa could pick me up.

"Umm," was all I could think to say.

Mom nodded. "Do you think you can try that?"

I nodded back, but I could feel my stomachache coming for an early visit.

"That's great! It would be so nice to have you stay. I *really* want you to like our house," she said, holding my eyes. "I want you to feel like our house is your house. And, with you starting school soon, I would really like it if we could tell your new friends and teacher that you live there with me, Pop, and Leo."

"Like…pretend?" I asked.

"Exactly like pretend!" Mom said. "You'll still live with Grandma and Grandpa, of course! Nothing about that will change. We'll just *tell* people you live with us. That would make me the *happiest*."

The request didn't sit right with me, but I didn't want to make my mom sad. If pretending I lived with them would make her happy, then I figured I should do it.

"Okay," I said.

"That's my girl." She reached over and patted my hand as Pop and Leo came back to the table. He helped Leo into the booth beside me and looked over at Mom.

"Everything okay?" he asked, as if sensing something amiss.

She smiled at him. "Absolutely! Kat and I were just talking about how she's going to try really hard to stay the night. And we think it would be a good idea for her to tell people at school that she lives with us!"

Pop frowned. "Sarah..."

"What?" Her voice was suddenly much colder than it had been just seconds before. I looked at Leo to see if he noticed, too, but he was busy picking pepperonis off his slice and making a tower of them on his plate. "*I'm* her mother, Anthony."

"And I'm her father."

They stared at each other for a moment, before Pop shook his head and looked down at me and Leo. "Should we go cash in these tickets for prizes?"

"Yay!" Leo shouted.

The lie was born that day. And it's been mine to carry ever since.

The lie has followed me through kindergarten, elementary school, middle school, and now high school. People always assumed I lived with my parents, so it was easy to let them. In time, the lie became part of my story, worn and familiar and completely untrue.

What was once a small fib slowly grew bigger than anything else in my life. I can't exactly take it back now. People don't realize that I'm not even really part of *my own family,* and I would look so sad and pathetic and weird if that truth ever came out.

Hari, Luis, and Marcus are the only ones allowed to know it isn't true, but I get so upset whenever it comes up, they never press. They just let it ride.

And that's why when I go to my parents', I *always* knock.

Right after my rapping, the house is filled with barking. (My parents' dogs: a tiny Chihuahua named Pepito, two pits named Shark and Daisy, and a beagle named Archie.) I hear fumbling behind the door, and when it opens, there are the dogs with my mom just behind, her mahogany hair pinned up in hot rollers. She's in a full face of makeup and an off-the-shoulder dress, holding heels and her phone in the hand that's not on the doorknob.

"Kat!" she exclaims.

I crouch down to greet the babies first. "Hiiii!" I coo, taking a second to scratch each of them and give an extra-long rub to Daisy, who is totally my favorite. She nearly knocks me over, and I laugh.

These guys are definitely the best part of my visits. Don't tell.

"Daisy," my mom says, a little sternly.

"It's okay," I say. Then, "Hi, Mom. You look nice."

"Thanks! Come in, come in." She opens the door wide to make room for me.

I step inside. The dogs circle me, wagging their tails.

"Should I have dressed up? Are we going out for dinner?" I glance down at the casual joggers and crew neck I'm wearing— which look fine but don't measure up to my mom's outfit.

"Oh, no, not at all! You're peachy. I'll just be a minute." My mom tosses her heels onto the floor, slips into them, and then hurries over to the hall bathroom to take her hair down.

I settle onto the living room couch, Daisy and Pepito clamoring to be in my lap. Shark is off in the corner chewing on his beloved bone; Archie, who gives off old-man energy, is already lying down and trying to get back to sleep.

I watch through the open pocket doors as my mom gazes into the mirror, pulling her hot rollers out and running her fingers through her hair to soften the curls. Instinctively, I reach up to my own hair, tugging at some baby hairs that managed to escape my bun.

And then I look away from her, petting Daisy with one hand and pulling out my phone with the other.

From the bathroom, my mom calls, "So, how's school?"

"It's fine," I say, tapping through some stories. Looks like Luis, Marcus, and Hari are out tonight, and I feel an irrational pang at being left out. They always end up coming back with some inside joke and I never know what they're talking about. Ugh.

"That's good," Mom replies, as she leans in closer to the mirror and touches up the makeup at the corners of her eyes.

There are a few beats of silence, with just the sound of Shark gnawing on his toy until I ask, "Where's Pop?"

Mom leaves the bathroom, shutting off the light behind her, and joins me in the living room. "Picking up the pizza. He should be here soon."

I nod. "And Leo?"

She waves her hand at me. "Oh, who knows?"

As if on cue, we hear footsteps coming down the stairs and suddenly there's my little brother.

LEO SANCHEZ:
3,000 FOLLOWERS AND COUNTING.

Leo is the kind of guy who never takes a selfie. Pics are taken *of* him. Tall, with a slim nose, high cheekbones, and silky hair, Leo definitely takes after my mom, though the boundless can-eat-whatever-and-never-gain-a-pound metabolism is all Pop. He's also annoyingly smooth, self-assured, and funny. He's just... *cool*. In a way I don't get, and can feel pretty envious of.

Maybe it's the confidence you get when your version of our family isn't so fractured.

"Hey, Leo," I say.

"Oh, hey." He lifts his chin at me in a greeting before bending over to say hi to the dogs, who have rushed for him. "Thursday dinner, eh?"

"Thursday dinner," I confirm.

"Well, there you are!" Mom says. "I thought you were leaving?"

"I'm on my way out." Leo looks over at me. "Sorry."

Something tells me he's not *that* sorry to be missing out on our family dinner. I mean, *I* probably wouldn't be, if I were him. I shrug. "It's totally fine."

"Remind me where you're going?" Mom asks.

"To Chelsea's house. I won't be too late." Is Chelsea his girlfriend? The name doesn't sound familiar. But maybe. I feel like I should probably know this, but I'm too embarrassed to ask and clarify. I'd have to admit I don't actually know.

"No later than midnight," my mom says. "It's a school night."

Leo grins like he thinks that's funny. My stomach twists as I realize that my brother—who is a year younger than me—has a curfew a full *two hours later* than mine.

I wish I could say this is because of my grandparents, who are just too overprotective for their own good, but no. All big, official decisions about my life—like curfew or permission to take trips or whatever—still fall to my parents, despite them only seeing me once a week. My ten o'clock curfew is all them.

Yet Leo gets to go out and do his thing till midnight. K.

Leo leans in to give Mom a kiss on the cheek. "Be home later." To me, he says, "See ya."

"Yeah, see ya," I reply, returning my attention to my phone.

The front door opens and all four dogs race toward it at once, erupting into a cacophony of eager barking. They jump and bounce and paw at Pop, who is carrying two pizza boxes. These dogs live for my dad: he's warm and kind to them, but also knows just the right amount of discipline and training they need.

"Down," he says to them, and they obey, tails wagging wildly. When he spots me, a wide grin spreads across his face, and he hurries to give me a kiss on the cheek. "Hey, Kat!"

"Can we get a photo of all of us?" Mom asks suddenly. Leo, who hasn't quite made it out the door yet, groans.

Right.

SARAH SANCHEZ:
1,500 FOLLOWERS.

Yes. My mom has more followers than I do. Gross.

Pop raises his eyebrows. "Now?"

"Leo's on his way out," she explains.

At that, Pop frowns, and I feel a little vindicated inside. At least someone else is also disappointed that this dinner, which is *supposed* to be time for our family to get together and catch up, doesn't apply to Leo. "Where you off to?" he asks.

Leo sighs. "Chelsea's. I already told Mom."

"But we're having dinner with your sister tonight," Pop says.

"Anthony, I already told him he could go," Mom says, giving him a look that says they'll discuss this later. Pop looks as if he wants to say something, but doesn't. Instead, he lets out a terse sigh, walks into the kitchen, and puts down the pizza boxes, letting his keys fall into a glass bowl.

"Where do you want the photo, Sarah?" he asks, voice tight.

"Right at the table is good." She corrals us into the kitchen and stands at the head of the table while the rest of us dutifully sit. "Lean in." Mom holds up her phone to take a few selfies of the four of us, then inspects the images to make sure they're okay.

"Can I go now?" Leo asks.

"Drive safely," Mom says, opening the top pizza box and taking a pic of the steaming food.

As Leo heads to the front door, my dad goes to the cabinet to retrieve three plates. "D'you want the honor of choosing the first slice, Kat?"

46

I nod, examining the pie and trying to ignore the irritation I feel over tonight's already-rough start.

Pop holds a plate out to my mom, who doesn't take it. "Actually, I'm going to eat at Stacy's house."

What? First my little brother bails, and now *my mom* does, too?

She continues, "I *know* we're supposed to be having dinner as a family, but she's desperate for company! She's going through a really tough time right now with the divorce!"

"Seriously?" Pop asks, but it's not really a question. It's a statement of his supreme annoyance, tied up neatly in one little word.

"Kat doesn't mind." Mom looks at me. "Right, Kat? You don't mind if I hang with Stacy? She *really* needs me. Besides, it'll be nice, just the two of you! Daddy-daughter dinner!"

The way she says *daddy-daughter dinner* makes my eye twitch, but I just shrug. "It's cool." I pick up a steaming piece and put it on my plate, Daisy nudging my wrist with her snout, desperate for a scrap.

"Thank you!" Mom gives me a quick side hug and then blows my dad a kiss. "I'll be back later!"

And in a poof, she's gone.

Pop looks down the now-excessive amount of food he brought home, shaking his head. "Hope you're hungry, Kat."

I give him a halfhearted laugh. "It's okay, Pop."

Even though it's really not.

We fill our plates and ditch the kitchen altogether, settling in the living room with the dogs.

Pop flips through the channels until we choose a rerun of *Parks and Recreation*. Shark, Pepito, and Archie all sit patiently near my dad, hoping he'll toss them a pepperoni now and again, which he totally does. Daisy cuddles with me, and I give her some pepperoni, too. We make small talk between commercials: I tell Pop a little about some of my classes, and he tells me a little about his job.

Sometimes I imagine asking him more than just the polite basics. I'd love to learn more about my dad beyond the fact that he enjoys sports, works with Grandpa, and grew up in Puerto Rico.

He's an enigma, my dad. So stoic and private. I know more about Marcus's sisters or Luis's Titi Rosa than I do about my own father. I always imagined he and I could be close, if things were different. Our eyes crinkle the same when we laugh, and if our complexions were crayons, our hues would be just beside each other. My mom has sometimes offhandedly made comments about how alike we are, but it's hard for me to gauge if that's even true when I know so little about him.

I know a decent amount about my mom—if not directly from her, then from the stories Grandma and Grandpa have told me. But Pop...I still wonder. I imagine it was difficult to move to a new place, get left behind by family, and bounce around from house to house with no roots until he had to sprout his own. How does he feel being so far from home? Why don't he and Tío Jorge talk anymore? Why haven't we ever visited Abuela? Does he miss Puerto Rico? Speaking Spanish? His family?

None of these questions ever venture beyond my thoughts. The one time I ever tried to ask him about his hometown, he just got sad and quiet. To *really* get to know him would take courage—and a sense of familiarity I just don't have.

Maybe, though, I could ask something small. But what?

I think for a moment, and then: "Do you have a favorite color?"

He chews thoughtfully. "Blue." He looks at me. "What about you? It used to be purple, right?"

I nod. "Yeah, it was. But now it's gray. Like the moon."

"Gray," he repeats. "I'll have to remember that."

And then we go quiet again.

The show continues to play and I scroll through my phone.

In my feed, a photo posted by Mom pops up. It's one of the selfies of the four of us and the caption reads:

So incredibly grateful for this beautiful little family. As my kids grow older, I remind myself to appreciate the everyday moments that I'll miss, like our long-cherished family dinners that bring us together every week! Around the table is where we unwind, connect, and share so much. ♥

I can't help but scoff, letting more air out of my nose than I intend.

"What's so funny?" my dad asks, already smiling.

"Mom posted a photo of us." I turn my phone so he can see. "Says we're all eating dinner together."

He rolls his eyes. "News to me."

Mom has tagged me, Leo, and Pop in the photo, and I click on Pop's handle.

ANTHONY SANCHEZ:
7 FOLLOWERS. DEFAULT GRAY-PERSON ICON. NO BIO.

"Kind of a bummer about tonight," I say.

He looks over at me. "Yeah, it is. I told her I really wanted to make sure we were all together tonight. But you know your mother." He gives me a little half shrug. "We'll try again next week."

I want to say:

We don't have to try again, you know.

We don't have to pretend.

We don't have to *lie*.

But instead I nod, knowing I'll be back here—same time, same place—next week.

Chapter Seven

"*You are about to* get absolutely *annihilated*," Marcus says, clunking his lunch tray down beside mine at our table.

I arch an eyebrow at him. "Excuse me?"

"I don't think you're allowed to hit a girl, man," Luis cautions.

Marcus shakes his head. "What? No, you utter fool. Austin Simmons just quit as photo editor for the school newspaper!" His eyes are twinkling as he says this, as if we should be just as pumped as he is.

"Okaaay...?" I say.

"Okaaay, and that means his position is now open. And we are both going to apply." He motions between me and him. "And I am going to destroy you."

Hari lets out a low whistle. "Damn, Kat. You're just going to take that?"

"For real, Sanchez. He's trying to fight you. In a dorky, weedy, nonphysical way, but yeah," Luis says. "Hold up, why are only you two applying? We're *all* in Photography Club!"

At this, Hari straightens in his seat and looks offended. "Yeah! Maybe I want to apply, too!"

Marcus just rolls his eyes. "Then I'll destroy all of you at the same time."

"No, no, no. *I* am going to destroy *you*," I say, pointing at Marcus, suddenly caring about this thing I was completely unaware of just seconds ago. "Once you tell me why this matters."

Marcus rubs his hand across his forehead. "You're joking."

"Sorry, I just don't see why we would want this job," I say. "We've literally never been involved with the student newspaper before and I'm imagining I'll have to go to football games and shit."

"Ooh, yikes, I'm out then," Luis says, going back to slurping Capri Sun.

"Same," Hari agrees. "I'd rather die than be at Dev's soccer games."

"No, no, no. There is a whole team of photographers that— you know what? Listen. This position is a *leadership* position. You're in charge of all the newspaper's photographers. You get to boss people around. You don't have to go to games or anything else that sucks."

I make a face. "So, the editor never actually takes photos?"

"You do both," Marcus says. "Assign and also capture."

A thoughtful look comes over Luis's face. "Aren't newspapers, like...dead?"

Marcus heaves a sigh. "Yes, but we still have a *school* paper, Luis. Have you never noticed it before?"

Luis shrugs. "No. Honestly, my level of investment in this conversation is shrinking with each passing second."

"Okay, okay, so getting back to this," I say. "We already have Photography Club. Why care about this?"

Marcus lets out a laugh. "This girl really said, 'We already have Photography Club.'" Then he turns to me, hands clasped. "Okay, if I need to spell this out for you, I will, because I want this to be an actual competition so I can feel real victorious when I win."

"Okay," I scoff. "Enlighten me."

"Right, so, as Luis said, newspapers are dead and all that shit, but photography is alive and well. Our photography club is great, no doubt. Hence why I founded that shit. You're welcome." Marcus looks between the three of us. "Anyway, it's awesome, but it's still just a club, meaning technically anyone can join. So, while it will look amazing on *my* applications, because I *founded* it, it's really just a fun thing y'all did. No hate."

"I don't even care about college, pendejo," Luis says as he takes a big bite of his apple.

"I am not even dignifying that with a response right now. Back to this photo editor position. Colleges want to see that we've *done* stuff, okay? They want to see us as leaders and shit—especially people like us. Those white admissions counselors are like, 'Aww, look at these cute little Black and brown kids being ambitious. They'll look great on our campus. Maybe we can use them on all our brochures!'"

Hari starts laughing. "Okay, that's the straight truth. My cousin Daya says her school is forever trying to get her to pose for pics for their website and stuff."

"Exactly! It's really messed up, you know? Because it's like, we already feel tokenized and alienated at PWIs, and the whole university system itself upholds racist ideologies, but then we get used as pawns to show quote-unquote *diversity* so that we can try and get other BIPOC students there. Which is why I'm not playing around and I'm going to an HBCU."

"Okay, this is all great analysis, Marcus, but can you please get to the point about the photo editor position already?" I ask.

"Patience, Sanchez," Luis teases.

"Eat me, Luis."

"As I was saying," Marcus continues, "colleges like to see us as leaders. This photo editor role is perfect. This shitty school isn't known for much, but the last two photo editors both got into good colleges. I'm just trying to make sure the same is true for us. *That* is why we need to apply, Sanchez. It'd be good for either of us—I *know* how serious you are about your photos." He winks. "Although, obviously, the job's already mine."

I try not to make it clear that Marcus has clearly spent way more time thinking about college, his future, and his goals than me, and nod. "I knew all that. Just wanted to waste your time."

Marcus laughs. "Shut up, stupid. So, you gonna give me some competition or what?"

"Of course I am! You think I'm just going to let your sorry ass talk to me like that?" I shake my head. "Hell no. This opportunity is mine for the taking. Plus, I'm also a girl—"

"*Barely* a girl," Luis interjects, poking at my arm.

I ignore him. "So I feel like it's extra important for me to show that I can lead. Let's do this." I stick out my hand to shake with Marcus.

He grips my hand tight and shakes. "I look forward to trouncing you."

I smile at him. "You're already dead."

* * *

Marcus's challenge lights a fire under my ass, which surprises me. I spend my next class looking up some of the old photo editors at my school. It's easy enough to track them down on social media.

And, as it turns out, Marcus is right: many of the students who held exactly that position have gone on to great schools across the country. One is even a photography intern for the *New York Times*. Damn.

I'm kinda embarrassed that most of what Marcus shared during his offhanded rant was stuff I hadn't even really thought about. I guess that means I should be focusing more on my future—fretting over college admissions, figuring shit out.

But, despite being a senior, I don't even know if I *want* to go to college.

It's not like this is something we've ever really discussed at home. I'd be the first one ever attending. My grandparents are always telling me I'll do big things, but there's not really a discussion of the path between where I am now and those big things. I *think* they assume

I'll go to college...but then again, they would probably support me in whatever I wanted to do.

Though my parents have asked about college here and there, it's always been in the polite-dinner-conversation-with-people-you-hardly-know kind of way. Even if they were heavily invested in my future, I'm not sure they'd know how to help me decide if it's worth it or what I need to do to go. They were teen parents. They had bigger things to worry about than Statistics I.

Honestly, it's *school* that grinds my last nerve with all the college talk. They act like there is no other path out there for you if you aren't heading to some lush green campus with brick buildings.

Not one person has ever really asked me what *I* want to do, where *I* see myself, what kind of future *I* picture, and I honestly haven't even really asked myself either. Up till now, I was just expected to stay out of trouble and get decent grades, and I was fine with that.

I know I love photography, but the portfolio I'm building is just so I can start working freelance when I turn eighteen. I hadn't ever really considered using it in an application. Or going to art school. Or anything.

But now that graduation is approaching, that's suddenly not enough.

Does everyone else have every part of their lives figured out except for me?

• • •

After school, I head to One Fur All for a shift, and make a mental note that this would def be considered an extracurricular. *If* I cared about that kind of thing, not all hope would be lost.

When I walk through the door, it's chaos, with dogs barking and running around everywhere. What the hell happened here and why are none of these dogs in their pens?

Imani is shouting directions at some of the workers to wrangle the dogs back into their areas, and the moment she sees me, she says, "Kat, go grab Cash!"

Cash, my three-legged bestie, is chasing another pit I don't know yet. I toss my bag onto one of the tables and sprint toward him.

"Hi, Cashy!" I squeal, watching his ears perk up at the sound of my voice. "Come here, baby!"

He hesitates for a moment, but another enthusiastic "Hi!" from me and he bounds right over. I give him plenty of scratches while also grabbing his collar and leading him toward his kennel. Once he's inside, I give him a kiss on the head before securing the gate behind me and rushing to help Becca with a husky. Eventually, we get the animals back to their places, though the dogs are still riled up like they want to get back out and play.

Imani waltzes over to the two of us with a long-haired Chihuahua in her arms. "Well, that was fun."

"What happened?" I ask.

"Cash figured out how to open the locks on the cages," Becca explains.

My eyes go wide. "I'm sorry, what?"

Imani laughs. "Yep! Smart boy, that one. I had kind of seen him eyeballing us every time we would go in and out of his cage, but today was the first time I saw him do it. Of course, by the time we realized, he had already escaped and gotten a few other dogs out of their pens, too."

I look over at Cash. "You're a dog genius? Why didn't you tell me?" He wags his tail in response.

"I guess we need to invest in some better locks—ones that aren't susceptible to a very smart dog lifting them with his snout," Imani muses. To the Chihuahua, she makes her voice high and says, "Not that you could ever reach, huh, Sammie?" Then she hands Sammie to me. "Might be best to do individual photos of the newbies today, like her. Let's keep the chaos to a minimum."

"On it," I say, taking Sammie and stroking under her chin.

"Can you start to water the dogs, please, Becca? I have some online lock shopping to do, apparently."

Becca nods. "Will do!"

I head into the office behind Imani and walk over to the stash of costumes I keep under the desk. After riffling through them one-handed, Sammie squirming in my grip, I emerge with some leaf crowns Becca and I made for the dogs.

One by one, I take the new arrivals out of their kennels, photographing each. By the time I'm done, I've got pics for Sammie the Chihuahua; Petal the pit; and Storm the husky. Plus, I absolutely took a few more pics of Cash to freshen up his profile. As much as I love him, I'd love more to find him a loving family.

While I edit the photos, Becca comes in and settles in beside me at the computer.

"All watered?" I ask.

"All watered. Show me whatcha got," she says. I spin my laptop toward her. "Oh my gosh! Cash looks so, so cute in that crown."

"Right? *Please* let this be the pic that finds him a forever home."

"Seriously. He's so lovable," Becca says. "If I weren't living in an apartment, I would take him home myself."

"I literally asked my grandparents if we could adopt him, but my grandma's legit terrified of pit bulls." I sigh. "We'll find him a home one way or another."

She nods. "We always do."

I go back to editing the photos. After a few beats, I ask, "We still down for pics tomorrow?"

She looks at me. "If you still need them, I'm in!"

"Great. Meet at Hart Park, then?"

"Actually, why don't you come by my apartment?" she offers. "Sixish? I'll text you the address and we can go from there."

* * *

When I get home, I spend some time on my homework before falling down a social media rabbit hole.

I never really mean to; it just kind of happens. In between writing a few words on Chaucer for my English essay, I sneak peeks at IG—peeks that become looks, looks that become stares, stares that become full-on focuses. It's not my fault everything there is so much more interesting than my actual homework.

I scroll like it's my duty. I study the photos, I watch the stories from people at school who have their shit so much more together than me, I ogle the posts from people I don't even *know*—so well lit, so aesthetically pleasing. Double-tapping like an obligation.

A notification from my mom pops up. I check it out and find that she's posted a throwback photo from when Leo and I were little. I stare at those two tiny kids—me, already plump, Leo, already tall—and let myself imagine for the millionth time what might've been.

I scroll through my mom's grid. All of it depicts a picture-perfect life. Her and my dad traveling; Leo lounging at the pool in their backyard; the dogs on hikes; the four of us at our dinners.

Annoyed, I switch to creeping her Facebook profile, which is even more convincing. In between photos, she peppers in inspirational quotes, text posts about how being a mom is everything, over-the-top odes to each of us, Man Crush Monday pics of Pop, and on and on and *on*. If you were just stumbling across either of her profiles, you would fully think she had the sweetest family life.

It would be impossible to know she and my dad were teen parents who abandoned one of their kids and then told her to pretend otherwise.

But that's probably for the best.

Chapter Eight

By Saturday, it's official: Hari's parents are away for the weekend.

He begs me to come over before I meet up with Becca to help "set up for the party," as he puts it. I gently remind him that it'll be fine; no one's expecting decorations.

But he's nervous, and I know setting up is just a goofy pretext, so I go—but I make a quick pit stop before I show up at his house.

I arrive with a ghost-shaped balloon and a pumpkin piñata.

The grin on his face when he sees the festive decorations makes the extra effort totally worth it. "You're dumb," he says.

I hold out the balloon to him. "You love me."

Hari gamely takes the floating ghost from me, then motions for me to follow him inside. "Come on."

The Shah household is a sprawling, spotless Spanish modern, but today the rooms look even bigger than normal. There doesn't appear to be a thing out of place—mostly because there doesn't appear to be much of anything, period.

"Is it just me or are things looking a little...different?" I ask, already knowing the answer. I know this house as well as I do my own, and I can already list off some of the pieces that are mysteriously absent, like the solid-glass coffee table.

"Yeah, so, while Dev is out getting drinks and whatever, I've been put on hide-everything-that-could-get-broken duty," Hari explains. "Oh, and good news: you're helping."

I make a face at him. "I already helped. The balloon? The piñata?"

He scoffs, but I hold the piñata high. "Where should we hang this? I feel like the center of the living room would work well, since it's so spacious now. Then we can all jump around when the candy falls out."

"Hilarious, you know that?"

"I do know that." Hari takes the piñata from me, shoving it and the balloon behind his bedroom door. "You're saving those for later, right? We'll bring them out once everyone's here?"

"Oh, yeah, of course," he says dryly. "I definitely want all my brother's friends to see me with kiddie decorations. That would help me be accepted and not at all taunted by my peers for eternity."

"I'm sayin'."

Hari motions to the dining room. "Can you help in there? There are tons of breakables."

"Of course," I say, and we get to work carefully storing away the glassware on display in the dining room hutch, as well as Mrs. Shah's collection of crystal figurines. We grab a couple of other stray items until the house is nearly desolate and drunk-partyer-proof.

But even with that done, Hari is still pacing around nervously.

"You've gotta relax," I say. "The party is going to be fine."

"Is it? Because I'm suddenly feeling real nervous about having my entire house full of whack-ass seniors who get belligerently drunk. There's no way we pull this off without my parents finding out. And you know whose fault it's going to be, right?"

"Parties are not new to Dev," I remind him. "He can handle this. Speaking of, what made him let us come this time, anyway?"

Hari smirks. "I threatened to tell our parents."

"Bold! I like it."

He sighs. "Yeah, well, I'm kinda regretting that now. How are you so calm? Aren't you a little worried about, like, fitting in?"

"Well, yeah, of *course* I'm stressed about that," I admit. "But it'll be fine, I promise. I feel like we may be overthinking this. And the booze will help."

Hari nods. "Right. The booze will definitely help. And yeah, I'm overthinking this, for sure. It's kinda my thing."

I laugh at that. "You? Never!"

He smiles at me. "I'm just really glad you decided to come here instead of hanging out with Becca."

I grimace. "Well..."

Hari narrows his eyes. "Hold up. You *did* decide to stay here with me while I have my epic preparty meltdown *rather than abandon me* for a coworker you barely know, right?"

"So, about that..."

"Kat!"

"Okay, well, in fairness, I was straight with you about my plans. You even said I should bring Becca, which I very reasonably understood to mean you were fine with me hanging out with her beforehand."

His shoulders slump. "Kat. Please. I need support, here."

"I'll be here! Okay? I'm meeting Becca for just a little while. We'll be back before Luis and Marcus even hit on anyone," I say, trying to make Hari laugh. But he doesn't. "Don't be pissed. I told you I had plans."

"Not pissed, just disappointed," Hari says.

"Wow, really? You're gonna hit me with an I'm-disappointed-in-you right now?"

"Well!" Hari huffs.

I hold up my hands to him. "Okay. Fine. But I will be here. Even if you're 'disappointed' in me." I check the time on my phone. "And, actually, I'm gonna head out so I can be back here sooner. Okay?"

Hari falls onto the couch with a thud. "Leave me here to die."

I pat him on the arm. "That's the spirit. Don't break out the piñata without me! I'll see you soon."

On my walk back to my house, I feel a twinge of guilt. I'm

kinda abandoning my friend in his time of need. But also, I fully had plans, and I told him, and he knew, so. You know.

* * *

Before I head to Becca's, I need to get ready. My current look ain't it.

Especially because when it comes to Becca, she's always wearing the kind of shit that gives off, I don't know, *effortlessly cool* vibes. Oh, this oversized T-shirt over some shorts so it looks like I'm just wearing it as a dress? No big. What, this vintage polo over some baggy jeans? It's whatever. Like, she's not *trying* to look good, but looking good finds her.

So…what the hell will I wear that can work for hanging out and taking photos but *also* translate right into Hari's party as a quasi-costume? (It *is* a Halloween bash, theoretically.) Probably should've given this some thought before now.

I sort through my closet, feeling more dejected with each item. Nothing in my wardrobe is hitting. Nothing seems *right*.

Unless…

I crouch down beside my bed and start to dig underneath, pushing aside lost socks, a journal I've never written in, and an old camera case until I reach a plastic bin of clothes. It's mostly where I keep old things I've loved so much that they're no longer wearable, but I *know* I also stuck some clothes in here that I got from Mom and Pop on my last birthday.

After rummaging around inside, I find what I'm looking for at the very bottom: a plaid overall jumper and a long-sleeved off-the-shoulder white shirt to go beneath it—wrinkled, but unworn.

It's the furthest thing I own from my normal ensemble. But tonight I'm looking for something different, so maybe this could work. If anyone asks, I'm an ambiguously brown background extra from the movie *Clueless* or someone who goes to private school.

I walk into the kitchen with the clothes in hand and pull out the ironing board from the nook between the fridge and the pantry.

I've got to revive this outfit as if it hasn't been shamefully balled up under my bed for months. I find the iron under the sink and plug it in.

The distinct screeching sound our ancient ironing board makes as I open it must alert Grandma to what I'm doing because before I know it, she's pushing my hands away from the iron and clothes and saying, "Let me take care of this for you!"

"You really don't have to."

"It'll just take a second," she insists, already pressing the hot metal to the fabric and smoothing it out. "Where are you off to tonight?"

"Nowhere special. Just taking some pictures for a friend and then I'll go over to Hari's," I say, carefully omitting the part about the dozens of other people who will be there, the drinking, the pot. You know. "It might be a little after ten before I'm back."

Grandma hesitates, handing me the freshly pressed jumper and laying the shirt down next. "Well, I don't want you staying at his house too late...."

"I won't be that late. Maybe midnight?" When she gives me a look, I protest. "Leo has a midnight curfew!"

Grandma raises her eyebrows. "He does?"

"You didn't know?"

She smooths the shirt on the board in front of her. "I assumed it was ten o'clock, like yours."

"It's not. I don't think it's very fair that my little brother gets to stay out later than I do," I say with a sigh. "Can we make my curfew midnight like his?"

"I don't know.... That's really a decision for Mom and Pop to make...."

"But why?"

"They're your parents." A simple, truthful statement that makes frustration bubble up inside me. This is the line I've been

fed over and over and over for years—a supposed obvious explanation for why my life is set up in such a fractured way. Live here,
but abide by the rules made up by the people over there. Don't ask
questions. We're *family*.

What if I'm sick of quietly accepting the way things are?

I choose my next words carefully, not wanting to cause a fight
but unable to swallow the annoyance like I normally do. "I think
you should be the ones to decide when I can come home," I say.
"Especially because the rules around curfew are clearly unfair."

Grandma considers this. "It does seem unfair to me."

"Sexist, even," I add.

She delicately pulls the shirt up, examining her work, and
holds it out for me. "So, midnight, huh?"

My lips spread into a big grin. "Midnight. Oh, thank you so
much, Gram!" I rush to hug her.

"Okay. Just be safe. There are a lot of unpredictable people out
there and Halloween weekend makes me nervous," she says, rubbing my back. "But I trust you."

I pull back, nearly giddy over this win. "Thank you."

"Have fun tonight," she says.

"I will!" And I head to my room to change.

I feel so victorious right now. Like I could do a little dance. For
the first time in my life, my grandma, the woman who raised me,
has been in charge of a big decision. I didn't realize how much this
had been weighing on me until now.

True enough, this may cause some friction between Gram and
Mom—they sometimes get into it whenever it seems like Grandma
is trying to have some authority in my life—but this has been a
long time coming. I just regret not bringing it up sooner.

When I pull on the shirt and jumper, they're still warm from
the iron, and they feel extra cozy going on. I throw my hoop earrings on for good measure.

I expect to look in the mirror and feel like an imposter. But I don't.

Maybe it's the thrill of a later curfew, or maybe it's that I've finally spoken up for myself (even if only in a small way), but when I take in my reflection, I look *good*! My bronze shoulders peek out of the shirt, the jumper nips at my waist and cascades over my belly, and once I sweep my hair into a topknot and complete the look with over-the-knee socks and my Doc Martens, I'm ready.

Let's do this.

Chapter Nine

I borrow my grandma's car and plug the address for Becca's place into my phone, following its directions as I hype myself up for whatever tonight will be. I don't know. Maybe I just want Becca to *notice* me—not as the girl she works with, not as the girl who bugs her to take photos, but as me, Kat.

Tonight could be that. I'm hopeful, anyway. I really want to be *actual* friends with her.

As I get closer to her place, I realize that she lives in the rich part of town. Her apartment complex looks like a smaller version of a stereotypical influencer house, with pagodas and balconies and palm trees and a pool and hot tub. *Okay,* Becca. Go off.

Once I park, get inside, and successfully locate her unit, I shoot her a text to let her know I've arrived.

The door opens a moment later, but it's not Becca. It's a petite Afro-Latina girl with tightly coiled hair half piled on top of her head, half free and covered in what looks like red hair dye.

"Hey!" she says warmly.

"Hurry!" I hear Becca's voice call from deeper in the apartment.

"Coming!" the girl shouts back.

She turns down the long hallway. I shut the door and follow her, a little overwhelmed by how spacious, modern, and *money* this place looks.

The girl takes a left and I do, too, finally finding myself in a white-marble bathroom with a stand-alone tub and walk-in shower. It must cost a small fortune to live here. I vaguely recall Becca mentioning her dad is a politician or something back East, so if he helps her financially I guess it makes sense. Lord knows we're not making bank at the dog shelter.

Becca is holding her phone and sitting cross-legged on a sprawling vanity, and her friend perches on a round stool just in front of her. Beside Becca, there's an assortment of beauty supplies, including a bowl and brush covered in the same red goo that's in her friend's hair.

"Hi, Kat!" Becca says brightly. "Oh my gosh, you look cute! But you're *so* early."

She moves past the kind words with such haste I barely have time to digest them. I give her a sheepish smile. "Oh, um, sorry."

"No, no, it's totally fine. Now you can join in on the fun. Cora's giving herself some gorgeous red hair," she explains in a singsong voice. "And I'm helping. Kinda."

"She's filming me," Cora explains, dabbing the brush at a curl.

Becca grins at me. "Cora's a *beautuber*." Her voice is playful as she says it.

Cora rolls her eyes. "I hate when you call it that."

"What am I supposed to call it? You do beauty videos. Kat, she's big on YouTube *and* TikTok!"

"You can just say it like that! You don't have to say *beautuber*. That skeeves me out." Cora shudders dramatically.

Becca shrugs. "Fair enough." She holds up her phone to film as Cora parts and sections her curls.

"I've been trying to convince her to come off her social media hiatus and be in the video with me," Cora says as Becca starts painting another dark curl red. "You know, relive her glory days."

"*Cor*-a." Becca's voice has an edge to it.

Cora frowns. "Sorry."

"What am I missing?" I ask.

The two exchange a look, and Becca sighs. "Well, you might as well tell her."

"Becca used to be on YouTube, too," Cora explains. "She was kind of a big deal."

"Not really. But, yeah, I used to be in the beauty community." Becca shrugs. "It's whatever."

Only it's not whatever. My mind is buzzing with this new information. Becca used to be a successful YouTuber? When? Why didn't she ever share this? Is this why she's so adamantly against social media now?

Cora shoots me a look in the mirror. " 'It's whatever,' says the girl who had thousands and *thousands* of loyal followers."

"Yeah, well, it got to be too much," Becca says tightly. "I thought about my view count all the time—it didn't matter where I was or what I was doing, I was thinking about *content* and *metrics* and *growth*. I spent hours moderating comments—hours. I was really hyperaware of how I looked, too, and I got into *such* a dark place with that. Worst of all, I got sucked into the drama and the cliques. The fucking cliques."

Cora nods. "There are a lot of cliques."

"Yeah. I ended up having a huge fight with another girl who I *thought* was my really good friend, and I just quit. Deleted my channel and decided to give it all up. Left it all behind." Becca nudges Cora. "Except for her."

"Thank God you kept me!" Cora says.

"You're amazing. The rest of it wasn't good for my mental health, to put it lightly. Do you know how many creepy men used to message me? How hard it is to actually get money out of sponsors? Fuck it, all of it. I have no desire whatsoever to go back to that lifestyle." Becca's expression is set.

"I'm so sorry that happened to you," I venture, shocked.

She waves her hand at me. "It feels like a long time ago now."

"Still, it sounds like it really, really sucked."

Cora nods. "It did suck. Especially because Becca was *amazing* at creating looks. She did so many makeovers on her channel! She would just go to Panera or whatever and do them for random girls—that was kind of her shtick. It was mesmerizing. She was an artist."

"Well, I stick to doing my own face now," Becca says firmly. "I sometimes miss doing makeup for other people, but that's all I miss."

We go quiet. I can't believe Becca never shared any of this with me, *especially* knowing how social-media-obsessed I am. Was she ashamed? Or just that scarred by whatever happened? It must've been an unbelievably stressful experience for her to walk away from thousands and thousands of followers.

I'm almost a little annoyed that she gave it up so easily. What I wouldn't give for that kind of visibility.

I push that thought aside and take in the way Becca's face seems to have fallen, a little gloomier than when I first arrived. Maybe I can cheer her up.

"So…I'm kind of a fresh palette over here." I motion to my face. "Want to give it a whirl for old times' sake?"

"Oh my gosh, *do it!*" Cora squeals.

Becca grins and puts her phone down. "Okay, you know what? Yeah. That'd be fun!"

Cora surveys her finished hair in the mirror. "While you guys do that, I'll get us some drinks."

"There's hard seltzer on the bottom shelf," Becca tells her. Then she leads me out of the bathroom and down the hall. We end up in her bedroom, where there's another vanity—this one covered in makeup, pristinely organized.

"I'm a little rusty," she admits.

I smile as we both take a seat on the vanity bench. "Guess it's a good thing I've never had anyone do my makeup before, then."

"Lucky for me."

She sits back and studies me and suddenly I feel exposed. So close together. Sharing a seat. Knees touching. She gently turns my chin this way and that, her fingers on my jaw, and a small jolt of electricity courses through me.

Cora pops in to bring us our drinks. She and Becca raise their glasses.

"Cheers," Cora says.

We clink and I take a big cold sip, needing it. Cora slips out of the room to rinse the color from her hair.

Becca leans in close, a black eyeliner pencil in one hand, and I breathe in the tropical smell of sunscreen. I close my eyes and feel the liner slide expertly across my lids, shivering a little when her warm breath tickles my collar.

I'm pretending that nothing is happening, that my pulse hasn't quickened, that I don't feel a thing while our legs touch, that I'm definitely not a little...into? whatever is happening.

A few steadying breaths ground me. I'm hoping she doesn't notice.

After a few minutes, Becca says, "Okay. What do you think?"

I come back into myself and look at my reflection. Becca has dusted peachy blush across my cheeks and collarbones, gelled my brows, drawn a dark, slick cat eye that helps elongate my lids, and finished with a nude lip gloss. I look amazing.

"Okay, Becca. You're good." I marvel at myself, turning from side to side in the mirror. "This gloss! Wow. So shiny!"

She holds the tube out to me. "It's called Sugar and Spice. And it's yours. The shimmer's never quite looked right on me." Before I can protest, she adds, "Anything else you want done at the salon, madam?"

I laugh, but my throat feels a little dry. Her radiant heat feels really...um...good. "I don't think so....I mean, if I could ever figure out how to get my hair to behave, that would be nice. But it's a mess up there. You *don't* want to see it down."

"Ooh, I can help with that," says Cora, who has appeared in the doorway.

"Cora is really knowledgeable about hair and makeup!" Becca says, encouraging me. "Tell her your problem and she can fix it."

"Oh, well…it's just that my hair is kind of frizzy?" I explain. "I don't know, it just never does what I want it to do. I see all these other girls who have their curls on lock and mine just don't listen to me."

"What's your routine?" Cora asks.

"Routine?" I repeat.

"Yeah, your hair routine. Like, do you use a microfiber towel to plop your hair? Are you strictly air-dry-only? Do you co-wash or go with a low poo?" Cora asks. "Like, I co-wash with sulfate-free conditioner so my curls can soak up a ton of moisture, but it's not for everyone. That plus some gel has been life-changing." Cora pauses and chuckles. "But by the look on your face, I'm going to guess I scared you with all that information."

I let out a small, embarrassed laugh. Uh, yeah. "Is it that obvious? I mean, I just wash my hair with whatever my grandma buys, brush it, and call it a day."

Cora's eyes nearly bulge out of her head. "You brush your hair? *Your beautiful, curly hair?* Oh, no!"

"What's bad about that?" I ask, eyes widening. I feel like I've been doing something really shameful without even knowing. (In fairness to me, I'm the only woman in my family with this hair texture! How was I to know?!)

"If you have curly hair, you do *not* need to brush your hair," Cora explains. "That'll just make it frizzy."

"That's why my hair always looks like shit?"

Becca laughs. "Kat! Stop, it doesn't look like shit."

"Oh, it def looks like shit. Don't even try to play right now," I say. "That's why a bun is my best friend."

"Okay, from here on out, instead of drying your hair with a towel and then *brushing* it, use a T-shirt to wrap your hair after your shower; squeeze out some of the extra water, then add some gel; and, finally, let it air dry," Cora explains. "I swear, it'll *change your life*."

"Yeah?" I ask, though I don't see how I'm going to remember all this. Just throw away the entire hair routine I've been doing my entire life? The one my grandma taught me? Sure, great. I love change.

"Yeah. I mean, it'd be best if you could ultimately switch over to a microfiber towel, but a T-shirt will do the trick. Anyway, we're going to show you," Becca says.

"I think I'm good," I protest.

"Come on, Kat!" Cora begs. "Please, please, please!"

These girls—who know what they're doing, who are confident in themselves, who seem to know exactly who they are—are trying to bring me into their circle. Share a moment. Bond. And I would like to know how to take care of my hair, so.

"Yes," I say finally. "Let's go the whole nine yards."

Cora claps her hands together. "Bec, can we borrow one of your T-shirts for Kat's hair?"

"I'll grab one," Becca says, dashing out of the room.

Before I know it, I'm back in the bathroom, I have a towel wrapped around my shoulders so I don't get wet, and I've literally let my hair down and draped it into the sink.

Cora massages some of Becca's shampoo and conditioner into my scalp—though this isn't, apparently, the stuff I should be using since Becca's texture is different, Cora insists that this will help reset my hair, and that I don't need high-end products to make my curls come to life. She assures me she has a video explaining all this on her channel.

After a thorough rinse, Cora uses the T-shirt to squeeze some of the excess water from my hair, making a scrunching—as she calls it—motion. She has me flip my hair over my head and then makes me try to scrunch. I do.

Amazingly, even wet, the curls in my hair start to take shape.

"Now, some gel," Cora says.

Becca hands her a bottle. "This is all I could find, but it should work."

Cora squirts some into the palm of my hand. "Rub your hands together, then scrunch, flip your hair back, and let it air dry. And you're done!"

I follow her instructions and look in the mirror.

There's a wet towel hanging off me and a few wet patches on my jumper, but my hair—my normally uncooperative, flyaway-prone, brittle and dry hair—is looking pretty damn good. There are even a few *perfect* curls; they're wet and still a little droopy, but they're there.

"Well?" Cora asks.

"Holy shit," I say, touching one of the MVP curls that is already emerging in a spiral. "Holy *shit*."

Becca squeals. "Kat! It looks beautiful!"

"Cora did such a good job!" I gush.

"She really, really did." Becca reaches out to touch the spiral curl near my face, her fingers grazing my cheek, and a small jolt of electricity courses through me. I don't know what's happening, but okay! "So gorgeous. Here, want to just touch up your mascara before we go?" She hands me a wand. "I'm gonna work on my own makeup for our shoot, okay?" She squeezes my shoulder, and my skin turns to fire. "Be back."

She gives me a little wave and disappears with a makeup bag, which I'm slightly grateful for because my heart is just now steadying back to its normal pace.

Seriously, what gives? Fluttery feelings, pulse racing, heart pounding? You'd think...

I nearly poke myself in the eye with the mascara wand.

Because no. No.

Right?

I mean. There's Hari, or whatever. And a few boys before. It's always been.

So this would be...

Hmm.

Tonight, this close to Becca, it's like I've seen her for the first time.

Chapter Ten

The sun is starting to set as Becca and I pile into her Jeep. She's wearing a full face of makeup and a floor-length, bohemian-style green dress, and we say goodbye to Cora, who has effectively changed my hair life forever.

Music's playing. Something folksy. I try to listen, but my mind is still buzzing a little over whatever earlier was—hard seltzer and the smell of sunscreen and unexpected touches.

I check my reflection in my phone to distract myself. I will admit: this makeup look is all I've ever needed. Along with the cute outfit and the flawless curls, it's like a whole new me. A hot one. I like it.

Who knew Becca was so talented with makeup?

Who knew she was a big deal on YouTube?

I've gotta look her up. While she's busy driving, I tilt my phone away from her and Google. Searching just her name doesn't give me much—some hometown honors from her high school days—but "Becca DuPont" and "beauty" and "YouTube" does the trick: I find a Reddit post with the title, "Whatever happened to Beauty by Becca on YouTube???"

It confirms what Cora said. Becca's channel had thousands of viewers, with her videos racking up *tens of thousands* of views. She had so many followers, people who waited for her new videos to drop, and then, out of nowhere, her channel was gone—and so was every trace of Becca.

The Reddit poster posits whether this could be related to a

group of YouTube beauty influencers having an epic falling-out. There are a few deleted comments and little else in the thread, except for a brief mention of Cora Mitchell, the girl behind the channel of the same name.

With nothing else to go on from that post, I turn to IG.

CORA MITCHELL:
470,712 FOLLOWERS AND BLUE-CHECK VERIFIED.

Shit. She really *is* kinda famous. A quick scroll through her profile and I can see sponsored posts, collabs she's done with other famous content creators, and a pinned comment from one of the all-time biggest influencers in the beauty realm.

How could Becca have given all this up because of a fight?

I give Cora a follow, wondering, briefly, if she'll follow me back. (Pathetic, maybe, but I can't help it.) And then the car is slowing and I look up to see we've arrived at Hart Park. I hurry to put my phone away.

Becca kills the engine. "So, where to?"

"Let's start by the river." Earlier in the week, I'd explained my vision for the shoot to her, confessing I had hoped we could get some of Hart Park's wild peacocks in our shots. "Thanks for doing this."

"No problem," Becca says. "I know how important a good portfolio is. Someday, I'll get to say I knew you when."

We get out of the car and walk to the river. The yellowing trees, dry landscape, and flowing water make a natural backdrop, even if it'll mostly be out of focus. I take out my camera and pop my favorite lens on it—I had to work so many shifts at One Fur All to get this, so I care for it like it's my baby—and adjust my settings. Then I take a few practice shots.

I crouch down to test the lighting, tucking my jumper between my legs. I'm not really used to the whole potentially-flashing-others thing, but I make it work.

"Let's have you do a few smiling ones to start," I suggest.

After that, I barely have to direct Becca; we've done this enough that she knows what to do, finding her best angles and trying out new poses. Once we get into a rhythm, I get lost in what I'm doing, blocking everything else out: Becca's past; Cora's fame; Hari's party; the attraction I felt earlier. The familiarity of being behind the lens, of framing each photo, of considering an angle steadies me.

We take our time and transition to different parts of the park. The soft luster of the setting sun is giving these photos an angelic glow, which gives me an idea.

"Becca, let's have you stand with your back to the sun, okay?"

She furrows her brow at me. "You are always lecturing me about how your light should never be directly behind your subject."

I grin. Who knew she was actually listening when I'd go off on my tangents? "As a general rule of thumb, yeah. But the sunset is so gorgeous right now, we can get a few interesting shots. You down?"

Becca claps her hands together. "Okay, where to?"

I point to where I'd like her to stand and model the pose I'd like her to try. Then I step back and peer through my viewfinder. The way the light is cast makes it so that the sun illuminates the edges of her hair, casting a golden halo around her. "This looks so good!"

"Because of your artistic genius," she says, pointing at me.

I roll my eyes. "Please."

A few shots later, I notice some movement in my peripheral and turn to see two peacocks ambling toward Becca. She looks over at me, eyes wide. "It's happening," she whispers.

"Be still!" I whisper back, watching as the male peacock walks a few paces behind the female. If we're lucky, he'll try to impress her, and we'll be treated to a gorgeous show of green-and-blue feathers. Sure enough, a few moments later, there he goes: tail splayed and shaking aggressively at the lady peacock, who is thoroughly unimpressed. Sorry, dude.

I whisper to Becca, "Get on one knee." She does, and looks at me for further direction, so I elongate my neck and show her the pose I want. Once she's successfully mirrored me, I snap a few photos and check the back of the camera. Yes! The adrenaline I feel when I capture the perfect image is *everything*. "Got it!"

Becca turns toward the peacock. "Thank you, Mr. Peacock. Best of luck on your journey to find true love." Then she tiptoes until she's a safe distance away, so as not to startle either bird, and dashes over to me. "Lemme see!"

I pull up the most recent photo, which shows Becca on one knee, her other leg extended forward. The flowy dress drapes across the withering grass in such a way that it resembles the peacock.

"Kat!" she practically shouts. She grabs my shoulders and shakes me. "It's perfect! Oh my gosh."

"I don't think we're going to top that one," I admit. "Should we pack it in?"

Becca nods. "Let's." I tuck my camera into my bag and sling it over my shoulder. "We should've taken a few pics of you. You look so pretty, Kat."

I flush at the compliment. "Thanks, Bec. The makeup is all you, though."

"But it's the whole look. The clothes!"

"Oh, this." I glance down at my outfit, sheepish. "It's supposed to be a costume. Like *Clueless*?"

"Right! Halloween. Duh! But, I mean, whatever," Becca replies. "It's so good on you! You have legs, girl!"

"Not really..." I shake my head, but I'm pleased.

"Trust me."

We get in the car and head back toward Becca's apartment. I'm high off the thrill of a good photo shoot, so when she turns her Spotify playlist on, I sing right along. We dance together at a stoplight and laugh. Around us, the sky begins to darken. By the time we arrive at her complex, it's later than I anticipated.

I check my phone to see several anxious texts from Hari asking where I am. I know I've got to head over there stat.

But first: I kinda need to ask Becca to come with me. After how much fun we've had, I'm feeling pretty confident that the answer will be yes.

"All good?" Becca asks, nodding toward my phone.

"I'm good. But..."

"What is it?"

And suddenly my heartbeat quickens, as if to remind me: hard seltzer. The smell of sunscreen. Her soft touch. *You look so pretty, Kat!*

Maybe...?

Before I lose my nerve, I blurt out, "My friend Hari is throwing a Halloween party. I was wondering if you wanted to come by? It's not a huge thing. Like, this is fully what I'm wearing."

Becca's eyebrows go up. She's looking at me like I'm the sweetest itty-bitty little thing she's ever seen.

Oh, no.

Oh...no.

"That is *so* sweet of you, Kat," Becca says, gently. "But I do have my own plans for tonight. Plus, I have to admit, I think it would be a little inappropriate for me to go to a high school party. The optics are...not great. I mean, I'm in college. I don't want people thinking I'm a creep or anything, you know?"

Oof.

The car suddenly feels small. "Yeah, for sure," I say, trying to keep my voice light. "Of course."

Becca smiles at me. "Okay, good. And, hey, thanks for today! I can't wait to see the new pics. When will you share them? I mean, not this evening, obviously, given that it sounds like you have a big night ahead of you! But maybe tomorrow?"

I nod, not so much at what she's said, but more to get me the hell out of this car. "That sounds good. I'll see you."

"Totally," Becca says. "Have fun tonight!"

Right. Something tells me that may not be the case.

Chapter Eleven

So badly, I want to drive home, curl up under my blankets, and sulk.

It's not easy being hardcore rejected from something you didn't even know you wanted.

But Hari.

His texts are getting more frequent, more desperate. He's not having fun. He's full-blown panicking. He needs me.

And, honestly, maybe it'll feel good to have *someone* need me right now.

I drop Grandma's car off at home, stow my camera gear, and offer a quick hug to my grandparents before leaving again.

On the short walk to Hari's, I find myself replaying everything that happened tonight. I guess I don't know what I was expecting with Becca today, but it definitely wasn't the roller-coaster ride that I got. I mean, we've always had a pretty friendly relationship, but tonight gave me the most unexpected *feelings*—and then. Oof.

How foolish was I to even consider?

When I near Hari's house, I can easily see why he's stressed. There are cars parked everywhere and the music, laughter, and shouting are carrying down the street. Nothing like making it really obvious that a party's going on. Smooth, Dev. Super smooth.

I go around back and start to weave through the throngs of people I recognize but don't know from school, searching for Hari.

But I stop dead in my tracks when I spot none other than Leo. My little brother.

He's wearing a skeleton T-shirt, so at least he's committed to the Halloween theme. He and his friends are standing around with Dev and Dev's friends, vibing like they all know each other, which is news to me. How is it possible that Leo is here in all his sixteen-year-old glory, laughing it up like he belongs?

Then again, maybe he does belong, in ways I won't ever really understand. Ever since he started high school, people have come up to me asking if I'm Leo's sister, even though I'm the one who was there first. It should be the other way around, except I'm a nobody. A few of our classmates have even straight-up laughed when they found out we're related, as if it's some huge joke. Me, fat, with my curly hair, pretending I'm hot shit but afraid I'm not anything at all, and then Leo—slim, tall, lighter-skinned, messy-haired, good-looking, and *actually* hot shit. No pretending necessary.

There's a girl in bunny ears hanging off Leo's arm. Guess that's Chelsea, his girlfriend. They're laughing with Dev, who is shirtless but wearing a firefighter's hat, as if that counts as a costume.

DEV SHAH:
10,403 FOLLOWERS.

Stubble. Muscles. Handsome like Hari but not nearly as kind. Gifted with so much confidence it should be illegal. He's essentially a walking fuckboi, the kind of dude who posts shirtless pics but pretends they're not thirst traps.

Distracted, I find myself not looking where I'm going. I almost *literally* run into Marcus and Luis, who are, predictably, trying to hit on some girls dressed as an angel and a devil. They all have red Solo cups in hand and it's clear to me that Marcus and Luis are working together at whatever weird pickup game they think they have.

As promised, Luis is without a costume, but Marcus is actually dressed up like Chris from *Get Out,* as he said he would be.

It's just a denim button-up, a gray undershirt, and his own camera slung around his neck, but still. He committed, and he looks really good.

"Kat?!" Marcus asks, eyes big when he spots me. He slaps Luis in the chest to get his attention.

Luis sways at him. "I'm a little busy here, man."

"You're gonna want to see," Marcus says. "Kat, you look—"

I put up my hands to stop whatever words are ready to come tumbling from his mouth. "Don't."

Luis finally peels his eyes away from the dark-haired girl long enough to look at me—I recognize her, a junior named Xiomara— and he bursts out laughing. "What the hell did you do?!"

My cheeks flush and I find myself tugging down the bottom of the jumper, trying to make it longer. What little confidence I'd had left is crushed under the cruel sound of Luis's cackling and the laughter from the girls he and Marcus are standing with.

I ball my fists. "Fuck you," I spit out.

Luis looks over at the girl. "She's so mouthy, that one. Don't even listen to her, Xiomara."

XIOMARA MARTINEZ:
722 FOLLOWERS.

"Run while you still can," I say to her.

"Stay out of this, *Sanchez*!" Luis hisses through gritted teeth.

"Can we get back to whatever this is?" Marcus asks, waving a hand at me. "Since when do you have legs?" And that makes the girl he's standing beside roll her eyes, grab Xiomara's hand, and start to pull her away. "Wait, no, Ava, I didn't say they were *good*, I—"

"No, no, no, no, no!" Luis says, reaching for Xiomara, but she shrugs and follows her friend and they disappear inside the house. Luis glares at me. "Ay, cabrón! The fuck is wrong with you?"

"The fuck is wrong with *you*?" I shout. "You're being an asshole!"

"Because I don't like your dress?"

"I mean, I don't mind it," Marcus offers.

"Because Hari needs you guys and you're out here trying to get laid instead of being there for him!" And, yeah, because you don't like my dress, but I'm not about to admit that.

Marcus furrows his brows at me. "What are you talking about?"

"For real. We haven't seen your boyfriend most of the night."

"That's my *point*. You're at his house and his party—"

"Dev's party," Luis interrupts.

"You haven't seen him all night and that's not concerning you at all?" I demand. Marcus and Luis exchange a look.

"We just assumed he was having a good time," Marcus admits.

"You know he gets anxious!" I say. "Some friends *you* are."

"You're the one who was off with *Becca*," Luis shoots back. He emphasizes her name as if he's a Valley girl. "Weren't you supposed to bring her, too? Where is she? I don't see that college girl you promised anywhere."

I shake my head. "She couldn't make it."

"A little sus…," Marcus muses.

"Very sus. Like, is Sanchez even cool enough to be friends with someone from college? We knew that shit was too good to be true," Luis declares. "Sad, Sanchez. What a liar."

And that feels like a slap in the face.

Luis can't possibly know that what he's said is eerily accurate, confirmation of my worst fears about myself. That I'm fake. That I pretend. That I lie. That I'm not wanted.

After Becca making me feel like a total reject, his teasing stings more than it should. He's right. I'm *not* cool enough to be friends with Becca the College Girl. I'm definitely not cool enough to hang with Dev and Leo. I'm not even sure I'm cool enough to be here right now, despite this being my best friend's house.

I ignore the lump in my throat. "I'm going to find Hari. Best of luck trying to find someone to lower their standards enough to sleep with you tonight."

Then I turn and rush toward the house.

Once inside, I weave my way around to Hari's room, letting myself inside without knocking. There he is: he's sitting on his bed, toying with the papier-mâché piñata I gave him earlier.

Hari looks up at me. "Finally!" he snaps.

I make a face, closing the door behind me. "I'm here, aren't I? Jeez."

"Sorry. I just thought you'd be here sooner." He throws me the piñata pumpkin and I catch it, finding that the once-smiling jack-o'-lantern is now missing its teeth altogether.

"What *happened* to this?"

"I've been picking at it," he admits, gesturing toward the trash. I see now where much of the papier-mâché has ended up. "This night has already been a disaster."

I set the piñata down on his nightstand. "How so?"

"Have you *seen* the number of people who've showed up?" Hari asks. "Someone barfed and I stepped in it. I spilled a drink on some girls. I tried to start a conversation with one of Dev's friends because she was painted like some Roy Lichtenstein art and she *just looked at me* and walked away."

"Okay, that's pretty bad," I admit. "But that one's not anything you did! Sounds like she was the ass."

He sighs. "Does that matter? I don't know anyone out there, Kat. They're all here for Dev and they clearly don't want me hanging around."

I give him a small smile. "I don't think they're here for Dev.

I think they're mostly here for the booze and the possibility of a hook-up."

Hari groans, burying his face in his hands. "Why is my brain dumb?"

I walk over to his bed and take a seat beside him. "Your brain is not dumb," I say. "Dramatic, sure."

He looks up and gives me a weary smile. "Seeing all these people who I know but don't *really* know, in my house, looking at me like I'm a little chump—I don't know, man. It set me off. And then Luis and Marcus were so fucking, like, *suave* out there."

"You think Beavis and Butt-Head were suave out there?"

He finally laughs.

"Seriously," I say. "When I got here, they were like yappy dogs trying to mark their territory." I make a face. "It was gross. They should be neutered."

"It'd be for the best," Hari agrees, smiling. "Hey, where's Becca? Weren't you going to bring her?"

I shrug. "She said she wasn't interested in a 'high school party.'"

He cringes. "*Savage.*"

"For real."

"At least I get you to myself this way," he offers.

"Yeah, guess you're stuck with me. But where's your costume?" He points at the HELLO, MY NAME IS...sticker on the lapel of his shirt, which I somehow missed. It reads LARRY in block print and I laugh. "Nice."

"And you are...a sexy schoolgirl?" he asks.

I roll my eyes, though I am embarrassed to admit I don't mind being called sexy. "Private school girl slash ambiguous brown background character from *Clueless*. Obvi."

"Right, right. Of course." Hari reaches under his bed and pulls out a bottle of Tito's. "You want to get shitfaced and listen to some music?"

"I have a better idea. Let's get shitfaced and then go listen to some music *out there*. You know, at your party."

"It's not my party," Hari insists.

I grin, feeling something like confidence begin to return. "It will be after we're done."

Chapter Twelve

The thing about drinking is that I haven't done it a lot and I have no idea how much is too much.

So, maybe I end up going from zero to shitfaced pretty quickly. Or maybe it took a long time. I don't really remember. All I know is that I'm here and *shiiiit* it feels good.

So much so that I'm able to coax Hari out of his room after, like, a couple of songs and two shots. We find ourselves in the backyard with everyone else, kinda like we belong, like we don't feel self-conscious while the music is playing and bodies are swaying.

Luis and Marcus spot us and ask if Hari's doing all right. When they see he's fine, they mutter something like an apology to me about being a little harsh about the dress.

But all I do is grab Luis by the shoulders and say, *"It's a fucking jumper!"* and grin and then my song comes on and I start to dance.

Because why not?

At least when I'm this deep in, I'm not worried about Becca not considering me a friend, or those deliciously fluttery feelings I felt when she touched me, or why my brother Leo has to be so obnoxiously cool, or why I can't figure out this whole "fitting in" thing, or why my family is a disaster, or why Marcus and Luis can't just give me a break. All those stresses float away with the burn of some cheap booze at the back of my throat.

Every so often, I find myself looking over at Leo—still chill as ever, still the center of attention, still vibing in Dev's circle under the palo verde trees—and drink a little more when I find it still stings.

"What are you looking at?" Hari asks, catching my not-at-all-subtle glances.

"Our brothers. Being annoying." I grin at him and grab his hand. "Come on."

"Kat, no, I—"

"We're going over there whether you like it or not!" I tug on his arm and Hari relents, following me over to the circle where both of our siblings are hanging out. Leo spots me and gives a small wave. I give him a forced hi-nice-to-see-you face scrunch and tap Dev on the shoulder.

He turns. "Ayy, Sanchez! Look at you!"

"Hi, Dev," I say.

"You dress up tonight just for me? You shouldn't have," he teases, and some of the people around him laugh. "It's these muscles, huh?"

"This," I say, motioning toward my body, "is for Hari. But thanks. That's really sweet." Then I smile. "Hari's going to do a keg stand. So, come on."

Dev laughs. "*Hari* is going to do a keg stand?" He looks over at his brother. "Is she serious?"

"Yes," Hari says boldly. "C'mon."

"KEG STAND!" one of the dudes from beside Dev yells, and suddenly people are chanting "keg stand" over and over as we all pile into the garage, where we find more drinks, snacks, red Solo cups, and two huge kegs.

"You really want to do this?" Dev asks.

Hari quickly glances over at me—I give him a nod—before he smirks at Dev. "Don't look so surprised."

Then suddenly two of Dev's soccer teammates are grabbing Hari and hoisting him upside down while his hands support him on the keg. It is at this moment I wonder: Could we be any whiter?

There's really no time to grapple with this, and instead I kneel down, grab the keg tap, and hold it up to Hari's upside-down face.

"You ready?" I practically shout over the chatter, music, and cheers.

"Hit me," he says, and I put the tap right into his mouth. Everyone starts to count.

One...

Watching Hari guzzle this terrible beer is pretty hilarious.

Two...

Like, I'm laughing pretty hard watching this whole scene unfold. It's some kind of surreal, out-of-body experience.

Three...

I'm still laughing.

Four...

Okay, now I'm getting a little worried.

Five...

Is it possible to drown from a keg stand?

Six...

Eh, it's back to being funny.

Seven...

Hari grunts, and I take that as my cue to remove the tap from his mouth. Everyone erupts into loud cheers and the boys put him right side up again.

He wipes his mouth as one of the guys who had been holding him up yells, "Hell yeah, dude!"

"Not bad!" Leo yells.

"You only lasted seven seconds?" Dev asks, before looking over at me. "So sorry, Kat..."

He's teasing, but I see Hari ball his fists. He steps closer to his brother. "Don't say shit like that to her."

Dev exchanges a glance with one of his friends and laughs. "Okay, Hari, calm down."

Hari takes another step toward Dev. "It's not a fucking joke."

"Hey, it's okay," I say, holding his elbow.

He rips his arm away from me and lunges toward Dev, shoving him hard into the crowd of people.

"What the fuck, man?" Dev shouts. He shoves Hari back and sends him flying into a table full of snacks. Chips and buns and Takis scatter everywhere.

I rush to help Hari up. But he doesn't need any help; he's made of pure anger and adrenaline, his eyes fixated on his brother, and he lunges again. "Fuck you!" he yells, and, in an instant, he's back swinging at Dev.

Dev lands a punch square on Hari's jaw.

There's so much shouting and yelling that I don't even think Hari hears me as I plead, "Stop! Stop!" and tug on the back of his shirt. Leo is suddenly grabbing Dev and trying to pull him back, too, as other guys rush in to help.

Though it's a struggle, we eventually get the Shah boys to separate, and Dev bellows at Hari. "You're insane, dude! Get the fuck away from me!"

"We're going!" I yell, shooting Leo a grateful look.

He nods at me, and as I turn to usher Hari toward the house, I hear Leo shout, "Everyone, relax!"

"Fuck that guy," Hari says loudly, glaring back at Dev while we stumble toward the house. He rubs at his jaw, which is already swelling.

"I know," I murmur, guiding him inside to the kitchen. "Sit." He slides onto one of the stools at the kitchen island, glaring at some of our classmates. Everyone vacates the room, leaving behind empty paper plates and overturned plastic cups. I lower my voice. "You're not making any friends right now."

"Good," he retorts.

I gather some ice from the freezer and wrap a dish towel around it. "For your face," I say, and I gently press it to the side of his jaw.

He winces. "Shit, that hurts."

"I know," I say again, softly. "What the hell happened out there?"

"I don't know," Hari admits. "What he said to you pissed me off. He's always clowning on me like that, I can't fucking stand it. When it's just him and me, it's one thing, but really? In front of all of those people?"

I nod. "I'm sorry he said that. But you really didn't need to go at him that way. What were you thinking?"

"I don't know."

"You don't know? You just got into a full-on fistfight with your brother. You'll be lucky if someone doesn't call the cops on you!"

"Okay, Kat!" Hari snaps. "Maybe you shouldn't have gotten involved! Just stay out of it!"

I scowl at him and pull away, ice pack in hand.

"Don't talk to me like that," I snap. "It's not my fault you guys were being stupid-ass machismo douchebags."

At that, Hari's eyes get big, and it's like he comes back to the Hari I know—not the testosterone-fueled Hari that speaks with his fists.

"Hey, no. I'm sorry." Hari reaches for my hand. "You're right. I'm just lashing out. I'm sorry." He pulls my hand back up to his jaw, leaning into the ice, and he looks at me with tired eyes. His thick brows are furrowed in an apology, and I find myself studying his face—his long eyelashes; his smooth brown skin; his jaw, sharp on one side and slowly swelling on the other; his full lips.

"Okay," I say quietly.

Because maybe I *did* stoke this fire, at least a little. I don't really know what I was thinking with the keg stand. I guess I was just hoping that it might let us show off for once, that it might make Dev and Leo (and, let's be real, everyone else here) not count Hari and me out so quickly. Just once, can't we be part of the crowd?

"This night turned into a mess," Hari says, as if hearing my thoughts.

I nod. "Yeah. A little. Sorry."

"No, Kat. You're good." He meets my gaze, a thoughtful look coming over his face. "You know, I didn't even get to tell you how beautiful you look." His face turns into my hand, and I feel myself tremble.

All day the only thing I wanted was to be noticed.

And here was Hari—noticing.

"Okay," I say again, nearly a whisper, not moving my hand away from his face. He softly kisses my thumb.

Maybe it's that Hari saw me. Maybe it's the sting of rejection from earlier. Maybe it's the relentless teasing from Luis and Marcus. Maybe it's the confusion over what I'm even doing. Maybe it's the alcohol. Maybe, maybe, maybe.

Something in me tells me to kiss him.

I know I shouldn't. I *shouldn't*.

I say this to myself as I move even closer to him, smelling a mix of his cologne and cheap beer.

As he reaches out and grazes his fingers across my exposed collarbone.

As my breath catches in my throat.

As I drop the ice onto the counter and lean toward his mouth.

As he envelops me in his arms.

As his lips are on mine.

I shouldn't.

But I am.

Chapter Thirteen

"*Kat* . . ." Hari's voice is hoarse as he pulls his lips away from mine.

"Yeah?" I'm distracted, wanting to go back to what we were doing and not bother with all the talking.

"We're drunk."

His voice is gentle, but still, shame creeps up my neck. I frown. "So?"

"So...don't you pay attention in Mr. González's class? 'Don't make reckless decisions when you're under the influence.' He's said that like a hundred times since the beginning of the semester."

I add furrowed brows to my already frowning face. Mr. González—pinched face, kinda unpleasant—is not exactly who I want to be picturing right now. And now, after my *second* rejection of the day, I have to be questioned as to whether I pay attention in class?

"I listen," I protest, annoyed. "But we're not that drunk, are we?"

He looks at me and gives me a small smile, our faces so close. "I did a keg stand."

"Right." I sigh and pull away from him. He puts his hand on my arm, gingerly tugging me back to him.

"I want this. But I just want us to be, like, I don't know. Sober. If we're going to do this thing for real. If..." Hari lets the latter half of his sentence hang in the air, full of weight.

I swallow. Though we've hooked up, we've never *hooked up*. And based on the fact that we made our way into his bedroom, into his bed, and he's shirtless, and his hands are on my thighs, he's right.

And suddenly the weight of that—of this whole day—comes crashing down on me, and a hot tear rolls down my cheek, and before I can stop it, there's another, and another.

"Hey, no, no, no," Hari murmurs. "I'm sorry."

I'm swiping sloppily at my face to push the tears away but they keep coming.

"It's not you—it's everything." I look away from him and down at my hands, which are now smudged in black makeup. "I just had a really bad day." Hari reaches down to grab his shirt from the floor and hands it to me. I wipe at my face with it, leaving mascara streaks behind, solid proof of this miserable day on the fabric scrunched up in my hands. And that makes me cry more. "Look," I squeak, holding the shirt up to him. "I ruined this too!"

"It's just makeup! It'll wash out," he assures me.

"I didn't even know that! I don't know anything about the perfect cat eye or beautubers or sulfate-free conditioner—"

"Sulfate-free conditioner?" he echoes.

"Or anything at all, ever, about being a girl or being normal or being like everyone else. I don't even have a normal family, Hari. My parents hate me. My own brother pretends I don't exist!"

"Okay, well, join the club there." Hari gives me a half smile, but concern reads all over his face. He takes my hand gently, like I'm made of the same kind of glass as the figurines his mother collects. "What is going on, Kat?"

"I don't know. I don't *know*." I bury my face in his chest. "I just had a horrible day."

"Okay. Tell me more about it, then." He reaches over to his nightstand and grabs the piñata, wiggling the mouthless jack-o'-lantern. "Better yet, tell him. He was really supportive of me earlier."

At that, I actually let out a laugh. "*He* never would've encouraged you to do a keg stand."

"I have major street cred now, okay?" Hari teases. "Seriously, though. Talk to me."

I glance between his crumpled henley in my hands; to his shirtless body, which looks so good I'm yearning for more; to my jumper that's askew, my shirt rolled down so far you can see my strapless bra; and I realize that I'm *such a mess*.

Everything I might share—that I showed up to take photos of a girl I've misread, that I am livid over the fact that my younger brother is exponentially better liked and more well-adjusted than I am, that I don't understand why my parents are uninterested in having me be part of their family, that all I want is a normal family, that Instagram tells me that everyone has their lives together so much more than I do, that I haven't given enough thought to college or my future, that Luis called me a liar and that stings me more than a thousand paper cuts, that I feel so devastatingly out of place every single day of my life—confirms that.

In fact, it makes my stomach churn.

"I'm okay." I sniffle. "I'm just drunk."

Hari nods. "Okay. Yeah. Me too. Let me walk you home."

I sniffle again, and suddenly I feel that distinct sensation of bile rising from my stomach. I close my eyes, swallowing hard.

"Okay. But I'm going to be sick first."

"Shit." Hari leaps from his bed and grabs a trash can just in time for me to barf—and not a cute barf, either, if there is such a thing. I feel like I'm in the fucking *Exorcist* over here, expelling literally everything ever, and it's maybe one of the grossest moments of my life. Yet Hari is rubbing my back and that makes me start to cry again. "It's okay," he whispers. "It's okay."

He leaves the room and I briefly think, Well, this is it. I've pushed him too far this time.

But he's back a minute later with some water and paper towels. I use the paper towels to wipe at my mouth and rinse with water, then take a long sip.

"We really should get you home."

I hold up the garbage can. "But I need to clean this up."

"No," Hari says, rifling through one of his drawers, pulling out a hoodie, and slipping it on. He yanks out another one for me, puts it around my shoulders, and holds out a hand. "Come on."

I know I look a mess, so I'm grateful when we leave the comfort of his room and see that there are way fewer people inside than before. Seems like most must've taken off after the fight and I don't blame them.

Unfortunately, the house itself is also legitimately trashed—abandoned bottles, random spills, and crushed food are everywhere. "Oh, no."

"Dev can deal with it," Hari says with a laugh. Then he winces and reaches for his jaw. "Especially after what he did to me."

We slip out the front door, avoiding the backyard, where we can hear a bit of laughter—likely where Dev and a few sycophants are still hanging out—and start toward my house.

The cool October night elicits goose bumps on my skin. I imagine this is what it's like to live in a place where the seasons actually change, where the leaves shift colors, where the snow falls—rather than here in Bakersfield, where one season rolls right into another: Hot, Hotter, back to Regular Hot, then Mild.

We pass a smashed pumpkin in the street; one of the neighbor's houses is flickering with purple and orange lights; another is guarded by a giant inflatable skeleton taller than the roof. As we walk, I'm comforted by how easy it is to hold Hari's hand. I don't let go, mostly because it feels like his hand is the only thing tethering me to this earth right now.

I disrupt the quiet of the night to say, "Thanks for taking care of me." Now that we're a ways from his house, my voice sounds far too loud on this otherwise empty street.

"Of course. Although..." He pauses, then glances at me. "We're good, right?"

I nod, but that makes me a little dizzy, so I stop to say, "For sure. We're good."

Hari breathes a sigh of relief, as if he's been holding it in this whole time. "Good. I mean, I *wanted* to, I really did. But I just feel like we should...I don't know. Figure this out first?"

"Yes." But I'm not listening as hard as I should. I just want to get home.

In the pocket of my jumper, my phone buzzes. I pull it out, praying it isn't Grandma texting. It's not quite midnight, so I'm not *technically* past my new curfew, but I can see her hunching over her iPad and typing out a message to me in gigantic font, just to check in.

The messages aren't from her, though. They're from Becca.

Becca: **I know it's suuuuuper late, but two quick things: One, hopefully I didn't offend you with the party thing. Yuo're cool, but you know, hanging with high schoolers is kinda weird when you're in college!!!**

Becca: **Omg typos**

Becca: **But two: I was telling my friends about the pics we took and we are all DYING to see them.**

Becca: **Do you think you can share them with me tomorrow so I can show them?**

Becca: **Pretty place**

Becca: **Please**

Becca: **Sorry, autocorrect**

Becca: **AND WINE**

Becca: **Okay tysm!!! Hope your party was fun! Happy Halloween!**
🎃 🕷 🕸

"Please tell me that's not Granny," Hari says, using the affectionate nickname he's given her.

"No, it's just Becca."

"Becca the Savage."

"That'd be the one."

"Is . . . is Becca the person behind the whole . . . ?" He motions at me, toward my hair and outfit and whole look.

My cheeks flush. Can this night just please end? "Kind of. She helped, anyway."

"I mean, there's nothing wrong with it! You look hot. As indicated by my—"

"Okay!"

He laughs and takes my hand. "Okay, but yeah. You look hot regardless."

"Regardless of?"

He shifts uncomfortably, trying to find the right words. "I just mean the dress is good, but what you wear normally is, too. Is good. It is good. This isn't really you, you know? I don't know."

I know he's trying to give me a compliment, assure me that I'm good as I am, but I don't want to hear it.

"I don't even really know who I am," I murmur.

We're at my house now and I'm so damn thankful. A definitive end to this garbage day.

"You gonna be okay tonight?" Hari asks.

"I'll be okay. Thanks for walking me home."

"Anytime." He squeezes my hand. "I'll text you."

We let go, and I wave before I tiptoe as steadily as I can into my backyard, hoist the unlocked window to my bedroom open, and climb inside. I may have a new curfew, but old habits die hard.

It's then I realize I still have Hari's hoodie draped over my shoulders. I toss it in my laundry basket, grab my robe, and slink to the bathroom. While I'm quietly having a shower, my phone buzzes. As soon as I'm out, I check it.

Hari: **You make it inside okay?** ♥

The heart emoji sends me to another plane of existence. Because now we're right back where we started. Aaaaaughhhh.

I shoot back a quick text that just says: **Yes.**

And then I feel a fresh tear roll down my cheek.

Tonight was *anything* but what I had expected.

And right now, I feel like I would give it all up to be someone else.

In my room, I try to sleep but fail, so I pull out my camera and start to transfer the photos of Becca to my laptop. Unfortunately, another pit forms in my stomach looking at them.

I don't stop, though, instead using every photo—of Becca in angled poses, of her with her head tilted back in a laugh, of her with that peacock, a prized shot, the one that I framed, the one that I captured, the ambiance I curated—as a reminder that some people have it so fucking easy.

Becca had the acceptance and adoration that I crave so badly. She had the world telling her she was perfect as she was. She had it all, and she threw it the fuck away. To make matters worse, these photos came out *so stunning,* maybe among my best work yet, and they won't even get posted anywhere.

I let out a bitter snort. She doesn't know how easy she had it. She was someone meaningful. Someone people envied. Someone people liked. *Someone,* period.

She doesn't even deserve these photos, I think to myself.

And you know what? They're mine, anyway.

I conceptualized them.

I took them.

I edit them.

So, technically, these belong to me.

Chapter Fourteen

There's a soft knock on my door. I see half of Grandma's face peeking out from behind it as I open an eye.

"Oh!" she whisper-shouts. "Didn't mean to wake you, Kat. Just wondering if you're hungry."

Normally, I am charmed by my grandma's inability to actually whisper. She always *thinks* she's keeping her voice hushed, but really, her words come out more like a breathy yell.

This morning, however—with my head throbbing and my body desperate for hydration—I am not as amused.

"It's too early," I groan.

She takes a step inside and grins. "It's early, but...Grandpa made omelets!"

Omelets do sound good, and my grandpa makes them with extra cheese and a generous slice of warm, buttered pan de agua on the side. I feel like shit. Hot food would probably be good.

I rub my face. "Okay. Be there in a minute."

Grandma raises her shoulders in a cute little shrug to indicate her excitement and waggles her fingers at me. "We'll keep your plate warm for you!"

I close my eyes, unsure how I'll will myself into being the peppy person my grandma would love to have at breakfast this morning. I don't even feel like I'm alive right now; I'm fuzzy and bleary and— oh, crap.

I sit up in bed, which is a terrible idea—blood instantly rushes to my head. Everything from yesterday comes rushing back to me. It hits me like a freight train.

The excitement over spending time with Becca.

The butterflies.

The sting of rejection.

The dread of Hari's party.

The drinking. Oh, God, the drinking.

Hari's fistfight with Dev.

The hookup that was almost sex.

The abrupt end to that hookup.

The shame.

The crying.

The barfing.

And, maybe the most unbelievable part of all, the grand plan to *use Becca's photos however I want.*

I lunge toward my phone on the nightstand, which is nearly dead because apparently I never plugged it in, and before I can even unlock it, I see…

A flood of Instagram notifications.

hellolovely721, leegendaryone, itssashaaaaa, and 470 others have liked your post.

Leah Tropp (leahtropp) started following you.

Star Wiley (writteninthestarz) started following you.

Greg The GOAT Batista (itsgregtheGOAT) started following you.

And on and on and on.

"Shit, shit, shit." I unlock my phone and navigate as quickly as I can over to Instagram, my hands shaking.

Sure enough, I'm logged in to a new account, with a photo of Becca's pouty smile as the avatar. The name on the account reads Max Monroe, like some kind of LA-based influencer in all her glory.

I throw my phone across my bed like it's teeming with fire ants.

I did that. I used Becca's photos and *created an entirely new person* on Instagram.

What have I done? I can't steal someone's face! What kind of nonsense is that?! Becca would absolutely *kill me* if she found out. Who does something like that? And *Max Monroe*? Seriously, Kat?

Okay, calm down. I can just delete the account. Like, immediately. No one will ever know.

I take in a deep breath and sit up straighter, reaching for my phone and unlocking it once more.

But before I can navigate over to the settings to delete the profile, I find myself shocked at the fact that this account already has 280 followers. In just a few hours! I click on the single photo that's posted.

And there is Becca in all her beautifully illuminated golden glory, fully looking like some kind of woodland goddess who possesses the ability to speak to animals.

There's also a long caption—complete with a longggg string of hashtags—to go with it. It reads:

The woman in this photo is powerful. Graceful. Beautiful. Inspiring.

The woman in this photo is privileged. Arrogant. Selfish. Cold.

She is all of these things at once, a reflection of the world around her—of the sky, sometimes serene and sometimes cloudy; of the ocean, sometimes calm and sometimes choppy; of the ground, sometimes lush and sometimes rocky.

Like us all, she chooses who to be based on how the world treats her.

Today, the world is cruel. And so is she.

Maybe tomorrow will be different.

Last night, I imagine I wrote this as some kind of introspective rant that I thought was pretty deep. Though I'm sure I was thinking of

Becca when I wrote it, in the light of day, I know it's about me, a testament to the tightly wound ball of emotions that I am.

I scroll down and note that there are a few comments on the post.

Three fire emojis from one person.

Love the peacock from another.

But it's the third comment that gets me: *These words are beautifully written. Well put. Thank you.*

A smile is tugging at the corner of my mouth. Sure, the photo is obviously Becca, and Max Monroe is very obviously "pretend," as Grandma would say, and all of this is a ruse.

But those words were all me.

"Kat!" My grandma's singsong voice breaks me out of my thoughts.

"Coming!" I call, plugging my phone in so it can charge.

Deleting the account can wait a little longer.

* * *

Grandpa's famous omelets are restorative, and the warm bread, slathered in butter, may be even more healing. At the very least, after some food, water, and Tylenol, I am a little more ready to sit down with what I've done.

And the list is... long.

For starters, I definitely hooked up with Hari again after *swearing* to myself that I wouldn't. (Obviously, that was just a lie.) Between that, the crying, the walk home, and the hand-holding, things with him are messier than ever. Already, I've gotten a **good morning queen** text, like maybe he's eager to have some kind of bigger discussion about "What aaaare we?" and ugh. What have I done?

I send him three crown emojis in response because what the actual hell am I supposed to say? *Hey, uh, sorry we hooked up again, but thanks for not letting us have sex because I'm actually NOT down for taking this thing any further. Besties?*

Right.

No doubt, Hari deserves my honesty. Yet pretending things are normal and That Thing Def Didn't Happen is way more tempting.

And, of course, I'm still dealing with the swift rejection from Becca, because duh. I'm seventeen and she's a freshman in college.

Then there's *this*. I glance down at the metaphorical ticking time bomb on my screen. Max Monroe AKA Becca Dupont AKA Kat Sanchez.

Shit.

But also…it's satisfying, having people actually read my words and *hear* me.

Like, I'm not out here trying to say that this is the type of thing people should be doing. I don't steal people's faces. I don't. And my lies are normally digestible ones—I live with my parents, my family is perfect, I'm totally comfortable with myself, et cetera.

This would be a lie to end all lies. The queen of lies. The Beyoncé.

If I kept this whole thing up, I mean. Which I'm not going to do.

Still, though, I find myself wondering…what if?

I muse on how it could be possible that *this* photo is one that has gotten much more attention than any photo I've ever posted when the style is the same as all my others—but the pit in my stomach tells me I already know the answer. Instagram, the internet, and the world all seem to have been made for beautiful thin white girls.

And these are *my* thoughts, after all, not Becca's. It's just her face I'm borrowing to share my very real feelings. Being vulnerable and opening up about some of these insecurities may not feel as scary if it's someone else's face that's attached. Everybody loves a pretty girl, right?

I find that there's a request for a message in my IG inbox and note that the photo of Becca has been shared by a New York–based photographer with a decent following, which likely helped the photo and account get noticed.

I scroll through the likes, the followers, the comments. All of these people are responding so well to Becca and to this post, but would they even care if they knew who was really behind the screen?

That it was some girl who has no idea who she is or what she wants?

Whose body is speckled with stretch marks? Who's destined to experience chub rub? Who has a sagging belly pouch?

Who often doesn't feel feminine enough?

Who is regularly reminded by one of her best friends that she isn't quite boricua enough?

Who can barely even speak what's supposed to be her own language?

Who somehow can't even impress her own parents? Or get them to love her? Choose her?

Who sometimes feels like an outsider in her own life?

Who watches the rest of the classmates on IG, Snapchat, Tik-Tok, *wherever*, happily living their lives with confidence?

Who is so insecure she hooks up with her own best friend just to feel a little loved?

There are more than a few tears now. I do not want to steal Becca's life.

But I come back to that comment, thanking me for sharing my thoughts, for being vulnerable, and think that maybe it might be okay if I borrow it. Just for a while.

Chapter Fifteen

While I'm still marveling over the response to Max Monroe's account, a text from the real Becca comes in. Seeing her name flash on my screen makes my mouth go dry, and I quickly switch to my own Instagram account, as if that will hide what I've done.

Becca: **Hey girl! So sorry for the string of weird texts last night. The merlot nearly took me outttt.**

Becca: **But I am super eager to see the pics! Do you think you'll share them at some point today? Not trying to be pushy, I swear, but I'm excited. I feel like they might've been our best ones yet!**

Even though Becca's text is innocent enough, I'm convinced she knows. She knows, right?

Frantically, I reread what she's just sent, searching for a clue that she's discovered my misbehavior, but there's nothing. She just wants to see her photos. So breathe, Kat. It's cool. She doesn't know. She's not even on Instagram—or anywhere, I remind myself.

With shaky hands, I text back, **So sorry! Things got kinda crazy last night. I'll get them over to you ASAP!**

Becca: **Same, clearly. Lemme know if you need some hangover cures!** ☺

Me: **Haha, I'm hydrating as we speak! Pics coming soon.**

Forty-five minutes later, I've rushed to edit all the images, forgoing perfection and settling for good enough. I upload them all to the cloud and text Becca a link.

Almost instantly, she writes me.

Becca: **OMG! These are even better than I imagined!**

Me: **I'm so happy you like them!**

I leave it at that.

Next crisis: There are several texts from Hari that came in while I was editing Becca's pics and I've yet to reply to them. He, Dev, and a few others are scrambling to clean up the house and restore it to the pristine state it was in before their parents left. I should probably be helping. And maybe playing referee? After last night's fight, it's probably only a matter of time until Hari vs. Dev: The Remix is under way.

I make the short walk over to Hari's and note Marcus's car outside the house. Good. He and Luis should be here helping, too. After a brief scan of the front yard to see if anything is amiss, I head inside and find the boys carrying a gigantic glass vase into the living room.

"Set it down gently, on three," Hari instructs. "One...two... three..." The vase thuds loudly as it hits the dark wood floor. "I said gently!"

"That shit is heavy as hell!" Luis protests.

"Oh, no—not Luis having trouble flexing his lil muscles," I tease. They all turn toward me, Marcus smirking, Hari grinning, and Luis scowling.

"Who invited this pinche payasa?" he asks.

"I'm here to help," I say. "And to make sure another brawl doesn't break out."

Marcus puts two fingers on his chin and squints his eyes at me, appearing thoughtful. "Correct me if I'm wrong, Kat...but didn't you help *start* the brawl last night?"

Luis practically cackles. "She sure did."

I scowl. "How would you even know? You guys were too busy chasing girls to care about anything."

"Don't blame us for people saying you're an instigator," Luis says with a shrug.

I narrow my eyes at him. "People aren't saying that."

Hari cuts in before either Luis and Marcus can say another word. "The whole thing is Dev's fault, not Kat's. And my fault, I guess. But he had it coming." He walks over to me and leans in. "Hey."

I think he's expecting a peck on the cheek. I give a half-hug instead. "Hey," I say, quickly. "So, what can I help with?"

Hari gives me a sideways glance, but doesn't say anything. I try to communicate with my eyes that I'm sorry and maybe we can talk later, but I don't know if my eyes can say all that. "Dev and his friends are out back taking care of the garage and everything," he says. "We just have the hutch left."

Luis groans. "That thing is so heavy." He flexes the muscles in his arms. "I need to save my strength so I can be good for my date later."

"Are you going to be lifting your date over your head or something?" I ask.

"I might."

"Okay, well, we need someone to grab all the stuff that goes inside the hutch and put it back. You can handle that, Luis," Hari says. "At least I think you can. Let me know if it's just too hard."

"I'll help," I offer, and everyone, including Luis, gives me a look. "What?"

"You gonna push me down the basement stairs or something, Sanchez?"

"Can't I just offer to help you, stupid?" Of course, my real motive is avoiding having a big talk with Hari.

Luis gives me a sideways glance. "Fine... but I'm watching you."

"Me too," Marcus agrees. For emphasis, he uses two of his fingers to point at his eyes and then at mine. I make a face at him.

We all move into the basement, Hari and Marcus figuring out how to get the massive hutch back upstairs, Luis and I starting to carry a few of the crystal angels and other assorted figurines. He balances a bunch in his arms, but I opt for just one in each hand. That boy is way too risky for my liking.

"Nice of you to finally show up, by the way," Luis says. "We've been here awhile already."

"You want a medal or something?" I ask.

"Maybe I do," he says, stomping up the basement stairs.

"You'll be waiting awhile, then." I place the two turtles I'd been carrying on the dining room table. "I love Mrs. Shah, but this collection is a little...well...tacky."

Luis bends his knees to carefully lower down all five million figurines he'd been carrying at the same time. He looks at the anthropomorphic mustachioed mushroom, the angel with her hands tucked under her chin, the baby holding a heart—and laughs. "I have never said this before, but you are absolutely right, Sanchez."

I laugh, too. "If I ever get old and start buying a bunch of tiny statues like this, please kill me."

"That's a promise," he says solemnly. Then he reaches a hand to the back of his neck and glances at the floor, like he's considering something. "So, yeah, sorry if I was too harsh with you last night. I was a little tipsy and just, like, surprised by your outfit—not that that's an excuse. But yeah." He's not looking at me, but at the silly little baby instead.

"You sure you weren't just trying to show off?"

He shifts uncomfortably. "Maybe a little."

"It's all right," I say. "Sorry if I was too hard on you about Xiomara. I wasn't trying to ruin your chances or anything."

He looks over at me and grins. "Oh, you absolutely *were*."

I smile back. "Okay, fine. Maybe I was. But I'm glad she didn't listen."

"Me too."

This is maybe the first time Luis has (soberly, because last night doesn't count) uttered the word *sorry* to me, and I appreciate it. I know that our relationship is pretty much all messing around, almost one hundred percent of the time, but a little sincerity here and there goes a long way.

"Also, since we're being honest and all, you think you could stop calling me fat all the time?" I ask.

Luis looks surprised. "But *you* call yourself fat."

"I do…but I mean it more, like, as a description of my body," I explain. "Whenever I hear you say it, I think you mean it like I should go die or something. It really feels like a judgment on me."

"Jeez, Sanchez!"

"Sorry! But it's true!"

He shakes his head. "I don't mean it like that. I just thought—I thought we were clowning, that's all. But I won't say it anymore if you don't like it."

"I don't really," I admit.

"Okay. Of course." Then he squares his eyes at me. "But I'm still going to call you a gringa."

I laugh. "Fine."

"Guys? A little help?" Marcus calls. We look over to see that he and Hari are struggling to angle the hutch the right way through the basement door.

We help them shimmy it through, careful not to scuff the floor, and get it back into its rightful place. Luis and I make another run downstairs to get the rest of the goofy figurines and set them all back where they belong.

Once everything is in its proper spot, we survey the house. It looks good. Hari thanks us all and Luis and Marcus leave pretty quickly, probably before they can get roped into helping with something else.

And then it's just me and Hari and whatever happened last night.

From the way he looks at me, I can tell he's hoping we'll talk. Like, *talk*-talk—not just about the almost-sex, but about us, our future, what we are, and what we want to be.

Maybe if I start it won't be so bad.

Rip it off like a Band-Aid, Kat.

"I wanted to thank you for last night," I say. "And also to sincerely apologize for throwing up in your trash can, which I can't imagine was fun cleaning up."

Hari grins. "I actually left it for you so you can handle it."

"Ew, stop!" I playfully shove at his arm. "I'm trying to be nice here."

"Right, right. Sorry. It's all good, Kat. Really, I feel like I should be thanking you. I was on the verge of a panic attack before you showed up."

"Yeah, but then I kinda made everything worse." I motion toward his still-swollen cheek. "You look absolutely busted."

His eyes go wide and he laughs, gingerly touching his jaw. "Damn, girl. You are ice-cold. *Absolutely busted.*"

I smile back. "I'm just thankful that you were so nice to me last night. I was clearly going through it, too. I couldn't ask for a better best friend."

When I say the words *best friend,* it's as if the glimmer of hope in Hari's eyes flickers out.

Maybe I really am ice-cold.

"Best friend," Hari repeats.

I nod at him, probably a bit too enthusiastically. "*Best* friend. Best friend in the world. Like, if there were an award for the most incredible friend ever, it would be you. Because—"

He interrupts. "Is this because I stopped us last night?"

"No! God, no, not at all. I'm glad you stopped us. We were so drunk—"

"I wasn't that drunk."

"Well, *I* was super drunk, and not thinking clearly, and just overall making bad decisions—"

"So our kiss was a bad decision?"

"I mean, not, like, bad, but I just feel like I don't know what might've happened if we kept going and *that* would've been horrible."

"Horrible," Hari echoes.

Nothing I'm saying is coming out right, but I can't stop. "No, no. Not horrible, like, *horrible*-horrible, as in *gross* or anything, but horrible, as in…this would not have been a very good thing for our friendship because it's been confusing enough with all the kissing and, like, we should probably stop that since we're better off as friends?"

The last part of my sentence comes out in a rush, almost a question, like I'm asking permission for this to be okay—even though that's not at all how I want it to sound. Because I'm certain. I've made up my mind. I don't want to keep doing this—whatever this is. I want us to go back to being the kind of friends that don't kiss. I want us to go back to normal.

Hari rubs his face wearily, letting out a long sigh.

"I thought you liked me, Kat." His voice is so small when he says this. "So, all those times we kissed were just…what?"

"Fun? Nice? Hot? And also a little weird? And a bunch of other things? It's not like I didn't want that then or even last night. That's what's so confusing." I take a breath, trying to sort out my own thoughts. "I just—I feel like it's not fair to you if we keep doing this without committing to something further. I don't want to hurt you, Hari. So, I—I don't know. I think we should go back to what we were. Before this summer."

His eyebrows furrow, his eyes growing glassy.

I swallow hard, feeling the slightest prick of tears at the back of my own eyes. "I'm sorry."

He looks away from me.

I should stop talking. Take a cue from Hari and also be quiet. Let him feel his feelings. Leave.

But instead, there is something nagging, words lodged in my throat that I can't seem to ignore. And suddenly they're out. It's a question so raw it's made of only desperation and fear. "You're not going to tell people at school I live with my grandparents, are you?"

I'm five again as I ask this, heart pounding, worried someone will know. That they'll find out the truth. Discover the lie. Realize I'm only pretending. Realize what a castoff I really am.

And that's it. That question I have the nerve to ask is what breaks him.

When Hari looks over at me, his face is contorted. "Seriously, Kat? You reject the hell out of me after almost having sex with me and all you can think about is whether or not I'm going to tell people you live with your *grandparents*?" He spits this out at me, each word angry, like the question is so disgusting he can't believe it even crossed my mind.

My cheeks flush immediately. "I didn't mean it like that," I say quietly, heat rising to my neck, my shoulders creeping up toward my ears in a pitiful shrug. "I'm just spiraling. I don't know! We've never been in a fight before and..."

"And you think I'm so vindictive I'd go on and blab about your family situation? Wow." He's shaking his head. "No, Kat, I'm not going to tell anyone your lame-ass secret. People wouldn't even care if I did."

The venom in his words sinks its teeth into me.

If I felt ashamed before, now I feel small. Not only was this the wrong thing to ask, but Hari, my best friend, the only person in the world who knows how deeply rejected I've felt by my parents, the one I've cried to about this more than once, thinks that piece of my story is an insignificant joke. A footnote. A blip. A nothing.

I swallow hard, no words left to say.

The sliding door to Hari's dining room abruptly slides open and Dev slips inside with one of his friends behind him. They're laughing, a sound that rings out like a taunt, given everything that's just transpired. They stop when they see me and Hari.

Dev narrows his eyes at his brother. "Don't mind us. Just finished cleaning up your mess from out back."

"My mess, right. Because *I* wanted to throw that party," Hari growls.

"You know, I've thrown plenty of parties while Ma and Baba have been away, and they've gone just fine every other time. Yet, *somehow,* this one gets majorly fucked up. What was different?" Dev looks over at his posse, dramatically tapping his index finger on his chin. "Oh, right. *You* were here. Seems to me like you and your little friends are the problem."

Hari squints his eyes at him, shaking his head. "Grow the fuck up, Dev."

"Be less of a failure, Hari."

Hari moves toward him in a quick, fluid motion, and suddenly they're in each other's faces again.

"Guys, come on!" I reach for Hari's wrist to pull him back. But he yanks himself away from my grip.

"Don't touch me," he snaps, cold and poisonous. "Just go."

I recoil, dropping my hand to my side. Dev and his friends exchange a confused look.

"Damn, Hari," Dev murmurs.

"Whatever," Hari says, pushing past Dev into his room and slamming the door so hard that the pictures on the wall shudder.

I feel my lip quiver and I rush out of the house, desperate for a breath I can't catch.

Outside, the tears that have pooled in my eyes brim over, cascading down my face without me giving them permission.

I tried to be honest with Hari, and for what? So he could make fun of something I'm deeply ashamed of? So he could hate me? So I could be the bad guy?

Fuck this. Fuck *all* of this.

Chapter Sixteen

Hari and I don't fight. Like, ever. The biggest fight we've ever had was when I insulted Drake after Hari admitted Drake was his favorite artist ever. We had just come home after a really long day at Disneyland, we were both tired, I was on my period, and we were just in terrible moods. We yelled at each other and I stomped away from him and *tripped* and then we both started laughing so hard we couldn't stop, because who gets into a fight over Drake?

That was pretty much it. There had been little tiffs here and there, I guess, but mostly we got along.

This is brand-new territory for us. He's angry. I'm angry. He's hurt. I'm hurt.

But what am I supposed to do?

Normally, he's who I'd be texting about this. We'd go somewhere, put on some music, make fun of whatever it was until we felt better, and laugh it off.

But he's the one I'm fighting with.

I feel so...alone.

And when I get back home, things don't get any better. Grandma and Grandpa are sitting at the kitchen table, deep in some discussion that I know I'm not supposed to be hearing.

"She's being unreasonable," Grandpa says.

"I understand that. But this was the agreement," Grandma explains.

"That we made more than fifteen years ago, when decisions were things like whether Kat could go to the park or take swim lessons. We're talking big things now, Bethie. If they wanted to have a say in those, then they shouldn't have left her behind."

A small gasp comes from Grandma. "Ray."

"I'm tired of it! If we think Kat is responsible enough to have a later curfew, that should be the end of it!"

"He's right," I say, and their heads swivel to me in the doorway. There is surprise on both of their faces.

Grandma gives me a small smile. "Kat. Hi, honey."

"It's not like I'm asking for the moon. I'm just asking to have the same curfew as my little brother," I continue. "If you guys are okay with it, then what's the big deal?"

A silence falls, and questions I've always wanted to ask swirl in the space between us.

Like: How often have Grandpa and Grandma had similar discussions like this?

How often have my parents tried to dictate how I'm raised despite not being here?

How did this dynamic where my parents call the shots even emerge? And why did Grandma and Grandpa agree to it?

Why is this still a thing when it seems like none of us are fine with it?

Why are we all pretending to be this perfect family when we're so far from it?

Grandma clears her throat, smoothing the ripples in the tablecloth in front of her. "Your parents are just feeling a little left out." Grandpa snorts, and she gives him a look. "But the new curfew stays. We don't want you to worry about it."

"You have enough on your plate," Grandpa says. "We'll handle it."

I don't know what he means by they'll handle it, but I'm too tired to question it. I just nod and turn to go into my room. I'm sure there was some kind of argument between my parents and my grandparents, though I never get clued in on what's happened. It's only by the sheer luck of walking in and hearing Grandma and Grandpa talking that I even know this is an issue. If they had it their way, they probably would've talked to my parents and tried to smooth things over without me ever really knowing.

And that's part of the problem, isn't it? I never get to be involved in any part of what goes on with my parents. I don't get to have frank discussions with them about how our family makeup makes me feel incredibly alone. I don't get to say that I'm trying and failing to feel like I'm part of the Sanchez family. I don't get to tell them that not having a real bedroom in their house feels like a purposeful statement. I don't have the chance to say, *Hi, Mom and Pop, I wish you loved me like you love Leo.*

Instead, I'm just the girl who carries the lie. The lie that I'm wanted.

* * *

I can't sit still with all this, so I don't. I leave the house with my camera, walk to the nearby bus stop, and go. I don't have a destination in mind. I just need to get away from everything about me for a little while. I put in my headphones and listen to some Bad Bunny.

That—combined with the hum of the engine, the hiss of the brakes at each stop, the sway as we motor down the highway— helps me recalibrate. Breathe.

I get off at a stop near Cal State, aka CSU, and walk toward the campus. It's easy enough to blend in here, to walk around and pretend I have a purpose, so that's what I do. The people-watching is prime. That's one of my grandma's favorite pastimes, and I like it, too; I got it from her, I like to think. Students spill out onto the walkways, sprawl on the grass with their laptops and phones, listen to music, laugh, read, whatever.

Soon, my camera is out and I'm capturing a little of everything. A group of friends petting a dog. A girl in a dress and Converse easily weaving through the crowd on her skateboard. A table under an arch-way made up of gold and blue balloons with signs that read CELE-BRATING FIRST-GEN. A boy in the dopest coral jacket I have ever seen.

It's easy to get lost in everything around me. That's part of what I like so much about taking photos. It helps me feel like I'm part of something, even if I'm just an observer. I'm petting the dog, too, or gliding through campus on my own skateboard. It gets me away from me.

Before long, the sun starts to droop in the sky—like me, tired from a long day. I get back on the bus to head home, thinking, once more, of the mess I've managed to make in just two days.

Nothing about my life feels like it's in my control right now.

Is it any wonder, then, that I've gone and made a fake person? At least with that I can call the shots.

My mind wanders as I imagine Max, imagine she's real. What might she post next? How might she feel about this situation? What would she do?

* * *

Back at home, I look through some old photos I've taken. In one, Becca's back is to the camera as she faces a cliff, the choppy ocean in the background. Gigantic, ominous storm clouds are rolling in, heavy with rain. Her pose is strong, powerful, almost defiant. Shortly after I'd taken this photo, it started pouring—thunder, lightning, wind, the kind of storm that felt angry, like the sky was seeking its revenge on the earth below.

It's perfect.

I open the image in Photoshop. Soon, I'm buried in the cathar-tic process of tweaking the photo, smoothing this piece of hair, getting rid of those tire marks in the grass there. It's soothing.

Once I'm done, I Airdrop it to my phone and open it on Max's Instagram.

I start to type.

Even when you can see the storm rolling in, the rain can still have a way of ruining your day.

I hurt someone I love, deeply. And they hurt me. And now, amid all that hurt, it feels like I've lost my way.

What do you do when you feel so alone?

What do you do when there's a storm inside you, crashing, thundering, striking?

What do you do when you're not okay?

My eyes are bleary with tears as I write this.

After Hari...after Becca...after my family...after everything, there is a part of me that's shattered.

I post, and a like comes almost immediately. When I feel a little validated, shame burns in my chest.

But I leave the post up.

Chapter Seventeen

With the rest of my night, I create an editorial calendar for Max Monroe.

First and foremost, this means I now know what an editorial calendar is, and I've got an Excel sheet brimming with ideas for her account—which is admittedly already more work than I've put into anything else I've done in a while.

But it's something to focus on, something to pour my energy into, and it gives me comfort. It gives me purpose. And she—she gives me a voice.

Every time a thought comes into my mind about how *maybe* I shouldn't be posting as Max, another like, follow, or comment comes in, smothering my doubts.

And…it's nice, you know? My phone is regularly buzzing as people respond to what I'm sharing. I'm hearing from people who seem to *love* the photos I've taken. In the comments, they offer words of encouragement, spilling things that have led them to feel similarly, leaving hearts to let me know they're there for me.

Finally, in this tiny corner of the internet, I feel a sense of belonging. I feel *heard*. Don't I deserve that?

Especially because I know I now have to avoid Hari at school, which is difficult given that he, Luis, Marcus and I spend ALL of our time together.

I've already planned my absence from the group tomorrow: I'll send a group text with a lie about how I forgot to work on my

English paper (there is no English paper), so I'll be holed up in the library every spare moment. It is a boring excuse, but it will work.

And, after a lie as big as the one about Max, little lies don't feel so bad. One by one, I'll just shove them into my pockets, collecting them, hoping I won't topple over under their weight.

Here's what I know about Max:

Like Becca, she's in college at CSU, because now I can try out what that feels like without actually committing.

She comes from a good family, a *normal* one, like the kind you might see in a TV sitcom. They talk. A lot. Their fights are only over the garage door being left open or someone tracking mud through the house—not over broken promises or unwanted babies.

Max is open and, though she may not have all the answers, she trusts her heart. She's the kind of girl you're low-key scared to talk to but who is actually super cool once you get to know her.

Her future is bright, teeming with possibility and hope.

And she gets to be *vulnerable*. To share her emotions openly and honestly.

I'm exhilarated by this idea that I get to decide every single thing about Max—her hopes, her dreams, her fears. Through her, I can just let go, let loose, and explore who *I* want to be.

With her, maybe I don't have to pretend I'm so damn tough all the time.

If it takes a fake account to allow me to express myself, who cares? I'm not hurting anybody. If anything, I'm simply taking a page out of my mom's book. If she can post all these photos of me, Leo, her, and my dad on Facebook, if she can brag about how perfect her life is with us, if she can make it seem like we've got our shit together, then why can't I have my little fiction, too?

It's only for a little bit, anyway. It's temporary.

That's what I tell myself.

At my next One Fur All shift, I find Imani in her office with a few other workers and volunteers, but no Becca in sight. Small miracles.

"Hi, Imani!" I say.

She looks up from her computer and smiles. "Kat! How are you?"

"Not bad." I take my bag off my shoulder. "How's Cash doing today?"

"He's good. Though I am starting to worry a little," Imani admits. "We haven't gotten any inquiries for that sweet boy."

I frown. "Still nothing? Not even with the new pics?"

Imani shakes her head. "Nothing. There was one call to get some info, and they even came down, but once they noticed he was missing a limb they went with another dog."

"Nooo, poor Cash! His feelings must be so hurt."

At that, Imani gives me a small smile. "I gave him some extra rubs under his chin, but I'm sure he'd love some more from you. That would help."

"Definitely," I say.

"Can you water everyone while you're back there, too?" she asks.

"Of course." I head toward the kennels. Most of the dogs who were here just last week are gone, but my little buddy, who is quickly taking up more and more space in my heart, is still in his corner kennel, lying down and watching some of the volunteers mill around. His tail starts to wag when he sees me, but he stays on his spot on the ground. Maybe he really is sad. I let myself into his kennel and hold up a harness.

"C'mere, Cashy." He gets up and comes toward me, and I connect the harness to his leash. "Who's a good boy, huh? Who's a good boy?!" I crouch down so we're eye to eye and I scratch behind his ears and under his chin until eventually he flops over completely, begging for some belly rubs. I laugh. "There's my baby. We're going to find you a home, Cashy. I promise you that."

He licks my cheek, as if accepting my promise, and I lead him into the fenced-in field so he can stretch his legs and play. I desperately need to figure out a way to get Cash to a good home, but I don't know how. If photos of him in a flower crown weren't enough to do it, what will it take?

Cash and I play fetch for a bit as I rack my brain. What if I started Photoshopping him onto silly backgrounds? Or what if I worked on some special training with him, so that he can do things like play dead and retrieve? That might make him more appealing. We could post videos of him doing tricks.

I pull out my phone and start to Google a few simple commands. As I do, some notifications for Max pop up, and I quickly check out her account.

A new comment has come in from someone named Elena, @elenabobena, on Max's recent post. Her comment reads, *Be kind to yourself. If you ever need to talk, let me know.* ♥

And I find myself smiling.

"What's got you so happy?" I drop my phone at the sound of Becca's voice.

She swoops down to grab it before I can, and I yell *"No!"* so loudly that she jumps. A bewildered look comes across her face as she hands it back, screen side down.

"I wasn't going to peek, Kat, God," she says, dangling it toward me. "Are you looking at nudes or something?"

"Yes!" I blurt out with an awkward laugh. "That's totally what I'm doing."

For sure. Def not using your pics, which you don't want on social media, for my fake profile. Would never. No no. Not me!

"Okay, weirdo," Becca laughs. "Anyway, thank you so much

again for those absolutely beautiful photos you took the other day. You're really talented, Kat. I'm in awe."

I tuck my phone into my back pocket. "Thank you! I'm really glad you like them."

She leans down to grab the Frisbee I'd been tossing to Cash and gives it a solid throw. "Also, I keep feeling that I offended you when I said I didn't want to go to your party. I'm sorry. Hopefully we're okay?"

"Oh, that," I say. "We're good. I get why you wouldn't want to go. It'd be a little sus, right?"

"Totally! It's just weird, I think. Like I said, *you're* great, but yeah." She shrugs. "But I did have a super-fun time with you, anyway! Cora had fun, too."

"The beauty tips were great," I say. "Thank you again."

Becca smiles as Cash brings her back the Frisbee, all slobber-covered with bits of grass. She takes it from him, then hands it to me.

"Gross," she says. "Gonna go wash my hands."

It's only as she disappears inside that my heart stops feeling like it's being squeezed in a vise. Because that was *so close*.

I take a second to log back into my own Instagram account, far, far away from Max's, and go back to something really meaningful: teaching Cash to sit.

Chapter Eighteen

I try to compose some kind of text to Hari, but fail. I can't decide if I want to apologize for hurting him or yell at him for hurting me. I've never had to put this much effort into being Hari's friend before and I can officially say it sucks.

But how am I supposed to be fine with not talking to my best friend?

Luis and Marcus have probably figured out that something's up, since neither Hari nor I was very active in the group chat last night. I had a hard time sleeping, too.

Without the right words to say, without Hari to talk this out with, without a real solid plan in place, I'm at a loss for what I should do.

I could go to school, but then I may have to face reality.

Nah. I fake sick instead. "Headache," I say when I walk into the dining room, still in my pajamas. Grandma doesn't even question it and immediately offers to call the school for me, instructing my grandpa to cook some breakfast.

Grandpa taps his index finger on his chin thoughtfully, squinting his eyes a little as if deep in thought, before he exclaims, "Waffles!"

Guilt-ridden, I watch as he starts to maneuver around the kitchen, pulling out the ingredients. "Can I help?" I reach for a mixing bowl.

Grandpa gently swats at my hand. "No. You're sick!"

"But—"

"Straight to bed with you," he says, winking at me.

"Are you sure?" I ask.

"Positive," he replies. "Shoo!"

TBH, Grandpa is a pretty incredible cook, so I'm sure I'd be of no help. He's always experimenting in the kitchen. Some of his creations—eggplant lasagna with a garlic sauce, pierogies stuffed with rice and ground beef like you'd find in a stuffed pepper—are fire. Others, like the blueberry gravy or the pepperoni-and-cheese crepes, not so much. But whatever. I make a point of trying *everything* he's created because he's always so damn proud.

Like these waffles he enters my room with awhile later.

"Breakfast, for the lady," he says, bowing down as he hands the tray to me. "I hope this cures that pesky headache."

"Your food really is medicine, Grandpa," I say, grinning. "Thank you."

He tells me he hopes I feel better soon and then leaves me to eat and rest. The food in front of me looks IG-worthy, for sure: a mound of blueberry waffles smothered in butter and syrup, a side of sliced strawberries, and some hash browns. Picture-perfect, I think.

And then it hits me.

I can post this as Max.

It doesn't get more aesthetic than this artfully arranged plate of food on a breakfast tray with a steaming cup of tea. I stand on my bed, angling myself perfectly above the tray, and snap a couple of photos.

Then, while the tea is still piping hot, I position it on my nightstand and take a Boomerang.

I add this text:

Under the weather, but nothing a little tea can't fix.

And I post that to Max's story.

While I eat, I pop a photo I took of breakfast into Lightroom, select one of my favorite presets—I'm going with, like, a creamy, bright look for Max because it goes super well with Becca's complexion—and post with a simple caption.

Just what the doctor ordered.

On my own IG, this caption would probably be mercilessly mocked by the likes of Luis and Marcus. But coming from Max, it works.

Plus, since I've started posting, Max's follower count is already over four hundred followers, meaning I've now surpassed my own account with only a handful of posts. My new obsession is checking back every day and watching the numbers slowly climb.

I hit Share on the latest post and refresh. Likes come immediately. A rush.

I scroll through IG while eating my meal, grateful for this kindness from my grandpa. I've always admired both his culinary skills and his generosity; I admire them even more when he directs them at me. Thank you, Grandpa.

As I eat, I consider how I might grow Max's following. Posting on IG Stories is a good start; it adds legitimacy to what I'm doing. And who doesn't love looking at stories? I could do some scenic Reels, too, so long as I don't show myself and I'm careful to avoid reflections.

I check my DMs and note that there's one waiting for me in my requests.

It's from Elena, or @elenabobena, who has diligently liked and commented on all my posts so far.

She's written, **Oh no! Hope you feel better.**

I smile at this sweet, unsolicited message from a stranger.

I write back, **Me too! Thanks so much.**

I'm surprised when Elena writes back almost instantly.

Elena: **Tea always cures my ailments, so maybe it'll work for you too.**

Me: **Keeping my fingers crossed! Maybe this oolong can chase my headache right away.**

Elena: **Let's hope. I'm kind of obsessed with tea. Darjeeling is my fave. But I'm not super picky, tbh.**

Me: **Same. Makes me feel kinda sophisticated to drink.**

Elena: **RIGHT?! It's the thrill of making a tea party real.**

Me: **I don't think I've ever had a tea party!**

Elena: **EVER? Omg. We need to fix that ASAP. Tea parties are the BEST.**

Me: **Do I need to wear something frilly?**

Elena: **Frilly clothes totally optional. Just need the tea. And a good imagination.**

Me: **Now that I've got.**

Elena: **It's one of the greatest traits out there.**

Elena: **Ahhh, calculus calls.**

Me: **There's no tea in the world that can help with that.**

Elena: **Ugh, tell me about it.**

I like her last message that comes through and smile again to myself. Curious to learn more about this person, I click over to Elena's account. My eyes nearly bulge out of my head when I see she has eleven thousand followers.

...And she's talking to me?

Or, well, Max. But Max only has a fraction of her followers and hardly any posts by comparison.

What the hell drew Elena to her?

And encouraged her to reach out?

And be so nice?

There's a pride flag in her bio, and she's listed herself as part of this year's graduating class, meaning she's a senior. She's an Aquarius. A fellow dog lover. And she's curated a beautiful, sweet-as-candy vibe throughout her profile.

All her photos have a soft, pastel hue—sweet pink carnations in one; lavender platform shoes in another; a teal mug (likely filled with tea, now that I know she loves it) with the words NOT YOUR BABY on it.

Elena has cherubic cheeks and one of the kindest smiles I think I've ever seen. Blue eyes; pale skin; perfectly pink full lips; a dainty double chin. (I didn't know double chins could be dainty, but on Elena, it totally is.) In one of her photos, she's wearing a shirt with a pastel rainbow emblazoned with the words FAT FEMME. And did I mention her hair? It's soft pink like bubble gum.

The whole aesthetic is sugary, but it's clear this girl is also bold, confident in who she is, and unafraid to speak her mind. It's no wonder she has eleven thousand followers.

In her bio, she links directly to her TikTok. I swap over to the app and check out what she has to say there, stunned when I see she has almost fifty thousand followers and nearly half a million likes.

There are videos of her giving a tour of her room—equally pastel—as well as tips for small businesses like hers. As it turns out, Elena runs a sticker business, where she makes feminist and social justice–based stickers celebrating women, nonbinary people, and bodies of all kinds.

I find myself watching video after video—everything from tips on Procreate to a peek at her in-room "studio" to a list of her favorite spots around her hometown of Irvine, just three hours away from me.

I almost follow her on TikTok, but stop just before my finger hits the button. I don't want to follow her as me, Kat. And Max doesn't have a TikTok. Because she literally can't.

I have to tell Hari.

Only...I can't. Can't really tell Luis or Marcus, either.

Instead, I navigate back to IG, my safe haven, and follow her there, still floored that Elena has been so interested in what I've shared as Max that she not only followed, but regularly interacts with me.

This feels like a big win, and I'm sorry that algebra class has cut our DMs short.

I switch over to my own account, which is dead by comparison, and start cycling through everyone's stories—Luis, Marcus, some kids from school, influencers. I look at Hari's, too, but it's just a repost of something from Shit You Should Care About. I may be angry at him and him at me, but that doesn't mean I'm not interested in what he's up to.

With a sigh, I head out to the kitchen with my dirty dishes so I can start to clean up. I find my grandma and grandpa both sitting in the living room. It's unusual that they're both home in the morning like this, but Grandpa is taking a well-deserved day off because his shoulder's been bugging him, and Grandma sometimes has the luxury of working from home for her data analyst job. So, just seems like the stars aligned this morning.

They're both watching TV, with Grandma's laptop on the arm of the couch. Grandpa has his reading glasses on, a crossword puzzle book in one hand and a pencil in the other.

Rather than heading right back into my room, I go over to the couch.

"Hi, Kat," Grandma says, smiling at me. "How are you feeling?"

"Okay," I say, even though any pain I feel is more because of my life and not because of my "headache."

She pats the couch beside her and I sit down close, snuggling right up. We actually used to fall asleep together on the couch like this, me holding her hand. It couldn't have been comfortable for her, but she never complained.

It stopped as I got older—my choice—but sometimes I miss this, the comfort of just being able to cuddle with her, of feeling so warm and safe, like literally nothing in this entire world can hurt me.

I rest my head on Grandma's lap.

Grandma seems surprised, but she doesn't protest. Instead, she grabs the blanket that's draped over the back of the couch and does her best to put it over my body.

"Want to pick something?" Grandpa asks, holding the remote out toward Grandma so I can take it.

"No," I say. "I'm good with whatever you guys were watching. I just want to hang for a bit."

Grandma lets out a little laugh. "That's nice," she says.

My grandpa smiles, too. "Sure. Let's hang."

She resumes her work, Grandpa his crossword, and I snuggle in closer. Life can wait. For now, this is just what I need.

Chapter Nineteen

The truth is, I do not know how to be angry at Hari Shah.

The more I've thought of what Hari said to me—about my secret being low-key dumb—the more I've worried that maybe he's right. Maybe I have blown this thing way, way out of proportion. It's just that I've carried this lie around with me for over ten years now and the weight of it is so fucking heavy. What it represents is so fucking heavy.

I need to get back in touch. Mostly because I miss him. And I can't fake sick again.

Can I get a ride? I text Hari the next morning.

But he doesn't reply, and that hurts. I try not to let it, but I guess that's not how feelings work.

I get dressed and drive myself to school, borrowing my grandma's car. I park near Marcus's and then walk over to where we normally hang out outside before the bell rings. Marcus waves at me, but Hari and Luis barely glance up from whatever they're looking at on Luis's phone.

"Feeling better?" Marcus asks.

I give a small shrug. "A little, thank you."

Luis snorts. "Well, you sure don't *look* better."

Hari erupts into laughter—more than he ever does when Luis is teasing me, and I know this is just to make a point.

I glance down at myself and sigh. "True."

That causes Luis to snap his neck toward me in surprise. "Excuse me? Are you agreeing with what I just said about you?"

He looks over at Marcus, who is wide-eyed. "She must still be sick."

"Just don't feel like arguing this morning," I admit. "I'm gonna head inside."

"And you're going to homeroom early?" Marcus asks.

Luis shakes his head. "Who is this chick and what have you done with Sanchez?"

Marcus snaps his fingers. "I know what's up. She's just trying to intimidate me! She's going to work on her photo editor application."

I give him a small half smile. "See you inside."

Truthfully, between Hari, Max, Becca, and my curfew debacle, I haven't given that application much thought at all and it's due this Friday. But I guess I should.

I head to the library instead of homeroom, so I can pull out my laptop without my homeroom teacher breathing down my neck. There I start going through the portfolio I've pulled together thus far. The photos I've collected are some of my best—but the more I think about this position, the less eager I am to apply. I don't feel like giving up my free time to manage a team of photo editors so that we can take pictures of sports and things like that. Honestly, I don't really care about the newspaper. I only really cared about beating Marcus. Maybe that might've been enough before, but now? I really want to focus on Max.

Still, I know I *should* apply. I read through the essay prompt again. In less than three hundred words, I'm supposed to write about what would make me the best person for this role, about how it contributes to my goals.

Only...I don't really have any firm goals. Unless dreams of IG recognition count.

I watch the cursor in my Google Doc blink at me, annoyingly, tauntingly.

I type, *You should pick me because I'm not Marcus Brown and if he gets this position, I'll literally never hear the end of it, man,* and then delete it.

I'm the best person for this role because my photos are dope. Delete.

I would make an excellent photo editor despite not knowing shit about newspapers, but I bet I could lie my way through that because I lie my way through everything and I'm super good at it. Delete.

Being a photo editor is all I've ever dreamed of.

Ugh. Gross. And a lie. Delete.

Why can't I make myself care about this? At my age, shouldn't I know what I want to do? What I'm working for? Where I'd like to go? Why is this so hard for me?

I think of Marcus, who knows exactly what his plan is: apply and be accepted by Howard University, study journalism, and become a prominent photojournalist.

Hari will study business, likely at UC Berkeley, if his parents get their way. Though Hari is not exactly thrilled by the idea, he says it'll be stable and working for any job under capitalism is total garbage anyway, so he might as well get his.

And Luis has already said he'll skip college altogether—it's a scam, he argues—and hit up trade school.

All those things sound really nice, but I guess I don't know if any of them is exactly *my* thing.

The cursor blinks at me until the bell rings.

* * *

Things with Hari are chilly at lunch, which makes me so grumpy I end up excusing myself and eating alone in my car, even though that's not technically allowed. The one solace to this is that I can check my phone in peace.

Last night, before bed, I posted a photo of Becca that I had taken of her blowing some soft pink glitter toward the camera. It was a fun (but super-messy) idea and this photo came out almost magical-looking. I chose to post it because I wanted to share something a little lighter after my first couple of heavy posts. Also, I was maybe hoping the sparkle would elicit another DM from Elena.

It worked. When I open IG in the quiet of my car, there's a red notification indicating a new message. I smile to myself when I open it and see the name Elena at the top.

Elena: **THIS. PHOTO.**

Me: **Hahah, tysm!!!**

Me: **It def has a "you" vibe to it.**

Elena: **It really does! Who is your photographer?!**

Elena: **Full disclosure: I've totally been stalking you and I noticed you live in the Bakersfield area.** 👀 **I'm in Irvine!**

I pretend I haven't already stalked *her* and that this is brand-new information.

Me: **Omg! We're kinda like neighbors.**

Elena: **Right?**

Elena: **Soooo if you're willing to share the photographer, maybe I can borrow them.** 👀 👀 👀

I gnaw on my lip, considering how best to answer this. Can I be truthful about who the photographer of these photos is without potentially blowing up my spot?

On the one hand, it's risky. If I'm honest and I tell Elena that I, Kat Sanchez, am the photographer, there is a small chance she could eventually connect the dots that I'm also Max.

On the other hand, the temptation to get more followers on my own personal account is great. Although, what are the odds that anything will actually come of this? We're just internet friends, after all, and *barely* that.

Before I can think too hard, I write: **It's my friend @itskatsanchez!**

I hold my breath after I hit Send. Then get a little mad at myself. What was I thinking?

Elena: **Ahhh, well, she's AMAZING.**

Elena: **It helps that she has a great model.** 💕

My face flushes at both compliments, even though only one is truly directed at me. Given how perfect her IG game is, it feels very validating.

Me: **Thank you.** ☺

Elena: **Thanks for sharing your photographer with me. It'll be our little secret. Pinky promise.**

I grin at that.

Me: **I don't mind sharing with you. You've been so sweet to me!**

Me: **Like, for real, I don't know what made you decide to follow me, but I'm real glad you did.**

Elena: **Ummm super easy follow. That first pic of you with the peacock and the golden sun?! To die for!**

Me: **Ahhh, thank you, thank you!!! I'm literally so obsessed with your whole aesthetic. It's next level.**

Elena: **Hahah thanks! It's been a long time in the making. I pretty much never grew out of being obsessed with pink.**

Me: **It's working for you!**

Elena: **Appreciate that so much!**

I glance at the clock in the corner of my phone. Shit. I missed the lunch bell.

Me: **Shit. Lunch is over! Talk later?**

Elena: **Duh.**

I tuck my phone into my pocket and hustle back into the school, severely late for my next class but with the tiniest pep in my step.

Chapter Twenty

The fun chat with Elena uplifts my spirits so much that I decide to extend an olive branch to Hari with something I know no one can resist.

To the group, I text, **Want to come pet some dogs later?**

This elicits an immediate and enthusiastic response from Marcus, who immediately writes, **HELL FUCKING YES, KAT!!!**

Luis simply texts a brown thumbs-up emoji.

Hari doesn't text back, but just emphasizes Luis's thumbs-up. I take that as a yes and tell them to meet me at One Fur All after school.

My mistake is that I don't specify a time, so I rush over and find myself annoyed when they aren't there immediately.

It's only been a couple of days, but I just want normal back so bad right now. I want Hari to not be mad at me. I want to be harassed by Luis. I want to compete with Marcus. I want my friends. But hanging with them won't be so easy if things are fragile with me and Hari. Luis and Marcus have already made it their life's mission to tease the two of us for being a couple; now that we're definitely *not* a couple and kinda fighting over it, the teasing will sting even worse.

Or, worse, they'll figure it out and pick a side. And I fear it won't be mine.

The idea of losing all three of my friends all at once makes my stomach churn. Without them, what would I even have?

While I wait for them to arrive, I spend a couple of minutes on my phone. No new messages from Elena, unfortunately, but there are tons more likes on Max's latest pic. I also add a graphic that shows up in my feed that reads, PROTECT TEEN GIRLS AT ALL COSTS, and share that to my story. It's pastel, so Elena will totally like it.

Not that I'm overthinking what she'll like or anything.

Although maybe I am. The way I felt at Becca's...

Out of the corner of my eye, I notice a car pulling into the lot and look up. Sure enough, it's Marcus. He is painstakingly slow when it comes to parking, a fact that drives me absolutely crazy, but he always insists he needs to park *exactly right* so that there is enough room on each side of the car to prevent someone from accidentally "hurting" Honey. Gag.

I'm out of the car with my arms crossed well before they are.

When the three of them emerge, they're all holding iced coffees.

"Seriously? Making me wait so you could get iced coffees?" I scoff.

"Sorry, sorry. I was trying to hurry us along," Marcus says.

"Damn, Sanchez, I really needed it! I was, like, dying," Luis explains. Then he smirks. "Xio kept me up late last night."

I make a disgusted face. "Ugh, gross. And you didn't even bring one for me?" I look over at Hari, who doesn't meet my eye.

"Why would we bring a coffee for you?" Luis asks.

Marcus sighs at him. "C'mon, man." He looks at me. "He was supposed to grab your drink."

"I don't recall this. Thought you were talking to Sanchez's boyfriend."

Hari's jaw—which I will admit is looking much better after the fight—tightens at that.

Marcus just sighs. "Of course we brought you a coffee. Hang on." He jogs back to his car, ducks inside for a sec, then emerges with a drink and holds it up into the air victoriously.

"Yes!" I pump my fist in the air in celebration.

Marcus hands the cup to me and then asks, "Can we pet some dogs now?"

"Just a sec," I say, snapping a quick pic of my iced coffee up against the blue sky.

Marcus and Luis exchange a look but don't say anything. I slap a preset over the pic and pop it on my story—and on Max's. I crop my brown thumb on the cup out of the pic on Max's because you know.

On mine, I tag Marcus, Luis, and Hari. *When you have evidence that @mrcsbrwn, @luistho, and @harishah care about you.*

I show it to them and Luis makes a face. "Take that down! I don't want people to think we're friends."

With a grin, I say, "Too late."

I nod toward the building, indicating that they should follow me. Though I don't have a scheduled shift until Friday, I know Imani won't mind that I'm stopping by. I'll put these guys to work exercising the dogs. It's free help, and even though Imani is huge on paying everyone she can for their time, volunteer work keeps this place running. So I'm officially volunteering the boys.

When we walk inside, Becca is sitting at her desk, but totally texting on her phone.

"Hey, Becca," I say, waving at her.

She glances up. "Oh, hey. You're working today?"

I shake my head. "Just visiting. These are my friends—Luis, Marcus, Hari. Guys, this is Becca."

"*This* is your college friend Becca?" Luis asks, eyes wide. He walks over to her, extending a hand. Becca shoots me a confused look but laughs and holds her hand out to him. He kisses it.

"Gross, Luis. Control yourself," I chide.

"And Xio?" Hari reminds him.

"Xio doesn't need to know," Luis jokes.

"Hi, guys," Becca says. Then she looks over at me. "So, I'm your college friend, huh?"

I roll my eyes. "They're just being stupid. We're going to say hello to some of the dogs, okay?"

Becca nods. "Help yourself. I should be updating the profiles for the new dogs." She returns to her computer.

The four of us head out to the kennels. I decide on letting out two dogs at once, Luis, Hari, and Marcus taking one to the yard and me taking another. I can tell Marcus is in his glory as he squats down and greets each dog warmly, scratching all along their backs. One is a sheltie, Skye, and the other a poodle named Bubby. Laughing, we play-wrestle and toss toys for them, trying to wear them out.

After half an hour, I return Skye and Bubby to their kennels and say I'll be right back with another dog. Marcus urges me to hurry.

Cash dramatically stretches his entire body when I let him out of his kennel. He gives me a big sloppy kiss—which I happily accept—before leading him outside.

"Ready to meet some of my friends?" I ask him.

Cash wags his tail excitedly. When I open the back door, he bounds into the yard, nearly tripping over his own feet.

Marcus grins. "Ayy, look at him go!"

"Right? Isn't he adorable?" I coo.

"You sound white as hell right now," Luis teases, mimicking what I've just said. " 'Isn't he adorable?' "

I shake my head. "There's nothing white about loving dogs."

"Oh, no, there's everything white about loving dogs," Luis says. "Titi Rosa would never let one of them into our house. They lick their own buttholes, Sanchez."

I scowl at him. "You're nasty. Don't say that about Cash!"

He shrugs. "I mean, they do."

"Loving dogs *is* kinda white, Kat," Hari says. Ugh. The first time he's really spoken to me all day, and it's to agree with Luis that something I love is too white. Fun.

"*Humans* love dogs," I argue.

"I mean, my mom would also never let me have a dog in the house. She says dogs belong outside because they're dirty. I love them, but I do kinda get it. It's like, they wear their shoes in the house—on your couch, in your own bed, if they sleep with you," Hari explains. "Kinda rude, don't you think?"

"They're dogs!" I argue. "Marcus, help me out here?"

Marcus has dropped to his knees and he's whispering something to Cash, with his hands on either side of his face. "What?"

"Tell them loving dogs isn't white."

"Oh, it's white as hell," Marcus says. Then he looks over at Cash and singsongs, "*But I embrace it.* Look at this cutie!"

"Hasn't he been here awhile already?" Luis asks. "I feel like you mentioned him a long time ago."

"So you do listen when I talk!"

He squints at me. "Just that once."

"Okay, fine. Cash *has* been here awhile, though," I say. "It's partly that he's a pit. There are a lot of pits that end up here and they're sometimes hard to rehome. But Cash is also missing a leg, so nobody wants to take a chance on him."

"Damn, Kat, don't say that too loud," Marcus scolds, putting his hands over Cash's ears. "Homeboy can hear you." He takes a nearby weathered yellow tennis ball and throws it hard across the field. Cash races after it.

"Yeah, Kat. Don't be so rude," Hari says.

I give him a sideways glance, narrowing my eyes. "I don't think I'm the one being rude."

We stare at each other for a second until Luis interrupts. "So, really, this is your job? You just get to, like, pet dogs all day?"

"I do a little more than that. Take photos of them, manage their social media accounts, make sure they get exercise, feed them, give them water...," I explain. "But yeah. There are lots of belly rubs, too."

Luis tsks. "Damn, you really lucked out."

I nod. "I really did. You guys want to meet a few more?"

"Immediately," Marcus says.

I leash Cash back up and lead him inside, where I introduce the three of them to some of the newest arrivals—Hunter, Sage, and Obi—one at a time, kennel by kennel.

"Who names them?" Marcus asks, cradling Obi, a Maltese with the silkiest coat of white fur, in his arms.

"Depends. Imani, usually, but sometimes she lets us do it."

"You know what would be dope?" Luis asks. "Naming them after rappers. But, like, making it funny."

I arch an eyebrow at him. "How so?"

"You know, like calling one of them Snoop Dogg. Or something like, I don't know. Notorious D.O.G."

"Okay, okay. I'm feeling this," I say, thinking. "Like...Missy Elli-pit?"

Luis's face lights up. "Yes! Exactly!"

"For a cat: Tupac Sha-purr?" Marcus offers.

"Oh my God," I laugh. "I love it."

"Cardi Flea," Luis says.

"Young Pug!" I shoot back.

Marcus adds, "Kendrick Lamarf!"

"Whiz Khali-paw?" Hari suggests.

"Yes!" I practically shout, and one of the volunteers shoots us a look. "Sorry." To the group I say, "Okay, we're def being too loud. Want to get out of here?"

Luis nods. "I *am* hungry."

"Of course you are." I roll my eyes.

We leave One Fur All and agree to eat at Holy Guacamole, a local food truck that Luis is obsessed with. My friends all pile into Marcus's car and I get into my grandma's, following close behind.

Before I get out of the car, I grab my DSLR. I need to get some more authentic shots to work into Max's feed, and the food here is always so delicious-looking. It'll be perfect.

But, of course, when I emerge, Marcus eyes my camera. "If you're trying to intimidate me out of applying for that photo editor position, this is not the way to do it," he teases. "Photos of your food are not going to be better than my photos of beautiful Black women."

"No intimidation here. I'm just trying to take some pics of the food," I say with a shrug.

Luis starts to laugh. "So, is this for the 'Gram? First the iced coffee, now this? Sanchez, noooo. You can't become the type of girl that posts pics of what she's eating!"

Hari laughs, too. "For real, Sanchez. Yikes."

I roll my eyes again, not at all loving that Hari just called me Sanchez, which is usually a Luis-only thing. "Forget you, all of you, and mind your business."

Luis makes a face. "Ooh, yeah, can't do that."

I sigh. "Just shut up and order me a taco."

Chapter Twenty-One

Despite a relatively nice time with my friends, it's obvious that Hari is still pissed. And I feel like I've done my part. There really isn't more I can do. I'm done trying.

I skip the next Photography Club meeting to venture out for photos on my own. If this is how it's gonna be, fine. I don't need them. I can do it all on my own.

It is lonely, though.

I don't make it any better for myself when I hastily text Pop and say I'm skipping this week's family dinner. After the curfew drama, I'm good to sit this one out.

I'd rather focus my time and energy right now on Max stuff, anyway. I bury myself in drafting some posts for her account. It takes effort to find just the right photos and to figure out what I'd like the captions to be. They're not just photos of Becca, either: they're photos of the city, of the neighborhood, of people. They're my *real* work. And finally, finally, I'm getting a response.

For whatever reason, the things I've been sharing on Max's account have been working in a way my stuff *never* has. I'm a little salty about it, for sure—my photos remain bomb, if totally invisible—but if this is what people want, then fine. Because it's working. I'm consistently posting, I'm being vulnerable, I'm engaging with people, I'm sharing my art, and my followers are growing. It feels productive.

Max's latest endeavor: posting about dogs.

Mostly because I love them, and so does everyone else. Plus, I have access to so many.

The latest post highlights a photo of Becca, with reflective sunglasses sitting skewed atop her head, as she crinkles her nose, mouth open midlaugh. One of our since-adopted dogs, Sly, licks her cheek. While also wearing sunglasses.

There's a stray hair of hers that I edit out, then I smooth down some of the flyaways, as well as the small pimple on her chin that I remember her obsessing over that day.

For the caption, I write:

I. Love. Dogs.

We like to think that everyone loves dogs, but the truth is this: nearly three million dogs and cats are put down every year because shelters are too full and there aren't enough adoptive homes.

If that feels grim, it's because it is. But I am so, so lucky to work toward making a difference, in whatever small way I can, through my volunteer work at my local no-kill animal shelter. There, we take in all kinds of animals—dogs, especially—and we rehabilitate them.

We give them their shots, we feed them, we sometimes nurse them back to health after months of neglect, we train them, and most importantly, we love them until they can find a good home.

Each dog's story is different, but they are all so deserving of warmth and kindness. My hope is to help bring awareness to their stories, to help dogs all over find families, and to help make it so that all pets are able to find the homes they deserve.

The caption comes easily, inspired by my actual job. And I'm weirdly proud. This post feels really meaningful. Maybe I can actually use Max to help make a difference.

With my brain buzzing with ideas, I start to make a list of

animal welfare content I'd like to share: Shout-outs to my favorite no-kill shelters, tips I've learned from Imani on caring for dogs, how to determine if a dog is a good fit for you, how you can volunteer.

I'm only interrupted when Grandma calls to see if I still want to run some errands with her and Grandpa. I meet them at the car.

"Ready to grab a new shower curtain?" Grandma asks playfully.

"And a new screwdriver," Grandpa adds.

I grin, buckling myself in. "Oh, goody!"

"Maybe we can even get something nice for you, too. If you're good." Grandpa grins at me from the front seat as Grandma pulls out of our driveway.

"A pony?" I ask.

"If we can find them at Target, sure," Grandma says. After a moment, she clears her throat. "So...we heard from your mother."

I roll my eyes, not looking up from my phone. "About the curfew? Again?"

"That, and also you canceling on tonight's dinner."

I lean my head back against the seat. "Oh. Well, I just didn't feel like going."

Although I can't see her face, I know Grandma's frowning from the driver's seat.

Grandpa fiddles with the radio, pretending like this conversation isn't really happening. I wish I could, too.

"It's just that I hope you're not trying to punish your parents over our disagreement," Grandma says slowly. "That's our issue, not yours."

I cross my arms. "I'm not trying to punish anyone. I've been having a really difficult week and I don't feel like smiling through a dinner no one even wants to be at."

There's an edge to my voice that I can't help.

Grandma glances back at me, surprised. "What do you mean by that?"

I shrug. "I mean, Mom and Leo weren't even there for dinner last week."

At this, Grandpa cuts off the radio. "They weren't?" He glances at Grandma. "So much for that photo Sarah posted on Facebook."

"Oh, right—Mom made us take a picture first to make it *appear* like we were having dinner together, but then she and Leo left." I look at the window, watching as we pass fire hydrants and parked cars in a blur. "Then it was just me and Pop eating dinner with the dogs. Big, happy family."

Grandpa sighs. "I'm sorry, Kat. We had no idea."

"It's not your fault. But I mean...do they even want me to come over for dinners if it's such a nuisance? What's the point?"

"Those are your parents," Grandma reminds me.

I feel myself stiffen. I've heard this thousands of times throughout my life. That's your mom. That's your dad. That's your brother. Reminders over and over again that they're my family, like I might wake up one day and forget.

Does she remind them of that, too? I'm their daughter? Their sister?

"You and Grandpa are the ones raising me," I say quietly.

Grandma gasps. "Kat."

But it's true.

And yet we never say that. Sometimes, it makes me feel like I've made it all up, like I'm confused about who loves me and who doesn't. Another lie by Kat Sanchez.

I feel it, though. The strain. The distance. The indifference. In their house, which has nothing of me in it. In the bedroom they said was mine, "in case you ever feel like moving in," that has slowly become a storage room. In our one-night-a-week dinners. In the way the conversations we have over those dinners take such effort, like a meal shared by strangers. In the impromptu beach trips they take that include my brother but not me. In the back-to-school shopping they do with just Leo. In the way they know nothing about my hopes, my dreams, my art.

I am far from the favorite child... but it's even worse than that. I barely even register *as* their child.

I want to say that this is about so much more than a curfew or a missed dinner. This is about what makes a family.

But I don't.

Grandpa reaches over and puts a weathered hand on Grandma's knee. He gently strokes it with his thumb as he says, "She's right."

The air in the car is heavy with the weight of what I've just said. It's weird how the truth can do that sometimes.

"I know you want me and my parents to be closer, Grandma." My voice is soft as I speak. "I want that, too. If wishing on dandelions were enough, then we'd be good. But it takes work, too. Why am I the only one ever going over there? And why don't we ever do anything together? They never call me. They never include me in anything. It feels like I have to put in all the effort, and I'm punished when I don't have the strength anymore. It shouldn't all be on me."

It feels good to say this. I'm tired.

Grandma takes in a deep breath. "She is right."

Then Grandpa turns around, giving me a look that says he wishes he could pat my hand, too—comfort both of his girls at once. "We're proud of you, Kat. And we'll talk more about this."

I nod. "Okay."

Grandma nods, too. "Yes."

A pause, and then Grandpa speaks. "Now... what color pony?" Grandpa winks at me, an effort to quell the tension that still lingers. I force a small smile, but my heart feels heavy from another half conversation.

* * *

That night, my fingers long to send a text to Hari. I can't. So, I shoot a DM to Elena.

Me: **Is your family fucked up?**

Elena: **Um, of course they are. Isn't everyone's?**

Me: **Maybe. I don't know. Sorry for the abrupt, random message lol.**

Elena: **No worries!**

Elena: **You good?**

Me: **Just a lot going on.**

Elena: **Let's talk, then.**

Me: **It's hard to explain it all by DM. I wish we could talk another way.**

Elena: **Why can't we?**

Elena: **Phones do more than DM!**

My heart starts pounding. Truth be told, I would love nothing more than to talk to Elena. I've been so disconnected from everyone and everything that I haven't gotten to talk—really talk—to much of anyone lately.

How could I pull that off, though? If I give Elena my number, I'm worried she'll be able to track me down and figure everything out.

I search really quickly to see if there's a way I can share my number without sharing my number. There is. Without thinking, I download an app, set up an account, and DM Elena back.

Me: **Just a call, if that's okay. No video chat. I'm a mess.**

Elena: **Of course. Calling now!**

There is an eon between when I get that message and when my phone actually rings. I hold my breath. I shouldn't have done this. This is a terrible idea. I won't answer.

But then my screen lights up and I do.

"Hello?" I say.

"Max?" the gentle voice on the other end says, sounding more nervous than I expected.

Which actually makes me feel less nervous. "It's me. Hi, Elena."

"Hi!" And then Elena laughs, and it's the sweetest explosion of joy, and I laugh, too. "This is so bizarre. Right?"

"Super weird," I say. "Phone calls always are."

"Totally! Usually, I'd rather die than talk by phone. But...you seemed like you needed a friend tonight."

I grip my phone tighter. "I do. I've just had a really terrible night—couple of nights, actually."

"Well, don't be shy. Tell me about it," Elena says, her voice kind and encouraging.

It's alarming how easily the next few lies slip off my tongue.

"My parents and I have been arguing a lot. They want me to major in something practical, like business. But I really want to study theater. They're livid over it. They say I won't make good money and acting is an impossible industry to break into," I say, fabricating. "Which I know is probably true. But it's what I love. I just feel like they don't even see me, you know? They don't even *hear* me."

At least the last parts are true.

"Oh, God. That sucks! I'm so sorry they're pushing you like that," Elena says. "They should respect your dreams for the future, because you'll be the one living it. Not them."

"Exactly. It hurts that they have this alternate reality of what my life should be."

"I imagine college is hard enough, but having your parents breathing down your neck about the future?" She sighs. "That must make it impossible."

I sigh, too. "It does. Are your parents supportive of what you want to do, at least?"

"Mostly, yeah. The stuff I get shit for is not so much what I'll do, but where I'll go to college. My sister Carys has big opinions on that," Elena says. "She's already a freshman and decided to stay home and commute. She wants me to, too, because it's financially responsible and we can share the experience and all that. I love her, but I don't know. The East Coast is calling to me."

"I've never been."

"Oh, I haven't, either." And then she laughs. "But movies tell me all I need to know, obviously. It's uptight. A little high-strung. But eclectic. Small. Quaint. There are tiny coffee shops that know you by name, and everyone seems to own a bakery or have some other rom-com type job, like florist or art curator."

Now I'm laughing, too, at this shamelessly idyllic vision. "I could see you having any of those jobs."

"Right? I'm so East Coast! And the seasons." Elena's voice goes dreamy. "The changing leaves. The sparkle of snow. The gentle blooming of the flowers. Summers on the Cape. I don't know what, exactly, the Cape *is,* but people over there seem to love it."

"I think it's just a bunch of beach towns?" I venture.

"That's perfect! Then I won't get homesick. See? I have it all figured out." Then she pauses. "At least I like to pretend I do."

"It's easier that way sometimes."

"It really is." She sighs. "But maybe I can be convinced to stay here. I don't know. Tell me about Cal State. What's that like?"

I think back to some of the random trips I've made to CSU, of my daydreams of being a student on campus, of snippets I've heard from Becca. I use that to support some of my answers, and the rest, I just make up.

Because what's one more lie if it means I get to get closer to someone like Elena?

Chapter Twenty-Two

We talked for hours. It didn't feel like it, though. One second I was a jumble of nerves waiting for a call from this girl I barely knew, the next my room was shrouded in darkness with only a soft blue glow from the moon.

In that time, I came to know so much about Elena.

She recently broke up with her girlfriend. She has dreams of working with kids someday. She's been obsessed with the color pink since she was a kid, went through a period of time where she rebelled against it because #InternalizedMisogyny, and then reembraced it fully in high school. Her hair is usually pink, but it's also been lavender. She collects teacups with foul language on them. She calls her sister Carys "a real pill" in one sentence, and in another, her voice grows heavy with love and adoration for her older sibling. They have a cat, but she wants a dog.

I told her things about Max, too. Some are fake. Some are real. The longer we talked, the harder it was not to give Elena pieces of myself, too. It only felt right.

Being Max is rewarding is so many weird ways. And, while I'm avoiding Hari, which means also unintentionally avoiding Marcus and Luis, it gives me something to focus on. Her life feels so much easier to think about than my own.

After my call with Elena, any thoughts I originally had of deleting this account have been shelved indefinitely. I really need some kind of connection. Elena is it.

* * *

I use my quiet Friday evening after my One Fur All shift to go through the photos I've taken of Becca, which are now meticulously organized and ready to be posted.

For this to work, though, I need fresh content, too.

Thankfully, Becca and I are scheduled to work together on Sunday, so I shoot Becca a text asking if she'd be interested in a photo shoot—both at work, and after? I explain that I'm trying to build up my portfolio for my school's photo editor position, ignoring the fact that my application is due tonight.

It doesn't take her long to respond: **I'm in!**

I promise to get her a creative plan for the day so she can come properly prepared. She's been so excited after our last shoot that she says she's open to whatever.

There's a soft knock at my door and I scoot off my bed to open it. Grandma is there holding some tea for me. We haven't spoken very much since our awkward car ride, so I imagine this is her version of a peace offering. Love languages and all.

"Thirsty?" she asks.

I nod. "A little."

She holds the mug to me and smiles. "For you."

I reach for it and take a small sip of the hot liquid. "Thank you."

She's still standing in the doorway, as if unsure whether she should come in or stay standing. I'm not really sure, either. But I sit back on my bed so I can at least do something.

"I wanted to say I'm sorry about last night," she begins. I look at the mug and its pattern of orange poppies as if it's the most fascinating thing in the world. She continues. "I know it was a lot for you to come out and share those things. It must've been hard. Must be hard. I should've said more."

"It is hard," I say, slowly. "I'm sorry if I upset you."

She shakes her head. "Don't worry about me. It's complicated, isn't it? This whole thing."

"Confusing, too."

"It always has been," she agrees. "I don't always know the right thing to do. Or to say. I want very much for you to have a good relationship with Mom and Pop. Leo, too.

"It's for more than wanting that, though, that I've always insisted you follow their rules. It's because that's what we agreed upon. To make this...arrangement. It came with the promise that your grandfather and I would help keep your bond with them alive, as best as we could. Maybe that was an unfair promise. I don't know," Grandma says. "But it's a promise I made. And I take that seriously."

This is the most I've ever heard about the origins of how my living situation came to be. It's not much, but it is something.

Grandma looks down at my tea, then up again. "If that sometimes means I'm a little pushy, or a little reluctant to rock the boat, then I'm sorry. I've always had this vision of the four of you being together and being really close. Every parent imagines that, I think. So I know it's complicated and sometimes strange to have things be this way, but I appreciate you doing your best. I really do, Kat. And we have to keep trying."

The way she's looking at me, her brown eyes saucers of coffee-colored hope, I feel the weight of what she's asking. Just keep trying to make this work. Just keep pretending.

I imagine all the guilt she must feel for not "doing more" to get my parents to take me with them, for "allowing" this to happen, for "interfering" with our family—all things she has said, small comments, just here and there, over the years. The words may have been brief, the thoughts fleeting, but I collected them all and still have them, turning them over in my mind late at night.

And so I swallow. Smile. Nod.

"Okay," I say. "We'll keep trying."

She smiles back at me and reaches over to squeeze my knee.

Then she's gone from my room and I can properly deflate the way I couldn't when she was here.

What a mess.

I sink back into my bed and pull out my phone, eager for a distraction. My finger hovers over the colorful Instagram icon, and for a brief second, I squeeze my eyes shut and hope to find a notification for Max.

When I open them again and look back at my phone, I see that there *is* a blue (*1 Request*) notification in the upper right-hand corner.

I click and do a double take when I see the name I'd been hoping for—Elena Powell—in the messages. How can this be? We've talked so much already that she shouldn't be showing up as a request.

Then my heart drops into my stomach when I note the name at the top of the screen. It's not Max Monroe. It's Kat Sanchez.

Why is Elena DMing me instead of Max?!

Tears spring to my eyes at the thought that this could all be over already. My secret out. My adventure as Max over. My budding friendship with Elena done. We've only just talked once! I knew that was a terrible idea.

I briefly consider deleting my own personal Instagram and never reading the message.

Only I know I can't. So I tap on the notification with a shaky finger. And then I laugh out loud when I see the message.

Hi Kat! Sooo sorry to be a stranger DMing out of the blue, but I got your name from Max Monroe (@maxmonroelives). I am TOTALLY OBSESSED with your photography skills! You are so good! I noticed you live over in Bakersfield and I was wondering if you're open to new clients? Looking to get some pics for a website. Let me know! Thank you so much!

I must be dreaming. Because there is no way that Elena, the girl

I've been chatting with as Max, has now DMed me, *the real-life girl who is one hundred percent lying to her,* to meet up and take photos.

I laugh again, rereading the message.

There's no way I can agree to this. No matter how badly my insides are screaming yes.

...Unless?

I turn onto my stomach, thinking. And thinking. And thinking. And thinking. I write not one, but two, three, four, five, and six versions of a response. Call it courage, call it entrepreneurial genius, call it complete and utter stupidity, call it whatever you want but I'm *this close* to saying I'm interested.

I'm running through all the scenarios in my head and desperately wish I had someone to talk this through with.

Part of me is screaming absolutely not. Say no! I'm already being weird enough as it is, taking Becca's pics and posing as someone who *doesn't actually exist.* I could meet up with Elena and completely misspeak. The truth could come tumbling out.

The other part of me insists this isn't a big deal: I can just say I'm interested, do the photo shoot, give Elena the photos, and be done. No harm, no foul. She gets beautiful pics, I get to see her.

Because that's what it boils down to, right? I want to see Elena.

I pace around my room, turning both decisions over and over in my mind. Then I hop onto Max's IG account and compose a DM.

Me: **Just saying hi!**

Elena writes back almost instantly.

Elena: **Oh heyyyy! How are ya?**

Me: **Pretty good! Whatcha getting up to tonight?**

Elena: **Just going out with a few friends. My friend has an outdoor projector so we're going to watch The Rocky Horror Picture Show and eat a bunch of junk food!**

Me: **That sounds amazing!**

Elena: **Right?! How about you?**

Me: **Nothing much. Working on a paper.**

Elena: **Ugh. Say no more.**

Me: **Totally random, but did you ever end up reaching out to my friend Kat?**

Elena: **Okay, freaky. I just DMed her today!**

Me: **I'm actually psychic. Did I not mention that?**

Elena: **Well, Miss Psychic, can you tell if your friend is going to be down to take photos of me or what?**

Elena: **I'm finally going to make a real website for my sticker business!**

Elena: **And, if all goes well, maybe senior portraits next year?**

All of that sounds so wholesome and sweet. Okay, maybe it really wouldn't be so bad if I agreed to this? I can absolutely handle some simple pics for her website.

Me: **Crystal ball says ... You may rely on it.** ✦ 🔮 ✦

Elena: **Okay, why do you sound more like a Magic 8-Ball than a psychic?**

Me: **Same thing, right? But I'll give Kat a nudge for you! She's not on IG much.**

Elena: **Thank you!!!**

Elena: **And let me know if you can use your psychic powers to figure out the lotto numbers. Capitalism is the worst, but we should get our fair share, you know?**

I heart her latest message.

Okay. So I'm doing this. I'll confirm as myself soon, but not yet. I don't want it to be too obvious that Max and I are *the same person.*

To kill time, I suppose I could finally finish the photo editor application given that I went and mentioned it to Elena and all. It's due tonight by 11:59 p.m. Three hours, but who's counting?

I shoot a text to the group.

Me: **Marcus, how did you submit your portfolio?**

Marcus: **I cannot believe you are asking me this.**

Marcus: **And I cannot believe you haven't applied yet!**

Marcus: **Kat.**

Me: **I know! I'm finishing everything up right now.**

Luis: **Get it together, coño.**

I send back an eye roll emoji.

Me: **Can you just tell me? PDF or what?**

Marcus: **I used my website.**

I frown. A website? Marcus never had a website before!

Me: **Are you serious?**

He shoots me back a link and I click. Sure enough, a website for Marcus Brown Photography loads on my phone and it's...gorgeous. There are pages for his portfolio, pricing, about, and a contact page.

How does Marcus always have his shit so together?

Marcus: **You can just link your IG. Or do something on WordPress.**

Marcus: **Not that I'm helping you**

Marcus: **But let's remember this when I get this job. That I did go out of my way to help you and I still got it.**

Luis adds a skull emoji and Hari laugh-reacts at Marcus's text.

Guess I have a long night of work ahead of me.

Chapter Twenty-Three

I check my phone first thing when I wake the next morning, as always.

My new portfolio loads and I study it for a moment. Last night, I sank a lot of time into it—choosing new photos, editing them, cutting old ones—and it actually came out pretty good. But it was late when I finished and I *still* hadn't touched the essay portion of the application. The prompt kept staring back at me, and no matter how much I tried to come up with a thoughtful answer, nothing came.

I ended up reading through the full position description again, trying to imagine myself committing to the after-school and weekend work it listed and ultimately decided . . . nah.

I didn't apply.

At least I got an updated portfolio out of this whole thing.

Before I get out of bed, and before I lose all my nerve, I reply to Elena.

Hi Elena! That's so sweet of you to say. And of Max to recommend me—wow! Just peeked on your profile and love your aesthetic. I would totally be down. I typically charge $50 for an hour-long shoot, which includes 30-50 edited images, but since you're a friend of Max's, happy to do it for free! Here's my website so you can take a look at my work. Let me know more about what you're envisioning and I can let you know when I'm available.

"Typically charge," as if I've ever worked professionally before.

And then I take a deep breath with the realization that *now I'm carrying on two separate conversations with Elena.*

I need a shower.

Once I'm clean and I've run through what very well may be every possible scenario of the way things could go wrong, I check my phone again. Sure enough, Elena has replied. Still in my damp towel, I flop onto my bed and start to read what she's said.

Elena: **Just $50? Are you kidding me? I mean this with so much love, but Kat! You are seriously lowballing yourself! I INSIST on paying at least $100.**

Me: **Whaaat? No, no! That's way too much?? I'm still building my portfolio. I'm a newbie.**

Elena: **With all due respect, your portfolio is already good. Have you looked at your own IG? Most photographers, especially in this area, charge like $150-$200 for the session ONLY. Pricing for digital or print photos is usually extra!**

Elena: **I'm sorry for pushing so hard, but I'm super passionate about ensuring that creative people (and, let's be real, ESPE-CIALLY creative women) get paid what they deserve for their work. Way too many people think this work is free or we can just do it for exposure and I'm not about it.**

Okay, businesswoman! Add this to the list of things I like about Elena. Not only is she super encouraging and warm and creative, but also passionate about ensuring that other creatives— even someone like me, with next to no followers—get paid.

Me: **Okay, you win! How soon were you thinking?**

Elena: **I'm free next Saturday.**

Oh! Okay! Soon! Not stressful at all!

We hash out the details, with Elena explaining to me that she's looking for a few professional head shots as well as some more fun photos for her IG. I envision an early-morning shoot, when the sun is still sleepy and low in the sky and the colors are so much more subdued, like they're not fully awake just yet.

With travel, it would mean a really early morning for me. But I can already see the photos in my head. It's got to happen.

We agree to meet up at Ventura Pier Beach so I won't have to battle through LA traffic and I give her my actual cell phone number so I can text her to confirm later in the week. By the time we're done going back and forth, a text from Hari comes in.

It's just to me, though, not the group, and all it says is **You have my hoodie.**

My brows furrow. I have his hoodie?

Then I remember the night of his party, when he draped a spare hoodie over me for the walk home. Right. I search through my dirty clothes hamper and come up empty-handed, but eventually find it neatly folded in my dresser. My grandma must have washed it for me when she was taking care of some of my other clothes.

Me: **Yep. Got it.**

Hari: **Can I come by to pick it up?**

Me: **Fine.**

Hari: **K. Be there in a few.**

The brief exchange has me all prickly and frustrated.

When my phone vibrates once more, I know it's a text from Hari letting me know he's out front. I step out onto the front porch, shirt in hand.

"Hey," I say.

"Hey," he replies, squinting down at his shoe. He clears his throat, then looks up at me. "My hoodie?"

I hold it out for him to take and he does. Then he turns to go.

"That's it?" I ask.

Hari stops walking but doesn't turn yet. "What?"

"You're really just going to take your hoodie and go?" I cross my arms. "Seems kind of cold."

At that, Hari whips around. "*I* seem cold?"

"Well, yeah! You've been ignoring me all week and now you get in touch just because you want your shit back?"

"You've been ignoring me, too," Hari snaps.

"I invited you to come see the dogs."

"You invited all of us to come see the dogs. And I went, even though I really didn't want to."

I frown. "So, we'll just keep not talking to each other?"

Hari sighs. "What do you expect me to do, Kat? Pretend everything's good?"

"Talk to me, at least!" I say. "We got into a fight, but that doesn't mean we just stop being friends."

He squints at me, and I expect him to yell. But his voice is so soft when he speaks. "You really hurt me."

My voice goes soft, too. "I'm sorry, Hari. I really am. But we hurt each other."

He shakes his head. "I'm sorry I called your secret stupid. I shouldn't have done that. But, fuck, everything that was happening hurt so bad. And you immediately assumed I'd tell people as some sick revenge because you don't want to be with me."

I swallow. "I never should've said that. You'd never tell people. I know that. I was just really scared."

"Well, I still think it was shitty of you."

"And I still think it was shitty of you to belittle that part of my life. You know how it makes me feel."

"You care more than anyone," Hari says. "Other people would understand."

I narrow my eyes at him. "It doesn't matter. I should be the one who gets to decide what other people know. And I don't want you, my best friend, to make me feel like I'm overreacting. Can you imagine if your ma and baba gave you up? But kept Dev? How would you feel?"

Hari frowns. "I'd feel like trash."

"Yeah. I do feel like trash. A lot." Indignant, I add, "This is *my* life. It's not about you."

But I immediately realize that was the wrong thing to say when Hari's face clouds. "And *that's* really the issue. It's not about me, okay, sure, but it's *aaaaall* about you." His voice is getting louder as he speaks. "I get that you think this is only your burden, but you make me, Luis, and Marcus lie for you, too, and about the smallest shit—all to cover this up. What's worse, you're always glued to your phone now! It's like you barely see us at all! You almost ditched me at a party you knew I was horribly anxious over, and then you broke my fucking heart and your biggest concern after that was whether I was going to sell you out! You barely even care about my shit with Dev and my parents. It's you, you, you! How selfish can you be?"

This accusation is dizzying, but I don't let his words fully settle before I feel myself getting defensive. It's not like his behavior has been perfect! "That's *not* true—"

"It *is* true. You only care about what's going on with *you,* how this affects *you,* how *you're* feeling. Seems like you really don't give a damn about your so-called best friend."

He sounds angry, but there is pain evident all over his face, in the way his brows are furrowed, in the way his eyes have narrowed, in the way his perfect jaw has tightened.

"Hari…," I start, but I don't even know what to say. What can I say? Because he's kind of right, isn't he? I have been distracted. I almost wasn't there for his party. I haven't really been there for him as he deals with the anguish of his parents and feeling like the less-good twin. And I did just…break his heart.

In my hand, my phone buzzes, and my eyes flicker to it before I can stop myself. There's a number I don't recognize, but the text says, **Hey Kat, it's Elena! Just texting so you have my number!**

"Wooooow," Hari breathes. "You can't even tear yourself away from whatever is happening on your phone long enough to have this conversation."

"I'm sorry! I'm just overwhelmed. I can't think!"

My phone buzzes again, indicating another text, but I don't look. And then there's another, and another, and another in quick succession.

"Go on, Kat. I know you want to." Hari lets out a bitter laugh, nodding toward my phone. He reaches into his back pocket to grab his. "I got that one, too."

"I don't care what it says or who it's from. I care about this conversation."

Hari reads the text and looks over his shoulder, then back at me. "You'll care about these."

Reluctantly, I unlock my phone to see a text from Marcus to the group that says, **Guess who we just ran into?**

Luis: **SANCHEZ'S HOT MOM**

Marcus: **Nasty.**

Marcus: **But yeah. She invited us to come over for dinner on Thursday.**

Luis: **FINALLY. BECAUSE YOUR RUDE ASS NEVER HAS.**

Luis: **We said yes. Only for the free food tho.**

I look up at Hari, wide-eyed. "Shit."

True that Luis and Marcus know about the whole not-living-with-my-parents thing. But they've never been to my parents' house before, and the idea makes me feel a little queasy. They'll see how dysfunctional we are in person; they'll see the room I don't have; they'll see the full shape of the truth. And that truth is so ugly. Even Hari doesn't really understand.

"Yeah. Shit." He looks at me. "That's going to be a lot to handle."

"I deserve it, apparently."

He softens. "I didn't say that."

"You might as well have. And I won't even have you to talk about it with because you hate me."

Hari meets my gaze. "Hey, I don't hate you."

"It feels like it." And then I'm sniffling. "I miss my friend."

He shifts from one foot to the other. "I don't know what to say. I need some time. And even if I didn't, I wouldn't be able to come to this dinner. I'm grounded."

"Wait, what? You're grounded?"

Hari shrugs. "My parents found out about the party."

"When?"

"Yesterday. Our neighbor ratted us out." Hari holds up the hoodie in his hands. "Getting this was my last adventure for a bit."

I frown. "Oh, no. How mad are they?"

"Pretty livid. My dad said I'll be lucky if they let me go anywhere besides my room and school before I graduate. So, yeah."

Without thinking, I reach over and put my hand on his. "I'm sorry. I'm so sorry. Are you going to be okay? Is there anything I can do? I can talk to your parents. I can tell them this was all Dev's idea—or mine, whatever! I can—"

"Kat, no. It's fine. They're at least a little mad at Dev, too." He doesn't hide the sly grin that tugs at the corner of his mouth. "So, that part's pretty satisfying."

"Vindication." I give him a small smile back. "But, seriously. What do you need?"

"A new life sounds pretty good right about now." Hari motions toward my phone. "So yeah. Whatever. Look, I'm sorry I can't join you during the dinner. I know it'll be a lot."

"Just that you thought of coming helps. The sentiment. I owe you just for that."

Hari shrugs again. "You're good for it."

Weirdly, a wave of relief washes over me hearing that.

"So, we'll be okay, then?" I ask, needing him to confirm it for me.

He drapes his hoodie over his shoulder and looks at me. "Probably. I'll be so desperate for human connection once I get out of being grounded, you'll seem great again." Hari is smiling as he says this, teasing me.

I smile back. "I'll work on some things while you're gone."

He nods. "Me too. I know I've been kind of a shit myself. See you after exile."

Chapter Twenty-Four

My annoyance at my mom for inviting Luis and Marcus over for dinner is strong.

Yet things as Max are pretty damn great.

How can things feel so irritating, confusing, and unsettling in one part of my life, yet perfect, hopeful, and idyllic in another? The cognitive dissonance is so real rn.

To Elena, I confirm that we'll meet up early next weekend, a surge of giddiness shooting through me when I do.

I tell Luis he better not call my mom hot again, unless he has a death wish.

And I tell Grandma about the dinner with Mom and Pop and my friends. She's so excited she wraps me in a huge hug, unable to wipe the grin from her face.

I also shoot Marcus a text and wish him luck on the photo editor role. He teases me about already admitting defeat, and I don't have the heart to tell him I didn't even apply.

And I reach out to Hari to wish him luck. I add some reassurances that he's a good person, and things will get better, because I think he needs to hear it.

Still—I can't stop the word *selfish* from taking up a lot of space in my brain.

I kinda have been. And that...sucks.

I'm mulling this over when I head to my next shift at One Fur All, lugging my camera gear and some props with me, full of regret for scheduling what has become a super-extravagant photo shoot with Becca. If I'm worried about being selfish, the definition would probably be: stealing photos from a friend who has sworn off social media, passing them off as portraits of you, and then lying about why you need more.

At least seeing the wagging tails of the dogs when I get into One Fur All lifts my spirits a bit and I'm reminded that not *everything* I do is bad. Just most of it. Right now, anyway.

I get to work, feeding, watering, and bathing the animals.

Becca shows up to start her shift awhile later, and she rushes over to me first thing. I note that her hair is done up and she's wearing makeup. She looks lovely and I resent the small twinge of excitement I feel at the thought that today's new photos will be perfect for Max's account.

Selfish.

She and I have already settled on three different locations with as many different outfits, not including the photos we'll shoot right here.

We start by taking a couple of the tamer dogs out into the yard, and, armed with a pocketful of treats so I can get them to listen to me, I set up this shoot. I'm going to take photos both of Becca with the dogs (for my photo editor application, I told her) and of the dogs on their own (for work).

Since it's the start of November, I take a few wintry pictures for the website and social media. Though there's no snow in Bakersfield, I've picked up some props, like knitted scarves and beanies for the dogs, that'll help suggest a chill.

We take a few photos, including some new ones of Cash, before a voice calls to us. "Girls!" Becca and I turn and see Imani, waving at us to come inside. "Staff meeting!"

Becca and I exchange a look. "Did we know about this?" I ask.

"I definitely didn't," Becca says. "Guess we should get these guys inside."

By the time we round up the dogs, the rest of the staff is already seated and making small talk around our conference table. Imani and her assistant manager, Myrna, are fussing with a laptop.

Imani motions toward a few of the empty chairs at the back of the room, near the vending machines. "Is that everyone?" she asks, her eyes surveying the room.

Myrna nods. "Looks like it."

"What's this about? We *never* have staff meetings," Jin, our office manager, pipes up. (He's easily one of my favorites here, though Cash is my most favorite, obviously.)

Imani smiles. "I know. They're not really my cup of tea. But this is an important one."

"Are we all fired?" Sandra asks. Then she answers her own question. "Wait, I'm a volunteer."

Imani claps her hands. "Okay. No one's fired. This is a good thing, really! Lights?" Myrna flips the switch in the corner while Imani takes a second to get her laptop and the projector it's connected to set up. "Drumroll, please."

A few around the long table lightly drum their fingers. I suppress a laugh and join in. Imani's laptop turns on and a graphic shows up on the projector with snowflakes, snow people, and the words *Inaugural One Fur All Winter Ball*.

Imani points up at the projection. "Ta-daaaa."

"A ball?" Becca asks, eyes big. "Like a dance?"

"Exactly like a dance! And a fundraiser and a fashion show."

Becca and I exchange a look. "A fashion show!" I grin.

"For the dogs," Myrna clarifies.

"We can work with that!" I say.

"That's the spirit!" Imani says. "We've been approached by our local TV station to host a Clear the Shelters event just in time for the holiday season. And it is going to be good." She starts to go through her brief presentation, outlining her vision for the event.

It's impressive and I start to get excited. A ball? Sounds so fancy. One Fur All has even lined up a couple of high-profile sponsors.

Then Imani drops a major bomb: the event is right after Christmas, aka in just a few short weeks.

"I know we're in a time crunch, but we can do this," she assures us. "We just need to work together. And, let's be real, bust our asses."

Imani doles out different assignments, telling Becca and me that we're responsible for the digital and social campaign, and then explains she'll have more details to us by the end of the day. "I know we're not normally an email place, but check your emails, y'all."

We're dismissed.

The room is buzzing with energy, part excitement and probably part terror. This is a lot to pull off in such a short time, and we've never hosted anything like it, at least not since I've been around. Most of the work will definitely fall to Imani and Myrna, but it's a lot of pressure to know that Becca and I will be solely responsible for the digital presence of this event.

We have lots of tickets to sell. And no time.

I express some of these concerns to Becca after we're back at our desks. "I mean, I'm not trying to sound like a downer or anything. Just nervous."

"But it'll be a ball, Kat," Becca says with a sigh. "Can you even imagine? It just sounds so dreamy."

"It does sound pretty dreamy," I admit. "Plus, we'll be clearing the shelter. Cash will finally get a home!"

I could do a lil dance just thinking of it.

* ✳ *

Becca and I finish up our shifts, then head out for our shoot. It eats up the rest of my Sunday and gives us time to hash out some of the plans to help promote the One Fur All Winter Ball. She takes some notes on her phone and emails it to us so we can refer back to it next time we're in.

When I get home, I settle in my room for the night to work on editing these photos and get some over to Becca. But first, I hungrily check my phone, which I've neglected all day. The afternoon left me so busy I haven't been able to do much, except to post a quick Boomerang of Becca with the dogs onto Max's story.

There are a few reacts to that in my inbox—heart eyes, fire, wow, plus some messages:

WHERE did you get that beanie?!

You are soooo gorgeous!

STUN!!!

I give each message a heart and respond to the one asking where the beanie came from. Then I check through some of the stories of people Max follows.

Elena's story is full of snapshots from her weekend adventures. Looks like she and her friends ended up at Disneyland, which is so perfectly Elena. I feel a pang of jealousy, wishing I were there, too.

Which I know makes no sense.

Still.

It's as if Elena can tell I'm thinking of her because a text comes in. It's a photo of her and her friends screaming on the Tower of Terror. Her eyes are squeezed shut and her mouth is stretched so big she could probably fit one of the Mickey Mouse pretzels in it without even blinking. It's hilarious, and yet she still looks adorable.

Elena: **New profile pic, right?**

Me: **If you don't use it, I'm going to be pissed.**

Me: **How was it?**

Elena: **Magical, just like they say.**

Me: **Kinda jealous.**

Elena: **You should come next time!!!**

Me: **I wish!**

Elena: **IMAGINE????????**

Me: **I can and am tbh.**

Me: **Sounds like heaven.**

Elena: **RIGHT?**

Elena: **Hang on.**

The dots on her end of the conversation disappear, so I know she isn't actively typing, but I still just stare at the screen anyway, waiting.

I don't know what's going on with us, but I am really enjoying it.

Elena: **I'M BACK.**

Me: **Hi, Back. I'm Max.**

Elena: **Lmao oh God.**

Elena: **Okay.**

Then an image pops up. It's the same Tower of Terror photo Elena just sent, only now Becca's head is poorly Photoshopped onto someone in the background.

Elena: **Now you don't have to imagine!!!**

Me: **Oh my GOD.**

Elena: **You can thank me for that one later.**

Me: **I don't know how I'll ever repay you.**

Me: **I've never looked more beautiful?**

Elena: **Seriously.**

Elena: **We're driving back now.**

Elena: **My bff Vanessa drives like shit.**

Elena: **She's named her car and all. It's extra.**

Me: **Omg my friend Marcus has named his car, too!**

And, oops. Apparently now Max knows Marcus.

Elena: **What is with that?**

Me: **Freaks, all of them.**

Elena: **But not us.**

Me: **No, no. Never us!**

Elena: **Just glad to finally be friends with someone normal.**

I smile sadly down at my phone. Normal. Right. Definitely normal. Definitely not lying. I can't bring myself to respond to that message, so I give it a heart instead.

Elena: **Wait!**

Elena: **Don't go yet**

Me: **?**

Elena: **Hearting the message is the universal I-saw-what-you-said-and-now-I'm-peacing-out.**

Me: **Lmao okay, true. Way to call me out!**

Elena: **Sorry!!! I'm extra, I know.**

Me: **And I like it. Tell me more about your weekend.**

Elena: **Even the part where I ate too much cotton candy, got on the Tower of Terror, and promptly threw up?**

Me: **EW.**

Me: **But also yes.**

Me: **Even that.**

I turn over in my bed, telling myself the photo editing can wait till tomorrow.

Chapter Twenty-Five

I'm embarrassed to admit how late I stayed up talking with Elena. We texted her whole drive home and then she called. I filled her in on my day, including the recent photo shoot with the dogs. We spent a long time dissecting a new artsy TikTok trend, and I told her all about Cash. She shared memories of her childhood dog, a Lab named Scooter.

We talked about mundane things, like school, and fun things, like the best movies to rewatch over and over. Before I knew it, it was nearly 2 a.m.

Now I'm awake for school and so tired my eyeballs feel like they're on fire. But it was worth it. I smile to myself every time I think of our conversation.

I keep sneaking my phone out between and in classes all day long, exchanging messages back and forth with Elena. I send her a pic of one of my classmates' shoes, a pair of hot-pink platforms that I think she'll adore. She sends me a doodle of Cash that she's drawn in the margins of her notebook. I screenshot it to save.

"Hellooooo?" Luis says. We're in the cafeteria with Marcus and Hari, my lunch untouched.

"What?" I ask.

"I said, are you gonna eat that?" Luis looks over at Marcus with pursed lips. "This girl never listens, I swear to God."

"Sorry, I'm just distracted," I say. "No, I'm not going to eat that."

"Thank you, damn." Luis reaches for the container of pasta

my grandpa packed for me and starts to go in. "Titi forgot to leave me lunch money this morning, so I'm really hungry."

"You're always really hungry," Marcus sniffs.

"I'm extra hungry today, okay?" Luis slurps a noodle into his mouth.

Hari makes a face at him. "Disgusting, bro." Luis just shrugs.

"So, what's up, man?" Marcus swats at Hari's arm. "You still grounded?"

He nods. "I am. For the foreseeable future."

Marcus frowns. "That's bullshit."

"Seems a little unfair considering you didn't even *throw* the party," I offer.

"My parents don't really believe their darling Dev was the one behind it," Hari says. "Regardless, I was there, too. We're just supposed to stay home and focus on our studies. If they even get whiff of fun, we'll be stuck at home till graduation."

Luis frowns. "Sucks."

"Eh." Hari shrugs. "Not like I had much going on otherwise." He turns to Luis. "Unlike this one. How are things with Xio?"

A grin spreads across Luis's face. "Good. Like, real good."

I scrunch my nose at him. "Must you?"

"Don't be jealous, Sanchez. Just because I'm gettin' some and you and your boyfriend are on the outs."

He looks knowingly between me and Hari. Hari scowls at him. "Sorry I asked," Hari mutters. Then he rises from the table and slings his bag over one shoulder. "I'm gonna go."

"Hey, don't listen to him, man," Marcus says, but Hari is already waving goodbye as he leaves. "Look what you did. Kid's already depressed from being grounded, now you're busting his balls."

"We always tease him about Sanchez!" Luis protests.

"Well, maybe you shouldn't," I say. "There's nothing going on between us."

Luis looks at me skeptically, but Marcus gives me a small smile. "I mean, yeah. The way you're smiling at your phone tells me that. You've obviously got something going on with someone else." He nods toward where Hari was. "Probably why Hari seems so down."

"Oh, shit, Sanchez, for real?" Luis gasps.

My cheeks flush. "What? No!"

"The lady doth protest too much," Marcus says knowingly.

"Yo, stop that immediately." Luis wags his finger at Marcus.

Marcus ignores him. "Who were you texting, then?"

"Nobody!"

Marcus narrows his eyes at me, pointing at my phone. "Sure were smiling a lot for someone talking to 'nobody.' But okay. Be shady. That's on you."

"Let's just be nicer to Hari, okay?" I say, changing the subject. I don't want to share too many details, since it's clear he hasn't told either one of them what happened between the two of us, but I also want to put an end to this relentless ribbing. I can only imagine how it makes him feel. Salt in the wound. "He's going through a lot. And there really is nothing going on between us. You need to stop." I keep my voice firm. "I mean it. Or I'll stop sharing my lunch with you."

Luis holds up his hands. "Okay, okay. Just don't hold your lunch hostage. It didn't do nothing."

"Didn't do anything," Marcus corrects.

"Whatever, Urkel."

"How do you even know that reference? That show is, like, thirty years old."

"My titi loves that show!"

The two of them start bickering, and I can return to my phone in peace.

After school, a Snap comes in from Marcus to me, Luis, and Hari. It's a photo of a nameplate badge that reads MARCUS BROWN and, beneath that, PHOTO EDITOR.

I write back, **Ayyy! Congratulations!!!**

He writes, **Thank you. Victory feels GOOD.**

I send him back a middle finger emoji.

Luis: **Watch where you point that thing, Sanchez.**

Luis: **Does this mean Photography Club is dead?**

Marcus: **What? No! I need that for my resume!**

Luis: **We haven't done shit for it in weeks. Mr. Griffin has noticed. Once the club advisor notices, you're fucked, yeah?**

Hari: **It IS kinda dead.**

Marcus: **NO!!!**

Marcus: **Aside from Honey, this is my other baby.**

Luis: **You let your baby die, bro.**

Me: **Murderer!**

Marcus: **We'll do something this weekend, damn!!!**

Me: **I'm busy Saturday.**

Hari: **Ummmm I'm still grounded???**

Marcus: **From SCHOOL PROJECTS?**

Marcus: **No.**

Marcus: **You're coming!**

Hari: **I'll see what I can do.**

* * *

The week passes, late-night conversations with Elena the new norm. How we don't run out of things to say, I don't know, but the back-and-forth comes so easily. Making fun of bad TV shows we've recently watched. Sending memes. Exchanging pics of adorable dogs. Sharing TikToks.

All the talking, and it still feels like there aren't enough hours for us to chat, especially because we're both juggling school, friends, and work.

I end up asking Elena to tell me more about her sticker business, and she is more than willing to divulge. She says she got into making stickers by watching tutorials online. Though she'd always been someone who doodled in the margins of her notebooks, it wasn't until her older sister gifted her with an Apple Pencil for her iPad that she got into Procreate. She says she got totally sucked into the world of small-business creators on TikTok, which helps to explain how she has so many followers there.

Elena: **It's sooo weird sometimes, though.**

Elena: **To have so many strangers follow you and know things about you.**

Elena: **And you don't know ANYTHING about them.**

Me: **Oh, totally. That's so bizarre to think about!**

Elena: **RIGHT?**

Elena: **Like someone could be following me and actually be a stalker.**

Elena: **Or my French teacher.**

Me: **Just as bad, right?**

Elena: **BASICALLY! So gross.**

Me: **It must be a little cool, though, no?**

Elena: **Oh, yeah, it is sometimes. People are mostly nice. Actually most of them are really nice.**

Elena: **And I now make a decent chunk of change from my store.**

Elena: **So that's cool.**

Elena: **I shouldn't make it sound like it's so bad. I have super nice followers.**

Me: **I've tried really hard to grow my followers and it's been super slow tbh.**

Me: **I want to share more of my photography.**

Me: **But it always flops.**

Elena: **Oh, you take photos, too?**

Ugh. Right. Shit.

Me: **Just starting to. Kat is showing me the ropes. There are a few on my grid.**

Me: **But I just can't imagine having so many followers???**

Elena: **I feel like unless you're in a niche group it's really hard.**

Elena: **In my experience, people like to see people, get to know you, feel like you're someone they can be friends with. If you're not doing that, I'm not sure how much someone's followers will grow tbh.**

Elena: **But you're doing all the right things! So they'll come.**

I nearly laugh out loud at that.

Here Elena is, thinking I'm authentic and putting myself out there and earnestly trying to share something real with the world. Which, I mean, in a way, yes. But there is nothing authentic about what I'm doing. It's cowardly, actually.

Couple that with the fact that Elena innocently asked the other night why Max's account had only recently been created. I had to scramble to think of an answer because I hadn't yet considered this as part of Max's backstory. But, yeah, it is a little sus when an IG account has randomly popped up when everyone we know has practically grown up on the app.

As Max, I explained that my old account was way too embarrassing because I'd posted a ton of things in middle school that I wanted burned to the ground. And, I said, there were far too many cringeworthy photos to delete, so it was easier to start up again. Elena seemed satisfied with that answer.

But how much longer can I keep this up?

Chapter Twenty-Six

I get ready for the family dinner slowly, reluctantly, hoping that if I drag my ass enough I might miss it altogether.

Maybe sharing this dinner with Luis and Marcus will make it better. Or maybe it'll be much, much worse.

On the walk to my parents' house, I pull out my phone, take a quick video of a tree swaying in the wind, and pop it onto Max's story. Then I switch to my account and see that Hari has posted a new story, too. It's a photo of a tower of books he's built on his desk, topped with increasingly smaller items from his desk until it peaks with a pencil, balanced at the top.

Me: **So, being grounded is going well?**

Hari: 😒 🔫

It makes me laugh, and there is a small ache in my chest. I miss him. I wish he were coming tonight.

I trudge up to the front steps of my parents' house, the decadent scent of my dad's rice and beans and whatever else he's cooking up getting stronger the closer I get to the door. My knock sets off the dogs in a raucous round of barking. It's a second before Pop greets me, all four dogs just behind him, tails wagging. He's wearing an apron I got for him for Father's Day a few years back that reads GRILLMASTER.

"Kat!" He grins wide. "My favorite part of Thursday."

I smile back. "Ha, for real?"

"Of course! Come on in." Pop opens the door wider so I can step inside, which ends up being a little difficult with the dogs. I crouch down to love on them and scoop up Pepito, who is begging to be carried.

"Wow," I say, looking around. The house looks neat and tidy, with even the dog toys in their proper places. "Looks great."

"Your mom really went crazy making sure tonight would be nice," Pop explains. "She insisted everything be just right for your friends."

As if summoned, my mom comes into the living room, and I note her wrap dress, her blown-out hair, the jewelry.

"Hi, Kat," she greets me. Then she motions toward the house behind her. "What do you think?"

"I was just saying to Pop that it looks great in here."

"I'm glad you think so! We really wanted to make everything special for tonight." Mom comes over to give me a hug.

"And we wanted to do something special for Kat," Pop adds, winking at me.

My phone buzzes in my pocket and I pull it out to see a text from Luis.

Luis: **We're here, payasa.** 😈

I open up the front door, still holding Pepito.

"Took you long enough," Luis says with a smirk. At the sound of his voice, Archie, Daisy, and Shark dart to the door, causing Luis to scramble behind Marcus. "Yo, yo, yo!"

Marcus and I look at each other and burst out laughing. Pop rushes to the door with an apologetic grin, reaching for Daisy's and Shark's collars to pull them back. "Sorry, sorry..."

"Don't mind Luis," I say. "And, yeah, he's a baby about dogs."

"Ay!" Luis shouts, but he's still behind Marcus, who is now kneeling down and petting Archie.

"And this is Marcus."

Mom joins us in the entryway with a warm smile. "Good to

see you both again! And sorry about them. They can be a bit much. Come on in."

Pop commands the dogs to go to their places, and I put Pepito down so he can scamper off to his bed. As Pop offers to get some drinks for everyone, Luis glares at me. "You could've warned me."

"I didn't know you would actually be *afraid*," I say with a laugh. "You were fine at the shelter."

"Yeah, with, like, two at a time. But this is a lot of dogs. Are you and your whole family crazy dog people or something?"

Though the question is meant for me, Mom chimes in. "Anthony definitely is. I wanted one. But Anthony is a softy, so we end up with any dog that needs a home. He's really good with them."

"Must be where Kat gets it from," Luis replies.

"We don't have any dogs, but I wish we did," Marcus says. "I didn't even realize you had so many pets, Kat. You never mention them."

I shrug. "Oh, yeah." Probably because they don't really feel like my pets.

My mom claps her hands together suddenly. "I haven't even shown you guys the spread for tonight! I hope you're hungry."

Luis grins. "I'm *starving*."

"You might have a tapeworm or something," Marcus says.

"Shut up, stupid."

Marcus rolls his eyes. "Whatever."

Mom ignores their back-and-forth and motions for us to follow her. We go into the kitchen, where she has set up a nacho bar—chips, of course, plus toppings like cheese, pico de gallo, olives, green peppers, and guacamole.

"I'm allergic to avocado, Mom," I remind her.

She makes a face. "Ooh, right!" Then she laughs. "Okay, well, don't have any of that! The rest should be okay."

Luis arches an eyebrow at me, but I just look away. How embarrassing is it for your friends to visit your parents' house for the first time and then have your own mom forget you're allergic to avocado and try to serve it to you for dinner?

"Well, I love nachos," Marcus says, his best attempt at smoothing things over.

"Me too," Luis agrees.

"And this is just to start! Anthony made us some of his delicious rice and beans, plus some beef stew." As Pop comes into the room with drinks, Mom asks, "What's your stew called again? I always forget."

"Carne guisada," he says.

"My favorite!" Luis explains. "My titi always makes that for us."

At this, Pop's face brightens. "Are you Puerto Rican, too?"

Luis proudly lifts his forearm to show off the underside, where there's a tattoo of the Puerto Rican flag. He turned eighteen in August, so he can get inked legally now. "¡Claro!"

And Pop's whole demeanor changes. His eyes light up as he starts to speak to Luis in Spanish, a conversation I can't really follow. I pick up the words *Ponce* and *Rincón,* but my rudimentary Spanish just isn't that good.

Still, I marvel at this version of Pop I rarely ever see. His conversation with Luis seems so easy, so animated.

Mom turns to me and Marcus. "So, should we start with a tour of the house, or with food?"

"I don't feel like we need to do a tour of our house," I say.

"Oh my gosh, nonsense! It'll be quick," Mom insists.

Marcus gives me a reassuring smile. "I don't mind."

"Let's go then!" Mom looks over at my dad. "Anthony? Sorry to interrupt, but I'm going to do a quick tour of the house for the boys, then we can get started on dinner. Okay?"

184

Pop nods, wrapping up his conversation with Luis. "I'll finish dinner and see you in a few."

"We really don't have to," I try again.

"We'll just take a peek." Mom heads toward the stairs. Luis, Marcus, and I follow, and she jokes that we've pretty much already seen everything there is to see downstairs, though she does point out the restroom and notes that the sunroom at the back of the house is her favorite spot.

Upstairs, she shows off Leo's room first, which is tidy but Leo-less. He's out, my mom explains.

Of course.

Then she shows us her and Pop's room, which is also remarkably clean, though she makes a show of apologizing for "the mess." I'm filled with dread as we near the third bedroom. The one that was supposed to be mine, but isn't.

As she reaches for the door handle, I say, "Mom, I think we've seen enough—"

"Ooh, you embarrassed or something?" Luis teases. "You got real girly shit in there? Or maybe it's a disaster?"

Marcus grins, too, suppressing a laugh. But he says, "It's cool, Kat. You've seen my room. It's a mess."

"No need to be ashamed of your room, Kat!" Mom says, winking at me. Then she pushes the door open and I wince, fully expecting to see her old clothes, Pop's overflowing shoe collection, and all the other assorted crap that ended up here over the years.

Only . . . none of that is there.

Instead, there's a real bedroom setup—with a bed that's made, a dresser lined with hair products, a few of assorted books, a rug.

It's pink. Like, a saccharine, so-sweet-it-might-give-you-a-toothache, strawberry-ice-cream-colored-pink room.

But it's a room. In my parents' house. And it's mine. My name's even on the wall.

"Oh, shit. It is! It's sooo girly! You're secretly a girly girl!" Luis playfully swats at my arm. "I never would've taken you for one. Like, at all!"

"Pink is not just for girls" is all I can think to say.

"I mean, yeah, but this is *super* pink," Marcus says slowly. "It's not like your other room at all, but I dig it if that's what you're into. Looks cute."

Marcus is trying to be so supportive right now, I could hug him.

Luis suddenly rushes in and points at the wall. "That's a BTS poster! Sanchez is into boy bands!"

He's suddenly doubled over in laughter, like this is the funniest thing he's ever seen in his life. Marcus starts laughing, following Luis inside the room, and my mom chuckles, too.

"How do you even know who BTS is?" I challenge.

Luis stops laughing. "Everyone knows BTS, Sanchez!"

I look at Marcus, then point at Luis, smiling dryly. "I see that Luis is part of the BTS Army. I can't wait to tell everyone about this."

"Wait, what?! No, Sanchez! *You're* part of the BTS Army!"

Marcus sucks in air. "I don't know, Luis…you recognized them awfully quick…"

Luis uses both of his hands to point up at the poster emphatically. "Hellooo?! She has a poster of them hanging in her room! She's the fan here!"

"Yeah, but you got really excited over it. So, what does that say about you?" I tease.

Marcus grins. "Kinda speaks volumes, don't you think? Guess my dude likes pop after all."

"Man, forget this. I want nachos!" Luis stomps out of my room and heads back to the stairs, Marcus in tow. Marcus is quizzing him on who the members of the group are and asking which song is his favorite.

That leaves just me and my mom. I survey the room again and look back at her. "Wow."

She gives me a shrug in an attempt at nonchalance, but I can tell she's *super* proud of this room, of this gesture.

Personally, I'm not quite sure how to feel. I keep it simple.

"Thank you," I say.

"Of course, Kat." She smiles. "Do you like it?"

I glance around again. "It's cute. It's pink. Super pink."

Mom's face falls.

"But I like pink!" I assure her. "I just prefer gray."

She sniffs. "I thought pink would be better." She glances around the room, too, but she doesn't say more. Guilt gnaws at me. Maybe I should be more grateful. "Dinner?"

"Dinner."

I'm relieved when we settle down for our meal, far, far away from the fuzzy carpet and BTS poster (I like BTS, but come on). I've imagined many times what it might be like to have a room in my parents' home. I could almost feel the soft comforter beneath me; I acted out the arguments I might have with Leo over how I'm not taking the trash out *again* because I just did it last week and it's *his* turn; I saw myself falling asleep under their roof in a big bed just for me.

But why now?

I've longed for proof that my parents want me to be part of their family. Yet now that I've finally gotten it, it feels...tainted. I only got that room so my parents—my mom especially—would look good in front of my friends.

And everything about that sucks.

Chapter Twenty-Seven

When I tell Grandma about the room, she's over the moon with excitement, talking about how this is such great progress for our relationship, and look how hard my parents are trying, and isn't this so wonderful?

I DM Elena.

Me: **Is it just me, or does today kinda blow?**

Our chat last night has me thinking she'll probably agree. Her Apple Pencil broke and that means she's unable to make any new art.

Elena: **UGH. It totally did. And yesterday, too.**

Elena: **Today's just like a sequel to yesterday's suckfest.**

Me: **Suckfest II: The Suckening**

Elena: **Suckfest: 2 Suck, 2 Suckious**

Me: **Suckfest Forever After?**

Elena: **Omg stoppppp.** 💀

Elena: **It wasn't great, but IT'S ALMOST FRIDAY.**

Elena: **And you know what'll make you feel better?**

Me: **This bitch session is already starting to make me feel better, tbh.**

Me: **But what did you have in mind?**

Elena: **Welllll, I am meeting up with Kat on Saturday to get some photos done. You should TOTALLY come!!!**

My stomach drops at the suggestion. There is absolutely no way this can happen. Like, it's literally impossible. I choose my response carefully.

Me: That's such a sweet offer! But I'm going to be busy this weekend. It's part of the suckage that's to come.

Elena: Wait, I thought you said you didn't have plans this weekend?

Shit. Did I? I frantically scroll back through our chats. Yep. Sure enough. On Wednesday, Elena asked what I was getting up to this weekend and I said I didn't have anything planned just yet.

Me: I forgot all about one of my assignments that's due! My professors are KILLING us before Thanksgiving break.

Elena: 🔫

Elena: The suckfest continues.

Elena: But we should meet up soon! Or FaceTime?

Oh, dear, sweet Elena. If only you knew.

Me: I would love that!

Me: I am really shy, though.

Me: What if you hate me?

Elena: I could NEVER.

Elena: Let's plan something, though. For real.

Soon! I type. When I read it over and that seems too cold. I add: **Promise!**

Because at this point, what's one more lie?

∗ ✱ ∗

"Oh my God, finally!" Becca says when I get to work for my next shift.

I laugh. "Good to see you, too."

"Two things: One, I have been absolutely kicking ass at finalizing our marketing plan for this winter ball thing. I think you'll be really excited by it." She turns her screen toward me so I can peer over her shoulder. I skim her list of suggestions.

"This is incredible, Becca!" I say.

She playfully blows on her nails. "All in a day's work. Thank you, Marketing 201. At least I'm getting my money's worth, right?"

"Totally. I'm super impressed." I scan the list again. "Should we start splitting some of this up and adding deadlines?"

Becca nods and I grab a seat beside her, pulling up the Excel sheet she's shared with me. We get to work.

Most of the social campaigns are given to me, whereas Becca offers to take on the email newsletters and some of the external outreach, like to local radio stations. It isn't long before we have a pretty full plan.

"That felt good," I say.

"Totally. So productive," Becca agrees. "Should we send it to Imani?"

"Definitely." I hit the Share button, type a brief message, and send it over. "So, what was the second thing?"

"Hmm?" Becca asks.

"When I came in, you said you had two things. But you only shared one."

Her eyes get wide with realization. "Oh! When can I see the newest photos?"

"Ahh, shit. I have them, but I forgot to share them. Sorry!"

"No worries. I'm just...I don't know, curious to see them, I guess," Becca says. "It's weird because I know I can't post them anywhere or anything, but still. Taking these photos reminds me a little of my old life."

"Are you considering coming back?"

It must be odd to have gone from someone with a big following to cutting it off completely. Doesn't she ever feel like she's missing out? Doesn't she wish she hadn't been so quick to delete everything? And, more importantly, are my days as Max numbered—just when she's on the brink of hitting a thousand followers of her own?

But Becca guffaws at that. "God, no! No, no, no. But it's some-times a little nice to get all dressed up and relive the glory days. I've missed doing my makeup just for fun. And you do such a good job capturing it. You have real talent. I love the photos because they're also art."

I smile at her, both relieved and grateful. "Thank you. I'll share them with you soon."

"That'd be great." Becca starts to pack up her bags. "Anyway, I better get going. I have a ten-page paper to write." She rolls her eyes. "Wish me luck."

"Good luck," I say, offering a wave. She turns to go.

The afternoon is slow once Becca leaves. I share the folder of photos with her and then, since I need to hear from Imani before I can get started on any of those marketing plans, I decide now's as good a time as any to work on some new Max content.

I pop my headphones in and start editing. Every so often, I check Max's Instagram, too. Seeing her grid in browser mode is a whole new experience. It looks really, really good. I deserve these 924 followers.

A sudden tap on my shoulder makes my blood run cold. I imagine turning around and seeing Becca. But when I look back, it's just Imani. Still, I slam my laptop shut and pull my headphones out.

"Hi, Imani!" I say, in a voice that's way too chipper.

"Is Becca finally on Instagram?" Imani asks. "I remember months ago when she was going on and on about how she'd *never* go back."

I laugh uncomfortably. "Oh, no, she's not on Instagram. That was just my photography portfolio I've been working on on IG. Becca's been letting me take some pics of her for practice, so, yeah."

"Oh," Imani says. "That's fun. I'm glad you guys have become such good friends."

"Yeah, same!"

"So, just wanted to chat with you a bit about the marketing plan. It looks great!" Imani says enthusiastically. "Got a sec?"

"Of course!" I practically shout, all too thankful for a subject change. She grabs a seat beside me and we pull up the document on my work computer so we can both see. We make a few tweaks, but the whole time, my heart feels like it's vibrating in my ears.

I cannot believe I almost let myself get caught by Imani. This is the second close call I've had here, so I need to get my shit together and maybe stop blatantly working on a fake account while I'm at work.

Damn.

After my shift, Marcus sends a group Snap reminding us all about our meet-up for Photography Club on Sunday, and Hari writes back to confirm that he can't make it. The schoolwork excuse didn't fly. Ugh.

I don't chime in because I'm too busy daydreaming about meeting up with Elena tomorrow. Finally, I'll get to see her in person.

I haven't really let myself think about this much over the last week, and the few times my mind has drifted to it, I've felt like I might just throw up. I figured it was a feeling that would pass. It hasn't.

For days now, I've been talking back and forth with Elena as Max. We've shared so much in such a short period of time.

Yet now, as *me,* I'm gonna step in and possibly complicate the good thing we had going. While still pretending Max is real. And that I know her IRL. And that she's definitely not me. I'll have to act as if I have no knowledge whatsoever of who Elena is or any of the inside jokes we've built together. I'll have to forget the details I already know.

Tomorrow, Elena is essentially a stranger.

And lately, I'm beginning to feel like one, too.

Chapter Twenty-Eight

It is far too early for me to be driving out to Ventura Pier Beach. In fact, it's still dark out, so I see a few twinkling stars as I drive. Yet here I am, barreling down a quiet highway in my grandma's car, eyes aching from the severe lack of sleep I've been getting, just me and my giant ball of lies sitting in the passenger seat. Don't worry; I made sure to buckle it in. Safety first.

Just get in and get out, and don't do anything stupid, I tell myself over and over on my drive.

The road is so empty that I make it to the exit I need early. I decide to stop and get some tea for me and Elena. But if I showed up with some Darjeeling, her favorite, it would be a very weird coincidence. I opt for two plain green teas instead.

The detour is a decent distraction, but I'm still a jittery mess when I arrive at the pier. Even the cool early-morning air and the sound of the waves crashing do little to soothe me.

Nervously, I toy with one of my hoop earrings, leaning up against Grandma's car. Headlights pull into the lot. My back stiffens as I watch a yellow VW Bug—the model Elena told me to watch for—slowly drive toward me and park in the spot beside mine.

Deep breaths, Kat. Deep breaths.

Only I'm not feeling real calm. I do the only thing I can think to do and duck into the car to get Elena's tea. When I stand up straight again, there's Elena's soft pink hair, falling in cascading waves that frame her face. She peers at me from the other side of the car.

"Hi! Kat?" Her voice is nervous, like the first time we spoke on the phone. It both comforts and terrifies me.

"Hi! Yes! You must be Elena." I do my best to conceal my fear, hoping, praying she doesn't hear Max in my voice. I've always sounded different on the phone than I do IRL—lower-pitched, or something. I hope that camouflages me now.

If she does notice anything, she says nothing. Just comes around the car toward me, smiling, suddenly in full view.

At once I am struck by how breathtakingly beautiful she is, even in this poorly lit lot.

She's wearing a Peter Pan–collar shirt that's stitched with the words INTERSECTIONAL FEMINISM OR DEATH. It's tucked into a high-waisted pink skirt with suspenders. Her pastel-pink hair is so much subtler in person—more stylish, even. Freckles like constellations are sprinkled across her nose and cheeks. And those cheeks! Round, cherubic, leading to a small double chin that looks like mine. Her eyes are so blue they remind me of morning glories.

I swallow, hard.

She's *so pretty.*

"That's me," she says, giving me a small, awkward wave.

We just stare at each other for a moment before I remember I'm holding a drink that's meant for her. I hold out the cup. "Tea?"

Her lips spread in an easy smile, revealing a dimple in her right cheek. "That's so thoughtful. Yes!" She reaches for the cup.

"I wasn't sure what you liked, so it's just green tea. Hope that's okay."

"Green tea is perfect. Thank you so much." She takes a tentative sip to check the temperature and turns her focus wholly on the cup in her hands. Without looking up from her drink, she lets out a laugh. "I have to admit. I'm *so* nervous."

And that makes me laugh, too. Same, girl. Same. But since this is technically a real, grown-up, for-money gig, it's part of my job to help make my client feel at ease, regardless of my own nerves. So, I remind myself that I should be focusing more on helping her relax and less on how I'm a big fat liar—or on how cute she is.

I force what I hope is a comforting smile. "Don't be. Really! It'll be fun."

"I'm sure it will be! I've just never had a photo shoot done before," Elena explains. "So this all feels super new. I'm worried this is going to go terribly and I'll have had you drive out all this way for nothing."

"Oh, God—don't stress about any of that. For real. We're going to get some good stuff today, I promise. And it's not like I'm a real professional. You're not gonna be wasting billable time or anything."

She gives me a look. "Haven't we already discussed this, Kat? Don't downplay your skills." Elena playfully swats at my arm, and I feel goose bumps where her fingertips graze my forearm. "You're *definitely* a professional. I've, like, stalked your IG, so I would know."

I let out another laugh and it feels good, as if through the sound, I'm exhaling at least some of my nerves.

This is still Elena, the girl I've been talking to for weeks. There's a reason we click. Some of our friendship may not be real, but our connection? There's no faking that.

"Well, thank you. This is going to be great." I glance into the distance at the sky, where the sun is only just starting to peek past the horizon. "Should we head to the beach to start?"

"Yes! Definitely!"

I grab my backpack from the backseat of the car and we walk toward the sand.

"I've definitely looked at your IG, too, as you know," I say as we walk. "From the photos, I didn't realize you had freckles!"

Her face flushes and her free hand goes to her cheek. "Oh, yeah. Sometimes I edit those out."

That, and the fact that I was fully convinced Elena was made of pastel when clearly she's flesh and bone (beautiful flesh and bone, but human nonetheless), gives me pause.

As a photographer, cognitively, I know that photographs are often snapshots of one millisecond, suspended in time like magic. On their own, they're only half-truths. You don't get to see anything but what the photographer wants you to see.

It goes even further, too, when we're making composites, or spending time selecting the right preset, or editing out a stray hair—even sometimes swapping a face from one photo to another (I might make that change if, for example, the person I've photographed is blinking in one photo but the rest of it is perfect).

All this, and it's still hard for me to remember that photos can be very distorted images of reality.

"I probably shouldn't edit my freckles out...," Elena admits, and I realize I've gone silent after hearing her confession.

Great. I look so judgmental right now when I'm the *very last person* who ever should judge.

"No, I totally get it!" I rush to say. "I mean. I like your freckles. And freckles are super trendy. But I get why people edit their photos. It's complicated."

She sighs. "Yeah. I've been coming more to terms with them lately. But I got made fun of for having spots growing up, so it's hard."

"Oh, I feel that. I've definitely gotten made fun of for being fat or not being girly enough or just, you know. Dumb things," I explain. "Like, I'm cute and all, but when I'm editing, I'm sometimes low-key tempted to just, like...smooth out a roll or slim down my face or whatever. Or not to post at all."

Elena frowns. "I've been there."

We're quiet for a beat. Then I laugh a little. "Well, now that we're thoroughly depressed...should we take some smiling photos?" That gets a little laugh out of her. "Seriously, though. We've got to loosen up. Hang on." I reach into my pocket and pull out my phone, navigating over to Spotify. I pull up a stupid early-2000s Eurotrash song that I know we both love (though I can't say *that* bit), hitting Play. "We're going to dance it out."

"Dance it out?" Elena asks, grinning.

"It's just us on the beach," I say. "And I swear this'll work. It'll make us feel real silly, but that's what we need. Trust me!"

"I do love this song," she admits.

"Who doesn't?" And then I start to dance—horribly, in an uncoordinated and exaggerated way, in an effort to get Elena to join in.

It works. Soon, she's dancing with me and we're both laughing.

At the right moment, I pull out my camera and start to take some photos, joining in with some dancing whenever she starts to look shy again. "Keep it up!" I shout. "These look really fun! Whimsical! Carefree! Perfect for you!"

Eventually, I start to give her some more direction—try this, do that, move over here, sit there. I face her toward the sun, so that it casts a soft glow on her face. It's tough to get some of those pink-purple clouds in the back, but I manage, and I have a feeling Elena will love these photos that blend so perfectly with her immaculately curated aesthetic. I even had her bring a couple of her stickers and designs so we could take a few photos of those on the beach as well—although, truth be told, Elena fully has her product photography on lock and doesn't need my help.

Between shots and songs, we talk, making our way to different parts of the beach, and, eventually, swing back to the pier.

It surprises me how easy our conversation comes, especially now that I don't need to keep any of Max's lies straight. The more Elena and I have talked over the weeks, the harder it's become to remember what I've said. I guess I hadn't realized just how entangled I'd become until now.

Today, I get to just be me, something I never thought I'd be happy about.

We use up all the sunrise until the sky turns blue and the sun is bright.

"We've gotten so many good ones. Your website is going to be amazing!" I say.

Elena watches as I pack up my bag. "I hope so!"

"So, tell me more about your sticker business."

"Sure! I'm a digital artist, so the easiest and cheapest thing to make is stickers, though I do some other stuff, too, like notebooks and prints." She tells me this as we walk toward our cars. "I also make custom commissions here and there, although that can be tough sometimes since no one ever wants to pay." She gives me a knowing look. "You know how it is. As if exposure pays for things. What's up with this idea that creatives should, like, give their talent and time away for free?"

I nod emphatically. "We all love art and entertainment and don't mind celebrities raking in millions, but for small businesses, it's another attitude entirely."

"I don't get it!" Elena says.

I pull out my keys. "Well. I'll have these over to you soon, so you can add them to your website. That was fun."

"It really was, Kat. I'm so, so glad Max recommended you."

The sound of Max's name, aloud, is kinda unsettling.

"I'm glad, too," I manage.

Elena's face brightens. "Hey! You want to get some breakfast?"

I smile big. "Really?"

"Absolutely! I'm starving." The way she says it reminds me of Luis and I laugh. "What? I am!"

"Just the way you said that reminded me of my friend."

"Well, tell me all about your friend on our way." She motions toward the nearby promenade. "Come on!"

Chapter Twenty-Nine

The two of us come upon a small diner, complete with a yellow-and-white awning out front and a flickering sign that just reads BREAKFAST. It looks great contrasted against the beachy boardwalk and the cerulean sky, and I find myself regretting that I tucked my camera away so soon.

Elena's nose crinkles as we get closer to the building. "Okay, so, I know it doesn't look like much, but I promise it's good."

"I'm so hungry at this point, I'll take anything," I say. "Plus, I kinda like the look of it. It's retro."

"That's one way of putting it." She grins and grabs the door to hold it open for me. "After you."

Inside, this little spot is already hopping. Though there is some indoor seating, the clear selling point is the massive back patio, which offers a generous view of the ocean sparkling in the sun. "Holy shit," I murmur.

Elena grins. "*Right?* The view is half the fun, but the food is amazing, too. Grab a seat as soon as one opens up. Finding a table is always a fight."

I nod, looking around the patio for signs that someone might be wrapping up. Another group comes up behind us, also looking for a place to sit, and Elena makes a sign as if she's cutting her throat. I stifle a laugh and pretend to glare at them. They're going down.

We wait and scan. After a few false alarms, I see a couple put their utensils down. I need to pounce. I pretend I don't see them, that I'm casually just walking by, but the second they get up to leave, I slam down into one of the now-empty chairs.

"Yes!" Elena whisper-shouts as she snags the seat across from me.

"Tell me why that was the most stressful thing I've ever had to do in a restaurant," I say.

"If you think that was stressful, just wait until you have to choose what to eat," Elena warns. "But I'll help you pick."

A waitress comes by to clean our table and hand us menus, which we start to look over. I really *am* having a hard time choosing, so I take Elena up on her offer and let her help me narrow it down to two choices. I go with something savory: eggs Benedict and fried potatoes.

Once we've ordered, Elena asks the question I always dread. "So, what's your family like?"

I almost blurt out the same story I've told everyone for years: that I live with my parents and my brother and I'm super close to my grandparents, who live right down the street.

But I stop myself.

Instead, for the first time in a long time, I say, "I live with my grandparents. They're amazing. My grandma is this tiny ball of energy—and sometimes anxiety, but still, she's full of so much love. And my grandpa is a contractor and, secretly, a great home cook. Super goofy, too. How about you?"

"They both sound awesome! I live with my parents and my older sister, Carys, who's a real pill sometimes." Elena rolls her eyes, and I hide a smile at this familiar phrase I've heard as Max. "Sisters can be a bit much."

"My friend Marcus says the same thing," I say.

"Oh! You know Marcus, too?" Elena asks.

"He's one of my best friends."

"Max has mentioned him before. He's the guy who named his car, right?"

Frustration at myself for making this so damn messy courses through me, but I do my best not to let on. I roll my eyes instead. "God, yes. He calls the car Honey."

"My best friend, Vanessa, has named her car, too. Beatrix," Elena says, rolling her eyes also. "But at least it's after Beatrix Potter. Vee's super into bunnies, so I guess it kinda makes sense. Still, though."

"I'm more of a dog person," I offer. "I actually work at a dog rescue center."

"Oh my gosh! Really?"

I nod, thankful that, in all the dog posts Max has done, I've been careful never to specify where the photos are taken. It lets me talk freely about my job without Elena suspecting a thing.

"Yeah. I do some of the communications for One Fur All, and they do amazing work. We've helped so many dogs find new homes. Although...one of my favorite little guys is having a tough time being adopted."

Elena frowns. "Oh, no! What happens if he can't find a home? He won't be...?" She lets the rest of her sentence drop off.

"God, no! No. We don't do that. We have a whole system where we transport dogs who can't find a home here elsewhere in the country so they have a better chance," I explain. "But only as a last resort. We really do our best to place them in or around Bakersfield."

She looks relieved. "Well, thank God for that. I love dogs, too. So does Max."

I bristle at another mention of Max in such a short amount of time. "Lots of dog people out here," I say, forcing a smile.

Our food arrives, and I'm glad to change the topic.

While I take a bite of my eggs Benedict, Elena checks her phone.

I'm about to say the diner was a good suggestion when she

blurts out, "Okay, so, this is like, breaking girl code or whatever, but I just have to ask: What's the deal with Max?"

I swallow, hoping to appear more thoughtful than panicked. "What do you mean?"

"I'm stumped," Elena says. "Like, okay, I know that obviously you take photos for her, but you're friends with her, too, right? Live in the same town kind of thing?"

"Sort of," I say. "Yes, I take photos for her, but we don't really hang."

Sort of true, right?

Elena frowns. "Oh."

"Why?" I press, though I should probably just let this go.

"Ugh. I don't know. Max and I have kind of had this back-and-forth thing going on for the last few weeks," Elena says. "We've been, like, texting every day and talking super late into the night. Now, I will admit, I *totally* slid into her DMs first and kicked things off, but..." Her voice trails. "I can't get a read on her. It just seems like sometimes she likes me and sometimes she's super distant. It's so confusing. I asked her to come today because I thought she'd want to hang out with you and finally meet me in person and she said no!"

"Oh..." I stall and take a sip of water.

Elena continues. "I know. I shouldn't be asking! And this is, like, fully not your problem. Sorry."

"No, no, it's okay," I assure her. "I'm just not sure what to say. Max is..." I search for the right words. "Complicated?"

"I would agree to that. I can't get her to commit to anything more than a phone call," Elena says. "I just want something definitive from her, one way or the other. It's cool if she's not into me in that way, but the flirty vibe has been confusing."

I bite my lip. There I go again, being wishy-washy with intentions.

If Hari were here, he'd be nodding emphatically along with everything Elena is saying.

"That's fair," I say. "Do you like her?"

Elena uses her spoon to push some of the granola around in her yogurt bowl. "I mean…she's really cute. And we talk a lot. And I get excited every time she sends me a message. And I keep mentioning her even when I don't mean to."

"You *have* been mentioning her a lot."

"See?!" She buries her face in her hands. "So embarrassing."

"Not even close," I say.

"But I don't even know if she's into girls. It would be just my luck."

I search for words that aren't lies, ways I can try and right this ship that is so close to hitting an iceberg it's not even funny. "All I know is that Max can be a little all over the place." (True.) "And I imagine she's probably wrapped up thinking about college and stuff." (Sometimes true.) "So, I don't know. Just a lot going on, I'm sure…"

Elena twirls a strand of her pink hair between her fingers, nodding. "Yeah, no. That makes sense."

This whole conversation makes me want to jump into the ocean and swim far, far away.

Knowing Elena likes Max?…Me?

It's what I've wanted, secretly. It's how I feel, secretly.

But nothing can happen. Max isn't real. I am.

This is so messed up.

"I'm sorry I don't have more for you," I say.

She shakes her head. "No, no. I shouldn't have even been asking you. I'm sorry." And I hate hearing her apologize. Not when I'm the terrible one here.

"Don't be."

She sighs. "I wouldn't blame you if you told her I was pumping you for info."

"I won't say a word." Then I hold out my pinky to her. "Promise."

It feels silly to do this—disingenuous, even. But what more can I offer? I'm barely making it through this conversation as it is. The least I can do is provide Elena some comfort.

Elena wraps her pinky around mine. "Thanks, Kat. I appreciate that." Then she pulls her hand back and narrows her eyes. "You're weirdly easy to talk to, you know that? Like some kind of emotional support person or something."

I burst out laughing. "An emotional support person? I guess I can get behind that."

"You're a good listener, I should say," Elena explains.

"I kinda prefer the former now." I smile. "And the feeling's mutual."

"You know, we should hang again," Elena says. "Not, like, for photos or anything. But for fun!"

As if I deserve that.

And yet, I say, "I would really like that."

Elena's whole face lights up, and warmth spreads in my chest. "Yeah? My friends are having a bonfire soon, if you're interested?"

"I'll have to check with my grandparents first," I explain. "But if they're okay with it, then why not?"

"Okay! Yay! Well, I'll text you details and maybe you can come," Elena says, grinning. "And now, I swear I'll shut up so you can actually eat your breakfast. It's totally getting cold."

We make it through the rest of our meal without any further mentions of Max, and I find myself happy and sad when I get back in my car.

Because now, not only do I have to worry about the fact that I've sort of agreed to meet up with Elena again, but I also have this knowledge that Elena likes Max.

And…given our late-night DM sessions, the times I find myself drifting off in class to think of her, the butterflies in my stomach every time she sends me a message, my agreeing to this *absolutely wild* suggestion that I meet up with her to take photos purely because I was eager to meet her in person, and the fact that I couldn't stop looking at her lips all morning long…

I'm pretty sure I like Elena.

Chapter Thirty

I like Elena. *I* like Elena. *I like Elena.*

And *she* likes Max.

Who is also me—though she doesn't know that.

Is it wrong to be jealous of myself? Shit. This is so confusing.

Fresh off a great morning with her, I can't help myself; I open my phone and text Elena, as Kat.

Me: **I'm STILL thinking about those eggs Benedict.**

Elena: **RIGHT? Same with my granola. Who knew it could be so good? We should've taken an order to go!**

Me: **Thank you for introducing me to my new favorite spot.**

Elena: **Oh, so the spot is yours now? I see how it is.**

Me: **I'm willing to share, but only if you'll meet me there again.**

Elena: **Easiest negotiation ever.**

Elena: **I'm literally never going to hear the end of it for going without Vanessa, but it was worth it!!!**

Elena: **It was so good we forgot to take pics for IG.**

Me: **You know it's good when.**

Elena: **Seriously!**

Me: **I'll edit your pictures soon and have them to you by the end of the weekend. I hope you like them!**

Elena: **I know I will.**

Elena: **And thanks for being so cool even when I was weird.**

Me: **That's what good emotional support people do.**

Elena laugh-reacts to the message and I switch over to IG. I see stories from Marcus and Luis that show me that they're off playing laser tag before meeting up for Photography Club. I navigate over to Hari's account, which hasn't been updated in days and has no new story.

From the window in my room, I can see Hari's house in the distance. His car, as well as his parents' cars, is in the driveway, but the space where Dev is always parked is empty. Which annoys me. Aren't they *both* supposed to be grounded?

I pull up Dev's Instagram account and sure enough, his story is updated. I swipe through to see photos of him and his friends playing basketball.

Without thinking, I get out of the car and start walking to Hari's. It's such a familiar path that it's as if my legs have a mind of their own. Before I know it, I'm knocking on their front door, perhaps more forcefully than I should.

Mr. Shah answers. "Hello, Kat," he says, a hint of surprise in his voice when he sees me. "You look well."

"You do, too, Mr. Shah. Good to see you," I reply. "Is Hari home?"

He tilts his head to one side. "He is, yes. But he's still grounded."

"I was afraid of that. This is because of Dev's party, right?" I ask.

I know it is absolutely not my place to be doing this, and I am not sure what's taken over me. I have never challenged Mr. Shah, not in all the years I've known Hari, even though the urge was sometimes really strong. I hated having to watch the very obvious preferential treatment for Dev. It hurt to see Hari so wounded. He'd always brush it off as best he could, but this? It's too much. Hari doesn't deserve to be stuck in his room, by himself, taking the heat for a party that Dev threw while Dev is out living his life.

Mr. Shah stiffens. "Because of *their* party. They were both responsible."

"I just feel like I need to tell you that that party was all Dev's idea, Mr. Shah. Just Dev. If you could've seen Hari beforehand, how stressed out he was, how anxious, you'd understand," I say calmly. "He absolutely did not want that party to happen. He wanted nothing to do with it."

His eyes narrow and there is a sharpness to his voice when he speaks now. "Regardless of whose idea it was, neither of them stopped it from happening, so they are both complicit."

I make a point of looking toward the driveway, where Dev's normal parking spot is empty. "With all due respect, may I ask where Dev is right now?"

Mr. Shah crosses his arms and I can tell he is losing patience with me. "He's at his SAT study session. What is this about?"

I shake my head. "Dev isn't at his SAT session."

"Yes, he is," Mr. Shah insists.

"But he isn't." I pull out my phone and go to Dev's story, passing the phone to him. Sorry, Dev. But this is about Hari.

Mr. Shah looks down, brows furrowed, as photos and video show him that his golden child is indeed *not* at an SAT study session. "Is this from today?"

"This afternoon," I say, pointing at the time stamp beside Dev's username that reads *1h,* indicating the first video went up just one hour ago.

He frowns deeply, the corners of his mustache turning downward, too. "Hold on." Then he looks toward the house and calls, "Aditi!" It's just a moment before Mrs. Shah appears.

When she sees me, she waves. "Ooh, Kat! It's so good to see you!" Her voice is sweet like honey.

"Hi, Mrs. Shah. Good to see you, too!"

"Jaanu," Mr. Shah says, using his pet name for his wife, "look." He points at my phone, which has cycled through Dev's story and is now on a makeup ad. I fix it and show Mrs. Shah.

"Dev isn't at his SAT study session," I say, gently. She shakes her head as she watches. "I don't mean to rat Dev out, but I just noticed

Hari's car in the driveway, and I have been feeling so sorry for him as I know the party wasn't his idea." Mr. and Mrs. Shah exchange a look.

"I told you," she says to him, and he sighs.

"I'm really sorry for coming over like this and causing trouble. I just really, really needed you to know."

Mrs. Shah hands me my phone and places her hand over mine. "It's okay, Kat. I am glad you told us."

"It's probably best if you go," Mr. Shah says.

I nod. "Yes, I'm sorry." I tuck my phone in my back pocket and see the door to Hari's room open, just a bit. We lock eyes and he gives me a small smile before I leave.

Everything might be a little confusing and all over the place right now, but if there's one thing I'm certain of, it's that Hari deserves to be treated better. I hope this small gesture helps to change things for him.

That night, in between reliving the fun of the boardwalk with Elena, the thrill of a budding new crush, and the pride of standing up for Hari, I find I return to something else from earlier in the day.

Elena's freckles.

Startlingly absent from her IG, yet prominent as ever IRL. The sheepishness in her voice as she explained, oh, right. She hides them away sometimes. Without a second thought. A part of herself gone.

It's a small thing. Who cares, right? It's not like Elena is doing something catastrophic, like pretending to be another person. The ripple effect it has in my mind feels huge, though.

How many of the photos I see on Instagram are tweaked, even in such a minor way, like that? A nipped waist, some smoothed skin, an edited background, a disappearing double chin. What counts as a lie, what counts as an omission, and what counts as nothing at all? How is it so that the lines between what's real and what's edited can be so blurred on social media? Do we even know anymore? Do I?

Chapter Thirty-One

I. Am. Free!!!

Hari's text comes to me, Marcus, and Luis first thing the next morning. I grin when I see it.

Marcus: **Ladies and gentlemen, Hari Shah has returned!**

Luis: **That's nice and all, but you just woke me up.** 😠 ✒️

Me: **Hari!!!!!!! How does it feel?**

Hari: **Well deserved. Who wants to hang out today?**

Marcus: **I'm out. Photo editor shit. Y'all wouldn't know about THAT.**

Luis: **Don't be fooled by this clown. He's stuck going to the Senior Center to photograph the theater kids performing "Rent."**

Luis: **But I'm out, too. Xio thangs. Now THAT'S what y'all wouldn't know about!**

Hari: **Damn, is there NO love for me???**

Me: **I have some things to take care of this morning, but later today I'm good.** 👻

Hari: **It's on, then!**

If that isn't a great way to start a Sunday morning, I don't know what is. I sit up in bed and stretch. Between helping Hari, reviving Photography Club, and meeting Elena in real life, yesterday was the best day I've had in a while.

I make the most of my morning by finishing the photos for Elena and sending them her way, then dashing to One Fur All for my shift. It goes quickly, especially now that we have so much to work on ahead of the upcoming ball. I finish everything as fast as I can so that I can race toward what I'm anticipating: reuniting with my MF best friend.

Yes, things have been weird, and yes, we have things to talk about, but I'd do just about anything at this point to have him back.

I don't bother with pretenses when I see his car pull into the Bluffs, our agreed-upon meeting spot. Once his car door has shut, I rush over to him and give him a hug, squeezing him hard. "Damn, Kat. It's like you missed me or something."

I laugh and pull back from him, giving his shoulder a playful swat. "You missed me, too. Admit it!"

Hari scrunches his nose at me. "I wouldn't go that far. But I guess I do kinda owe you after you sprung me out of Shah jail."

"Tell me *everything*."

"Come on," he says, motioning toward the nearby trail so we can walk and talk.

Hari does most of it, at least to start. He shares how isolating it's been the past few weeks, how depressed he was getting, how he couldn't stop thinking about how unfair it was that he was having to pay for Dev's extravagance, how he tried to talk to his dad several times but without much luck, how he was shocked to hear my voice when I showed up yesterday, how he pressed himself up against the crack of his bedroom door and listened to everything, how it inspired a looooong conversation with his parents and with Dev, how though he's not grounded anymore, how Dev is finally, deliciously, *extra* grounded.

"He's not happy," Hari laughs.

"Who cares?! He punched you," I remind him. "And you've got your life back!"

By now, we're at the top of one of the hills and sitting in a grassy area, cross-legged, facing each other.

He nods. "I do. Which is good because I was on the verge of pulling out my old Legos. I'm just really relieved my parents actually heard me out this time. I mean, who knows if this will cause any meaningful change, but it's definitely something." Hari looks up at me. "Thank you."

"You don't need to—"

He cuts in. "But I want to. I haven't been a very good friend lately. I was so caught up in my disappointment over us not, you know, becoming something that I ended up lashing out and saying some stuff that wasn't cool."

"Hey, it's fine," I say, but he shakes his head.

"It's really not. I know how much everything with your parents hurts you. It's really not my place to say shit otherwise, no matter how I was feeling."

"Okay, but my timing with that ask was not great."

Hari laughs. "Oh, absolutely. Your timing was horrible."

And I laugh, too. "Yeah, it was. And..." I glance down, twirling a blade of grass around my finger. "I said some shit, too. I hurt you." I look up to meet his eyes. "I'm so sorry, Hari."

He gives me a small, crooked smile. "I know you are. But it's all good. I am, too. I did a lot of thinking while I was holed up in my room. And, I mean, it's for the best. How we ended things."

"Damn. You're over me already?" I snap my fingers. "Just like that?!"

"Not *just* like that, but I mean, yeah, in a way," Hari says. "I want to go back to being best friends who get into hijinks and take photos together and shake our heads at whatever weird things Marcus and Luis are up to, you know?"

I grab Hari's shoulders. "This is music to my ears, Hari. I've missed you so goddamn much."

He smiles. "I've missed you, too. Really."

"I will miss the making out, though," I say, and that takes Hari by surprise.

He laughs and scratches at the back of his head. "I mean, yeah, same. But I'll find someone else to make out with. And I'm sure you will, too." He reaches for the hem of my jeans and tugs at it. "But what's been up with you? I've done so much talking."

I sigh dramatically and flop back into the grass. "You don't want to know."

"Oh, boy…"

As I look up at the sky, my mind runs through all the weird and wild things that have taken place over the last few weeks. Where do I even start?

"Well, I've been working on this pretty cool winter ball thing for work. Cash is still up for adoption. My parents made me a pink room in their house. My grandparents feel guilty about me living with them. Oh, and I stole my friend Becca's photos and made a fake account on Instagram pretending to be a new person, and as that new person, I met a girl, and now I think I like her?"

Hari grabs my hands and forcefully tugs me into the sitting position, eyes wide. "I'm gonna need a repeat of all that."

I smile. "Thought you might." I start to talk and *everything* comes tumbling out. Elena, most of all. The late-night DMs and the Snap streaks and the meeting-Elena-as-me and my grand plans to just ghost as Max and try and have Elena get to know me as me instead.

Hari interrupts here and there to ask a clarifying question but, for the most part, remains silent, taking everything in. When I'm done, he lets out a big puff of air, looks away at the distance for a moment, and then back at me.

"So…while I spent the last few weeks rotting in my room, you went and created a whole-ass person?"

I wince. "Kinda?"

"And you fell for a girl? You like girls?"

"I didn't *fall* for her," I insist. "But…yeah. I do like her. It's new."

"And you thought I moved on fast."

I raise my eyebrows at him. "Are you mad?"

"I'm not. I meant what I said about us being better as friends," Hari says. "I think I'm more in disbelief over how much happened in such a small slice of time. I missed a lot."

"You're all caught up now, I promise."

He wrinkles his nose at me. "You realize you're catfishing someone, right? It's a little on the nose, don't you think? Kat the catfish?"

"I like to think of it as catfishing with a *K*. Katfishing."

We stare at each other for a second and then start cracking up. Waves of laughter come again and again, and soon we're both cackling so hard we're crying and I can barely catch my breath.

"I really missed this," I say, once we've calmed down.

"Me too." Hari swipes at his eyes and takes in a deep breath. "So, what the hell are you going to do?"

"About which part?"

"Touché. Um, about the account, I guess?"

I chew on my bottom lip. "I've been thinking about that. I don't have a good answer. I was giving myself until the winter ball to decide."

"Hmm."

"Unless you have a better idea?"

"I mean…" He tilts his head from side to side, as if considering the options. "Ultimately, it needs to go, right? Like, what are you even…doing with it?"

"Pretending to be a white girl?" I joke.

"I'm serious, Kat."

"I know, I know. I've been wrestling with this. I don't know what I'm doing. The way I see it, I have a couple of options." I hold up a finger and start to list them off. "I can delete the account entirely. Just, poof. Gone."

"Sounds pretty tempting," Hari says. "Maybe a little cowardly."

"Yeah. And unfair to…"

"E-*le*-na," Hari sings.

"Don't!" I warn. "But yes. Super unfair to her."

"Sooo, what, then?"

I hold up a second finger. "Come clean and make it right."

He winces. "I don't know, man. Maybe you *should* just delete it and ghost. I mean, I'm not trying to be rude here, but do you think coming clean isn't going to ruin everything?" Hari pulls up grass, agitated for me. "You straight-up lied. There's really no coming back from that, regardless of what you decide."

I frown. Up until now, I haven't wanted to think about the repercussions of what I've been doing, or just how messed up this has been—to Elena and to Becca. Leave it to Hari, my best friend, to help me see things as they are. Not yet willing to admit the gravity of my actions, I playfully suggest, "Maybe I can just tell Elena Max died or something?"

"Oh, sure. Cover one lie with a bigger lie. Great idea." Hari rolls his eyes. "What about Becca?"

I can't meet his gaze now. Yes. What *about* Becca? The one who will be hurt the most by what I've done? I disregarded her wishes and used her image to lie. I know this. More than regret, I feel shame—deep, ugly shame that twists and knots in my gut and makes the tips of my ears burn when I think of it.

"I know."

"She's the biggest victim here! You're using her photos, without her permission," Hari reminds me.

"I know," I say again.

"You've gotta get rid of that account." His voice is forceful. "Sooner rather than later."

My throat suddenly feels dry. Hearing the thoughts I'd been struggling with spoken aloud is dizzying. It's like I've been climbing a mountain of lies pretending a deep pit of hurt wasn't waiting for me on the other side.

"Well, shit," I murmur.

Hari's nodding. "Shit."

I let out a long groan. "I'm fucked."

"Royally," Hari agrees. "But, hey! At least you have me to remind you of that now. Doesn't that make you feel so much better?"

I narrow my eyes at him. "I'm delighted."

"Thought you would be." Hari rises to his feet and holds a hand to me. "Should we head back?"

"But my life is still in shambles," I say.

"Sure is. But if I'm going to help you figure it all out, I feel like you owe me a coffee or something."

I roll my eyes but take his hand and get to my feet, too.

As we walk back to the car, I consider my choices. Hari's right: I need to get rid of Max ASAP. Deleting the account very much seems like the easiest option, but Elena will ask me what happened to Max, and then I'll have to lie. Again. I don't want to do that.

But what choice do I have here?

Hari reaches over and squeezes my elbow. "Hey. It'll be all right. Okay?"

"Okay," I agree. "I'm thinking of changing my name and going into hiding. That should work, right?"

"That's exactly what I was thinking," Hari says. "I hear Denver is really nice."

I swat him, but I smile, thankful to have this back. And I know he's right. Max needs to go.

But I have to figure out what that looks like with the least damage to Elena. She and Max are so close.

She and *I* are so close.

And as for Becca—well. I don't even want to think about that right now.

So...maybe I'll still give myself until the One Fur All Winter Ball. It's just a few weeks.

I'll figure out the rest as I go.

Chapter Thirty-Two

I go days without logging in as Max.

When I finally work up the courage to do so, I see just one unread message.

Elena: **Aren't you going to ask me how everything went with Kat?**

I stare at the DM, bemused at how trippy it is to read a message from a girl I now know in real life, sent to a girl we're supposedly mutually friends with, referencing me. It's enough to make me dizzy.

I start to type.

Max: **I was going to**

Delete.

Max: **I meant to reach out but**

Delete.

Max: **So sorry! I've been super swamped. Hopefully everything went well and you had a nice weekend! Kat said she had an awesome time.**

Guilt starts to sprout in my chest. None of these are lies, per se. But they don't feel like truths, either.

To make up for it, I text Elena.

Me: **I heard a rumor.**

Elena writes back almost instantly.

Elena: **What about?** 👀

Me: **You.**

Elena: **A rumor about me?!**

Elena: **From who? What'd they say? I'm ready to fight.**

Me: **They said that you get people addicted to indie break-fast spots and then they can't stop thinking about the deliciousness. All other breakfasts are ruined forever.**

Me: **That's just what I heard.**

Elena: **God, I'm such a life destroyer.**

Me: **Yep. Now you have no choice but to let me ruin tacos for you by introducing you to the BEST food truck in Bakersfield.**

It's a bold text, and I've sent it before I can tell myself I'm playing with fire. I need this, though. Our days are numbered.

Elena: **Kind of a far drive for tacos...**

My heart sinks.

But then.

Elena: **Saturday? That'll give me enough time to break up with the other taco places in my life.**

Me: **Tell the other taco places it's over.**

I can feel myself smiling as I look down at our exchange. How badly I wish we'd met this way instead of the other—just Kat and Elena, never Max and Elena. But at least now I have Saturday to look forward to.

"This payasa is always on her phone," Luis jeers.

I look up and switch my grin to a scowl. "So are you!"

"Yes, but I have a girlfriend I need to keep happy," he explains.

Hari's face lights up. "Hey! You made it official?"

Luis grins. "I'm wifed up now."

"And happy about it," Marcus adds. "Our boy is growing up."

"Never thought I'd see the day," I say, smiling. "Congrats, dummy. You finally found someone to put up with your shit full-time."

Despite my teasing, he beams. "She's the best. I can't wait for you all to meet her."

"We've gone to school with Xiomara since the sixth grade," Marcus points out.

"But you don't know her as *my girl*," Luis says. "It's different."

"It is different," I confirm.

"See, even Sanchez is on my side." Luis turns to me. "But don't think that's going to make me stop teasing you about your phone obsession. It's, like, a *real* addiction at this point."

I roll my eyes. "Shut up."

"Did you know that people will spend five years and four months of their lifetimes on social media?" Marcus asks. "I feel like it's even more severe for you. Like, twenty years."

"See, the weird thing to me is that I never see this girl post shit." Luis is talking to Marcus as if I'm not there now. "Like, what is she even doing on that phone?"

"Unfortunately for me, I spend a lot of time texting you idiots," I sniff.

"But not when we're right here! What gives, Sanchez? You in some kind of secret fanfic community?"

Marcus snaps his fingers. "For BTS!"

Luis starts laughing. "Oh, shit! That's right!"

Hari shoots me a quizzical look and I shake my head. He missed the whole BTS poster saga, and I'm not about to fill him in.

"But I mean, if not fanfic, what?" Marcus asks sincerely. "You've even stopped sharing your photography. It's weird."

I furrow my brows. "Didn't think anyone would notice."

"Of course we noticed," Marcus replies.

"Even *I* noticed," Luis says.

"How would you know? You don't even follow me!" I argue.

Luis shakes his head. "Your profile is public, stupid. I can just look you up."

"That's so much more work than just following me."

"I don't follow nobody!"

Marcus waves a hand at us to try and get us to stop bickering. *"Plus,"* he continues, "you've been MIA in real life, too, Kat."

"What is with this attack right now?" I ask, bristling.

Luis squints at me. "I'm convinced you're living some kind of secret life."

Hari laughs knowingly and I shoot him a look. "If this is your way of saying you want more of my attention, Luis, I am flattered."

"Nobody said that," Luis replies.

"I will make more of an effort to be around you." I reach over to Luis and pinch his cheek. He swats me away. "And you." I reach for Marcus's cheek to do the same, but he dodges out of my way. "And you," I add, pointing at Hari, who I can't reach from my seat.

"Well, all I know is now that we've revived our club, we need to be regularly doing shit, otherwise we can lose our funding," Marcus says.

"Wait. We get funding?" Hari asks.

Luis looks confused. "Yeah, what? We get money?"

"Not much, and I mostly use it for gas money, since Honey and I are always the ones carting your sorry asses around," Marcus replies.

"So, you steal money from the school so that you can fill Honey with premium gas and use Photography Club as an excuse?" Luis teases.

Marcus points a finger at him. "That's not what I said!"

A playful look comes over Hari's face as he says, "I didn't even know we were a real club."

"You *know* we are," Marcus continues. "And, as the club's founder, I've been the one attending meetings with our beloved club advisor, so that we can prove we're legit and qualify for what little funding we get and also get our picture in the yearbook."

I arch an eyebrow at Marcus. "Why have we literally never known any of this?"

He lets out a frustrated grunt. "I've told you all this multiple times!"

Hari looks over at me. "He's never said a word about this."

Luis shakes his head. "This is all news to me, my dude."

"Seriously. You should try to communicate a little better," I add.

Marcus gets up from the table and grabs his lunch tray. "Forget all of you. We are having a mandatory club outing on Sunday, and you will all be there."

"Wait, wait, wait." Hari reaches for Marcus's arm to stop him from leaving the table. "What club again?"

We all start laughing and Marcus rips his arm away from Hari. "I'm going to the library!" He leaves in a huff.

"That was fun," Hari says.

Luis grins. "Agreed. I'm glad y'all two are friends again." He nods toward the two of us. "Makes clowning on Marcus so much easier."

Hari and I smile at each other. Same, Luis. Same.

Later that afternoon, at home, I log into Max's messages. While Elena and I have been texting back and forth throughout the day, I've been too chicken to see if she'd replied to Max.

When I pull up the message, I feel extra bad for ignoring her.

Elena: **I did have a nice time, thanks.**

Elena: **Are you mad at me or something?**

The second message came in in the early afternoon, so it's been sitting, unread and unanswered, for most of the day, while she and I have been exchanging random TikToks and joking about celebrities we hope get canceled just because they're annoying.

All that playfulness in one conversation, and so much bad energy in another. Poor Elena.

Me: **I'm not mad at you at all! I've just got so much going on right now. I'm thinking of taking a break from social, actually, so I might be a little more absent than normal. Just FYI.**

Maybe a slow fade as Max is spineless, but I've been weighing all the scenarios in my head and I'm not sure there's another way. Not without ruining absolutely everything.

Chapter Thirty-Three

My marathon texting sessions with Elena have shifted from Max over to me. If she thinks it's bizarre that Max has dropped off the face of the earth and in her place is a new girl named Kat who types suspiciously similarly, she hasn't said as much.

Thank God.

Because talking to her and getting to be myself is so much more fun.

Plus, knowing that my reign as Max is coming to an end makes me way less jumpy around Becca, which is good, because the closer we get to the One Fur All Winter Ball, the harder the two of us need to work together to create content for the website and its social media channels.

One afternoon, I come home to what appears to be an empty house. I find Grandma in her room, where she's occupied herself with a book. She puts it down on the bed and sits up when I enter.

"Hi, chickadee. How was your day?"

I flop onto her bed like it's my own. "It was okay. Happy to be done with work. Did I tell you about the ball that's happening?"

"I don't think you did." She reaches out and strokes my hair as I fill her in on what's going on at work, and she listens intently. When I finish, she asks, "So, will you take Hari with you as your date?"

I sit up. "Hari?"

Grandma raises both of her eyebrows at me and leans in. "You two seem to spend an awful lot of time together."

"I mean, we do, but Hari and I...we're just friends."

"Oh. Hmm." Grandma doesn't seem convinced. "It's just that I could've sworn I saw you two holding hands when he walked you home a few weeks ago." When I don't say anything, she adds, "You know, around Halloween?"

My eyes practically bulge out of my head. "What? You saw us?"

She smiles. "I may be old, but I'm not dumb. Your mother used to come home late with your father like that—though I was much stricter back then." A little sigh. "Hari is a wonderful young man. I really do like him. He's so good to you, Kat."

I let out a laugh. "I can't believe you spotted us! You never said anything!"

Grandma shrugs, looking down at her bedspread. "Well, I don't want to seem overly interfering, Kat. I've learned that being too strict can sometimes drive the people you love away." Her voice is melancholy as she says this, sharing the tiniest glimpse of life before me. But when she meets my gaze, she's smiling again. "So, I was imagining things, then? No hand-holding?"

"Not exactly," I admit. "I mean...we had been holding hands that night. But things didn't really work out. We're better as friends."

She clucks her tongue. "That's too bad. But I do understand. Good friends are hard to come by."

"They really are." I hesitate. "I guess while we're talking about it, though..."

Grandma meets my gaze. "Yes?" she asks, prodding me along.

"There is someone." I pick at the chenille coverlet like it's suddenly so interesting. I should have rehearsed this, especially now that my heartbeat is beating so hard I can feel it in my ears. Just say it. Say it before you lose your nerve, Kat. I swallow. "A girl."

"A girl," she repeats, the inflection in her voice indicating surprise. Good surprise? Bad surprise? It feels like a lifetime between that and when an easy, reassuring smile spreads across her lips. "Tell me about her! Do you know her from school?"

A relieved sigh escapes me, the faintest hint of happy tears springing to the corners of my eyes. Of all the things my grandma could have chosen to say, she's gone with a genuine question about how I met Elena.

"Not exactly. I met her on Instagram," I admit. "But she's amazing. So kind and warm and smart."

"Pretty?" Grandma asks.

"The *prettiest*," I gush. "She doesn't know I like her yet. But soon, maybe. I don't know. She did invite me to a bonfire."

"Is that so? That sounds like fun."

"Yeah?" I grin. "So, I can go?"

"Of course," she says. Her face suddenly brightens. "Maybe she could be your date to the ball!"

I laugh. A little harder than I intend. It's just all so much! I'm shocked by—and so, so grateful for—the sudden shift in conversation from *hey, I like a girl* (and therefore I am bi) to *this girl should be my date for an important event* (and therefore my grandma is already so on board with it she's imagining scenarios where this girl comes with me to a thing!).

"Maybe…"

"Either way, you'll need something to wear," Grandma adds.

And my heart nearly floods with joy as I realize she's hinting at one of our infamous Kat-and-Grandma shopping trips where we buy way too much. This is her way of letting me know: I see you, and I love you, and we should celebrate.

"Right now?" I ask.

"Right now." There's a twinkle in her eye as she says it and I could hug her. So, I do.

* * *

Our shopping trips are something I've always treasured. We don't do them that often, but when we *do,* we go all out: hitting the nearby outlets, buying way too much, splitting a huge pretzel dog, and hitting every single store that looks even mildly interesting.

We like to play games, too. In one store, we pick out the ugliest clothes we can find and bring them over to each other.

I hold up a fishnet top and show Grandma. "I found this for you."

She laughs. "Goodness! You want me to give everyone a show?"

Then she holds a long flannel nightgown out to me. "This one's for you, then."

And on and on. The silly finds are amazing, but I do find a few new clothes, too—a jumpsuit, some new Doc Martens, a long jean skirt. In between the stores, we chat about Grandma's circle of friends (the Golden Girls, she calls them; they all regularly meet up for walks and gossip); school; Grandpa's cooking; and Cash, including my fervent hope that this ball will be his ticket to a loving home.

Finally we take a break and settle together on a bench.

"I love to people-watch," Grandma says. With her chin, she motions toward a couple who are walking with their hands in each other's back pockets.

"Gross!" I laugh.

She laughs, too. "My thoughts exactly."

I point at a man who is dressed like a quintessential tourist (loafers, socks, Hawaiian shirt) and we both giggle. There's also an adorable little kid who says "Hi!" to every single person he sees, a woman who is totally trying to conceal the fact that she has a dog in her backpack, and two boys around my age who definitely stole one of the shopping carts from a store and are now taking turns joyriding in it.

"People are so weird," I declare.

"That's what makes the watching so good. Look."

Grandma points behind me. I turn—as subtly as I can given that we're gawking—and see an older woman, a little younger than Grandma, holding hands with a tiny curly-haired girl.

I watch them for a minute: the gentle way the older woman leans down to speak to the girl and listen to what she has to say; the little girl reaching up for the woman's hand to hold; the girl's toddling walk. I can't help but smile to myself. "That looks like us."

Grandma reaches over and pats my hand. "It sure does."

I pull out my camera and take a photo, wanting to capture the sweetness between the two. Then I turn the camera to Grandma and snap one of her.

Her hand goes up in front of her face to stop me. "Being with you is like being with the paparazzi."

"I have to do it this way! You'd never let me get your picture if you had warning."

I review the photos I've taken. In Grandma's photo, her expression is soft and serene. I show it to her.

"Not bad considering the subject," she chuckles.

I give her a look. *"Grandma."*

She smiles at me. "It's lovely, Kat."

"Check this one out." I navigate back a few photos till I find one I took the other day of Grandpa. His weathered hands are on full display as he works on fixing our mailbox. Always the ham, once he realized I was taking his photo, he crossed his eyes and puffed out his cheeks.

Grandma laughs when she sees it. "We should frame that."

"It would look great in the living room," I joke.

We sit there for a moment longer and I go through all the photos on my camera. Looking at them all lined up like this—this sweet woman and the little girl; my grandpa; my grandma—my heart floods with so much love and appreciation for these two incredibly strong people who raised not only their kid, but then their kid's kid. We may not be a perfect family, but I'm so lucky to be loved by them. That much I know.

"Do you think Grandpa will be okay with it, too? With me liking a girl, I mean."

Grandma smiles at me. "If you told your grandfather you liked a space alien, I think he wouldn't bat an eyelash. You can do no wrong in his eyes. Or in mine."

I scoot closer to her and rest my head on her shoulder, taking her by surprise. She squeezes my arm. "I love you. We both love you. You can share things with us, even if they feel..." She searches for the right words. "Big. Or scary. We want you to feel comfortable doing that. We'll try to share more, too. No matter what, you'll always be my little chickadee."

I squeeze her arm back. "I love you, too. Thank you. And no matter what, you'll always be my...chicken?" I offer.

This makes her chuckle. "Chicken?"

"I don't know! I was trying to think of the older version of a chickadee."

And she laughs some more. "Oh, jeez. Well, we'll need to work on that. But the title of Grandma is all I really need." Then she motions toward the stores. "Shall we get back at it?"

I get to my feet and hold a hand to help her up. "Let's."

Chapter Thirty-Four

As Grandma predicted, Grandpa is more than happy to receive my news, offering me a hug, a handshake, and a request that I model some of the new things I've just bought.

One thing's for sure, though: I will not be sharing this news with my parents yet, especially not at our mandatory dinner tonight.

If I'm honest (and I'm working on being honest more often), their house is the last place I'd like to be right now.

But a promise is a promise, and I promised Grandma I'd keep trying. So here I am.

Mom's here, too, and so is Leo. With me and Pop on one side of the table, them on the other, and the four dogs sitting around us hoping for scraps, we're just one, big happy family.

Only the awkward silence that lies heavy between us makes it painfully obvious that it isn't so.

This all feels so...fake.

"So, how's everything going, kids?" Pop asks with forced cheerfulness.

Leo pushes his food around on his plate. "It's going."

"I got a B on my chemistry test," I offer. "Which is better than I thought I'd get."

Pop smiles at me. "That's great, Kat! Future chemist?"

I let out a strained laugh. "Hardly. Chemistry isn't really my thing."

"She's a pretty great photographer, though," Leo says. "Maybe she'll do that."

I steal a glance at him. I didn't even know he knew I took photos. "That would be awesome."

Mom wrinkles her nose. "You can't really go to college for photography, though."

"I mean, you can," I object.

"Art school is a thing, Mom," Leo reminds her.

"Hmm," is all Mom says in response.

"I'm sure whatever Kat decides will be great," Pop says.

It's weird like this for the whole dinner. Pop offers to clean up and do the dishes, so I go up to my room—both in an attempt to show I appreciate the space, and for a moment to breathe.

On the bed, surrounded by pink, I see Leo come into the doorway.

"Some room, huh?" he asks.

"Some room," I agree with a laugh.

He glances around it. "There is nothing in here that I would ever imagine you picking out for yourself." He shakes his head. "Feels like they don't even know us sometimes."

I don't hide my surprise. "You feel that way, too?"

"Of course. Mom once tried to set me up with horseback riding lessons." He smiles wryly. "Do I look like the horseback-riding type?"

I grin. "Not sure I know what a horseback-riding type looks like, but it's not you, that's for sure."

"Thank you," Leo says, bowing.

"I want to appreciate that they've done this. But it feels wrong, you know?" I stare around. "This isn't my room."

Leo nods. "Yeah. They should've made you one a long time ago. Now it's like, who are we trying to fool?"

"Exactly. Like, *I'm* not fooled."

"Wouldn't expect you to be."

It's new, talking to Leo like this. So frankly. So openly.

But I like it. Maybe we have more in common than I thought.

* * *

Once I'm back home, I take out my phone and open Max's IG. I'd been waiting for some kind of response to Max's message that she was going to take a break. Like, I don't know—a please-don't-go or a hope-you're-okay kind of thing. Nothing, though.

So, as me, I shoot her a text.

Me: **How are you?**

Elena: **Ugh.**

Elena: **Kinda bad, actually.**

Me: **Oh no. What's wrong?**

Elena: **My friend Vanessa and I got into an argument.**

Elena: **Over Max.**

At this, my heart nearly stops. Max is having far too many real-life consequences for my liking.

Me: **Oh no! What happened?**

Elena: **She's just been really weird with me lately, totally pulling back, barely talking to me. We went from ACTUAL PHONE CALLS to her ghosting me. It had me so upset I cried. And then Vee got mad at me because she WARNED me that Max seemed off.**

Elena: **No offense. I know she's your friend!**

Me: **No offense taken. I'm so sorry!**

Elena: **Literally after going super silent, she reappeared JUST to say she's taking a break from social.**

Elena: **It's all so weird.**

Me: **I've been noticing some weird vibes, too.**

I mean…yeah.

Elena: **Really?**

Me: **Yeah. I don't really know what's going on.**

Elena: **Well, I hope she's okay.**

Me: **I'm sure she's fine. She just kinda has a history of coming and going from social media.**

Elena: ☹ ☹ ☹

Me: **At least we met, though? I totally owe her for that.**

Elena: **Ugh, so true! If nothing else, this has been super great.**

Me: **I know what'll cheer you up.**

Elena: **PLEASE.**

Me: **You. Me. Tacos. Sunday!**

Elena: **YES!!!**

Elena: **Ugh. You're the best. I can't wait.**

If I'm going to hurt the girl, the least I can do is try to heal her, too.

Chapter Thirty-Five

"*Well, that was a* disaster," Becca mutters.

An older couple who had been considering adopting Cash came by One Fur All to meet him in person. The match seemed so promising: the two older gentlemen were retired (able to devote all their time to Cash!); athletic (perfectly capable of tiring Cash out!); and kind (willing to give Cash all the love he deserves!).

But one giant kiss from Cash and one half of the couple broke out in hives. Dog saliva allergy, apparently. A shock. Couldn't possibly adopt. Goodbye.

And now we're back at square one.

I groan. "We were *so* close."

"We won't give up just yet," Imani says. "We'll find something." When I look over at Cash in his kennel, he wags his tail at us hopefully. "In the meantime, I'm going to make some calls."

Becca and I nod, but once Imani's gone, I deflate. "This sucks."

"It really does," she agrees. "But...we could totally use this as an excuse to dress him up as a turkey and take new photos?"

I grin. "It's like you're reading my mind."

One extensive photo shoot with Cash, a meeting about the upcoming ball and its ticket sales (which are looking great!), and plenty of dog cuddles later, my shift is over, and I'm left to count down the minutes until Elena arrives—*here*, in *my* town.

We agree to meet downtown, so I occupy myself with my camera. There are some incredible new street murals that have just been painted and I've been dying to get some photos of them. They'd make a cool backdrop, I decide, but who should the subject be?

Since I'm alone, I guess it'll be me. I grab my tripod from my car and set up my camera, pull up the app on my phone that lets me take photos via Bluetooth, and pose. It's been a minute since I've taken any photos of myself, but I feel cute today.

"Okay, model!" a voice calls out.

My eyes land on Elena. She's in a mint-green sweater dress and matching leaf-shaped earrings. Suddenly there are butterflies in my stomach.

"Oh *please*," I say. But my lips tug into a small smile as I reach for my camera to take it off its tripod.

"Wait! Take one of us both first!" Elena says, joining me in front of the mural.

I'm taller than she is, so I prop an elbow on her shoulder like I'm leaning on her and we mug for the camera. She jumps on my back for another pose, and in the next we're laughing, hard, at the silliness.

"Want one of just you?" I offer.

"Sure!"

I slip my camera off the tripod and resume my preferred position behind the lens, getting a few candids of her smiling.

"Okay, make a funny face," I instruct. She wrinkles her nose and I snap. "Perfect. So cute."

"Stop." She's grinning. "Hi, by the way."

"Hi! I'm happy you're here." My voice is cheerful and light. Something about being around this girl is both exhilarating and low-key terrifying. I pack away the tripod and camera. "You ready for tacos?"

"I didn't drive all this way to *not* get tacos!" Elena says.

"Follow me."

After a quick pit stop at Grandma's car, where I stow my camera bag, I lead us toward where Holy Guacamole has parked today. We smell the garlic and onions before we see the truck, and Elena breathes it in. "Okay. I haven't even tasted anything yet and I'm already sold."

I smile at that. "See? I wouldn't lie to you."

Again, anyway.

We order a lot of tacos and some drinks, and I nod toward a little park. While Elena balances our food, I dig into my tote, pull out a blanket, and spread it out on the grass in front of us.

"Fancy," Elena teases.

I laugh. "Well, you did come all this way."

I sit down, and I'm surprised when Elena sidles up right beside me, cross-legged, so that our knees are touching. The smallest shiver runs down my spine. I do my best to ignore it by taking a taco from our shared plate.

Elena does, too, and I watch as she tastes it. She closes her eyes as the flavor hits, which is the kind of bliss any good food should bring to you.

"Well worth the drive," she proclaims. "Do you come to this place often?"

"Constantly. It drives around the area, so part of the fun is figuring out where it'll be. My friend Luis is convinced he was the one to discover it, but that's just him rewriting history; Marcus was actually the first. But we let Luis have this one. You know."

She nods, pushing a strand of her pink hair away from her rosy cheeks. "As good friends do." Then she peers at one of the tacos in particular. "What's that one?"

"This is a birria taco. Bite?" I hold it out to her.

Elena doesn't take it from me and instead leans in to taste it while the taco is still in my hands. Her mouth touches the tip of my thumb and I nearly jump back from the electricity that shoots through me.

"So good," she murmurs, and I wonder, just for a second, if she did that on purpose. It takes everything in me to pry my eyes away from her mouth, those lips, and regain my composure.

"My grandma said yes, by the way." I wipe my fingers on one of the napkins near me. "To the bonfire."

Elena playfully smacks my arm. "Why didn't you lead with that?!"

"I was distracted by tacos!" And your face, but I won't say that. "I'm really excited."

"Me too!" She practically squeals. "You'll get to meet all my friends and I know they're going to love you. Also: fires on the beach are just the best. It'll be fun."

"If you're there, I know it will," I say. She meets my gaze and holds it. I look away at the blanket beneath us. "So, uh, how's your sister doing?"

Not my smoothest line, but Elena and her sister have been fighting a lot, and it's all I could think to ask.

"She's okay. A little stressed over her finals," Elena says. "Kinda makes me dread the idea of going off to college."

"Well, it might be a little bit better if you're living on campus rather than still at home."

She rolls her eyes. "Tell that to Carys. I sometimes wish she'd picked a college that wasn't within driving distance so we could've had time apart and I'd have a chance to miss her."

"That's fair. I've always wondered what it would be like to have a sister. Or a sibling at all, really."

Elena takes a sip of her drink. "I thought you had a brother?"

"I do. But because we don't live together, I don't feel like we have that close relationship the way a lot of siblings do," I explain.

"I mean, not that living together is some guarantee that you're going to get along."

"Clearly," Elena jokes.

"Right. My best friend, Hari, doesn't really vibe with his brother, either. Still, though. I imagine living together makes you feel a little closer than not."

She nods. "Most definitely. As much as Carys drives me absolutely crazy, I also adore the shit out of her. We fight like hell and then two seconds later, drive off together to go shopping or she'll be in my room helping me package sticker orders. We're all over the place, but I think it's mostly out of love. I'd actually be pretty devastated if she went away for college."

"Totally. Sometimes I just feel like I barely know my own brother, you know?" I shake my head. "The most we've talked recently has been when my parents made this whole new room for me in their house and it was, like, not my style at all, and we both thought it was a little much. But we don't really talk other than that."

"Could you start?" Elena asks. "I mean, easy for me to say, I know. But you're both old enough now that you could probably start working on a relationship that's separate from your parents."

I consider this. "I guess we could do that."

"I mean, I'm not trying to say it'd be so easy. It would take work, like any relationship. Might be worth it, though."

Yeah. I think it would. I smile at her. "You're kinda smart, you know that?"

"I was actually a child prodigy," she whispers.

"Shut up!"

She grins. "I swear! I was in classes for the gifted and everything!"

My eyebrows rise; I'm amused. "I had no idea I was in the presence of such greatness."

"I'm an enigma," she says, pleased with herself. "So, what should we do next?"

I laugh a little to myself. "I set us up with something stupid."

Elena grins. "I *love* stupid."

"How do you feel about escape rooms?"

♥

Chapter Thirty-Six

My mouth hurts from all the smiling I did around Elena.

Your girl has a serious crush. (So, bisexuality confirmed.)

I practically float through the week, revisiting small moments: our knees brushing, an accidental mouth on my thumb, texting each other something and saying *this made me think of you,* loaded glances across a silly escape room. I'm already daydreaming about getting to see her again at the bonfire. The dizziness of those feelings makes other parts of my life feel boring by comparison.

But I make it through Thanksgiving with the fam. It goes fine, as far as mandatory-family-holidays-that-celebrate-colonizers go. I make it through another week of school, which also goes fine. And I make it through another week of Max's account being up, *without* catastrophe.

Finally, it's Bonfire-With-Elena Day.

After school, I hurry through my shift at work, then speed home so I can get ready to leave for Corona del Mar State Beach— two and a half hours away, not including LA traffic.

Thankfully, I've already laid out what I'll wear: high-waisted black jeans, a cropped sweatshirt with a jean jacket over it, and Doc Martens. I get dressed and put my big hoop earrings on, then pull my hair back into two buns, with my baby hairs laid down. Thanks to a YouTube makeup tutorial, I've got some mascara, eyeliner, and a little Sugar and Spice on, too. I bring my camera bag with me—partly so I can take some photos of the night, and partly because it'll give me something to do with my hands.

My stomach is doing somersaults the entire drive up and I question so much about what I'm wearing, what we'll do, what I'll say, whether Elena's friends will like me, if we'll be able to successfully avoid talking about Max, how this whole night will go.

When I near the beach, I text Elena.

Me: **Almost there!**

Elena: **OMG yay!!!**

Elena: **We're leaving in a few so I'll see you soon?**

Me: **Can't wait!**

Elena: **ME NEITHER!**

Elena: **Text me when you get here so I can come grab you!**

It doesn't take long.

I spot her before she spots me. The pink hair makes it easy, and she waves both hands excitedly when she sees me. I wave back, a bit shyly, and tuck my phone into my back pocket.

As she nears, I take in everything about her all over again: long pastel hair in mussed, beachy waves, as if she's been lounging on the shore all day; lips in a nude matte lipstick; and freckles, out in full force. They're so prominent and cute, tiny kisses from the sun. She's wearing an oversized sweatshirt the color of a primrose with a white collared shirt peeking out and it's paired with a pleated skirt, tights, and some fresh high-top Converse.

I'm overtaken by the urge to wrap my arms around her.

Instead, I say, "Hi! You look so *good*. Like, really, really good."

I know I'm gushing, but I don't even care.

"Why, thank you!" Elena smiles so big at me and does a little twirl. "*You* look so good!" My insides turn to mush at the compliment. Before I can thank her, she reaches for the collar of my jean jacket. "So smart of you to wear a jacket, too. It's going to get cold later."

"Yeah," is all I can manage, her fingers grazing my neck.

"I want you to meet everyone," she says, leading me toward a crowd of people our age. "We've staked out the best bonfire spot."

Elena runs up to someone and grabs their arm, interrupting the conversation and pulling them toward me. "Kat," Elena says. "This is my absolute best friend in the whole wide world, Vanessa."

"The universe," Vanessa corrects.

"Right, the universe. Vanessa, this is Kat, the girl I've been telling you about!"

Vanessa's eyes flit over me, as if able to read who I am just with a glance. She extends a hand to me. "This girl has been talking about you *a lot.*"

I feel my cheeks flush and Elena waves a hand. "Ignore her!"

"It's so nice to meet you, Vanessa. I've heard only the best things about you, for real." I take her hand and shake.

Vanessa shrugs. "I am a gift."

"I love your look," I say, meaning it. She somehow manages to be both menacing and adorable in her way-too-big-sweater paired with a choker, black lipstick, black nails, and a tattooed clavicle.

At that, Vanessa gives me a smirk. "Same." To Elena, she says, "But who wears combat boots to the beach?" I sheepishly glance down at my shoes and when I look back up, Vanessa is gone, once again talking to the tall, adorable, flower-crown-adorned brown boy she'd been with when I arrived.

Elena laughs and looks at me. "She's like this with everyone. I promise Vanessa is thrilled you're here. And I like the boots."

Elena introduces me to a few others, starting with the person Vanessa had been talking to, named Javier; Javier's boyfriend, Angel; a girl Elena describes as "everyone's favorite pint-sized lesbian," Samantha; and a soft-spoken Black girl I immediately take a liking to named Harmony.

I am surprised by how truly kind and welcoming this group is, just as Elena promised. I mean, aside from Vanessa, who is giving me some well-deserved side eye. Respect.

The fire is already roaring, emanating heat. But the camping chairs are all spoken for. "Where should I sit? I didn't bring anything."

"With me!" Elena gestures to a checkered blanket. "We can share it."

"Not that we'll be sitting all night," Angel interjects. He bends down to rifle through his leather backpack and retrieves some Bluetooth speakers. "Because we need to dance."

Javier reaches for his phone. "Ooh, let me pick!"

"Obviously," Angel says.

And moments later, music pours from the speakers and Javier starts to twerk.

"Is this twerking music?" Vanessa asks, skeptically.

"It is now," Javier says.

"He's obviously been enjoying Sunny a little too much," Harmony quips.

I raise both eyebrows at her. "Sunny?" She points to a bottle of sunscreen.

"Only our best friend," Javier explains. Then he cups a hand on the side of his mouth and adds in a loud whisper. "It's not really sunscreen."

We laugh and Elena holds up a tube. "This is ours." She unscrews the cap and takes a sip, then holds it to me. I take a drink without thinking, eager to calm my nerves. I'm jittery as hell and I can't help it. Elena looks so beautiful, and I really, really want her friends to like me.

The playlist suddenly switches to a reggaeton song I recognize as one of Luis's favorites. Javier whoops. "This playlist is soooo good!"

"Didn't *you* make it?" Elena asks, laughing.

He grins. "That's *why* it's so good!"

And it *is* so good. So good that, slowly, most everyone abandons their seats and begins to dance in the sand. Javier holds out a hand to Elena and pulls her into the thick of it. She glances back at me, urging me to join with her eyes, so I follow.

As it turns out, Javier can actually dance and he puts the rest of us to absolute shame, but that's okay because we're having fun anyway. The movement keeps us nice and toasty as the sun slowly sinks to kiss the ocean. It's a breathtaking sight, really, made all the better by the laughter and the dancing and the closeness to Elena. Every so often, her hand will brush against mine or she'll shimmy into me. The contact feels like lightning.

"I need some water," Vanessa announces suddenly. "I left my water bottle in the car. Kat, come with?"

I hesitate, but Elena smiles and turns to cheer for Harmony in a dance-off against Javier, so I nod. "Okay, sure."

We start to walk toward the parking lot, the chill in the air deepening the farther we get from the fire. It's night now, the last of the sunset almost gone. I make an attempt at small talk. "Javier is really good, huh?"

"Mmhmm," Vanessa replies.

"And the music is super great."

"Yep."

After a moment, I venture, "I'm so glad you all let me come."

She gives me a tight smile. "Well, my vote on that was vetoed."

That catches me by surprise. "Oh."

Vanessa doesn't speak again until we've reached Elena's Bug. Then she turns to me. "Here's the thing. I find it all a little odd."

I swallow. "What do you mean?"

"It's just weird, right? Elena stumbles upon this freshly created account for someone named Max Monroe and is, like, smitten."

My heart starts pounding at the dreaded mention of Max. "I mean, yeah, Max is this beautiful girl and Elena falls really easily. That's her fatal flaw, really—that and how trusting she is. I can say that because I'm her best friend."

"Right. Of course."

"Soooo, obviously, when she shared some of the posts with me, I did my research. Only Max Monroe living in Bakersfield is eerily absent from Google. Like, what the hell? Is she living in witness protection or something? A *murderer*?"

I let out a nervous laugh. "I really doubt that..."

Vanessa narrows her dark eyes at me. "Well, *you've* obviously met her. You're her trusted photographer. Yet Max wouldn't even entertain the idea of meeting up with Elena, she was completely resistant to FaceTime, and after a couple of weeks taking up a lot of Elena's emotional energy, she basically disappeared. Then *you* show up in her place. Saying all the right things. Comforting her. Making her laugh. It's a pretty big coincidence, if you ask me. And I'm not trying to see my best friend's senior year get fucked up by someone playing games. So, what gives, Kat?"

Panic sets in. I run through so many things I'd like to say—*lies, lies, lies*—but nothing feels right. I should've expected this possibility, but I didn't. I was too busy thinking about seeing Elena again, maybe holding her hand, kissing her.

"I can see how it might look weird," I begin.

Vanessa crosses her arms. "Right."

"It's just that..." Think, Kat. Think! And suddenly, I'm blurting out, "She's got horrible acne."

Vanessa looks taken aback and, frankly, I am, too. "Acne? Like, she's scared to show her face kind of thing?"

"Yep! I edit the crap out of all her pictures—at her request, of course. But she's sooo embarrassed about it. She'd kill me if she knew I was sharing this, actually," I explain. "And Monroe is her middle name. She really didn't want anyone to be able to Google her and see real photos of her. So, yeah."

At this, Vanessa frowns. "Oh. That's…really sad, actually."

"It really is," I agree. "I keep telling her she doesn't need to do this, but…"

Vanessa taps her chin, looking at me closely, and I see her skepticism return. Lots and lots of skepticism.

"I know this is a lot. For what it's worth, I've stopped associating with Max, too. And I'm sorry for whatever she's done. I really am," I say. "But I would never intentionally hurt Elena. I like her too much."

And there it is. The truth.

She squints at me. "Okay," she says, slowly. "At the end of the day, Elena is her own person and she can do what she wants. But I will absolutely kill you if you hurt her."

"Consider me as good as dead if I do."

"Good." Vanessa ducks into Elena's car and retrieves her water bottle. Then she locks up and nods toward the beach.

As we walk, she says, "Oh. One more thing."

"Yes?" I ask.

Vanessa grins sweetly at me. "If you ever hear from *Max* again, tell her she's a fucking asshole."

"There you are!" Elena shouts when she sees the two of us nearing the bonfire. "Have you been grilling Kat?"

Vanessa's hand goes to her mouth, which opens in mock surprise. "Me? I would never!"

Elena tsks Vanessa, pointing a finger, and then grabs my arm. "You probably need more to drink after that."

"*Please,*" I murmur.

"Come on." Elena pulls me over to her blanket and sits down. I sit beside her, but a little farther away than I normally would, stuck between being terrified of Vanessa and thrilled to be back near Elena. She closes the space between us by scooting toward me. "It's *freezing*. We need body heat!"

"We can get closer to the fire?" I suggest, glancing over at Vanessa. But she's sitting beside Samantha, who has pulled out some nail polish and is repainting Vanessa's nails.

"No," Elena says. "We don't need it."

I look over at her, the glow from the fire illuminating her delicate features. "Here." I shrug off my jean jacket.

"Oh, you don't have to," she says, but I'm already handing it to her. We're about the same size and I know it'll fit. Elena tugs it on and snuggles into it, like it's a cozy blanket. "Thank you."

Our eyes meet and suddenly the conversation I had with Vanessa is gone. All I feel is the urge to reach over and kiss Elena.

"Let's play a game!" Javier suddenly shouts.

Moment over.

"What kind of game?" Samantha asks.

"No, no games," Harmony insists. "The last time we played a game on the beach, y'all ended up burying me in the sand and *abandoning* me."

"Oh my God, you're so dramatic," Angel says. "It was for, like, a second! We just went to get Popsicles! And we *brought you one!*"

Harmony crosses her arm. "It felt like an eternity."

"Fine! How about telling ghost stories?" Javier offers.

"Halloween is way over," Samantha scoffs.

"Ghost stories are good year-round!" Elena insists. "Let's do that."

Angel shoots his hand up in the air. "I've got one!"

"Ooh, yes, babe!" Javier grabs Angel's hand. "Terrify us."

"Okay, so, when I was like, nine years old or something, I was having a really hard time going to bed. At the time, we were living in this one-story house except for mine and my little brother Junior's room, which was up in the attic."

"Already creepy," Harmony says. "Go on."

Angel gives her a knowing look. "Tell me about it. So, Juni and I are in our beds, and we had, like, this old decrepit rocking horse in the corner of the room, which I always thought was stupid spooky. The house is dead silent, pitch-black, so I can't see much. But my eyes are open and I'm staring at the ceiling. All of a sudden, out of the corner of my eye, I see the rocking horse start to gently rock back and forth, back and forth, back and forth."

"Ugh, no!" Samantha squeals.

"It's soo subtle at first, I swear I'm imagining things. I can't even bring myself to really look, right? But then, I swear to God, the horse starts to rock harder, and it starts to move!"

"Hate this," Harmony says.

"Dead-ass! It went aaaaall the way across the room till it knocked into our desk and then just stopped completely. But I know I wasn't imagining it because the sound of it bumping into the desk startled Juni awake!"

Elena gasps, grabbing my arm. "This is terrible! Keep going."

Her holding on to my arm definitely isn't terrible, though. I put my hand over hers and look over at Angel. "Then what happened?!"

"I tried to be tough and just told Juni to go back to sleep but then buried myself under the covers because I was so scared I wanted to pee myself. I barely slept that night, I swear, but come morning, the horse was back in its regular spot—like it had never happened. I thought I dreamt it," Angel says. "But then, I went downstairs for breakfast, and my ma was so pissed at me. She was like, 'I heard y'all doing God-knows-what upstairs last night. There was so much creaking you kept me up!' So, she obviously heard whoever—or *what*ever—it was messing with the rocking horse."

Javier shrieks and shakes his hands in front of him. "Babe! You never told me this!"

246

"Because it's scary! I'm not even done! That night, same thing happens. Slow rocking back and forth of the horse, till it got so violent."

"Then what?!" Harmony demands.

"And then BOOM!" Angel claps his hands together and we all jump. "The horse knocks itself the hell over. Mami comes running upstairs and turns on the light."

Vanessa leans in. "Aaaaand?!"

A grave look passes over Angel's face. "And...the horse is splayed out, and when Mami moved it upright, she said she knew it was one of us messing around because the handles were warm like we'd been touching it. But we hadn't!"

"Oh my God," Samantha murmurs.

"I know! I know. Neither one of us had gone near that wretched thing, yet here was Mami, saying it was warm to the touch. We were hoping it was nothing, that we'd imagined things, or maybe that our cat, Chico, was playing with it and doing something stupid. Anything but the terrifying realization that there was nothing in the room except for me and Juni and whatever was playing with that terrifying horse!" He shivers, as if a chill is running down his spine. "That same night, I swear we heard the sound of giggles, but in the morning, after we swore up and down it wasn't us, Mami took the horse to the curb." He makes a cross over his chest. "Gracias a dios."

"And you never found out what it was?" I ask, wide-eyed.

Angel shakes his face. "Nope. But sometimes I still wake up in the middle of the night and feel like I hear creaking."

We let out a collective yell—part terror, part thrill, part disbelief, part holy-shit-your-rocking-horse-was-haunted.

As we collect ourselves, Javier shakes his head. "I can't believe you never told me that!"

"It's terrifying, and we both know you're a scaredy-cat, babe."

That earns Angel a playful nudge from Javier, and some good-natured teasing from the others.

"Well, now that I'm thoroughly spooked, I'm too scared to go to the bathroom alone," Harmony says. "Anyone want to come?"

Vanessa and Samantha hop up while Javier and Angel say they'll stay by the fire.

"You want anything?" Elena asks me.

"Nah," I say.

She leans in toward me. "Good. Let's go for a walk."

"Won't you be cold?"

She smiles at me. "In your jacket? Never."

I get to my feet and hold out a hand to help her up. She takes it, and we don't drop hands once she's standing. My heartbeat quickens.

She leads the way toward one of the rock formations, the waves lapping on the sand beneath the mass of stone. "Careful not to get too close to the water. It's like ice," she warns.

"You say that like you know from experience."

She sighs. "I may have been dared to jump in the water last fall. And I may have stupidly agreed to do it."

I laugh. "Why on earth would you agree to that?!"

"I take dares *very* seriously," she says, giving me a beady look. "Oh! I wonder if it's still there? Follow me!"

Before I can ask, Elena is racing off ahead of me. I jog after her and find her squatting near one of the rocks.

"What're you doing?"

Elena points, and I look to where her index finger is. "That's me!"

"E-B-P?" I ask.

"Elena Brynn Powell," she explains. "And yes, I drew a heart around my own initials. Self-love and all."

I grin. "Here for it."

"What's your middle name?"

"Isabel. So, Katherine Isabel Sanchez. *K-I-S.*" The letters are so close to a word I've been thinking of all night that I feel my cheeks flush, especially when Elena's gaze meets mine. I change the subject. "This sky is so beautiful right now." I lean against a spur of rock and tilt my head toward the sky. It's a cloudless night, and the twinkling stars are clear in the dark abyss.

"It is," Elena says, looking up, too. "But if you *really* want to see the sky, Joshua Tree is supposed to be incredible."

"That's on my list!" I exclaim. "Just haven't had time to go yet."

It's so peaceful being here, like this. Elena; laughter and music in the distance; the sound of waves rolling in. It almost makes me wish I had my camera on me so I could capture this moment—her and me and the ocean and whatever's happening. But maybe it's even better without the distraction.

"I'm really glad you invited me out tonight," I say quietly.

She meets my gaze. "I'm really glad you came."

Whether it's the way she's staring at me—so intently, so deeply—or the chilly air, I don't know, but I can't stop a visible shiver from snaking down my spine.

"Cold?"

"Just a little," I admit. She takes off my jacket and holds it out. "No, I'm good! You keep it."

"How about...?" Elena doesn't finish the rest of her sentence, but just moves in to drape the jacket over my shoulders. I glance down at the sand, then up at her: her eyes, her freckles, her mouth. "So, Katherine Isabel Sanchez?"

I nod slowly. She leans closer to me.

"*K-I-S...S...*," she whispers.

My breath catches in my throat. I can feel my heartbeat pulsing in the tips of my fingers.

Elena gently tugs the collar of the jacket—and me—toward her.

I bring my lips to hers.

It's a tentative kiss at first—unsure, a little awkward as we find our footing, but so *sweet*. I find my hands on her hips, pulling her closer. It's Elena who deepens the kiss, and I feel dizzy, tasting her, breathing in her scent with its faint hint of citrus.

I pull back first, all nerves and tingling energy and giddiness. A serene smile crosses her face, and we both laugh. "I've been wanting to do that all night," I admit.

She wrinkles her nose at me. So adorable. "Me too."

I eye her. "Dare you to do it again."

She grins, but doesn't hesitate. Her mouth meets mine, and I'm trembling all over, reaching up to hold either side of her face.

In the distance, I hear a call for Elena, and we finally, reluctantly separate.

"We should probably get back," I whisper, breathless.

Elena touches her nose to mine. "I guess so. But only if I can have your jacket back."

I grin at her, shrugging it off and handing it over. "It's yours."

Elena smiles at me—sweet, sparkling, blissful.

I hold out my hand. She doesn't hesitate to lock her fingers in mine.

Chapter Thirty-Seven

I am glowing the entire ride home, my body is tingling from head to toe.

Two kisses weren't enough.

But they have to be, for now. Because in order to make it home at a decent hour, I had to leave shortly after Elena and I went back to the bonfire with playful smiles and intertwined hands.

Grandma and Grandpa are already in bed when I get home, thankfully, so I am able to go to my room and text Elena in peace.

And maybe take a cold shower.

She's still at the beach when she writes me back, sending a photo of Javier juggling their now-empty sunscreen bottles, and I'm sorry to be missing out.

Elena: **Wish you were here.**

Me: **I wish I was there, too.**

Me: **My heart is still racing.**

Elena: **TELL ME ABOUT IT.**

Me: **You didn't tell me you were such a good kisser?**

Elena: **I know some things.** ☺

Elena: **Oh, God. That was terrible.**

And I laugh out loud.

Me: 💀

Me: **I'm dead.**

Me: **But still into you.**

Elena: **From beyond the grave?**

Me: **Boo!**

Elena: **Tooootally into you too. Even if you're a ghost.**

Elena: **As if THAT wasn't obvious.**

Elena: **Shit, we're about to leave and I'm driving.**

Me: **Drive safe. Text me when you get home?**

Elena: **Promise.**

I lie in bed an absolute giggly, ecstatic, delighted mess. While I wait for Elena to text me that she's made it home all right, I go through some of the photos we snapped tonight. She and I took one of just the two of us in front of the bonfire, flushed, but so happy, fire blazing behind us. We also got a couple of group shots, with Javier insisting we hold him up so he could drape his whole body across our arms. He even let me try on his flower crown and took a photo of me. I make that my new profile picture on IG and share some of my favorite shots, selecting the one of me and Elena as the first.

A text comes in not long after from Elena.

Elena: **Home safe. ♥**

Me: **Sweet dreams. ♥**

Elena: **The sweetest.**

* * *

In the morning, I wake and immediately text Elena.

Me: **Good morning. How'd you sleep?**

Elena: **Soooo good.**

Elena: **How about you?**

Me: **The best sleep I've had in a really long time.**

Elena: **I do have that power.**

Me: **Like magic.**

Elena: **We should kiss more, no? Since it has so many benefits?**

Elena: **I mean, sleep is really important.**

Me: **Oh, of course. It would be for my health.**

Elena: **Today???**

Me: **I have work. ☹**

Elena: **Noooooooooo**

Elena: **Fine. Guess you'll just have to wait!**

Me: **It'll be worth it.**

Elena: **It better be.**

Grinning from what feels like ear to ear, I get ready for the day and head to work. But make no mistake: there is a whole lotta pep in my step. I'm cheerful AF.

"Good morning!" I practically sing when I arrive.

Becca eyes me as I settle into my desk. "Someone's in a good mood."

I sigh. "The best mood."

She swivels her chair to face me. "Okay, spill."

"There's a girl," I say, smiling.

Becca claps her hands. "Tell me *everything*."

The joyful smile that spreads across her face—and her genuine interest in what's going on in my life right now—tugs at my heart. If she only knew. But I can't go there right now.

I gush about Elena instead. Becca listens and reacts at all the right places. And then she asks, "So, how'd you meet?"

Oof. Well...

"On Instagram," I say simply. "Enough about me, though. What have you been up to lately?"

She tells me about how she absolutely can't wait to be done with the fall semester; how she spent Thanksgiving at Cora's house and got to meet Cora's super-hot boyfriend; how she's talking to someone from her marketing class. Once we've caught up, we get to work on some of the marketing for the winter ball. But I find it hard to focus, picking up my phone every so often to text Elena.

While Becca is in the middle of having me read over an email she's just written, I hear Imani's voice call from her office. "Kat? Can you come here?"

"Oooh," Becca teases.

I stick my tongue out at her and head to Imani's office. "Hi," I say, lingering in the doorway. "What can I help with?"

She looks away from her computer and gives me a smile, gesturing to the chair on the other side of her desk. "Actually, can you sit for a second?"

I take a seat. "Sure."

"So, there's something I wanted to talk to you about. It's about Cash."

"Oh?" I ask. "Is he okay?"

"Yes, yes. I should've started with that. Sorry," Imani says. "Cash is totally fine. As goofy and adorable as ever. But, as you know, he has had a real hell of a time trying to find a good home."

"I know. Poor thing."

"We've had almost no bites, despite him being a truly lovely and wonderful dog. I've been giving this a lot of thought and...well, I've decided that we're going to make use of our match program and send him to another shelter, one where his chances of being adopted are much higher than here." Imani keeps her voice soft when she says the next thing. "So, he'll be leaving us soon. I wanted you to hear it from me because I know you're very attached to him."

Instantly, tears start to well in my eyes at the thought of Cash being shipped to another area of the country—alone, having to start all over, without a guaranteed home. Without any of us there to help him. Without me.

"But Imani, there has to be another way," I choke out.

Imani smiles sadly at me. "I've tried to think of some other way, I really have. But there are just too many pits in the system in Southern California. There's a stigma against them, they're one of the least-adopted breeds, most apartment complexes prohibit them...It makes placing one really hard. And it isn't fair to Cash to keep him here on a hope and a prayer. He deserves a real life, a real home, and a real family."

"Maybe I can adopt him," I blurt out.

"That's very sweet of you, Kat, but you know the adoption age is eighteen."

"I can ask my parents again?" I suggest, even though I highly doubt they'd say yes. And when I asked Grandma and Grandpa ages ago, it was a gentle but firm no. (Grandma is pretty uncomfortable with big dogs.) But I'm desperate.

"I don't want you to do that," Imani says. "And I've even considered adopting him myself, but I have three, plus the kids."

"Right," I say. "That would be a lot."

"We gave it our best effort, Kat. You should be proud of how much you did for him. It would have been nice to have him live locally, so we could keep in touch, but ultimately he'll do better somewhere else."

I swipe at a tear as it falls down my cheek. "I understand," I manage.

"Oh, Kat." Imani reaches for a tissue box and hands it to me.

"Can we just have until the winter ball?" I ask. "That's almost here. It'll also give me a chance to spend some more time with him." She sits back in her chair, thinking this over. "Please. I promise, if he doesn't get adopted by then, I'll personally help you with whatever it is we need to do for him. Just—please."

"Well..." She sighs. "Okay."

I leap from my chair and rush around her desk before she can stop me. "Thank you, Imani! Thank you," I say, giving her a hug.

She smiles. "You're welcome. Now back to work for the doggos."

I join Becca back at our desk and she asks if I'm all right. I get choked up again as I explain, and Becca—bless her—quickly offers to take on more responsibility for the ball, so I can try to come up with new ways to get Cash's story out there.

I spend the rest of the afternoon posting features of Cash on the One Fur All social pages. Aside from that, I start to work on a more heartfelt, personal post about Cash, including all the special things I love about him and why he would make a good addition to any home. I include quirky things to know; specific instructions for giving him the perfect belly rubs and ear scratches; treats he loves; everything.

Before I leave for the day, I stop in to say hello to Cash and give him lots of kisses.

* * *

Elena and I FaceTime after my drive home and I tell her all about Cash. She asks if there's anything she can do and I promise I'll tell her if I can think of anything.

I also text Hari, Luis, and Marcus to fill them in, as I know they each took a liking to Cash, too. (Maybe not so much Luis, but he can deal.) I beg them to ask around and see if they may know of anyone looking for a dog.

I text Pop juuuust to double-check that they're good on dogs.

Me: **So, remember when I asked if you wanted to add a three-legged dog to your legion of pups?**

Pop: **How can I forget? You made us look at pictures of that dog all night! Super cute.**

Me: **He is! Are you sure you don't want to adopt him?**

Pop: **Your mother would kill me.**

Ugh, fine. I even ask Grandma once more, just in case, and she very generously offers to "think about it." Which is totally a no.

Hari texts me separately a little while later.

Hari: **I'm sorry, dude. I know Cash is your favorite.**

Me: **Thank you.** ⊕

Me: **If you can think of anything, let me know.**

Hari: **I definitely will!**

I'm determined to do something. If I need to dedicate the next couple of weeks to this, then so be it. Cash is *going* to get adopted. That's a promise.

Chapter Thirty-Eight

I'm due to meet up with the boys for Photography Club. When it became clear we didn't have a solid plan for our outing, I offered to take the lead. Borrowing Grandma's car for the day, I make a quick stop at the store, load up on tons of snacks and drinks, then drive to One Fur All. When I get there, I enter through the visitor entrance rather than the employee entrance.

Jin grins when he sees me. "Hi, Kat! Whatcha doing here, girl?"

"I'm just a visitor this morning," I say. "I want to take Cash on a field trip for the afternoon."

These dog field trips are something Imani allows with trusted volunteers. It's a way to get the dogs away from the shelter for a bit, usually to explore a new park or spend an afternoon lounging at the volunteer's home. Today, though, I'd like to take a small road trip with Cash—a little for him, a little for me.

"Well, you know we have very strict guidelines for volunteers here. We don't let just anyone take our dogs for the day," Jin explains, playfully raising both eyebrows at me. "Do you think you're qualified for this?"

I suck in some air and make a face like I'm nervous. "God, I don't know. I hope so!"

Jin reaches for a clipboard with paperwork and holds it out in front of him. He grabs a pen, clicking it dramatically, and clucks his tongue. "I will put my professional reputation on the line and trust you. Name?"

"Katherine Sanchez," I say.

"Okay." He scribbles my name down, then glances at me and narrows his eyes skeptically. "Reason for this sign-out today?"

I clear my throat and lean in toward his desk. "I'm planning a heist."

Jin snaps his fingers and nods enthusiastically. "Right, right, right. Okay. Well, everything seems to be in order, then." He whips the clipboard toward me and I see that he's just scribbled HAVE FUN across the application in giant letters. "Enjoy!"

"Thank you, Jin!" I say with a grin. A few polite hellos to colleagues and a quick bathroom break (for Cash) later, the two of us are in my grandma's car, ready to go. I roll down the windows a touch so Cash can enjoy the breeze on this gorgeous morning.

I start the car and then turn to him. "We're going to have ourselves a day." He looks at me and wags his tail, his behind moving side to side, too, and I laugh. "Yes! Loving this energy, Cash."

We head to Hari's. He starts to laugh when he walks toward my car, noting the passenger.

"I see why you volunteered to plan today's activities. Marcus loves dogs and all, but he'd *never* let Cash in Honey," he says through the rolled-down window.

"Get in!"

Hari motions for Cash to scoot to the middle so he can sit in the passenger seat. For the first time ever, I am thankful for Grandma's beast of a car: Hari, Cash, and I can easily all fit in the front, with plenty of room for Marcus and Luis in the back.

"Should we go pick them up?" I ask. "And, full disclosure: I may use this as a chance to fill them in on—well, everything."

Hari gives me a thoughtful smile. "I think that's a great idea. I'll text them and let them know we're on our way."

We drive across town and grab Marcus, and I fill the boys in on my plan. We'll take Cash with us down to Wind Wolves

Preserve—which is still in Bakersfield, but far—and take lots of photos. I tell him it'll be good for Cash *and* for us, but Marcus hardly needs an explanation.

"I've got free snacks, a dog to pet, we're heading somewhere beautiful, and I don't have to drive? That's a win for me," Marcus says.

But when we get to Luis's house, he refuses to get inside the car.

"Oh, come *on*!" I urge.

"Absolutely not. I am not about to be trapped in this metal box with that huge beast," Luis argues.

Marcus covers Cash's ears. "Yo, do not call him a beast. He is a gentle little baby."

"Why's he even here?!"

"We're giving him a nice day away from the shelter. We're going to do some of his favorite things. I even brought his favorite toy." I hold up a weathered tennis ball.

Luis arches an eyebrow. "*It* has favorite things?"

"He," Hari corrects.

"Whatever," Luis says.

"Yes, he does. He likes parks and running and exploring, and since we're going to be outside anyway to take some photos, I don't see why he can't come," I say. "This is what I have planned for the club meeting today. Take it or leave it."

Luis shrugs at me from outside the car. "Leave it."

"Wrong answer," Marcus says. "As president of Photography Club, I believe I called this a mandatory meeting. All of its members must attend."

Hari points at Marcus. "The man has a point."

Luis shakes his heads and throws his hands up in the air, a mix of frustration and defeat. "Ugh. Fine! But tell him to stay in the front." He climbs into the backseat and Cash immediately turns around to sniff at him. "Ugh!"

The drive takes about an hour. When we arrive, Cash is teeming with excitement. He hardly lets me leash him before he's bounding toward a small river, splashing and lapping up the cold water.

Wind Wolves Preserve is sprawling and picturesque: yellow fields of grass and brome rise to rolling hills that ripple off into the distance. In the spring, the wildflowers here seem to go on for miles, vibrant petals dancing in the breeze. It's a different kind of beautiful in late autumn, one of faded greens, browns, and yellows, but beautiful nonetheless. I chose this place so Cash could enjoy a wide-open California valley, possibly for the last time before being sent to another part of the country. Here, he can run around, sniff at wildlife, and live his best life.

Plus, there are *tons* of great spots, so the park is prime for photos. Our latest assignment in Mr. Griffin's art class is to take portraits of each other, and we can easily get those here.

We let Cash take the lead. He's darting all over, so strong it sometimes feels like he might yank my arm out of its socket. I give him a few treats, remind him of his commands ("Heel," "Easy"), and after a while, he starts to relax a little.

"Damn, that vista." Marcus points to the horizon. "We need to take our portraits up there. Come on."

He takes Cash's leash from me and we follow him up a trail that ends in an overlook. It's not yet noon, so the light isn't too harsh, and there are a few valley oaks for shade: decent conditions for photos, though not ideal by any means.

When we reach the top, it's breathtaking—a panorama of endless golden slopes. I sit with Cash while the boys take turns snapping portraits of each other, and then it's my turn. They each snap a shot of me, and then I take a photo of each of them.

As I return Marcus's camera, I ask, "Will you take one of me with Cash? He'll only sit still for a few seconds at a time, but I know you love a challenge."

"Absolutely. Prepare for the best photo of that dog you've ever seen," he answers. "You have my advance permission to print and frame it at the shelter."

I roll my eyes, but we start off together, moving away from the other boys for our mini-shoot. Ever the professional, Marcus asks, "What're you envisioning for this?"

"I just want a nice photo or two of me with Cash. If this is going to be the last time I get to spend time with him for—" I can't bring myself to finish the word: *forever.* I try again. "It would just be nice to have."

Marcus gives me an understanding nod. "You have that tennis ball?" I retrieve it from my canvas bag and hold it up. "Play fetch and pretend I'm not here. I gotchu."

I nod back, then dangle the tennis ball in front of Cash. "Ready, Cashy? Go get it!"

He chases after his beloved toy and brings it back to me. We go back and forth like this for a while, until he takes his toy and unexpectedly jogs over to Luis. Luis is thoroughly disgusted by the slobbered-on tennis ball, so Hari scoops it up and tosses it.

"How about some of those tricks you've been working on?" Hari asks.

"Oh, we've got tricks, all right." I command Cash to show off some of our newest: roll over, high five, and shake—all impressive, but I save the best for last. "Dance!"

Cash hops up on both hind legs and wobbles around. I think it looks charming. I even go on and make a total fool of myself by joining him, sticking one of my arms in the air to match his.

The sight of this makes Luis, Hari, and Marcus erupt into laughter.

"I think that might've been the winner," Marcus announces.

Luis shakes his head, amused. "You're such a weirdo, Sanchez."

"And yet this is probably the least-weird thing I've done

recently," I say with a laugh. "Anyway, should we head to the car for some snacks?"

Luis takes off without another word.

We follow, and Marcus gives me a soft smile. "I got a lot of good ones, Kat. I think you'll be happy."

I return the smile. "Thank you."

Back in the car, chip bags crinkle, sodas are unscrewed, and the heat is turned on. After a very sweet photo shoot, an impromptu dance party, and a lot of laughing, I figure now's as good a time as ever.

I clear my throat. "So, yeah, speaking of weird things. I have some stuff I'd like to tell you guys."

My gaze meets Hari's. He gives me an encouraging nod. Luis and Marcus deserve to know what's up, and frankly, I could use their advice and support.

"Please tell me it's Sno-Caps," Luis says.

"Ew, no, it's not Sno-Caps. You like those?"

Luis gives me a sheepish grin. "I doooo."

I shake my head. "No. It's not a food, period. It's, like, information about my life."

He waves a hand toward me. "Eh, pass."

"Ugh. Fine. I'll just tell Marcus then." I turn to him. "So, you know how you guys have been on my case about my obsession with my phone?"

"Mmhmm," Marcus mumbles, biting into a chip.

"Well, it's because I stole someone's face."

He nearly chokes. "I'm sorry, *what?*"

"Don't just drop that bomb!" Hari interjects. "Start at the beginning!"

"Okay, so...I may have had a really bad night a few weeks ago...and instead of engaging in more *typical* self-destructive behavior, I took some of the photos I'd had of Becca, and... well..." I inhale. "I made a fake Instagram account named Max, started sorta-kinda unintentionally catfishing a girl *as* Max, then met up with that girl as *me,* pretended we both mutually knew Max, had Max ghost that girl while simultaneously texting her as me, got totally sprung on her, kissed her, kissed her again, and continued to work with Becca as if I didn't steal her image after she has explicitly told me she has *no* interest in being on social media *ever.* Oh, and instead of deleting the account, like Hari advised me, I've just kinda done nothing with it and it's still there!" I look to Hari. "Does that about cover it?"

He nods. "Yeah, think you nailed that."

Marcus is nodding, wide-eyed, long after I'm done talking, like he can't quite process all that. Which is...very fair.

"Hold up," Luis says finally.

"I thought you weren't listening?" Hari teases.

"Well, I did, and now I gotta know. You told Hari all this, but you've been keeping it from us?" Luis is scowling at me. "That... sucks."

I wince. But he's not wrong. "Yeah. It does suck."

He crosses his arms. "We're supposed to be your friends, Sanchez."

"You are my friends," I insist. "My best friends in the world."

Luis narrows his eyes. "Says the liar. What else have you been lying about?"

My eyes meet Hari's. He nods. "Let's just tell them."

"Hari and I hooked up," I say plainly.

"But it's over now," Hari adds.

Marcus lets out a low whistle. "Well, *shit.*"

"You really have been living a double life!" Luis says. "I called that!"

"Okay, Kat and I needed to figure things out for ourselves first," Hari explains. "We didn't want anyone else knowing until that part was sorted."

Luis makes a face. "Whatever, liars."

"Personally, I don't really care about that part. I kinda get it. But the other stuff...Kat...wow." Marcus's eyes meet mine. "Why keep all of that from us?"

I sigh and look away. "I don't know. I really don't! I guess because it was easier than explaining over and over again what was going on. And because I was scared." I wasn't expecting to get choked up, but I start to. "I'm sorry."

"You're playing with fire, Sanchez," Luis warns. "Why haven't you deleted the account yet?"

"I'm *going* to, I swear! I just. I don't know. I don't know." I bury my head in my hands, doing my best to keep it together. In a muffled voice, I say, "It's the first time people have appreciated my photography. And appreciated my voice—what I have to say. I feel visible. I feel like my work is *reaching* people." I sniff. "But that's not an excuse. I don't *have* a good excuse. I'm sorry I'm such a fuckup." Cash nudges me with his nose. "I shouldn't have done any of this."

"Okay, true, but you're not an evil person." Marcus's voice is gentle when he says it. "I mean that. Yeah, it sucks that you kept us in the dark about this struggle you're having, but mostly because we could've, like, *helped* you."

Luis crosses his arms. "Speak for yourself."

"We're friends. We're supposed to tell each other about the hard stuff. The shitty stuff," Marcus continues. "All of it."

"Honestly wish you'd mentioned the whole you-being-bi thing sooner, if only because it makes you more tolerable. Kinda cool, almost," Luis says.

Marcus ignores that. "As I was saying, you can tell us things. We care about you. And, you know, *we* see you. *We* appreciate you. You don't need a fake profile. You don't need to be dishonest.

But lies...well, they're not great, but lies sometimes happen. I may have exaggerated some truths in the past myself."

"You have?" I ask.

"It is possible that I do not use all the Photography Club funding on gas," he says, nonchalantly. "Maybe I sometimes use it to get Honey detailed."

Luis points at him. "I *knew* it!"

"Umm, okay, well why don't you tell them where you *really* go on Tuesday evenings when you claim you're at Xio's house?" Marcus retorts.

He scowls. "Ayy, man, that was supposed to be a secret!"

"You can't make Kat feel bad for being secretive and then not be truthful with her," Hari says.

Luis sighs. And then, quietly, he admits, "I've been taking dance lessons."

I blink. "I'm sorry, what?"

Hari cups his hand around his ear as if to hear better. "Yeah, I couldn't really make that out."

"I *said* I've been taking *dance lessons*! Xio wants me to be part of her little sister's quinceañera, so I told her I would do this for her. Damn! Y'all are nosy!"

"Okay, but that's actually legit sweet," I say, making a face at him like he's precious.

He puts his hands up for me to stop. "Get outta here with that!"

"I've been talking to a girl I met in my SAT prep class," Hari blurts out.

All three of us turn to him. "Excuse me?" I ask.

"Yeah, I didn't know how—or when—to bring this up, but... since we're sharing, now seemed as good a time as any? She goes to Garces Memorial," he says. A private Catholic school nearby.

Marcus raises both eyebrows. "Is that your kink, dude?"

"Oh, it totally is! Those plaid skirts and lil uniforms," Luis says enthusiastically. "I get it."

"You're talking to someone?" I ask, a smile spreading across my lips as I reach back to muffle Luis.

He gives me a sheepish grin. "Her name is Iris."

"*Yeah it is!*" Marcus whoops, and we all laugh.

Then, totally overcome with emotion over how understanding they've been and how excited/relieved/delighted I am to hear that Hari is really and truly over me, I give him a hug.

"I just love you guys!" I shout, getting Cash excited.

"Don't be gross," Marcus says.

Luis grimaces. "It's too much, Sanchez."

But Hari smiles at me and I smile back at him, goofy, happy, and a thousand pounds lighter.

"Wait," Luis says. "How did we gloss over the fact that Kat is legit *cat*fishing people?"

"I said that, too!" Hari laughs. "Katfishing, though! With a *K*! Get it?"

"Guys!" But I laugh along with them, because it *is* ridiculous. And after so much lying, I deserve to be roasted for it somewhere in my life.

Luis is practically cackling. "This is all so stupid!" Then he turns to Cash, still grinning. "Aight, pooch. Since everyone else ran their mouth, is there anything *you* want to share, too?"

Cash leaps into the front seat and licks him.

Chapter Thirty-Nine

Hari: **I may have an idea for Cash.** 👀

I immediately FaceTime him, like it's not 6:30 a.m., and he answers right away. He blinks when he shows up on the screen. "Nice hair."

I reach up to touch the microfiber towel my hair's wrapped in to preserve my curls. "Thanks. It's new. Now spill!"

"What if you made a post as Max about Cash?" Hari suggests. When I look hesitant, he continues. "Look, you haven't deleted that account after having literal fucking weeks to do so. I checked it out and it's gotten up to, like, almost five thousand followers. Before you went dark, you'd been posting about dogs there, so I feel like the audience is right. You're bound to have some dog lovers following you—her—whatever."

"Luis has more followers than that account," I point out.

"He can share the post! We all can. Him, me, Marcus. Leo. Maybe I can get Dev to do it, too."

The wheels in my brain are turning as Hari lays this all out. Yes, Max has been dead these last few weeks. But I haven't deleted her. I couldn't figure out what I was saving her for, but maybe it's for this. A final post of "her" with Cash could be nice if it meant he finally got adopted. It would definitely help me feel like this wasn't all for nothing.

It's risky, yes—but Becca isn't on Instagram, our circles don't overlap, and none of the people Hari or I know have followings that are *that* big.

As far as I'm concerned, the potential rewards win out here.

"Yep," I finally say. "You're a genius. I'm gonna do it."

I don't hesitate. I've had what I wanted to say about Cash written up since this weekend, so why lose any time? (Sure, I wrote it for the One Fur All socials, but Max is better: more reach.) I select a beautiful photo of Becca and Cash, apply my preset filter, and post.

I try not to obsessively check Max's account throughout the day. I had only just started getting out of the habit. But it's hard not to peek and watch the likes climb; my dopamine sparks with each one. Old habits die hard.

A while ago, I had converted Max's IG to a business account so that I could see the insights behind the posts. The impressions of this post are climbing even faster than the likes: 5,271 impressions by Spanish class; 7,803 by lunchtime; more than 10,000 by the time the day is through.

I double down and post as me, too. Although I have, like, two followers, you never know. I select a photo of me and Cash, write a heartfelt caption, provide One Fur All's phone number and email, and share.

Please, please, please let this work.

* * *

After school, I go straight to One Fur All and march right into Imani's office. "Any calls for Cash?" I ask.

She shakes her head. "Nothing yet."

I frown. "Oh. My friends and I just started a pretty big social campaign for him. I was just hoping."

Imani gives me a gentle smile. "Don't lose hope just yet."

"Yeah," I sigh. "I won't."

There are a couple of DMs on the One Fur All Facebook page for me to respond to, so I busy myself doing that, answering questions about how old you need to be to adopt from our shelter (eighteen), whether we have any llamas available (whaaaat?), if we sell dog food or not (why?). There's even someone who just keeps saying, "I have a question" but never follows up with the actual question. Ugh.

Thankfully, a text from Elena rescues me from my stress.

Elena: **Today was the Mondayest of Tuesdays everrrrr.**

Me: **TELL ME ABOUT IT.**

Elena: **Can we please just go back to Saturday?**

Elena: **At exactly 8:27 p.m.?**

Elena: ☺ ☺ ☺

I grin at my phone like a dummy.

Me: **Is that the exact moment we kissed?**

Elena: **I definitely didn't sneak a peek at the time so I could remember it.**

Me: **How are you so CUTE?!**

Elena: **No . . . you.**

Me: **I wish I could drive out right now and see you.**

Elena: **Can you?**

Elena: **Or I can drive to you?**

The idea is so, so, so tempting. But I'm stuck here until at least seven, and it would take two and a half hours for either of us to get to the other (not including LA traffic.). Blehhh.

Me: **This weekend FOR SURE.**

Me: **But probably not today. By the time we got to each other, I feel like we would only get two minutes and then whoever drove would have to turn around and go home.** ☹

Elena: **You're right but** ⓦ

Me: **I do have another idea.**

Elena: **Gimme!**

Me: **It's weird.**

Elena: **I'm in.**

Me: **We could have a date? But, like . . . long-distance?**

Elena: **A DATE!!!**

Me: **What's your favorite movie?**

Elena: **To All The Boys I've Loved Before, no question.**

Me: **I've never seen it!**

Elena: **ARE YOU KIDDING ME KAT**

Elena: **ksjdfkjsdfsdf**

Me: **OKAY BUT I WILL SEE IT TONIGHT**

Me: **With you!**

Me: **We'll both get some food, hang out in our rooms, and watch this movie. While FaceTiming.**

Elena: **Stoppppp.**

Elena: **That's so cute, I can't.**

Me: **Is that a yes?**

Elena: **I NEED THIS NOW!!!**

Me: **I'll be home in a bit! Let's plan for eight?**

Elena: **Okay!!!**

Elena: **Guess I better clean my room.**

I laugh-react to that message, but behind my phone I swallow hard at the thought of getting to see Elena Brynn Powell's room. Seeing-a-cute-girl-in-her-room-on-our-first-date anxiety has entered the chat.

Especially because... I have not been on a real date before.

So, what gives me the RIGHT? I swear my heart sometimes does things without waiting for my brain to catch up to think it through.

In this case, though, it's pretty great. We have a date!

* * *

Elena told me she thought my pigtail buns were "super cute" at the bonfire, so I take my time to pin my hair back similarly tonight. And I need something cute but relaxed to wear—like I'm not trying too hard, but just casually look good, you know?

Eventually, I settle on a plain Nike crew neck over some leggings. Since she won't see the full 'fit, I might as well be comfy on the bottom. I add some brow gel and lip gloss.

Just before eight, I set up my laptop with the movie Elena has requested and have a small bowl of popcorn—freshly popped by Grandpa with a sprinkle of salt—set beside it.

Then I call her.

I suspect this feeling is a little like what I'd be experiencing if I were picking her up on a real date.

I'm pleased when she answers, and I can tell she tried to dress up a little on the DL, too. She has her pink hair pulled back into a tousled braid, draped over her shoulder; pink glasses; and an over-sized lavender sweater.

"Hi," she says, sounding shyer than I've ever heard her sound.

I feel myself smiling without even meaning to. "Hiiii."

Elena's room, or at least the bit I can see behind her, is exactly how I might've imagined: a pastel explosion. Above her bed, there is a shelf decorated with big string lights, an assortment of her art prints, and a sweet owl stuffed animal.

"Don't think I got a ticket for the owl to join us," I tease.

She swivels her head around and rips the owl off her shelf, then throws it out of view. "Oh my *gosh*."

"What?! I thought it was cute!"

"It is a he, thank you very much. *Whoo*-bert," Elena explains, her cheeks turning a shade that matches her hair. "That's embarrassing."

"It's really not," I assure her.

"You don't have a stuffed animal in *your* room."

"Not true. I just hid mine under the bed before I called you."

She laughs at that and pretends to wipe some sweat off her forehead. "Phew!"

I check my phone for the time. "Oh, show's starting soon."

"Right, right. We have tickets for eight ten, yes?" Elena asks, playing along.

"Yeah, and these were killer to get. So I hope you're sneaking in some snacks. No time to wait in the concessions line."

"Oh, I've got snacks, all right." She turns her camera to show me a spread of Red Vines and chocolate-covered pretzels. "You want anything?"

"Chocolate-covered pretzel would be good."

"You've got it." Elena turns the camera back to her, waving a pretzel at the screen and popping it into her mouth. "Now: can we hit Play yet or what?"

"Let's do it!"

The movie starts with the familiar sound of the Netflix logo unfolding on-screen, and I reach over to flick off the lights in my room as Elena settles back against her pillows to get comfortable.

"Please note," Elena begins, pointing to herself. "I am a Lara Jean Covey stan. Know that."

I grin. "We respect a stan."

"And isn't her room just absolute goals?" Elena sighs. "Okay, sorry." She makes a motion like she's zipping her lips.

"I don't mind," I say, enjoying watching her get excited over the movie even more than watching the movie itself.

Elena lets out a squeak when the camera pans out and shows Lara Jean's room in full view. It's so cute I pull a pillow into my lap and give it a gentle squeeze.

All of this is almost too much.

I swear I spend half of the movie just watching Elena watch, but eventually I settle in for the ride along with Lara Jean and Peter and their fake dating. By the time the end credits roll, I'm *all in* on this precious relationship.

"Sooo?" Elena asks. "What'd you think?"

"I loved it!" I say. "You really do give me all the Lara Jean energy, you know."

Elena grins big and she puts her hand over her heart. "That is *literally* the nicest thing anyone has ever said to me." We laugh. "You can be my Peter, then."

I bite my lip and nod. "I could be that."

"There's just something so romantic about love letters." She sighs wistfully. "Can you imagine? A letter. A real-life, hand-written letter that requires a stamp, and an envelope, and good penmanship, and forethought? The waiting. The waiting *alone* is dreamy. We've just gotten, like, so used to being able to text and DM each other, and it takes no effort at all, no patience. But a love letter? You're basically putting your heart and soul on paper, then hoping it gets there, hoping your person reads it, hoping they write back. It's like the ultimate declaration that you love a person and you will wait for them."

I chuckle, but honestly, she's moved me. "I've never thought of it like that."

"It's just so, so, *so* romantic," she gushes.

It's then that Elena glances offscreen. I hear a voice. "You were supposed to do the dishes, Elena!"

"I *will*," Elena insists to someone I assume is Carys. "I'm a little *busy* right now."

"I hardly think watching Netflix counts as being busy," the voice retorts.

"Don't, Carys! Go away!"

"*Do the dishes!* I'm not doing them again."

"Okay, okay. I'll be right there." Elena scowls and then turns back toward her phone. "Ugh. Sorry about that."

"It's okay," I say. "You've gotta go?"

She nods. "Unfortunately. My gremlin of a sister is being a real pill tonight."

I smile at her. "Hey, that's totally fine. I'm just glad we got to do this."

She smiles back at me. "Me too. It was really fun. Text you later?"

"Definitely. Good night for now, Lara Jean."

"Good night for now, Peter." She wiggles her fingers at me, laughs, then turns her camera off.

I flop back onto my bed and let out a satisfied sigh.

I almost don't want to ruin this by checking on Cash's post and possibly being disappointed. I'd put my phone on Do Not Disturb while we were watching the movie so I could really focus. But I suppose I should peek.

I unlock my phone and see red notifications on both my phone and messages apps. I check the phone notifications first and see three missed calls from Becca.

Ahh—maybe this is good news about Cash? Could this night get any better?

Quickly, I tap over to my messages to see that all four unread texts are from her, too. The last one, which I can see from the preview screen, just says FUCK. I open them up.

Becca: **You STOLE my FUCKING FACE?!**
Becca: **WHAT**
Becca: **THE**
Becca: **FUCK**

Chapter Forty

There is a clawing, visceral, sick feeling in my stomach.

I read and reread the messages from Becca, staring at them in utter disbelief. I knew this could happen anytime. But I didn't really believe it would.

I find myself breathing heavily. I rush out of my room and toward the front door.

"You okay, Kat?" Grandma asks from the living room.

"I'm fine," I lie, jamming my feet in some sneakers. "I left something at Hari's. Be right back."

I don't wait for her reply before I'm out the door and running. The chill in the early-December air nips at my exposed skin, but I keep pumping. There is a burn in my legs, an ache in my lungs, but the pain feels good.

I knock harder than I intend when I get to Hari's, as if my body is in control and I'm just along for the ride.

Mrs. Shah answers. "Kat! What are you doing here so late?"

"I need to talk to Hari," I say plainly.

She frowns at me. "I'm so sorry, sweetie. But Hari is out with Iris tonight." She looks at her watch. "He should be getting home shortly in order to make curfew."

"Oh," is all I can muster. "Oh."

"Would you like to come inside?" Mrs. Shah's brow furrows with concern. "You don't look well."

I shake my head. "No, no. I'm okay. I'll just text him. Thanks. I've gotta go."

I turn on my heel and quickly walk back home, fighting the urge to sprint. I can tell Mrs. Shah is watching me go, and I don't want to totally freak her out. When I get back to my porch, I take a seat on one of the wicker chairs outside, burying my face in my hands and trying to catch my breath.

Only I can't.

It's like a fist is trying to erupt out of my chest. My skin is prickling with heat despite the cold. My hands are trembling.

This can't be happening. How did she—?

How? *How?*

"Kat?" a voice asks. It sounds so far away, I barely register it. "Bethie!"

The voice says a few more things I can't make out before I register that my grandpa is kneeling before me, his hands on my knees.

"Take a deep breath through your nose," he's saying. "It's okay. You're okay." I try to do as he instructs, but it's difficult. My head is spinning so much.

"I—can't—" I manage.

"Okay. Okay. I'll do it with you. Okay?" And he's taking a long, deep breath in through his nose and then there are extra hands on my back, rubbing it in slow, soothing circles.

"Okay," I croak. I take in a ragged breath through my nose, my chest quivering as I do.

"Good, good." His voice is calm and even. "And out." He lets the air out in a steady puff and I do the same, watching as my hot breath comes out like a puff of smoke.

"That's it, Kat," Grandma murmurs.

"Again," Grandpa says, inhaling. I nod and mirror him. "Good." We do this a few times together until the ache in my chest starts to dull and my breathing feels less labored. Grandpa rises to his feet and helps me to mine. "Come on," he instructs, and he guides me inside and over to the couch.

276

Grandma drapes a blanket over my shoulders and looks at me with wide eyes. "Better?"

"A little," I say.

"I'll get you some water." She disappears again and Grandpa sits beside me.

"Keep breathing," he reminds me.

I close my eyes and sit back on the couch, focusing only on inhaling and exhaling. When I open my eyes, Grandma is standing beside us with an ice-cold glass of water for me. I reach out to take it and gulp a sip down.

"Okay," I whisper. "I'm okay."

"What's going on?" Grandma asks, but Grandpa shushes her.

"Let's get her to bed, Bethie." He looks at me. "We can talk in the morning, yeah?"

I nod. The last thing I want to do right now is explain to my grandparents what's going on. Grandma nods and takes my arm, leading me to my room. I feel numb as she gently guides me to my bed and stands over me, starting to work on taking my hair down. She uses her fingers to gingerly remove the hair ties before guiding the hoops from my ears and placing everything on my nightstand.

Grandpa comes in with a cup of what I assume is tea.

"Sleepytime," he confirms, setting it down. Then he hands me a pill. "Melatonin."

"It'll help," Grandma promises.

I put it in my mouth and then take a tentative sip of the still-hot tea. It burns a little, but that's okay.

Grandpa gives me a kiss on my forehead. "Good night, Kat. I love you. Rest."

I nod again, just about the only thing I feel I can do now. Before he leaves my room, he reaches down to retrieve my phone from the floor and place it on its charger, giving me and Grandma one last look before closing the door behind him.

Grandma pulls my blankets back on one side and motions for me to climb in. Once I'm settled in bed, she turns the overhead light off and squeezes into the bed beside me. She guides my head so it rests on her shoulder and gives me her hand.

I don't protest.

With her other hand, she strokes my hair, and whispers, "It'll be okay. Whatever it is. It'll be okay."

I'm not convinced it will be. But it's nice to hear, anyway.

* * *

In the morning, I wake with a start, gasping for air. For a moment, I have no idea where I am or what happened. But then it rushes back to me all at once.

I close my eyes, wishing desperately I could just go back to sleep—maybe forever—rather than write Becca back.

But it was already cruel enough that I never wrote back to her last night. It takes everything in me to reach for my phone and unlock it. With shaky hands, I open my messages. There are a few unread ones now, from Hari and from Elena, but I go straight to the unread messages from Becca. There are only two.

Becca: **I can't believe you're not even going to reply.**

Becca: **FUCKING PITIFUL!!!**

The tears that fall are hot as they streak down my face.

Me: **I'm so, so, so, so, so sorry. I don't even know what to say. There is no excuse for what I've done. I fucked up. I'm so sorry. I'm so sorry. I'll delete the account right away. And I'll delete all your photos, too. And if you never want to talk to me again, I completely understand. I'm so sorry, Becca.**

Delivery confirmations between my messages never show. I try to call. Straight to voice mail. She's blocked me. Without another thought, I pull up Max's account and delete it. Something I should've done long, long ago.

I check the other messages:

Hari: **Hey, you okay?**

Hari: **My mom said you stopped by and seemed out of it.**

Hari: **Hey. Just checking in again.**

Hari: **You still want a ride this morning, right?**

Elena: **Dishes are officially washed and Carys can pound sand!**

Elena: **Thank you for tonight.** ♥

Elena: **Good morninggggg.** ☺

I don't reply to any of them. I need to get in touch with Becca. I need to tell her how sorry I am, I need to explain myself, I need to apologize over and over and over, I need to grovel, I need, I need, I need. Once again, I am flooded with my own needs, and I'm crushed under the weight of the reality of how selfish I've been. A fresh round of tears comes. Fuck.

But school. I leave my room, bleary-eyed, and find Grandma perched at the dining room table, as if she'd been waiting for me to wake.

"Chickadee," she says, her voice gentle. "How are you feeling?"

"Horrible." I sniffle.

"Do you want to talk about it?"

My face crumples. "I messed up."

Grandma comes to me, enveloping me in a hug, and everything comes tumbling out. My shoulders heave with sobs as I tell her, and I'm not even sure she can understand everything I say, but I have to keep going and share it all. It all has to *go,* like I'm purging myself of this horrible, horrible thing I've done.

"And now I don't know what to do because everything is such a mess," I finish.

I fear she will be disgusted with me, that she'll yell at me, tell me I should be ashamed of myself. But she doesn't. She just holds me and rubs my back.

Once I've calmed down a little, she pulls me to the dining table so I can sit.

"I'm so sorry" is the first thing she says.

"Why are *you* sorry?" I ask, sniffling.

"It seems like you've been dealing with a lot," she says. "All on your own."

"I just wanted to be in control of one thing in my life," I admit, shame burning up the back of my neck. "I just wanted people to hear me. Appreciate me. Admire my art. Except it wasn't even me they were seeing, Grandma. It's all so stupid."

"It's important not to mistake lies for control." Grandma's voice is gentle but stern. "But...I am not going to sit here and make you feel worse than you already do. You'll have quite a difficult time making things right. If you even can. But you have to try."

A few more tears roll down my cheeks. She's right. Regardless of why I did it, *I still did it.* I am not the first person in the world to feel these things, yet I'm the only one I know of who decided to steal and deceive. And the damage is done.

"I need to tell Becca I'm sorry," I say. "But she blocked me."

"Maybe she doesn't want an apology." When she sees my face fall, she adds, "Not yet, anyway. It could change."

"I was thinking of driving out to see her to say sorry in person."

Grandma shakes her head. "Who would you be doing that for? Her? Or for you?"

Right. Becca's made it clear she doesn't want to talk. And who could blame her? After what I've done?

"So, what do I do, then?" I ask. "I'm supposed to work with her tomorrow."

She purses her lips. "I don't really have a good answer for you, Kat. I wish I did. I think this is just going to be something you'll have to figure out."

I groan. "Do I have to?"

Grandma chuckles. "Yes. And, sorry, but you'll have to do that at school."

Great. I shuffle to the bathroom and take a long, hot shower, then Grandma drops me off and writes me a note for being tardy.

All day long, I stare at my phone.

I try texting Becca again, but once more, no delivery notification comes.

I pull up my messages with Elena next and know I need to respond before she begins to worry. Stalling, I send her a message that just says **Good morning,** adding a heart emoji to the end of it, knowing it will probably be my final heart emoji to her. Ever.

The realization is like a gut punch. I close my eyes and think of last night. Of how sweet and perfect it felt. I think of the bonfire. Of the kisses. The late-night chats. The relationship we've been working on building these last few weeks.

It doesn't surprise me when my eyes well up, right there, in the middle of Spanish class.

My phone buzzes and I open my eyes.

Marcus: **You good, Kat?**

Hari: **We're worried.**

Luis: **They're worried. I'm annoyed. You blew us off this morning!**

Me: **Sorry. Becca found out.**

Hari: **FUCK.**

Marcus: **That sucks. I'm so sorry.**

Luis: ☹

Hari: **Tell us everything at lunch.**

• ✳ •

Midday, I am sitting in Honey with Marcus and Luis up front and Hari beside me, filling them in on the few short hours during which my whole life unraveled.

Marcus has instructed Luis that he is not to eat in his car under any circumstances, so Luis is leaning out the window, slurping the beef stew Grandma packed me from my thermos. I have no appetite, unsurprisingly.

"You're letting all the cold air in," Marcus whines.

"You could just let me eat with my head *inside*!" Luis snaps.

Hari rolls his eyes. "Guys, can we please focus? Kat is going through it." Luis scowls at him but obliges, snapping the container shut and sitting back down. Marcus rolls up the window and Hari turns to me. "Are you going to tell Elena?"

"You don't have to, you know," Marcus points out. "I mean, the account's gone now, right?"

I nod. "It's gone."

"She *will* find out. Trust me on that," Luis warns. He turns to me. "You gotta tell her yourself."

I wince. "I don't want to."

Luis reaches for my phone in my hands. "Call her now."

"Now?"

Hari gives me a sympathetic smile. "Maybe it's best to just get it over with."

"She's at school," I protest. I'm stalling.

"But she's probably on lunch, too," Marcus says.

I think back to what my grandma said, about how this is all gonna hurt.

Bad.

I take in a shaky breath and pull up Elena's contact. My finger hovers over the call button.

"Do it," Hari says firmly.

Without thinking, I do. It rings a few times but she picks up.

"Hey!" Her voice is sweet and bubbly and warm on the other end and there is a pang in my chest. "This is new. I like it."

"Hi, Elena." I sound shakier than I'd like and it's obvious.

"Everything okay?"

I let out a little laugh. "Not really, no."

"What's going on?" she asks.

My eyes dart around the car, looking from Marcus to Luis to Hari, who are all mustering their best looks of encouragement for me.

"I need to tell you something," I begin.

"Okaaaay…" She already sounds guarded.

"Um, first, I'm so sorry. What I'm about to say is really bad." My voice cracks despite my best effort. Hari pats my knee.

"What is it?"

"Okay. Um. I know I told you that I was friends with Max. But I lied."

"What?" Her voice is exasperated. "Why would you do that?"

"Because I've been lying a lot. And…in fact, I made Max up. She's not real." I don't let her reply before continuing in a rush. "I'm so, so sorry for lying to you. I didn't mean for it to go this way. It wasn't my intention to string you along and as soon as I started catching feelings, I tried to fix it, but it was just—a mess. I made a huge mess of things. I'm so sorry."

I'm crying now, unable to look at my friends.

There is a long, painful silence on the other line. "Elena?" I ask.

"I can't believe you," she says. "*Don't* call me again."

The line goes dead.

It's over.

Slowly, I take the phone away from my ear and place it in my lap, still looking out the window.

Luis is the first to talk. "At least it's done."

"Yeah," I croak. "It's definitely done."

"You did the right thing by telling her," Marcus says.

Hari squeezes my knee. "You really did, Kat. She's upset, but it's better that she knows."

I sniffle, rubbing at my eyes. "That's true." A sob tries to escape my throat but I hold it in. The lunch bell rings. "We should get back."

"But it's been so long since we skipped," Hari says, giving me an encouraging smile. "Right, Luis?"

"Hell yeah," he says. "I've got a test I didn't study for that I'd *love* to miss."

"It's settled, then," Marcus says, facing forward and revving the engine. "Tacos?"

Luis whoops and yells, "Tacooooos!"

* * *

Truth be told, no amount of tacos can make my situation better. But they do help a little. The laughing and the joking with Marcus, Hari, and Luis make it so that I feel less like my world is crumbling in around me, even if it's only for an afternoon.

Grandpa greets me with a firm hug once I get home. "You doing okay?"

"I'm doing okay," I confirm.

"Quite a scare last night, huh?"

"Yeah. I'm sorry about that."

"No need to be sorry. I'm just glad you're all right."

"Thank you. I think I was having a panic attack." I've been there when they've happened to Hari before, and I knew they were bad, but I'd never experienced one myself. They're no joke.

Grandpa nods at me. "I think so, too. I'm just glad you came back home so we could help you." He reaches over and touches his finger beneath my chin. "Keep your head up, okay? It'll get better."

"Thanks, Grandpa. Mind if I hang out for a few? I don't feel like being by myself."

He smiles at me. "I could use a sous-chef for my French cassoulet."

Grandpa hands me a spare apron and we spend the next hour

working together in the kitchen, me chopping herbs and vegetables for Grandpa while he does the seasoning, stirring, and creating. Grandma comes home awhile later, armed with grocery bags.

I help unload everything before retreating to my room, where I check my phone with dread.

Still nothing from Becca or Elena.

I take a moment to send a text to Elena.

Me: I cannot say sorry enough. I am so deeply remorseful for what I've done. I'm so sorry for the hurt I have caused you. You would be more than justified in never speaking to me again, honestly. If there is anything I can do to make this up to you, please. I'll do anything. I'm so sorry. So, so sorry.

Though it's a long shot, I wait to see if a response will come. It doesn't, but the text beneath my message changes to delivered, so I know she hasn't blocked me. At least not yet.

I notice I have a missed call from Imani. I return it immediately, praying that it's good news about Cash. I could really use that right about now.

"Hello?" she answers.

I force myself to sound chipper. "Hey, Imani. It's Kat. Sorry I missed you."

"Oh, Kat. Hello." On the other line, Imani's voice sounds thick with emotion. "Listen, I'm calling regarding a few things."

"Sure. What's up?"

"First, I wanted to share that we got a few calls inquiring about Cash, so I'm feeling really good that one of these will pan out and he'll have a home soon."

Joy surges through me. "That's amazing, Imani!"

"It is. Thank you for all the work you and your friends did to help make this happen. So, the other thing…" I hear her take a deep breath. "You've done great work for us, Kat. You really have, especially with this whole fundraiser I just threw at you guys. But it's come to my attention that you've engaged in some activities on social media that are, well, shocking, to say the least."

A lump forms in my throat. "I can explain—"

"No need," Imani says, cutting me off. "I already checked through our social accounts and it's clear you didn't do anything there. But given that your actions have directly affected one of your colleagues and that this serious lapse in judgment involved social media, which is under your purview here, I really have no choice. Effective immediately, you will no longer be working at One Fur All. And I am going to have to rescind your invitation to the upcoming ball."

"Okay," I say quietly. "I understand."

"I've really loved having you here, Kat. And I'm sorry to see you go. I'll be discreet about everything and you can leave knowing you've likely found Cash a good home." This is more kindness from Imani than I deserve.

"Thank you," I whisper. "I'm so sorry to have let you down."

There is a pause on the line before she says, "Be well, Kat."

"You too."

She hangs up. Goodbye, Becca. Goodbye, Elena. And now, goodbye Cash and goodbye job I loved.

Chapter Forty-One

It's a quiet couple of weeks. I go from the happiest I've ever been to absolutely devastated.

And I deserve it.

Hari, Luis, and Marcus check in on me but respect my wishes to be mostly left alone. I try texting Elena a few times, but each apology goes unanswered. I try to call Becca and go straight to voice mail each time.

I busy myself with some Christmas shopping, though I'm feeling anything but festive. For Grandma and Grandpa, however, I go through the motions. It's the least I can do.

When Christmas itself arrives, the three of us have an early morning of opening gifts under the tree, per tradition. I gifted Grandma and Grandpa photos of each other, which they both loved. Grandpa got a photo I'd taken of Grandma during our shopping trip weeks ago, while Grandma got a framed photo of Grandpa making a silly face. I made them black-and-white, and each photo is in a double frame, so the portraits are juxtaposed with similar photos we had from when they were young. It took me a long time, but it was time well spent.

My grandparents spoil me with gifts I don't deserve—a new camera bag; a pair of 14K gold hoop earrings; a fresh tube of my Sugar and Spice lip gloss. I cry when I open them. I beg them to take them back.

But they just hug me.

We stay in our pajamas till noon, toiling away in the kitchen, until it's time to shower and get ready for the family meal. (On Christmas, my parents come here; we don't go to them.)

I'm surprised when Mom, Pop, and Leo show up with Daisy in tow. Usually, the dogs stay home.

"She's a little under the weather," Pop explains.

I crouch down to pet her. "You and me both, Daisy."

Mom joins my grandparents in the kitchen, but Pop lingers near me.

"You doing okay?" he asks.

I shrug, not really wanting to discuss it. I wish Grandma hadn't told my parents all about this shit, but whatever.

He pats my shoulder. "Well...you'll figure it out. And it'll be okay."

"I hope so."

"I know so." Then Pop slips into the kitchen, while I join Leo and Daisy in the living room.

"How ya been?"

"Good, good. And you?"

I flop on the couch beside him. "Been better."

"Yeah...Mom told me what happened."

"Oh, yeah?" I ask. "Which horrible, awful part?"

Leo laughs. "Whatever you told her, I guess."

"I didn't tell her anything." I sigh. "Must've been Grandma."

"Oh, shit. Well, I'm not trying to be a narc or anything. Just wanted to say I'm sorry."

"Thanks." I give him an appreciative smile. "Gotta admit that I did it to myself, though."

"Yeah, well." He steals a glance toward the kitchen, then lowers his voice. "It's not like we've had the best role model when it comes to being truthful on social media. Mom is forever lying in her posts. Forever lying, period."

I'm surprised he says this, even though it's true. "Yeah. But it's no excuse."

Leo shrugs. "Fair enough. Maybe I'm just annoyed because she told me I could take a New Year's trip with Chelsea's family, but after they booked everything, she and Pop changed their minds." He shakes his head. "I'm surprised you couldn't hear the argument from here."

"What the hell? That's awful!"

He shakes his head. "Tell me about it. It was too late for them to cancel, so now I'm just out that money. Mom and Pop don't even care."

Before I can formulate a proper response, Grandpa pops his head into the living room and lets us know that dinner is ready. Ugh. Timing.

"I'm so sorry about that," I say to Leo.

He waves a hand. "It's all good."

It's not, though. That's really bad behavior.

What I did was terrible, yes. But our family problems—the lying, the weird power plays, the pretending everything is perfect? I'm over it.

I follow Leo into the dining room, where Grandma and Grandpa have set up an extra table just to hold all the food they've made. While everyone loads up their plates, Daisy follows beside me, her snout poking at my hand as she begs for bites of whatever I take. When no one's looking, I sneak her some ham.

We eat and talk, though I'm not really feeling up to much of either, especially not now that I'm annoyed at my parents for pulling the rug out from under Leo. He should get to spend New Year's with Chelsea, and in silent protest, I join him immediately in the living room once we're done eating. I just need to make it through a few more hours, I tell myself. Then I can go back to sulking.

I text my friends to see how their holiday is going so far, but look up when I hear Mom clear her throat.

"Kat, should you really be on your phone right now?" Her arms are crossed as she says this.

"What do you mean?"

"I think you know what I mean. You've done plenty of damage with that phone, don't you think?"

"Sarah," Pop says, surprised.

My cheeks burn. "I'm just texting my friends."

Mom holds out a hand and motions for me to give her my phone. "Hand it over." But that just makes me pull it to my chest. "I mean it."

Pop reaches for her hand gently, guiding it back to her side. "Kat's learned her lesson. Her regret is very sincere. And she needs that phone for safety when she's out."

"She should've had her phone taken away the instant what she did came to light." Mom shoots Grandma and Grandpa a pointed look. "But now is better than nothing." She turns to me. "Give me your phone."

I look over at Grandma, who glances away. "But—"

Mom rises from the couch and walks over to me. "Don't make me take it."

"Sarah!" Pop exclaims.

Mom is in front of me now, reaching toward the phone. "I don't want an argument from you." I stare at her, hard, feeling everyone's eyes on us. "Come on. Give it to me." At once, I'm that little girl at Pirate Playscape: helpless, confused, desperate to run and hide. Daisy is whining beside me. Reluctantly, I hand my mom my phone. She gives me a tight-lipped smile. "There. Was that so hard?"

"Okay, that's enough. No need to gloat," Grandpa cuts in.

"*Ray*," Grandma says.

Mom tucks my phone into her purse, smiling. "I'd be a terrible mother if I let my kid get away with lying."

Leo lets out a laugh. "That's interesting."

We all look over at him.

Mom narrows her eyes. "And why's that?"

"Don't you lie all the time on Facebook?" Leo asks, eliciting a gasp from Grandma. "And Instagram? Everywhere, basically?"

"Ex*cuse* me?" Mom asks.

"Hey," Pop says sternly. "Let's be respectful."

"No, I want to hear what Leo has to say. I lie all the time?" She crosses her arms smugly. "Please, enlighten me."

"Well, for starters, how about the New Year's trip with Chelsea?"

"Not this again." Mom rubs at her temples. "Your *attitude* is what made me change my mind about that, so I'd hardly call that a lie."

He looks down at his phone and taps a few times. A post comes up. A post from Mom. "Yet you posted on Facebook that I was 'incredibly thoughtful and trustworthy' and 'deserved' this trip—and you made it sound like *you guys* were paying!"

"First of all, I *was* going to pay before you started talking back to me!"

"I wasn't talking back to you!" Leo insists.

But Mom isn't listening. "Yes, I did write about how it's been emotional for me to watch you grow up because all of a sudden you're talking about taking trips with your girlfriend—but you're not too old for me to take that away."

"All I'm hearing is you, you, you in all of this," I say. "What about Leo?"

Mom glares at me. "What *about* Leo? He was incredibly disrespectful when I asked him to do one little thing! *That's* why he's not going on his trip!"

"You asked me to miss my best friend's final game of the season to clean up the backyard so your friends could come over!" Leo argues. "I told you I'd help but that I couldn't do that to Martín!"

"Jeez, Mom, that is ridiculous!" I cry.

"Kat," Grandma warns.

"What? It is!" I insist. "And we wouldn't even be having this discussion right now if you didn't tell them."

Her eyes go big, but her voice small. "What was I supposed to do? They're your parents."

"No, you and Grandpa are my parents. These people are the ones who left!" And just like that, with that simple truth spoken, the air gets sucked out of the room.

Mom's eyes instantly go teary. "Why would you say that? After we made a bedroom for you?"

"You made that bedroom to make yourself look good," Leo says. "It wasn't about Kat at all."

She wipes at her now-wet cheeks. "Well, I'm sorry I'm such a bad mom, then." And she rushes out of the house.

Pop's nostrils flare and he shakes his head. "Are you guys happy now?" Then he meets my eyes. "I expected more."

My fists clench. "Me too," I spit. "I expected more my whole life."

He says nothing. Just follows Mom out of the house.

Grandpa reaches over and pats Grandma's hand. Then he glances to me and to Leo. "Okay. Let's take a breather. Why don't you two go for a walk?"

We nod and grab our coats, stopping for a second to leash Daisy and take her with us.

Once we've fallen into a steady rhythm walking along the street, I speak. "So...that was a lot, huh?"

"Yeah, and also a long time coming," Leo says.

"Thank you for sticking up for me back there."

He smiles at me. "Yeah, of course. Thank you for having my back, too."

I tuck my hands into my pockets for warmth. "That's what sisters are for."

"It's weird to think we grew up in different houses, but we have the same issues with Mom and Pop. The lying. The weirdo behavior. Don't even get me started on the other shit."

"What *other* shit?" I ask.

"The constant arguing. The nasty sarcasm. The punishments that never match what I've actually done." Leo's grip tightens around Daisy's leash. "Did you know that over the summer, my friends and I got pulled over by the cops, had the entire car searched top to bottom, and got screamed at in broad daylight, and when I came home with a ticket for 'excessive noise' because we'd been listening to music with the windows down, Mom said I deserved it? Acted like I was a full-blown criminal after one of the most humiliating experiences of my life. I got grounded, they took away my phone, and she made a crack about me embarrassing her in public. Her!"

My stomach tightens hearing this. It's scary enough to be brown and get pulled over by the cops, but to be punished on top of that? "That's awful. I had no idea. I'm so sorry."

"It's all good. I just...avoid her whenever I can. That whole house, actually."

"Pop, too?"

Leo sighs. "By default, mostly. He's just spellbound by Mom, always making excuses for her. You know? Like tonight. He took her side so quickly, without even thinking. He didn't even hear us! He was so fast to tell me to be respectful. And after Mom came at us both so hot!" He shakes his head. "It's like I don't even get the chance to be close to him because he's busy trying to keep Mom happy."

I nod. "Yeah. That makes sense."

"But of the two, I'm definitely closer to him. Every time it's just the two of us, the house feels... I don't know. Lighter? It's weird." He looks at me. "Sometimes I wonder what it might be like if Mom wasn't, like, this invisible force keeping us apart."

"Well, he has autonomy," I say. "He could make the effort. Stand up to her."

"He won't, though." Leo chews on his lip, as if considering something. He chooses his next words carefully. "We talk sometimes. He's told me about his life before he came over. It was rough, apparently. He's been really focused on not repeating some of the same mistakes his dad did. He says he never wanted his kids to have a broken home, and... maybe I shouldn't say this."

"Say it," I urge.

Leo turns to me. "Okay. Well... One night, he told me he wished he had pushed Mom harder to take you with them."

"Oh," I say.

"Yeah."

I'll admit that that was the very last thing I ever thought Leo was going to share. I don't know how to feel hearing it. Because the reality is, regardless of any wishes my dad had, he *didn't* push harder.

"But it's kinda shitty of him to say that, and to dump it on me," Leo says. "It's, like, a way to cope with the guilt, I think. Doesn't change a thing."

"No. It doesn't. I've spent my whole life wondering what might've been, feeling like it was my fault they left, telling myself I was the one who wasn't good enough." I swallow. "Yet I'm just supposed to act like that didn't happen. It's like I was a couch and they were trying to decide if I went with the decor. I don't know."

"I'm so sorry, Kat. I shouldn't have said anything."

"No. I'm glad you told me. I always thought maybe Pop and I could be close, if only..." I let my sentence trail off, because I don't even know how to finish it. "I've just had such a hard time watching them—with you—be so close, and yet feel so unbearably far away. So invisible. I wanted to belong so badly. But now," I say softly, "I'm realizing it wasn't sunshine and rainbows for you, either. I was always jealous, you know."

Leo's eyebrows go up. "Of me?"

"Of course! To me, you were the special one. The chosen one. The one they wanted." I wrap my arms around myself. "I wondered what that felt like."

A puff of air escapes Leo's lips as he processes this. "Wow. Yeah. Yeah, I can see why you'd be jealous, then." He steals a glance at me. "You want to know something funny?"

"What's that?"

"I've spent a decent amount of time being jealous of you, too."

"You're joking."

"I'm not. Not that I think Grandma and Grandpa are perfect, but they seem pretty damn close. I wondered what it was like to live there sometimes, with them. They just seem like they'd be great parents. Really caring and open, you know?" Leo pauses. "Plus, then I'd have had you, too."

When I hear this, my eyes ache with tears. I'd never once considered Leo might've been imagining a life where we were together.

"You do have me," I say finally. "We have each other. We don't need to live together to be closer."

Leo rubs his chin. "That's true, huh?"

"Yeah. We don't need our parents' permission to forge a relationship. Maybe we can get really wild and have huge fights like other siblings do."

He laughs. "Be prepared for me to get so frustrated with you for, like, hogging the car."

I grin. "Well, I'm gonna be really pissed at you for being so much cooler than me all the time."

"That one I can't help," Leo says with a laugh. "I do like this idea, though. Talking to each other more. Away from the bullshit."

"I think we can both agree we've had enough of that."

We've rounded the block by now, and Daisy starts to pull herself in the direction of her home. Which means a natural point of separation for Leo and me. He'll go home and so will I.

Leo nods to Daisy. "I should take her back."

"And I should probably take myself back," I agree. "Will you be okay? When you get home, I mean."

"I'll be fine. Promise."

I nod. "Okay. But text me when things cool down?"

He smiles at me. "I will."

Chapter Forty-Two

I'm about seventeen years overdue for a long talk with my grandparents.

When I get home, I find them both in the kitchen, waiting for me. Wordlessly, Grandpa hands me my confiscated phone, and Grandma pulls me into a hug.

"I'm sorry," I say to her.

She strokes my hair. "I'm the one who should be sorry."

"Let's go for a drive," Grandpa suggests. "We have a lot to discuss."

We're quiet as Grandpa drives into the still night, no destination set. I go over my conversation with Leo once more. How many minutes each day did I spend wishing that I lived with my parents? How many minutes were wasted?

Because the only family I need has always been right in front of me.

Grandma clears her throat from the front seat. In the dark of the car, her voice is soft. "They were children when you came along. We didn't know about your dad up till that point. We were pretty strict with your mom; she wasn't allowed to go many places or do much of anything."

"She was our only baby," Grandpa says. "We were overprotective."

"Maybe that's what drove her to sneak around...to get into things she'd never in a million years want us to know about...to lie. I don't know. What I do know is that we suddenly went from parents of one to parents of two frightened seventeen-year-olds—one with no family to speak of—and the sweetest little baby we'd ever seen."

Grandpa continues. "Your dad was such a good kid. He wanted to prove to us that he was going to stick around and do right by you and your mom. But they were so young. They had no idea what they were in for. Just kids themselves."

"Our presence helped, but..." Grandma sighs. "Your mom and I fought a lot. A lot, a lot. It was ugly sometimes. I was just so mad at her. I had envisioned a future for her that involved college and a good job and stability and I felt like all that had been ripped away. I carried so much hurt and anger...but then I'd look at you, my sweet little chickadee, and my heart would bloom. You brought so much joy into our house."

"So much joy," Grandpa says. "Remember how hard she used to laugh whenever one of us said the word *watermelon*?"

"Gosh, that sweet, sweet laugh. It was music."

"So what happened then?" I ask.

"Well, they ended up pregnant again," Grandpa says. "It was...a surprise. To everyone, I think."

"There wasn't enough room in that house for us, them, two babies, and everyone's anger." As Grandma says this, Grandpa eases the car off the road, pulling into a deserted lot. "Therapy wasn't as talked about then, but I think we needed it. To process. Your mother especially."

Grandpa clears his throat. "They loved you. But they were just barely eighteen. They wanted their independence, and weren't sure they could have it with two babies."

"So you stayed," Grandma says.

"And we loved you," Grandpa says. "We don't regret it an ounce."

Grandma shakes her head. "I *do* feel guilty that I agreed sometimes. But I have no regrets about raising you. Not ever." She sighs.

"Now. What questions do you have for us? Anything you want to know about that time, or your parents when they were younger— just ask."

"No questions. But also a million questions," I say. "Can we... can we just drive? For a little bit?"

"Of course, Kat." Grandpa turns on his blinker to get back on the road. "You still like looking at the stars?"

"Yeah. I do."

He nods. "Okay. Let's take you to them."

I imagined if I could only know how everything came to be, my life would magically be fixed. Like the "why" would be the iron on my wrinkly life, and one warm, smooth stroke could make it flat.

As it turns out, that's not even close to the truth.

But here are my truths.

I grew up in a warm and loving household, raised by two resilient and kindhearted people who showed me nothing but support. These versions of my grandparents may not have been the same versions my mom had known. That's okay.

My parents did love me. But they chose to leave me behind. I don't want to make excuses for that. They chose Leo over me, and it will always be that way. But I don't think I need them like I used to. My *real* parents are here in this car.

Most of all, what happened seventeen years ago wasn't my fault. Even though it sometimes felt like it was.

We reach a grassy valley and get out. In the cold dark of night, standing shoulder to shoulder, with only the stars to hear us, Grandma, Grandpa, and I agree to some family therapy. Just to get it all out there. It feels good and healthy and right.

Chapter Forty-Three

The day after Christmas I meet up with Hari, Luis, and Marcus. We exchange our gifts at Luis's house, sharing his Titi Rosa's arroz con dulce. It's nice.

But when I get home, a web of apologies sit in my chest, and I still need to untangle them all. Remorse, guilt, sulking—none of that actually fixes what I've done.

I need to actually make the effort.

I try my luck and call Becca.

To my absolute shock, the phone rings. I hold my breath, hoping.

"Ready to explain yourself now?" Becca's voice is cold.

"Only if that's what you want," I say. "I can also crawl into a hole and die, if you'd prefer."

"Tempting," she says. "I only unblocked you because I checked and saw that account was gone."

"And it will stay gone. That's a promise."

"I'm really fucking mad at you, Kat."

"As you should be."

"But I'm also really confused. I deserve some answers."

"You do. You absolutely do," I say. "I'll tell you everything. Whatever you want to know."

She's quiet on the other end. "Fine. Let's meet up."

We decide on a place—a park—and she tells me to bring my laptop and any other device where I stored her photos. I agree in an instant.

I arrive first. It takes so long before Becca shows that I begin to think she never will. But, eventually, there she is.

Becca walks toward the picnic table I've commandeered and sits across from me. "Well?"

"I am so, so, so sorry, Becca. I don't know what I was thinking."

"You weren't," she cuts in.

"You're absolutely right. I wasn't thinking. But that also makes it seem like I had no control over this thing I did, and that's not true."

"But why?" Becca shakes her head. "You really violated my trust."

"I know. I know! I don't really have a good reason or excuse. I was struggling with some really dark feelings—feeling invisible, feeling unloved, feeling rejected, feeling unacknowledged—and I dealt with them in the worst way possible. It doesn't really matter. It was wrong."

"So, when, then?" she asks. "How long has this been going on?"

I bow my head. "Since Halloween."

"Fuck. After that nice day we had?"

I nod meekly. "I know. It's so fucked up."

"Beyond fucked up!" she spits. "I was doing you a favor posing for you and you used that against me! You *knew* how much social media hurt me. You *knew* it destroyed my mental health. And you *still* did this to me. God, Kat. You're heartless."

My voice cracks when I reply, but I don't want to cry. I don't want to make her feel sorry for me. "I know. I'm so sorry."

"Can you, just, for like, a second, imagine how horrified I was? When Cora sent me that smiling photo of me and Cash, on some profile I didn't recognize, filled with pictures of my own goddamn face...I nearly cracked in half. I thought it was some cruel joke by that terrible group of people that drove me away from beautube. Not something done by someone I know." She sniffles. "Not by someone I thought was my friend."

It gets harder to keep the tears back. "I have no excuse. I'm just so very sorry. And I know that's not enough."

I pull out my phone and show her my camera roll. "I deleted every single photo of you that I have. I pulled them from my portfolio." And I reach into my bag and pull out my laptop to pull the site up. "See? I scrubbed everything. There's nothing in the iCloud, I emptied my recycling bin, I cleared my SD card. I promise you I don't have anything. Except for this." I hold up a USB stick. "These are your photos. Not mine. Oh, also." With my free hand, I dig into my jacket pocket and pull out a scrap of paper. "These are my logins. You can check everything. That's my email, the cloud, Google Drive, Dropbox. My own Instagram, my Snapchat. The login for—" I glance up at her, not wanting to say it. "You know."

"Yeah, I get it," Becca says, taking the paper and USB.

"Okay, yeah, so it's just all gone. And I've deleted your number from my phone, plus our text chain, and I deleted my Google Maps so I have no idea how to get to your house anymore," I explain. "I think that's everything. Obviously, I will fully leave you alone. But if there's anything I can do to make it up to you, I'll do that. I would offer to come in and work your shifts for you and give you the money, but I don't think I'm ever allowed to set foot back in that building. Rightfully so."

Becca crosses her arms. "I'm not sorry for getting you fired."

"You shouldn't be."

"But the dogs will miss you."

"I'll really miss them, too."

Becca rises from the table and shoves her hands into her pockets. "I hate everything you did."

"So do I," I say. "I'm sorry I ruined everything."

"You should be." She squints at me. "I'm gonna go. But I wanted to share one last thing. Imani told me Cash has found a home."

My eyes widen. "Really?"

Becca nods. "Can't say for sure how they found out about him. Maybe it was Max." She slings her bag over her shoulder. "Anyway."

"Thanks for meeting up with me," I say. "I didn't deserve it."

"No, you didn't," Becca agrees. "But I did. Bye, Kat."

"Bye, Becca."

I watch as the girl whose face had become as familiar to me as my own walks away. It's hard to imagine never seeing it again.

I'm deeply ashamed by how things have ended, all the more remorseful after Becca extended such a kindness by agreeing to meet up with me...hell, for not pressing charges against me. Her grace has taught me a lot about who I want to try to be in the future.

I've got a long way to go.

Chapter Forty-Four

The evening of the One Fur All Winter Ball arrives and it pains me that I'm not there. Instead, I'm watching the event unfold on IG Live, which I assume Becca is now in charge of. The venue Imani chose is breathtaking—classy, yet accessible, and still appropriate for what this really is: an event to raise money and get some pretty damn adorable dogs new homes.

Each of the adoptable dogs is dressed to the nines in a tuxedo or a dress and they are charged with leading the attendees to their tables (though I can see on the video that they have the help of a volunteer). It's perfect.

I watch for a bit before tucking my phone away. With how beautifully everything came together, and knowing that tickets to the event were so coveted that they even ended up with a waiting list, I'm confident One Fur All will meet its goal of clearing the shelter. It's what Imani deserves, it's what Becca deserves, and it's what all those animals deserve.

It does make me think of Cash. I'm sorry that my horrible actions mean that I never really got to say goodbye to him. He had no idea how much he'd come to mean to me.

But all that really matters is he's found a family that will love him.

In my own family, we're doing our best. Thursday dinners are on hold, or maybe canceled—whatever. I have Leo now, though. And therapy with my grandparents. So, even if the progress is slow, even if there's always a small piece of me that wonders, this is a start.

There is one pastel piece of this puzzle I can't stop thinking about, though.

I can't blame Elena for icing me out. I deceived her. There's no building a relationship together when that's how things begin.

Even though I had dreams of bonfires and breakfast, of road trips and hand-holding, of star gazing and laughter, of comfort and stability, sometimes dreams get shattered. All you can do is pick up the pieces and try again.

* * *

"Kat!" I hear Grandpa's voice ring out.

I rise from my bed and poke my head out of the door. "Yes?"

"Grandma needs help with the groceries. Can you run out?" He motions toward the dishwasher he's emptying. "I'll be out in a minute."

"On it!"

Quickly, I shove my feet into Grandpa's oversized loafers, toss on a hoodie, and shuffle out to the car—which is moving side to side ever so slightly, as if someone is jumping or shifting inside. I approach with caution.

Grandma opens the driver's-side door and I shoot her a confused glance. "Why is the car so...bouncy?"

"Hmm, doesn't seem that way to me," she says, walking toward the trunk. "Maybe you're imagining things. Bags are back here."

I shrug and meet her around the back of the car. Grandma puts her key in the hatchback and turns it, the door lifting easily into the air. I expect to see our familiar reusable bags brimming with food in there.

Instead, there is a green-eyed dog with three legs.

"Cash!" I scream.

He leaps out of the car and onto me, knocking me fully over and into the grass. He licks my face again and again, covering me in spit. "Cashy! Oh my gosh! I've missed you!" I rub his belly, and scratch his ears, and kiss him, his bottom half wiggling to and fro with the excitement of seeing me.

I look over at Grandma, who has been joined by Grandpa at her side.

"Did you guys arrange for me to hang out with Cash today before he goes to his new home? This is amazing!"

"We know that these last couple of weeks have been really tough," Grandma says. "So we wanted to do something nice for you."

"This is the *nicest*!" I turn to Cash. "Isn't it, Cashy?" He wags his tail and licks me again. "We'll be so good, I promise. Do you know what time I need to bring him back?"

"It's an overnight," Grandma says.

"The first of many, we'll say." Grandpa is practically beaming as he says this.

I turn toward them both, understanding slowly washing over me. "Wait..."

"Merry Christmas, Kat," Grandpa says, coming over to us and scratching Cash's back. "And welcome home, Cash."

"But...Cash is a *big* dog," I protest, looking over at Grandma. "And you're afraid!"

Grandma just smiles at me. "Your grandfather and I have been talking about this for a while. I even asked your parents to bring Daisy over on Christmas for a trial run of sorts. And it went well."

"*That* part went well," Grandpa quips.

"Hush, you," Grandma says. "We know how much you've wanted a dog of your own. This one, especially."

"Can't think of a better addition to the family!" Grandpa gets down on the ground with Cash, who barks in excitement.

I can't help it; I start to cry.

"Oh, Kat!" Grandma exclaims, coming to my side and helping me to my feet.

I wrap her into a tight hug. "Thank you," I say, sniffling. "Thank you both." Grandma rubs my back in reassuring circles, and Grandpa comes over and scoops us both into a giant bear hug.

"I'm just excited to have another man in the house," he jokes.

Cash runs over to us and jumps up on my back, joining in this group hug. "See? He already loves you guys! You won't regret this. I *promise*."

"We know we won't, Kat. We've never regretted a decision we've made," Grandpa says, and my heart tightens. This is all so thoughtful and perfect that it's almost too much for me to take. "Oh! And one more thing."

Grandpa retrieves something from the car and holds up a familiar box. I know exactly what this is because I helped make them—it's the care package One Fur All sends home with each adopted dog.

We go inside and I settle on the floor with Cash, pulling out the contents: a collar, harness, and leash; a toy; doggie bags; and a toothbrush and some dog-friendly toothpaste. I smile when I see a note at the bottom in a familiar, loopy scrawl.

Happy for you and your bestie. Take good care! —Jin

"Well, isn't that nice," Grandma muses.

"But you'll need more than that, won't you?" Grandpa scratches his chin, sizing Cash up. "How about a nice sweater for our new friend?"

"It's like you're reading my mind." I pull out my phone and start a list of things I want to buy ASAP to help Cash feel comfortable.

Grandpa keeps tossing out suggestions for our list and I start to get the sense that he really is every bit as excited about our new addition as I am.

*   *   *

That night, I text the boys a photo of Cash snuggled up at the foot of my bed.

Me: **Guess who found a new home?!?**

Hari: **OH SHIT**

Hari: **Did you adopt Cash after all?!?!**

Me: **My grandparents surprised me!!!!!**

Me: ☺

Me: **I would DIE for him.**

Marcus: **Yoooo, we are coming over tomorrow FIRST THING so I can get some well-deserved doggie therapy in!**

Marcus: **I'm fine, just always looking for an excuse to pet dogs, you know?**

Luis: **Please tell me you're not letting him sleep in your bed.**

Me: **He definitely will be.**

Luis: **Nasty as always, Sanchez.**

Luis: **Glad to know some things never change.**

Chapter Forty-Five

Cash and I are snuggled up in the living room because I've commandeered the TV. It's frigid out, with the forecast even calling for possible snowflakes. It's a long shot, but still!

The cozy vibe is definitely amplified by the lingering Christmas decorations, which don't get put away till after the new year. There's the glittering tree; the white lights strewn on the mantel; the little cactus on an end table that wears a Santa hat.

Cash is even wearing a knit sweater that Grandpa and I picked out because he might get cold, too, you know?

The gentle rise and fall of his chest is soothing and I use his body as a heater, tucking my feet beneath his belly. He doesn't wiggle away even though my feet are like ice.

Grandma and Grandpa are treating themselves to a very nice and very rare evening out, so Cash and I are waiting on Luis, Marcus, and Hari to visit. With college application season over—and Grandma and Grandpa's blessing for me to take a year to work and figure out what I want to do—we've been longing to get together and just relax.

It's not long before there's a knock on the door. Cash leaps up and rushes to the entryway, then sits nicely just like I taught him. I grab a treat for him on the way to my door and toss it. Cash catches it with ease.

"Good boy," I coo. "Stay."

I pull the door open and smile when I see my friends standing before me.

"Hey!" Hari says brightly.

"Are you going to invite us in or what?" Marcus blows on his hands dramatically. "It's freezing out here."

I move aside to let them in. "Come on in." They pile inside and I lock up behind them. "Watch this." I turn to Cash. "Cash, take a bow!" With my hands, I make the corresponding gesture I've taught him. He bows with his chest to the ground and his tail in the air.

"Ayyy, that's pretty impressive!" Hari says. "Not as impressive as your dance, but still great."

"Not bad at all. Huh, Cash?" Marcus bends down to greet him.

Luis shrugs. "It's aight."

I roll my eyes at him. "Whatever, man. We're in here." They follow me into the living room and Luis immediately kicks off his shoes. "Make yourself at home, I guess."

"Don't mind if I do, Sanchez."

"Can I get you all anything?" I ask. When Luis goes to open his mouth I cut him off. "Not you."

He shakes his head. "Hilarious."

"I know. Hot chocolate work for everyone?" I suggest.

Marcus's face lights up. "I haven't had hot chocolate in forever!"

"I'll take mine with extra marshmallows, please," Luis says.

"Hari?" I ask.

"I'll come help you," he offers, and I smile. We walk toward the kitchen, Cash in tow. Hari pulls out mugs while I gather the ingredients and a large saucepan. I start heating some milk on the stove. "How're you doing?"

"I'm okay," I say, unwrapping the chocolate and breaking it up into smaller pieces. "I'm focusing on social media less and just trying to be a kinder, more honest person. Things are getting better. Slowly. Especially with Cash here." I sneak a glance toward the living room, where Marcus and Luis are arguing over who gets to sit in Grandpa's armchair. "And you guys."

Hari looks toward the living room and laughs. "You sure about that?"

"They are who they are. I can't change that." I add some chocolate to the already-hot milk. It starts to melt. "Hey, I've been meaning to ask: How's Iris?" Hari looks down at the floor bashfully. "Oh my God. You're sooo into her."

He rubs his hand on the back of his neck. "*Kiiinda*, yeah."

"Oh, Hari. I'm so happy for you," I say, meaning it. "Can we hang out soon? Just you and me? I know I've been a little MIA getting Cash settled in and all, but I legit want to hear everything."

Hari grins at me. "I'd really love that."

"Me too," I say, gently stirring the mixture. Once it's combined, I turn off the burner. "I think this is done."

Hari holds out one of the mugs to me. I pour. "So . . . have you heard from her at all?"

"No. Don't think I will, either."

"Damn. I'm so sorry."

"Yeah," I say, as I scrape the bowl so the last of the hot chocolate goes into the fourth mug. "It sucks."

Hari pulls a mini-marshmallow out of the bag and holds it out to me. "Consolation prize?"

I pop it in my mouth and smile. "Thank you."

We walk back toward the living room with the hot drinks, Marcus sitting in Grandpa's armchair, clearly victorious.

Hari pulls the bag of marshmallows out from the crook of his elbow and sprinkles a few in our cups. When he gets to Luis's, he drops a huge handful into the mug and the extras spill into Luis's lap.

"Mira, you're making a mess!"

Hari shrugs. "You asked for extra marshmallows!"

"You did," Marcus says.

Luis huffs but pops some of the stray marshmallows into his mouth. "Fine. What are we watching tonight, anyway?"

"I'm so glad you asked." I use the remote to find what I'm looking for.

"Are you shitting me right now?" Marcus asks.

"I am not."

On-screen, the title card for *To All The Boys I've Loved Before* is pulled up.

"You know…I watched this with Xio before, and it's actually kinda good," Luis admits.

Marcus whips his head toward him. "What?!"

"Sit back, relax, and give it a chance," I say. "If you hate it after twenty minutes, then we'll bail."

"Well, *I'm* excited," Hari offers.

The movie starts. I'm taken back to the first night I watched it. It's not as if I am *pining* for Elena with this film choice. But, okay, yeah, maybe I am a little. The movie reminds me of when things felt *so good*. If I want to relive that for just one night, I think that should be okay. Especially because I get to watch it with my perfect new pup and my three amazing and obnoxious best friends.

We have as great a night as possible, given everything, but after they leave, I climb into bed, numb and sad. Why can't everything just fix itself like it does in the movies?

I'm especially thinking of Lara Jean and Peter and how *they* managed to make it work. Love letters seemed to do the trick.

I sit up in bed.

A love letter. I need to write Elena a love letter.

She was so moved by the power of a love letter, by the fact that there is nothing instant about it, that the very act of writing a love letter is vulnerable and requires patience and a willingness to show you're putting yourself out there.

To be fair, it is a long shot. The longest of long shots, really. But I have to try.

I pull out my laptop and start working on a draft of what I'll say. I make a folder. I drag in some photos. I write. I rewrite. Cash watches me with one eye, my super-sleepy sidekick who at once wants to cheer me on and wonders why I can't just go to bed.

"I know, bud," I whisper. "If this works, though, I promise it'll be worth it."

He gives me a sluggish tail wag.

When the written portion feels complete, I dig through old craft supplies scattered around my room till I find exactly the right paper, just the pen I'm looking for, an envelope, and some photos I'd printed. It's the middle of the night by the time I'm done. But I have it. When I wake, I can add a stamp, and seal it with hope.

I only hope it isn't too late.

Chapter Forty-Six

I wait, and I wait, and I wait.

Love letters require patience, after all.

The more time that passes, though, the less sure I am that I deserve another chance with Elena.

Still, I remember the late-night conversations. The phone calls that connected us. The secrets we shared. The picnic and the escape room. The blanket by the bonfire. The kisses under the moon.

So, I hope, and I hope, and I hope.

Days later, a letter arrives. My familiar handwriting is scrawled across the front. The envelope, once crisp and clean, sealed with hope, arrives tattered and bruised. Across the front, in huge letters, are the words RETURN TO SENDER.

And I finally understand. I shouldn't have tried. I will never be the person who tries to break a boundary again.

Chapter Forty-Seven

It's cold as hell but Cash's walks wait for no one. Not even on New Year's Eve.

I get into my coat and bundle him up, too, doggie booties and all. We take our time winding around the neighborhood, a route that's already becoming familiar to him.

As we round the corner back home, I see Pop walking Shark, Pepito, Archie, and Daisy in the distance. He stops dead in his tracks when spots me. We haven't spoken since Christmas.

Part of me wants to take Cash and run the other way. But the other part of me, the part that sees his feeble wave, the part that still…I don't know…hopes?, imagines some kind of connection. Some kind of *something*.

Pop decides for me when he and the dogs get closer. I tell Cash to heel, and he obeys.

When Pop nears, I bend down to greet the dogs first, then rise to meet his gaze.

"Hi," I say, keeping my voice quiet.

"Hi, Kat. It's good to see you."

I squint at him. "Is it? Because I haven't heard from you since Christmas."

His eyes fall to the pavement in front of us. "I know. I'm sorry." When I don't say anything, he continues. "And I'm sorry—for what I said, and for immediately taking your mom's side. Just, for, I don't know. Not giving you or Leo a chance to speak. I'm sorry…" He reaches for the back of his head and scratches. "For a lot of things, actually."

"Yeah."

"I've been doing a lot of thinking. About everything. I feel like we missed out on so much with you, you know?"

"You did," I say. "You hardly know me at all."

Pop nods. "I know. It kills me. You're nearly grown. You'll be leaving soon for whatever future awaits you." His eyes glisten as he speaks, his voice wavering. "It isn't right. How everything happened. How we treated you. But, if you'd be willing, I'd like to work on things. I have been with Leo."

"Yeah, I know. We talk."

"Right, right. Good. That's good. I'm happy you guys have been getting closer," Pop says. "And I would really like that for us, too. Someday."

I pull my coat tighter around me. "We'd have to start from scratch, you know."

"Absolutely."

"It would take a lot of work."

"I agree. But it's the most important work I can ever imagine," he says. "I'll do most of the heavy lifting."

"And Mom?"

"Your mother—she, well." He shakes his head. "She has her own things to work on. And that's her choice. But *I* would like to try to make things better with you. I've failed you, Kat. And I feel like I have a lifetime of apologizing to you. If you'll let me. I just… I want to know more about you than your favorite color." He sighs. "I don't need an answer now. But I hope you'll consider it."

"I'll think about it," I say, crossing my arms.

He nods at me. "Thank you." Then he motions toward the dogs, who are getting restless. "I'm going to take these guys home. I love you, Kat. You've always been my favorite part of Thursdays."

I don't say anything, so he turns to go.

"Pop!" I call after him. He turns. "What's my favorite color?"

He smiles at me. "It used to be purple. But now it's gray. Like the moon."

I smile at him. "Yeah. Like the moon."

"Happy New Year, Kat."

"Happy New Year, Pop."

Chapter Forty-Eight

"*Have I mentioned how* absolutely *dumb* this whole thing is?" Luis grumbles. "Because it's dumb. Stupid dumb. People write sonnets about how dumb this is."

Hari shoots him a look. "You know what a sonnet is?"

"Man, I don't need that right now. We've been driving forever and I'm *starving*."

"You're always starving!" Marcus points out. "I really think you need to get checked out or something."

"Seriously, Luis. You good? You getting all the nutrients you need?" I ask. "Because I have been giving Cash some dog supplements and maybe that could work for you, too."

He shoves his hands in his pockets and stomps away, leaving us to unload the car. Cash chases after him.

"Hey, wait, I'm gonna stomp away, too, and then I don't have to help with anything," Hari jokes.

"Right?" His girlfriend, Iris, has a playful smile on her face. She's a pretty girl with kind eyes; smooth, dark hair that cascades all the way down her back; and quiet one-liners that outwit us all. Hari practically looks at her with heart eyes whenever she's around, and it's the greatest thing ever. "I think he secretly knew what he was doing."

As I survey all the bags I've stuffed into Grandma's SUV—camera gear, camping equipment, a bag I may have overpacked for Cash—I do wonder, briefly, if maybe Luis is right. Is this stupid?

It's not like I've been camping in Joshua Tree National Park before. And we're not exactly camping people.

Then again, I didn't really think we were Halloween party people or friends-who-talk-about-feelings people, and now look.

As if sensing my doubt, Xiomara grins at me, giving my arm a squeeze. "This is gonna be so fun!"

I smile back. "I hope so!"

She wanders off to follow Luis.

The sun is going down and there is a slight chill in the just-barely-spring March air, but it's not so bad. And even if it were, I wouldn't admit that. We're gonna do it; we're *finally* gonna see the stars under the sky. I didn't research for months to make this happen for nothing.

"Here, hand me the tent and I'll get started with that," Marcus says.

"Over by the rocks should be good." I slip the tent out of the car and pass it over to him with a grunt. "It's heavy."

"I've got it." With ease, Marcus carries the tent toward a nearby rock formation. "How's this?"

Iris nods. "That should work. I did a little research before we came, and I read that the rocks should shield us from the wind and then cast a nice shadow over our camp when it gets hot."

I grin at her, impressed. Hari looks at Iris with awe. "My girl is the smartest in the world."

"Y'all can stop making googly eyes at each other at any time and help me out," Marcus says. He glances at me. "How'd we end up being the only single ones here?"

"Speak for yourself," I say. "I brought Cash."

Hari makes a face. "Looks like you're the only one sleeping alone tonight," he teases.

Marcus shakes his head. "Wooow. That's cold."

"I'm happy to share Cash, though," I assure him. "And the campsite only accommodates six, anyway."

Hari nudges me, motioning into the distance. "Check it out." I watch as Luis pops a Taki in his mouth, and one in Xio's mouth, and then shares one with Cash.

I roll my eyes. "And he claimed he didn't like dogs."

While Marcus, Hari, and I put the tents up, Iris gets a fire going. By the time we're done, Xio and Luis have rejoined us.

"I saw you sharing your snacks with Cash," I say. "Admit it: he's grown on you."

"I will never admit any such thing," Luis argues, but I stick out my tongue, knowing I've already won.

"Luis, why don't you make yourself useful and get started on dinner?" Hari asks.

"Yeah, Luis. Prove your worth," Marcus teases.

"Lucky for y'all, I've been practicing my skills. Over winter break, Titi Rosa taught me everything she knows." Luis puffs up his chest. "Prepare your taste buds."

She may have taught him everything she knows, but Luis clearly didn't retain much. He burns the burgers. We eat them anyway. As Marcus and Hari are on cleanup, Iris and Xio set up the sleeping bags, and Cash plays fetch with Luis—his new, Taki-wielding pal—I take a chance to slip away to get my camera set up.

I make my way toward an arched rock formation. I'm hoping I can try to capture the Milky Way behind it. I have a very specific photo in mind, one that shows off some of my favorite things, and I hope it'll come out right. I decided to take a gap year and try working as a freelancer, then apply to CSU Bakerfield, probably as an arts major. So I need good work for the ol' portfolio.

The moon is just a sliver tonight, which will be good for the photos, but not so great for safely navigating around. Using my phone's flashlight, I set up my tripod and take a few test shots with my camera. Then I can't help it; I glance up at the sky. If I thought it was clear and beautiful before, out here? It's next level.

Someone bumps me. Hard. I nearly fall, but a hand steadies me.

I scowl, ready to shout at who I assume is Luis messing with me, only to see a petite girl with cascading coiled hair. Her curls are bathed in moonlight, as if she herself is made of space.

"Sorry!" she says. "I was totally not looking where I was going. Blame the sky. It's fucking gorgeous."

And I laugh. "It really is. No worries. I get distracted by the stars, too."

She looks up again and takes in a breath. "It's so pretty it almost makes me weak." Then she looks back at me. "I'm Deja, by the way."

"Kat," I say. "I'm staying over there with my friends." I motion behind me.

"I'm here with friends, too. That way." She points in the opposite direction and smiles at me, big and warm and inviting, and I find myself smiling, too.

"There you are!" Hari's voice echoes through the desert. "You disappeared. Are we still getting that picture?"

The girl waves at me. "See you around."

I wave back at her before turning to Hari. "Yeah. Yes," I say. "Let's do it."

Xiomara goes over to my camera. "So, this is all set up, right?"

"All set up," I confirm. "Just push this button right here."

"Between the two of us, we'll figure it out," Iris assures me.

"We'll just be a second," Hari says. He gives her a quick kiss, and then he, Marcus, Luis, and I head toward the nearby arch. We start to scale it.

"This seems dangerous," Luis says.

"It'll be worth it," Marcus replies.

Hari nods. "Just trust us."

Luis scowls at him. "When have I *ever* trusted you?"

With a shrug, Hari says, "Well, then, don't trust us. Just be quiet and do it anyway."

"Fine."

I hop from one rock to another, Cash easily making the jumps right with me. Once all five of us are at the top, I look out at the desert. Yeah, this should work. All I want is to capture a photo-silhouette of my favorite people—and my favorite dog—against the stars. Something to show how far we've come. To pay tribute to what we've been through. To remember this night. To remind us that, through everything, we were there for one another. To prove we could stand still and quit (lovingly) bickering for just a moment. To look back on. To commemorate all the adventures that still lie ahead.

"How's it look?" I call to Xio.

"It's great!" she calls back. "You ready?"

I look from Hari to Luis to Marcus and then down at Cash. "Are we?"

Hari nods. "Let's do it."

"Okay, Xio!" I shout. "On three!"

"On three, what?" Luis asks.

I roll my eyes. "Strike a pose and say cheese, dummy."

Together, beneath the starry sky, we count down from three and shout, "Cheese, dummy!"

Acknowledgments

I've always thought that books are magic, and now I know that the art of creating them can be pretty magical, too. There are teams and bloggers and indie booksellers and bookstagrammers; there are publishers and agents and copy editors and illustrators; there are friends and families and dog snuggles; there are memes and Twitter chats and communities; there are the stars and planets aligning; and there's everything in between.

Writing this book during a pandemic while parenting and working full-time has been no small feat, and so, my first acknowledgment goes to privilege, without which I would not be able to pursue this beautiful thing that I love and that I get to share with others, too.

And now, to give sincere and heartfelt thanks.

Thank you to my family and in-laws for their endless love, celebrations, and support. I appreciate everything you've done and continue to do for me, Bill, and Maya. We are so lucky.

A special thank you to my brother, Renz, for allowing me the space to write about something so personal in this book. You're one of the funniest and best people on this planet, and forever my chaotic Gemini birthday twin.

Thank you to Writers Row—Judy, Jane, Cait, and Kerri—for always sharing friendship, grammar jokes, joy and woes, laughter, hugs, and drinks. Cheers to you all.

Thank you to all of my amazing friends, with special shout out to Kate Albus, for her unrelenting warmth and kindness; Liz and Sanya, for being my OG internet besties; Samm, for all the drone jokes and clown and Pingu memes; chingonxs literarias for the feeling of community and also the fun lil DMs; Angela Velez, for her shared love of glitter; my JBs Mozza group, for all of the laughter and support as a new mom; and the Nasties, who traveled to me in the middle of a global pandemic to celebrate my first book when the world was shut down and popped champagne with me (literally or metaphorically) in the snow: Paige, Cait, Laraine, Kerri, Brosh, Veatch, Deleney, Anne, Nikki, Annie, and all our littles.

Thank you to my writing and author friends, old and new, and specifically #The21ders and Las Musas, who send me memes or let me talk through ideas or get on chaotic IG Lives with me.

Thank you to every single podcaster, bookstagrammer, blogger, booktuber, booktoker, Book Twitter (I don't think there's a cutesy name for you all but let's workshop that), and book lover who showed kindness and appreciation for me and my books in ways I never imagined. You make the YA community what it is and help connect stories to the people that matter most.

Thank you to the readers who recreated my book cover, which remains one of the greatest things to ever happen to me.

Thank you, always, to teachers, librarians, and indie booksellers, some of whom have shown so much love to me and my stories that it brings tears to this sensitive lil baby author's eyes. I am humbled by your support and generosity in welcoming my stories into your classrooms, libraries, and bookstores across the world. My characters are more well-traveled than I'll ever be, and I couldn't be more grateful. Your work is immense, underappreciated, and meaningful, and you light the way for lonely little kids (like I once was) to see beauty and hope in the world.

Thank you to my higher ed communities and friends, including my friends from Springfield College and UMass Amherst, for their warm reception and support.

Thank you to everyone who's purchased, borrowed, shared, exchanged, tweeted about, felt something for, smiled when thinking about, amplified, or celebrated my books (eBook, audiobook, hardcover, paperback—all forms of reading are valid!).

Thank you to anyone, everyone, who has reached out with a kind word to say about my work.

Thank you to my literary agent, Tamar Rydzinski—a cheerleader and force I greatly admire. I appreciate all that you do to support my career, me, and my work. You're always championing for bigger and better things, and I'm eternally grateful.

Thank you to my TV and film agent, Lucy Stille, for believing in Charlie and working tirelessly to get her story out there.

Thank you to my editor, Mora, for adding wit and charm and precision to my stories in ways I never could have imagined.

Thank you to Sara, my forever pen pal who understands my Lizzie McGuire obsession, for helping to keep me organized, sane, and not getting sick of me.

Thank you to illustrator and artist Ericka Lugo for lending your stunning artwork and vision to my books, and stopping readers in their tracks when they see your gorgeous creations. Your art constantly blows me away and I've heard from SO many who feel the same way.

Thank you to the incredible team at Holiday House, including Derek Stordahl; Sara DiSalvo; Mora Couch; Terry Borzumato-Greenberg; Michelle Montague; Mary Joyce Perry; Mary Cash; Elizabeth Law; Alison Tarnofsky; Amy Toth; Pam Glauber; Barbara Perris; and Kerry Martin. I can't thank you enough for seeing the value in my work and doing everything possible to ensure that my babies go off into the world ready to thrive.

Thank you to fat girls everywhere. We deserve the best.

Thank you to TikTok and Animal Crossing for keeping me sane during the pandemic.

Thank you to Dunkin Donuts for never making iced coffee the same, literally ever, and always making every sip a surprise.

Thank you to one-star reviews for keeping me humble.

Thank you to all of the dogs who have let me pet them.

Thank you to em-dashes, exclamation points, and parentheses for existing.

Thank you to childcare, without which I would not be able to write. And, of course:

Thank you to Obi for always being a real-life teddy bear and humoring me when I want to dance with you around the living room.

Thank you to my sweet Papaya, for giving the best hugs, for showing us tenderness that makes me weep, for offering silliness that makes my belly ache. Rediscovering the world through your eyes is one of the greatest gifts.

Thank you to my Bubby—my heart, my soul, my boulder—for the endless laughter, spontaneous dance parties, Gilmore Girls rewatches, unmatched thoughtfulness, never-ending Dunkin runs, the snuggles that turn into naps, and the unfettered joy that you bring me every single day. You've got my only heart.